"Konar describes her subject beautifully, lyrically, in the language of a fable.... Readers who allow themselves to fall under the spell of Konar's exceptionally sensitive writing may well find the book unforgettable."
— Ruth Franklin, *New York Times Book Review*

"*Mischling* is a luminous tale of hope in the shadow of the Holocaust."
— *Vanity Fair*

"Konar is an astonishing and fearless writer, whose great gift to us is this book. With incantatory magic, she marches through the most nightmarish of landscapes, swinging her light."
— Karen Russell, author of *Swamplandia!*

One of the Year's Best Books

A *New York Times* Notable Book • An *Elle* Best Book of the Year
A *Flavorwire* Best Book of the Year • An Amazon Top 20
Book of the Year • A Barnes & Noble Discover Pick
An Indie Next Pick • A *Publishers Weekly* Best Book of the Year

"There isn't a page in this novel that isn't also shining with hope and love, and that's what makes this beautiful book worth reading."
— *Book Riot*

"Konar makes the emotional lives of her two spirited narrators piercingly real.... Their ability to hang on to hope and kindness in the face of the most awful suffering—to remain, in Elie Wiesel's words, humane 'in an inhumane universe.'"
— Michiko Kakutani, *New York Times*

"Triumphant." — Alice Whitwham, *O, The Oprah Magazine*   "Luminous." — *Vanity Fair*

"Astonishing." — *Elle*   "Unforgettable." — Ruth Franklin, *New York Times Book Review*

"TRIUMPHANT"   "UNFORGETTABLE"   "LUMINOUS"   "ASTONISHING"

Dear Target Book Club Readers,

I am immensely grateful to you for reading the story of Pearl and Stasha Zamorski, twins whose childhood imprisonment fails not only to break their sisterly bond but to diminish their belief in humanity. Given that subject, I'm often asked how I was able to bear writing the novel. I always reply that the sisterhood between Pearl and Stasha was a great comfort to me, a truly living thing; their love made the effort of writing feel worthy and possible. In them, I found two heroines who, for many years, taught me who I wanted to be. They are brave, resilient, imaginative, but, most important, they confront the question of how one might resume a life so disrupted by sorrow and trauma. Theirs is a childhood defined by loss, and their adulthood won't be the adulthood enjoyed by others, but they are determined to live beyond the shadow cast by Mengele. Their revenge is to find meaning again in a world that stripped them of it, to search for loving-kindness and beauty as a way to honor their family, and to bear witness.

I hoped this novel would be seen as a tribute to the many remarkable books and poems that informed my perspective. But as the novel has journeyed out, I've heard from survivors and their descendants, men and women whose days are captive to memories no human should have to bear. With the growing loss of direct witnesses, many of these people—who know these horrors with a terrible authority—have said that perhaps we have arrived at the right moment for fiction, that maybe characters like Stasha and Pearl can approach these stories with a different urgency, successfully immersing the reader in events too often described as "unimaginable." The possibility that *Mischling* could be considered worthy of playing a small role in that remembrance is humbling, and I can only think that your willingness to embrace the novel underlines the fact that we must keep this history, with its many horrors and bitter triumphs, in our sights. Because the world may be full of beauty, as Pearl and Stasha would say, but it is redeemed only by our commitment to make it so.

Yours in gratitude,

Affinity Konar

"Powerful. . . . *Mischling* grapples with how to articulate unspeakable horror, how language and narrative can bear the unbearable, what happens when words fail. . . . A heartbreaking novel about compassion and cruelty, brutality and beauty."

—Anita Sethi, *The Observer* (UK)

"A piercing novel written with chin-up virtuosity, as powerful as the best mythic stories of the masters of old."

—Chigozie Obioma, author of *The Fishermen*

"A truly original story."

—*Marie Claire*

"This novel, haunted by history and the unknowable power of family, is made bearable—indeed, necessary—by the spectacle of a literary imagination that observes no limits. Konar has produced a tremendously unsettling work of art."

—Ben Marcus, author of *The Flame Alphabet*

"Konar makes every sentence count. This is a brutally beautiful book."

—*Publishers Weekly*

"*Mischling* transported me to another world. It's a world that's part of our history, of course, but Konar's genius is that she allows us to see it anew. Brace yourself for a novel unlike any you've ever read."

—Cristina Henríquez, author of *The Book of Unknown Americans*

"This searing work deepens our understanding of the Holocaust. It is highly recommended for that reason and for its stunningly original approach."

—Edward B. Cone, *Library Journal*

"Taking what is, on its face, a horrifying topic—the Holocaust—and somehow finding beauty within it is just one of the many small miracles Konar pulls off in this absorbing, heartbreaking novel." —Preston Jones, *Fort Worth Star-Telegram*

"Affinity Konar's masterfully told and lyrical novel, *Mischling,* may be the year's most poignant book."
—David Gutowski, *Largehearted Boy*

"*Mischling* is a phenomenal book—harrowing and heartbreaking, intimate and epic—and Affinity Konar is a wise and compassionate writer with talent in spades. An achingly beautiful novel that will stay with me for a long, long time."
—Molly Antopol, author of *The UnAmericans*

"It's to Konar's credit that the novel manages to be as much about the perils of sisterhood as it is about the tragedy of genocide.... Moments of beauty emerge unexpectedly and stick with the reader long after the book is over." —*Shelf Awareness*

"A spare, stunning debut that's a must-read."
—Sona Charaipotra, *B&N Reads*

"While the ugliness of the story might push readers out, the spell cast by the author's verbal wizardry pulls them back in. Daring in concept and method, Konar's novel has homed in on the perfect blending of inspiration, vision, and technique to pen a unique masterpiece." —Philip K. Jason, Jewish Book Council

MISCHLING

A Novel

AFFINITY KONAR

A LEE BOUDREAUX BOOK

BACK BAY BOOKS

NEW YORK BOSTON LONDON

Copyright © 2016 by Affinity Konar
Reading group guide copyright © 2017 by Affinity Konar and Little, Brown and Company

Lee Boudreaux Books / Back Bay Books
Hachette Book Group
Little, Brown and Company
1290 Avenue of the Americas, New York NY 10104
leeboudreauxbooks.com

Originally published in hardcover by Lee Boudreaux Books / Little, Brown and Company, September 2016
First Lee Boudreaux Books / Back Bay Books paperback edition, May 2017

Lee Boudreaux Books is an imprint of Little, Brown and Company, a division of Hachette Book Group, Inc. The Lee Boudreaux name and logo are trademarks of Hachette Book Group, Inc.

The publisher is not responsible for websites (or their content) that are not owned by the publisher.

The Hachette Speakers Bureau provides a wide range of authors for speaking events. To find out more, go to hachettespeakersbureau.com or call (866) 376-6591.

ISBN 978-0-316-30810-6 (hardcover) / 978-0-316-46417-8 (large print) / 978-0-316-46684-4 (signed edition) / 978-0-316-30809-0 (paperback) / 978-0-316-51158-2 (Target edition)
LCCN 2015958011

10 9 8 7 6 5 4 3 2 1

LSC-C

Printed in the United States of America

For Philip and for my family

Mischling / misch•ling /, hybrid; half-breed. Used by the Third Reich to denote a person of mixed blood.

PART ONE

CHAPTER ONE

World After World

We were made, once. My twin, Pearl, and me. Or, to be precise, Pearl was formed and I split from her. She embossed herself on the womb; I copied her signature. For eight months we were afloat in amniotic snowfall, two rosy mittens resting on the lining of our mother. I couldn't imagine anything grander than the womb we shared, but after the scaffolds of our brains were ivoried and our spleens were complete, Pearl wanted to see the world beyond us. And so, with newborn pluck, she spat herself out of our mother.

Though premature, Pearl was a sophisticated prankster. I assured myself that it was just one of her tricks; she'd be back to laugh at me. But when Pearl failed to return, I lost my breath. Have you ever had to live with the best part of yourself adrift, stationed at some unknowable distance? If so, I am sure you are aware of the dangers of this condition. After my breath left me, my heart followed suit, and my brain ran with an unthinkable fever. In my fetal pinkness, I faced this truth: without her, I would become a split and unworthy thing, a human incapable of love.

That is why I followed my sister's lead and allowed the doctor's hands to tear me out and smack me and hold me to the light. Let us note that I never cried during the ruptures of this unwanted transition. Not even when our parents ignored my wish to be named Pearl too.

I became Stasha instead. And with the chore of birth complete, we entered the world of family and piano and book, of days that baffled by in beauty. We were so alike—we were always dropping marbles from the window onto the paving stones and watching them descend the hill with our binoculars, just to see how far their little lives would take them.

That world, teeming with awe, ended too. Most worlds do.

But I must tell you: There was another world we knew. Some say it was the world that made us the most. I want to say that they are wrong, but for now, let me tell you that our entry into this world began in our twelfth year of life, when we were huddled side by side in the back of a cattle car.

During that journey of four days and four nights, we cheated our way into survival under Mama's and Zayde's instruction. For sustenance, we passed an onion back and forth and licked its yellow hide. For entertainment, we played the game Zayde made for us, a game called the Classification of Living Things. In this form of charades, you had to portray a living thing, and the players had to name the species, the genus, the family, and so on, all the way to the encompassing brilliance of a kingdom.

The four of us passed through so many living things in the cattle car; we postured from bear to snail and back—it was important, Zayde emphasized in his thirst-cracked voice, that we organize the universe to the best of our too-human ability—and when the cattle car finally came to a stop I stopped my charade too. The way I remember it, I was in the middle of trying to convince Mama that I was an amoeba. It's possible that I was portraying some other living thing and that I am remembering it as an amoeba now only because I felt so small in that moment, so translucent and fragile. I cannot be sure.

Just as I was about to admit defeat, the door to the cattle car rolled open.

And the incoming light was so startling that we dropped our onion on the floor, and it rolled down the ramp, a smelly and half-eaten moon that landed at the feet of a guard. I imagine that his face was full of disgust, but I couldn't see it—he held a kerchief over his nostrils while issuing a series of sneezes, and he stopped sneezing only to hover his boot above our onion and cast an eclipsing shadow over the tiny globe. We watched the onion weep as he crushed it, its tears a bitter pulp. He then resumed his approach, and we scrambled to hide in the shelter of Zayde's voluminous coat. Though we had outgrown Zayde as a hiding place long ago, fear made us smaller, and we contorted within the coat folds beside his dwindled body, leaving our grandfather a lumpy, many-legged figure. In this shelter, we blinked. Then we heard a sound—a stomp, a shuffle—the guard's boots were immediately before us.

"What kind of insect are you?" he asked Zayde, rapping each of the girlish legs that emerged beneath the coat with a walking stick. Our knees smarted. Then the guard struck Zayde's legs too. "Six legs? You are a spider?"

It was clear that the guard had no real understanding of living things at all. Already, he'd made two errors. But Zayde didn't bother to point out that spiders aren't insects and that, in fact, they are possessors of eight legs. Traditionally, Zayde enjoyed issuing playful, singsong corrections, as he liked to see all the facts put to rights. In that place, though—it was too dangerous to express any intimate knowledge of creatures that crawled or were considered lowly, lest you be accused of bearing too much in common with them. We should have known better than to make an insect of our grandfather.

"I asked you a question," the guard insisted while issuing another rap to our legs with his stick. "What kind?"

In German, Zayde gave him facts: His name was Tadeusz Zamorski. He was sixty-five years old. He was a Polish Jew. He ended there, as if all were told.

And we wanted to continue for him, we wanted to give all the details: Zayde was a former professor of biology. He'd taught the subject at universities for decades but was an expert in many things. If you wanted to know about the insides of a poem, he would be the one to ask. If you wanted to know how to walk on your hands or find a star, he'd show you. With him, we once saw a rainbow that ran only red, saw it straddle a mountain and a sea, and he toasted the memory of it often. *To unbearable beauty!* he'd cry, eyes abrim. He was so fond of toasts that he made them indiscriminately, for nearly any occasion. *To a morning swim! To the lindens at the gate!* And in recent years, there was this, his most common toast: *To the day my son returns, alive and unchanged!*

But as much as we would have liked to, we said nothing of these things to the guard—the details caught in our throats, and our eyes were tearful because of the death of the nearby onion. The tears were the onion's fault, we told ourselves, nothing more, and we wiped the drops away so that we could see what was happening through the holes in Zayde's coat.

Encircled in the portholes of these flaws were five figures: three little boys, their mother, and a white-coated man who stood with a pen cocked over a little book. The boys intrigued us—we'd never seen triplets before. In Lodz, there had been another set of girl twins, but a trio was the stuff of books. Though we were impressed by their number, we had to admit that we trumped them in terms of identicality. All three had the same dark curls and eyes, the same spindly bodies, but they wore different expressions—one squinted at the sun, while the other two frowned, and their faces fell into similarity only when the white-coated man distributed candy into each of their palms.

The triplets' mother was different than all the other mothers of the cattle car—her distress was neatly tucked away, and she stood as still as a stopped clock. One of her hands drifted over her sons' heads in some perpetual hesitation, as if she felt that she no longer had the right to touch them. The white-coated man did not share this attitude.

He was an intimidating figure, all shiny black shoes and dark hair of equal polish, his sleeves so expansive that when he lifted an arm, the fabric below billowed and winged and claimed a disproportionate measure of sky. He was movie-star handsome and prone to dramatics; kindly expressions swelled across his face with obviousness, as if he was eager to let everyone near know the extremity of his good intentions.

Words passed between the mother and the white-coated man. They seemed like agreeable words, though the man did most of the talking. We wished we could hear the conversation, but it was enough, I suppose, to see what happened next: the mother passed her hands over the dark clouds of the triplets' hair, and then she turned her back, leaving the boys with the white-coated man.

He was a doctor, she said as she walked away, a falter in her step. They would be safe, she assured them, and she did not look back.

Our mother, hearing this, gave a little squeak and a gasp before reaching over to tug at the guard's arm. Her boldness was a shock. We were used to a trembling mother, one who always shook while making requests of the butcher and hid from the cleaning woman. Always, it was as if pudding ran through her veins, making her constantly aquiver and defeatable, especially since Papa's disappearance. In the cattle car, she'd steadied herself only by drawing a poppy on the wooden wall. Pistil, petal, stamen—she drew with a strange focus, and when she stopped drawing, she went to pieces. But on the ramp she discovered a new solidity—she stood stronger than the starved and weary should ever stand. Was the music responsible for this alteration? Mama always loved music, and this place was teeming with bright notes; they found us in the cattle car and drew us out with a distrustful cheer. Over time, we'd learn the depths of this trick and know to beware of the celebratory tune, as it held only suffering at its core. The orchestra had been entrusted with the deception of all that entered. They were compelled, these musicians, to use their talents to ensnare the unwitting, to convince them that where they had arrived was a place not entirely without an appreciation for the humane and the beautiful. Music—it uplifted the arriving crowds, it flowed beside them as they walked through the gates. Was this why Mama was able to be bold? I would never know. But I admired her courage as she spoke.

"It is good here—to be a double?" she asked the guard.

He gave her a nod and turned to the doctor, who was squatting in the dust so that he could address the boys at eye level. The group appeared to be having the warmest of chats.

"*Zwillinge!*" the guard called to him. "Twins!"

The doctor left the triplets to a female attendant and strode over to us, his shiny boots disrupting the dust. He was courtly with our mother, taking her hand as he addressed her.

"You have special children?" His eyes were friendly, from what we could see.

Mama shifted from foot to foot, suddenly diminished. She tried to withdraw her hand from his grasp but he held it tight, and then he began to stroke her palm with his gloved fingertips, as if it were some wounded, but easily soothed, thing.

"Only twins, not triplets," she apologized. "I hope they are enough."

The doctor's laugh was loud and showy and it echoed within the caverns of Zayde's coat. We were relieved when it subsided so that we could listen to Mama rattling off our gifts.

"They speak some German. Their father taught them. They'll turn thirteen in December. Healthy readers, the both of them.

Pearl loves music—she is quick, practical, studies dance. Stasha, my Stasha"—here Mama paused, as if unsure how to categorize me, and then declared—"she has an imagination."

The doctor received this information with interest, and requested that we join him on the ramp.

We hesitated. It was better within the suffocations of the coat. Outside, there was a gray, flame-licked wind that alerted us to our grief, and a scorched scent that underpinned it; there were guns casting shadows and dogs barking and drooling and growling as only dogs bred for cruelty can. But before we had a chance to withdraw farther, the doctor pulled aside the curtains of the coat. In the sunlight, we blinked. One of us snarled. It might have been Pearl. It was probably me.

How could it be, the doctor marveled, that these perfect features could be wasted on such dour expressions? He drew us out, made us turn for him, and had us stand back to back so he could appreciate the exactitudes of us.

"Smile!" he instructed.

Why did we obey this particular order? For our mother's sake, I suppose. For her, we grinned, even as she clung to Zayde's arm, her face lit with panic, two drops of sweat tripping down her forehead. Ever since we'd entered the cattle car, I'd avoided looking at our mother. I looked at the poppy she drew instead; I focused on the fragile bloom of its face. But something about her false expression made me acknowledge what Mama had become: a pretty but sleepless semi-widow, faded in her personhood. Once the primmest of women, she was undone; dust streaked her cheek, her lace collar lay limp. Dull gems of blood secured themselves to the corners of her lips where she'd gnawed on them in worry.

"They are *mischlinge?*" he asked. "That yellow hair!"

Mama pulled at her dark curls, as if ashamed of their beauty, and shook her head.

"My husband—he was fair" was all she could say. It was the only answer she had when asked about the coloring that made certain onlookers insist that our blood was mixed. As we'd grown, that word *mischling*—we heard it more and more, and its use in our presence had inspired Zayde to give us the Classification of Living Things. Never mind this Nuremberg abomination, he'd say. He'd tell us to ignore this talk of mixed breeds, crossed genetics, of quarter-Jews and kindred, these absurd, hateful tests that tried to divide our people down to the last blood drop and marriage and place of worship. When you hear that word, he'd say, dwell on the variation of all living things. Sustain yourself, in awe of this.

I knew then, standing before the white-coated doctor, that this advice would be difficult to take in the days to come, that we were in a place that did not answer to Zayde's games.

"Genes, they are funny things, yes?" the doctor was saying.

Mama, she didn't even try to engage him in this line of conversation.

"If they go with you"—and here she would not look at us—"when will we see them again?"

"On your Sabbath," the doctor promised. And then he turned to us and exclaimed over our details—he loved that we spoke German, he said, he loved that we were fair. He didn't love that our eyes were brown, but this, he remarked to the guard, could prove useful—he leaned in still closer to inspect us, extending a gloved hand to stroke my sister's hair.

"So you're Pearl?" His hand dipped through her curls too easily, as if it had done so for years.

"She's not Pearl," I said. I stepped forward to obscure my sister, but Mama pulled me away and told the doctor that, indeed, he had named the right girl.

"So they like to play tricks?" He laughed. "Tell me your secret—how do you know who is who?"

"Pearl doesn't fidget" was all Mama would say. I was grateful that she didn't elaborate on our identifiable differences. Pearl wore a blue pin in her hair. I wore red. Pearl spoke evenly. My speech was rushed, broken in spots, riddled with pause. Pearl's skin was as pale as a dumpling. I had summer flesh, as spotty as a horse. Pearl was all girl. I wanted to be all Pearl, but try as I might, I could only be myself.

The doctor stooped to me so that we could be face to face.

"Why would you lie?" he asked me. Again, there was his laugh, tinged with the familial.

If I was honest, I would have said that Pearl was—to my mind—the weaker of the two of us, and I thought I could protect her if I became her. Instead, I gave him a half-truth.

"I forget which one I am sometimes," I said lamely.

And this is where I don't remember. This is where I want to wander my mind back and under, past the smell, past the thump-bump of the boots and the suitcases, toward some semblance of a good-bye. Because we should have seen our loves go missing, we should have been able to watch them leave us, should have known the precise moment of our loss. If only we'd seen their faces turning from us, a flash of eye, a curve of cheek! A face turning—they would never give us that. Still, why couldn't we have had a view of their backs to carry with us, just their backs as they left, only that? Just a glimpse of shoulder, a flash of woolen coat? For the sight of Zayde's hand, hanging so heavy at his side—for Mama's braid, lifting in the wind!

But where our loved ones should have been, we had only the introduction to this white-coated man, Josef Mengele, the same Mengele who would become, in all his many years of hiding, Helmut Gregor, G. Helmuth, Fritz Ulmann, Fritz Hollman, Jose Mengele, Peter Hochbicler, Ernst Sebastian Alves, Jose Aspiazi, Lars Balltroem, Friedrich Edler von Breitenbach, Fritz Fischer,

Karl Geuske, Ludwig Gregor, Stanislaus Prosky, Fausto Rindon, Fausto Rondon, Gregor Schklastro, Heinz Stobert, and Dr. Henrique Wollman.

The man who would bury his death-dealing within these many names—he told us to call him Uncle Doctor. He made us call him by this name, once, then twice, just so we could all be acquainted, with no mistakes. By the time we finished repeating the name to his satisfaction, our family had vanished.

And when we saw the absence where Mama and Zayde once stood, an awareness collapsed me at the knees, because I saw that this world was inventing a different order of living things. I did not know then what kind of living thing I would become, but the guard didn't let me have a chance to think about it—he grasped my arm and dragged me till Pearl assured him that she'd support me, and she put her arm around my waist as we were led away with the triplets, away from the ramp and into the dust, onto a little road that led past the sauna and toward the crematoria, and as we marched into this new distance with death rising up on either side of us, we saw bodies on a cart, saw them heaped and blackened, and one of the bodies— it was reaching out its hand, it was grasping for something to hold, as if there were some invisible tether in the air that only the near-dead could see. The body's mouth moved. We saw the pinkness of a tongue as it flapped and struggled. Words had abandoned it.

I knew how important words were to a life. If I gave the body some of mine, I thought, it would be restored.

Was I stupid to think this? Or feebleminded? Would the thought have occurred to me in a place free of flame-licked winds and white-winged doctors?

These are fair questions. I think of them often, but I have never tried to answer them. The answers don't belong to me.

All I know: I stared at the body, and the only words I could summon weren't my own. They were from a song I'd heard played on a smuggled record player in our ghetto basement. Whenever I'd heard the song, it had improved me. So I gave these words a try.

"'Would you like to swing on a star?'" I sang to the body.

Not a sound, not a stir. Was it the fault of my squeaky voice? I tried again.

"'Carry moonbeams home in a jar?'" I sang.

It was pathetic of me to try, I know, but I had always believed in the world's ability to right itself, just like that, with a single kindness. And when kindness is not around, you invent new orders and systems to believe in, and there, in that moment—whether it was stupidity or feeblemindedness—I believed in a body's ability to animate itself with the breath of a word. But it was obvious that these lyrics were not the right words at all. None of them could unlock the life of the body or were powerful enough to repair it. I searched for another word, a good word, to give—there had to be a word, I was sure of it—but the guard wouldn't let me finish. He pulled me away and forced us to press on, anxious to have us showered and processed and numbered so that our time in Mengele's zoo could begin.

Auschwitz was built to imprison us. Birkenau was built to kill us. Mere kilometers bridged their attached evils. What this zoo was designed for, I did not know—I could only swear that Pearl and I, we would never be caged.

The barracks of the Zoo were once stables for horses, but now they were heaped with the likes of us: twins, triplets, quints. Hundreds upon hundreds of us, all packed into beds that weren't beds but matchboxes, little slots to slip bodies into; we were piled from floor to ceiling, forced into these minute structures three or four bodies at a time so that a girl hardly knew where her body ended and another's began.

Everywhere we looked there was a duplicate, an identical. All girls. Sad girls, toddler girls, girls from faraway places, girls who could have been our neighborhood's girls. Some of these girls were quiet; they posed like birds on their straw mattresses and studied us. As we walked past them on their perches, I saw the chosen, the ones selected to suffer in certain ways while their other halves remained untouched. In nearly every pair, one twin had a spine gone awry, a bad leg, a patched eye, a wound, a scar, a crutch.

When Pearl and I sat on our own bunk, the mobile ones descended on us. They scrambled over the rickety corrals with their straw mattresses and appraised our similarities. Demands of our identities were made.

We were from Lodz, we told them. First, a house. Then, a basement in the ghetto. We had a grandpapa, a mother. Once, there had been a father. And Zayde had an old spaniel that could play dead when you pointed a finger at him, but he was easily brought back to life. Did we mention that our father was a doctor who helped others so much that he disappeared one night, that he left us to tend to a sick child and never returned? Yes, we missed him so much we could not even divide the weight of our grief between us. There were other things we dreaded too: germs, unhappy endings, Mama weeping. And there were things we loved: pianos, Judy Garland, Mama weeping less. But who were we really, in the end? There wasn't much to say beyond the fact that one of us was a good dancer, and the other one tried to be good but wasn't really good at anything except being curious. That one was me.

Satisfied by this information, the others offered their own in a clamor of sentence-finishing.

"We get more food here," began Rachel, a girl so pale that you could nearly see through her.

"But it's not kosher and it eats your insides," her equally transparent half pointed out.

"We keep our hair," noted Sharon, pulling on her braid for show.

"Until the lice come," added her shorn sister.

"We get to keep our clothes too," contributed one of the Russians.

"But they put crosses on our backs," finished her double. She turned so I could see the cross that blared in red paint on her dress, but I needed no illustration. A red cross stood between my shoulder blades too.

The children hushed abruptly, and the uninvited silence hung over us all—it was as if a new cloud had installed itself within the rafters of the Zoo. The many doubles looked at each other searchingly—there had to be something, their faces said, something more than food and hair and clothes. Then a voice piped up from the bunk below us. We craned to see the speaker, but she and her twin were curled up together, flush with the brick wall. We never came to know her face, but her words stayed with us always.

"They keep our families safe for us," said this unseen stranger.

At this, all the girls nodded their approval, and Pearl and I were overwhelmed by a new rush of conversation as everyone congratulated one another on belonging to families who would remain intact, unlike so many.

I didn't want to ask the obvious. So I pinched Pearl to make her ask for us.

"Why are we more important than the others?" Her voice shrank as it approached the end of the question.

A flurry of answers rose, all having something to do with purpose and greatness, with purity and beauty and being of use. We didn't hear a single one that made sense.

And before I could even try to understand this concept, the *blokowa* assigned to look after us entered. Behind her prodigious back, we called this person Ox; she had the appearance of a wardrobe with a toupee and tended toward foot-stamping and nostril-flaring when caught in one of her passionate rants, which our supposed disobedience frequently inspired. When Pearl and I were first introduced to her, however, she was just a figure popping her head in at the door, half shrouded in night and offended by our questions.

"Why are we called the Zoo?" I asked. "Who decided this?"

Ox shrugged. "It is not obvious to you?"

I said that it was not. The zoos we'd read about with Zayde were sites of preservation that presented the vastness of life. This place, it cared only for the sinister act of collection.

"It is a name that pleases Dr. Mengele" was all Ox would say. "You won't find many answers here. But sleep! That's something you can have. Now let me have mine!"

If only we could have slept. But the darkness was darker than any I'd known, and the smell clung within my nostrils. A moan drifted from the bunk below, and outside there was the barking of dogs, and my stomach wouldn't stop growling back at them. I tried to amuse myself by playing one of our word games, but the shouts of the guards outside kept overpowering my alphabet. I tried to make Pearl play a game with me, but Pearl was busy tracing her fingertips over the silver web that embroidered our brick corner, the better to ignore my whispered questions.

"Would you rather be a watch that only knows the good times," I asked her, "or a watch that sings?"

"I don't believe in music anymore."

"Me neither. But would you rather be a watch—"

"Why do I have to be a watch at all? Is this my only choice?"

I wanted to argue that sometimes, as living things, as human-type people who were presumably still alive, we had to treat ourselves as objects in order to get by; we had to hide ourselves away and seek repair only when repair was safe to seek. But I chose to press on with another query instead.

"Would you rather be the key to a place that will save us or the weapon that will destroy our enemies?"

"I'd rather be a real girl," Pearl said dully. "Like I used to be."

I wanted to argue that playing games would help her feel like a real girl again, but even I wasn't sure of this fact. The numbers the Nazis had given us had made life unrecognizable, and in the dark, the numbers were all I could see, and what was worse was that there was no way to pretend them into anything less enduring or severe or blue. Mine were smudged and bleared—I'd kicked and spat; they'd had to hold me down—but they were numbers still. Pearl was numbered too, and I hated her numbers even more than mine, because they pointed out that we were separate people, and when you are separate people, you might be parted.

I told Pearl that I'd tattoo us back to sameness as soon as possible, but she only sighed the sigh traditional to moments of sisterly frustration.

"Enough with the stories. You can't tattoo."

I told her that I knew how to well enough. A sailor taught me, back in Gdańsk. I'd inked an anchor onto his left biceps.

True, it was a lie. Or a half-lie, since I had seen such an anchor-inking take place. When we'd summered at the sea, I spent my time peering into the gray recess of a tattoo parlor, its walls bordered with outlines of swallows and ships, while Pearl found a boy to hold her hand near the barnacled prow of a boat. So it was that as my sister entered into the secrecies of flesh on flesh, the pang of a palm curled within one's own, I schooled myself in the intimacies of needles, the plunge of a point so fine that only a dream could light upon its tip.

"I'll make us the same again someday," I insisted. "I just need a needle and some ink. There must be a way to get that, given that we are special here."

Pearl scowled and made a big show of turning her back to me—the bunk cried out with a creak—and her elbow flew up and jabbed me in the ribs. It was an accident—Pearl would never hurt me on purpose, if only because it would hurt her too. That was one of the biggest stings of this sisterhood—pain never belonged to just one of us. We had no choice but to share our sufferings, and I knew that in this place we'd have to find a way to divide the pain before it began to multiply.

As I realized this, a girl on the other side of the room found a light, a precious book of matches, and she decided that this scarcity would be best put to use making shadow puppets for the audience of multiples. And so it was that we drifted off to sleep with a series of shadow figures crossing the wall, walking two by two, each flanking the other, as if in a procession toward some unseen ark that might secure their safety.

So much world in the shadows there! The figures feathered and crept and crawled toward the ark. Not a single life was too small. The leech asserted itself, the centipede sauntered, the cricket sang by. Representatives of the swamp, the mountain, the desert—all of them ducked and squiggled and forayed in shadow. I classified them, two by two, and the neatness of my ability to do so gave me comfort. But as their journey lengthened, and the flames began to dim, the shadows were visited by distortions. Humps rose on their backs, and their limbs scattered and their spines dissolved. They became changed and monstrous. They couldn't recognize themselves.

Still, for as long as the light lived, the shadows endured. That was something, wasn't it?

CHAPTER TWO

Zugangen, or Newcomers

Stasha didn't know it, but always, from the very beginning, we were more than we. I was older by only ten minutes, but it was enough to teach me how different we were.

It was only in Mengele's Zoo that we became too different.

For example: On that first night, the marching shadows comforted Stasha, but I could find no peace in them. Because those matches illuminated another sight, one accompanied by a death rattle. Did Stasha mention the dying girl?

We weren't alone in our bunk that night. There was a third child with us on the straw mattress, a feverish, black-tongued mite who curled up beside me and pressed her cheek to my cheek as she died. This wasn't a gesture of affection—our proximity rose only from the fact that there wasn't an inch of room to be spared in our matchbox beds—but in the days ahead I found myself often hoping that this twinless, nameless girl took some comfort in being close to me. I had to believe that it was not a lack of room alone that put her cheek to mine.

When the rattle stopped, the Stepanov twins, Esfir and Nina, the eleven-year-olds in the bed slot below us, leaped up to our mattress and stripped the girl of her clothes. They performed this task with an unnerving deftness, as if they'd been undressing corpses all their lives. Esfir joyously flung a sweater around her shoulders; Nina shimmied into a woolen skirt. The disapproval on my face must've been obvious, because Esfir offered me the girl's stockings, thrusting the unraveled, grayed toe beneath my nose, in a gesture of appeasement. When I waved this gift away, she—a veteran, or Old Number—employed the insult used for us New Numbers, or newcomers.

"*Zugang!*" she hissed at me.

If I hadn't been so lost over the death beside me, I might have defended myself, but I cared little at that moment. The Stepanovs exchanged wily glances with each other, and then Serafima winked at me, as if to acknowledge the great favor she was about to perform on my behalf. Without a word of negotiation between them, the two took hold of the girl's body by its head and its feet and slid its meager weight from our bed.

"She can stay." I reached out and put a hand on the still-warm chest.

"She is dead," they argued. "See the trickle from her mouth? Dead!"

"So? She still needs a place to sleep, doesn't she?"

"It's against our law, *zugang.*"

"What law?"

They were too busy carting the body down the ladder to the floor to answer, their movements illuminated by the same scant light that produced the shadowy animals. I wished for utter darkness then. Because I saw the girl's eyes fly open as her body thumped past the rungs and to the floor. All of the children turned in their beds so as not to witness the exodus, but I saw the girl's hair fan over the threshold as her bearers dragged her out, and I tried, as she disappeared from view, to remember her eyes.

I thought they were brown eyes, as brown as my own, but our acquaintance had been so brief, I couldn't be sure.

All I could be sure of was the sprightliness of the twins. When they reappeared at the door, they were clapping the grime from their hands. Nina twirled in the skirt, and Esfir plucked lint from the stolen sweater. They were enlivened by these new possessions. Nina ambled over with a bundle in her hand and tossed it in Stasha's direction.

"Take the stockings," she spat at my sister. "Don't act so superior."

Stasha regarded the stockings where they lay, so limp and forlorn, in her lap. I advised her to give them back, but Stasha had never been good at taking anyone's advice, even mine. She thrust them onto her hands like mittens, much to Nina's pleasure.

"You're resourceful," Nina said approvingly before retiring with her sister to the bunk below, where the two of them rustled about in their straw like the scavengers they were, doubtless planning their next acquisition of goods.

Everyone survived by planning. I could see that. I realized that Stasha and I would have to divide the responsibilities of living between us. Such divisions had always come naturally to us, and so there, in the early-morning dark, we divvied up the necessities:

Stasha would take the funny, the future, the bad. I would take the sad, the past, the good.

There were overlaps between these categories, but we'd negotiated such overlaps before. It seemed fair to me, but when we were done with the partitioning of these duties, Stasha had misgivings.

"You got the worse deal," she said. "I'll trade you. I'll take the past, and you take the future. The future is more hopeful."

"I am happy with the way things are," I said.

"Take the future. I already have the funny—you should have the future. It will make things more even between us."

I thought of all the years we'd spent trying to match every gesture. When we were small, we'd practiced walking the same amount of steps every day, speaking the same number of words, smiling the same smiles. I started to retreat into these memories, but just as I'd begun to calm, Ox resurrected our dread. Cool and efficient, a drab figure in an oatmeal-colored cloak, she picked her way through the barracks with the dead child, now clothed in mud, held aloft in her arms. Wordlessly, she carried the girl over to our bunk and laid her back beside me, placing the cold hands over the concave chest and crossing the legs at their ankles. Tongue thrust between her teeth in concentration, she performed this endeavor with the manner of one arranging flowers for the room of a beloved houseguest.

"Who did this?" Ox demanded after she'd completed her work and the girl stared sightlessly up at the rafters.

No one would answer, but Ox didn't much care for answers, preferring any opportunity for intimidation. "I recommend that you children find a better way to amuse yourselves than by dumping bodies by the latrines. You all know that Dr. Mengele requires that every child in the Zoo must be counted in the morning. If this body goes missing again—"

She allowed the possibilities to dangle in the air, all the better to frighten us, and then, her mission completed, she turned and left with a dramatic flap of oatmeal-colored cloak, pausing only to confiscate the matches from the girl making the shadow puppets. All was dark once more, though not dark enough to obscure the death that lay beside us.

"She looks hungry even now," Stasha observed. She skipped a stockinged finger across the girl's still cheek. "Do you think she has feelings anymore?"

"No one has feelings when they are dead," I told her. But I wasn't quite convinced of this myself. If there was ever a place where the dead might still feel their tortures, it had to be the Zoo.

Stasha took the stockings from her hands and tried to pull them over the girl's feet. First the left foot, then the right. One stocking crowned at midcalf, while the other slipped easily over the knee. Frustrated by this difference, Stasha tugged at the woolens to make them align, and I had to point out to her that the pair were mismatched, that there was no way to force them into sameness. Nothing was fixable; we could only make do.

"Please," I whispered to Stasha as her efforts inspired a new hole in one of the stockings, "let me have the past, and I'll take the present too. I just don't want the future."

That was how the role of keeper of time and memory came to be mine. From then on, the acknowledgment of days was my responsibility alone.

September 3, 1944

In our former life, I was used to doing the talking for us. I had been the outgoing one, the one with proven methods of getting us out of trouble, the one who negotiated exchanges with peers and authority figures alike. This role suited me. I was everyone's friend, and a fair representative for us both.

We soon found out that Stasha was better fit for socializing in our new world. A fearlessness had entered her. She set her teeth with severity when she smiled, and she walked with a girlish approximation of a swagger, like a movie cowboy or a comic-book hero.

On our first morning, her chatter was endless. She asked questions of anyone she could, to try to ease our adjustment. The first to receive her inquiry was a man who introduced himself to us as Zwillingesvater, or Twins' Father. He saw us respond to the oddity of this name with curious faces, but he did not try to explain it except to say that all of the children called him this—the Zoo, we would find, had a habit of assigning people new names and identities, and even adults were no exception to this rule.

"When do we see our families?" Stasha asked Twins' Father as he sat on a crate recording all our facts for Mengele's use. We were sitting with him behind the boys' barracks with an irrelevant globe idling at his feet in the dirt. The travels of this globe— a relic that was usually kept in the storehouse—were much envied by us all, as the object was able to move from camp to camp, while we remained pinned within the Zoo. One of the boys—a Peter Abraham, whom Mengele had dubbed "a member of the intelligentsia"—served as one of the doctor's messengers, and in this position, he was able to steal this little globe, to tuck it beneath his coat and toddle from block to block as if afflicted with some strange pregnancy. Peter stole it in the mornings, and in the evenings, one of the guards stole it back. In this way, the world was possessed and repossessed, and over time, it grew more battered in its travels. Holes appeared, borders were blurred, whole countries faded away altogether. Still, it was a globe, and it tended to be a useful thing to have around, because during interviews like these, one could focus on its surface instead of Twins' Father's face, though I suppose both were equally worn and discouraged in appearance.

"We see our families on holidays," Twins' Father told her in his patient way. "Or so Mengele says."

Twins' Father was twenty-nine years old and a veteran of the Czech army. He carried himself like a soldier still but had a weariness that was likely exacerbated by his charges. Impressed by his military pedigree and German fluency, Mengele had entrusted him with overseeing the boys' barracks and processing the paperwork of all the incoming twins, paperwork that was later sent to the genetics department at Berlin's Kaiser Wilhelm Institute.

If it could be said that Mengele ever did a good thing, that good thing was appointing Twins' Father to his post. The boys loved him;

they clung to him as he taught them lessons—German and geography, mostly—and he kicked a rag ball around the soccer field with them in odd little fits of games. There were mothers of newborn multiples who were permitted to live in the Zoo in the interest of assisting the development of their babies, and they cooed over Twins' Father, saying that he would make a fine head of the family someday, but the man winced at this praise, and just carried on in his gentle and resourceful way. We girls were quite jealous of the boys for this ally, having only Ox as our designated authority. We learned nothing of where we were from Ox. From other girls in the barracks, we learned that Mengele's Zoo had once been near the Romany camp. But now, the Romanies were dead, as every last one had been exterminated on August 2, 1944; their eradication was seen as a necessity by camp authorities, who were appalled by the rampant disease and starvation among them. This was not a problem of proper rations—the adults were clearly withholding food from the children. Romanies would rather sing and dance all day than address their filth. All that could be done with such a people was to end them.

There were rumors that Mengele tried to intervene. Whether this was true, no one knew. We knew only that the Romanies were gassed, and we, the twins of Auschwitz, remained. Directly before our compound, there was an empty plot of land where the Germans collected the dead and the near-dead. This plot filled and emptied in terrible repetition. This was our immediate view.

We could also see birches in the woods beyond the thirteen-foot-high electric fences. And we could see women prisoners in the adjacent field; if the girls saw their mothers among them, they could throw their bread to them, hoping that they would not loft it back, as our rations were greater than anyone else's in the camp. We could see the labs we were taken to on Tuesdays and Thursdays and Saturdays, the two-story buildings of brick, but the rest of our view was limited. If someone had cause to pluck us up and take us somewhere, then there was more we might learn of Auschwitz, but otherwise, we did not see the section of the camp called Canada, which featured a series of warehouses so overwhelmed with pillaged splendor that the prisoners named it after a country that represented wealth and luxury to them. Inside Canada's structures, our former possessions loomed in stacks: our spectacles, our coats, our instruments, our suitcases, all of it, even down to our teeth, our hair, anything that could be considered necessary to the business of being human. We did not see the sauna where inmates were stripped, or the little white farmhouse whose rooms were passed off as showers. We did not see the luxuriant headquarters of the SS, where parties took place, parties where the women of the Puff were brought in to dance and sit upon Nazi laps. We did not see, and so we believed we already knew the worst. We couldn't imagine the greatness of suffering, how artful and calculated it could be, how it could pluck off the members of a family, one after the other, or show an entire village the face of death in one fell swoop.

The day after our arrival, Twins' Father remained efficient and stoic as he approached our paperwork, but there were times in which his uncertainties seemed to surface as he considered the import of every answer and the effect it might have on our lives. I watched his hand waver between one box and another before imposing a hesitant check mark.

"Now tell me," he asked, "which of you came first?"

"This matters?" Stasha had never been fond of this question.

"To him, it all matters. My sister Magda and I, we don't know who came first. But we say that I did, just to please him. So tell me, Pearl, who was first?"

"I was," I admitted.

As Twins' Father and I continued with the details, Stasha directed her questions to Dr. Miri, who was waiting to collect the finished paperwork and deliver it to the laboratory. Dr. Miri was a beautiful doctor—like a lily, people were fond of saying, a solemn and thoughtful kind of flower. She reminded us of Mama a little, with her dark hair and too-big eyes and crooked mouth, but she was more doll-like, and the expressions that crossed her face often struck me as very strange because they were so distant, so far away. They were not unlike the expressions one might have while under-water watching disturbances occur on the waves above.

Even more remarkable than Dr. Miri's beauty was the fact that Mengele allowed it to remain untouched. Most of the beauties who entered Mengele's view emerged from it much changed, as he could not bear admiring them. He put beauties on one of two paths—the Ibi path or the Orli path. If you were on the Orli path, you might be beautiful on the day of your arrival, but on the very next you'd be given a disguise; Mengele would puff up your belly and swell your legs to sausages, or he'd turn your skin to wax and set it to run with sores. If you were on the Ibi path, you could go to work in the Puff; you could lean from the window and flutter like a rare, colorful bird and listen to the madam negotiate your price with the men knocking at the door. Dr. Miri's path, the path of a Jewish doctor respected by Mengele, was the rarest one of all.

Orli and Ibi were Dr. Miri's sisters. She didn't see them much. If a person wanted to make Miri cry, all he had to do was mention Ibi and Orli. Mengele did this from time to time, whenever he found her work in the laboratory unsatisfactory or wanted to compel her to do things she did not want to do. I would come to witness such exchanges frequently in the days ahead, but on that first day, there was only Dr. Miri, standing there, waiting for our file.

"When do we leave?" Stasha asked her. A pause hung in the air.

"There are plans for that," Dr. Miri said finally, after exchanging a look with Twins' Father, the kind of look that adults use when approaching delicate subjects that they've approached many times before and still have yet to resolve. "We've started the plans but we don't know—"

She was saved from answering when a woman appeared in the doorway with her infants in her arms, two bundles swaddled in gray cloth, their faces tucked away from view.

Sometimes, when twins were still babies, their mothers were allowed to live in the Zoo alongside them to serve as nursemaids. Clotilde was one such mother. Everyone knew who Clotilde was because her husband had killed an SS man; he'd seized a pistol from the guard, issued a fatal shot, and led a flicker of an uprising. Three SS were felled before the end of this siege, and care was taken to ensure that the hanging of this rebel was witnessed by all. But instead of inspiring fear, his death bred a hero's tale. Her children would always have that legacy, Clotilde was fond of claiming, but their father's fame was apparently of little comfort to the babies. They whimpered and kicked their tiny feet against their dingy wrappings, as if to protest their patriarch's violent end.

Stasha drew close to Clotilde and tried to inspect the bundles. I was afraid she would ask to hold the babies—she tended to think herself more capable than she really was—but thankfully, she remained interested only in her own questions.

"What do we eat?" she asked Clotilde, who passed one of the babies to Dr. Miri to admire. I saw Dr. Miri stiffen at the sight of the child, but Clotilde seemed blissfully unaware of this reaction, too invested in answering Stasha with a tone of educational bitterness.

"Soup that isn't soup!" she proclaimed with glee.

"I've never heard of such a soup before. What's in a soup like that?"

"Today? Boiled roots. Tomorrow? Boiled roots. After that? Boiled roots and a bit of nothing. Does that sound good to you?"

"There are things that sound better." Stasha nodded at the babies. "Your twins are lucky not to have to eat soup like that."

"Pray for better, then," Clotilde instructed. "And if your prayers aren't answered, then eat your prayers. Prayer alone can keep a body full." The babies saw the absurdity of this, and their whimpers assumed the turbulence of ear-piercing bawls.

"We don't pray," Stasha told her, raising her voice to be heard above the wails.

We'd stopped praying in the fall of 1939. November 12. Like many who stop praying, it was a familial event, spurred by disappearance. Although, to be most accurate, I should say that prayer experienced a surge for one week, then two, and it wasn't until the first thaw that it died entirely. By the time the bluebells thrust their heads up in the soil, prayer had become a buried thing.

I wasn't about to explain this to Clotilde, whose eyebrows were already arching disdainfully at us. She regarded the heads of her babies and covered them with her scarf, as if hoping to protect them from our lack of faith.

"You will reconsider your position when you get hungry enough," she muttered, and then she and Twins' Father had a quick conversation in Czech, the meaning of which was unknown to us, but my impression from the blunt ends of their words and their shattered delivery was that each was telling the other to know his or her place. As the fray mounted, a torn and fearful look entered Dr. Miri's face—not unlike the expression a child has while witnessing her parents fight—and she stepped between the two quarrelers.

"But maybe," she suggested to us, her voice winsome despite the fact that she had to shout to be heard, "maybe, instead of praying, you will wish. You do wish, don't you? You can have as many wishes as you want here."

Her manner was so even, so practiced, that I realized that much of Dr. Miri's work in the Zoo had to involve easing similar conflicts to a halt. She was successful in this case. Clotilde spat on the floor, signaling her surrender in the argument, and Twins' Father smiled a little at the fanciful nature of this proposed resolution before returning to our interview.

"Where have you lived?" he asked us. "Any other siblings? Your parents—both Polish Jews, yes? Your birth—natural? Cesarean? Any complications?"

We could hear the travel of his pen as he sorted out all the details we gave him, and then, right as we were nearly finished, a troop of guards flooded past; the dust rose, the dogs barked, and Twins' Father threw his pen to the ground with a force that made us jump a little. The babies' wails increased. The man put his head in his hands, and we thought he might be going to sleep forever, that he'd decided to stop living altogether, just like that. We'd heard that such phenomena had a habit of occurring in this place. But after we'd watched the top of his prematurely gray head for a minute, he looked back up at us, thoroughly alive.

"Forgive me," he said with a weak smile. "I ran out of ink. That's all. I am always running out of ink. I am always—" For a second, it appeared as if he might sink again, but then he righted himself, just as suddenly as he had before, and smiled at us broadly while waving his hand. "Go, now, for roll call."

We began to turn away from him, obedient, but then he gestured for us to wait. He made a point of looking directly into our eyes. It was obvious that what he said to us was something he repeated often, to any child who would listen.

"Your first assignment for class is to learn the other children's names. Recite them to each other. When a new child comes, learn that name too. When a child leaves us, remember the name."

I swore I would remember. Stasha swore too. And then she asked after his real name.

Twins' Father stared down at the papers for one minute, maybe two. He seemed lost in the answers he'd so carefully composed, as if all the check marks and little boxes he'd inked in black had blacked him out too, and then, just as we'd resigned ourselves to leaving without an answer, he lifted his eyes to us.

"It was Zvi Singer once," he said. "But that is not important now."

———

We stood for roll call in that early-morning light, our noses twitching in an effort to shake the stench of ash and the unwashed. September's heat lingered in the air. It bounced off us in waves, haloed us with dust. This roll call was the first time I saw all of Mengele's subjects gathered together: the multiples, the giants, the Lilliputs, the limbless, the Jews he'd deemed curiously Aryan in appearance. While some regarded us innocently, others held suspicion in their stares, and I had to wonder how long we would be considered *zugangi*. We did our best to ignore these looks as we sawed through our hard heels of breakfast bread and drank our muddy, fake coffee. Most of my bread I gave to Stasha. But I drank all of my fake coffee, which was very sour, like it had been brewed in an old shoe at the bottom of the river, according to my sister. When Stasha drank her coffee, her throat took offense and she was compelled to spit into the distance. Unfortunately, the Rabinowitzes were contained in that distance—they were all lined up to receive their breakfast—and Stasha's spittle insulted the eldest son of the family, as it landed squarely on the lapel of his suit coat.

The Rabinowitzes were Lilliputs. There was a whole family of them, complete with a baton-wielding patriarch, and they all still dressed in the velvets and silks of their performance costumes, colorful garments edged with gilt and lace and swinging with tassels. The hair of the women was pompadoured high, and the wavy beards of the men streamed behind them like banners in a parade. They were an ostentatious sight, and though I didn't share the sentiment, I could see why others resented them. For one, where else could one find an intact family in Auschwitz? And for two, they were among the grandest beneficiaries of Mengele's attentions. His marvel over the family not only put them in a superior state of mind but blessed them with a spacious room to themselves in the infirmary, and their quarters brimmed with elusive comforts: Tables draped with lace and a window frilled with pink voile curtains. A full tea set painted with a willow-tree pattern. A miniature armchair in plush leather, big enough to seat a lamb. Mengele had even given them a radio, which Mirko, the eldest son, a teenager, was entrusted with. Mirko always sang along with that radio, even when there weren't words to the music; he'd invent words, just to have something to sing. He was the one Stasha was unfortunate enough to strike with spittle.

"You take care who you spit on, *zugang*," Mirko said to her through gritted teeth.

I tried to wipe the spittle from his coat as I apologized, but he withdrew, as if doubly insulted by my efforts, and addressed the fabric with a swipe of his hat brim. Stasha stared at him all the while, mesmerized, her eyes spreading themselves wider than I'd thought our eyes could go. They grew as if to make more room to inspect the curiosity before her, and her appraisal was obvious, verging on ill-mannered.

"Haven't seen my kind before, have you?" Mirko challenged.

"You are not our first," Stasha lied. "We've seen shows, lots of shows. We used to go to the theater all the time. We saw a whole troupe of people like you once."

I often had to wonder where she summoned these lies from. They came so easily to her, as if she had another nature devoted strictly to fabrication. I can't say that I wasn't unnerved by her deceit, but she appeared to know how to draw in people like Mirko, who suddenly lost his defensive stance. His balled-up hands relaxed at his sides, and once the disgust left his face, I saw how handsome it was. He had features that a girl reading a romance novel would have projected onto the imaginary hero, and I'm sure he was well aware of its powers, because he made a gentlemanly point of turning to Stasha, and allowed me to blush with some degree of privacy.

"I would hardly have mistaken you for sophisticates," he said to her. "But I suppose that even young ones like you may have use for the theater. Do you have any talent between you?"

"My sister is a dancer," Stasha said. She made her usual mistake of pointing to herself while saying this. I grasped her pointing finger and put it in my direction.

"Oh?" Mirko's gaze then focused solely on me. "Where have you danced? May I suggest a collaboration? Performing keeps the doctor very happy. We give him private shows from time to time, entertain his friends. Like Verschuer. Have you heard of Verschuer? He is the doctor's mentor. Even Mengele, yes, he has a mentor. If you are a good dancer, perhaps I could mentor you?"

He performed an impromptu jig and then concluded with a proud bow.

"I come from a long line of dancers, and my grandmother, she was a tall woman, like you. We've danced all over, for kings and queens. We tell jokes too. Would you care to hear one? You would? What kind of joke would you prefer?"

Before we had a chance to answer, the palest woman we'd ever seen, white hair blazing at her back like winter, descended upon this small person in a colorless and incandescent glory. She swooped down and pummeled him; she stomped on his tiny feet as he yowled. She asked him who he was to think himself better than tall people, human people like us, even if we were just a pair of weak *zugangi*. Stasha tried to intervene—she pointed out that he wasn't bothering us in the least—but the insulting angel was too preoccupied with her torture to listen. She chased him off, stepping on his heels as he ran, and threw a couple of rocks at him for good measure.

"You ugly ghost! You better watch yourself in your sleep," Mirko threatened before retreating behind the boys' barracks.

"Try it, tadpole!" his tormentor shouted. "I'd like to see you make me hate my life. If they can't do it, how will you? Every day, I wake ready to burst, because I am filled with poison and vigor and plans for revenge. Just try to complete my suffering! Try!"

After concluding this outburst, the angel beamed triumphant and then fell to dusting off her sullied clothes with an aggravated sweep of her hands. She wore once-white pajamas of frayed silk and was so lean and tall that she resembled a pillar of salt. The eyes in her pale face were bordered by bruises that lent her the look of a panda. This was curious enough until one noticed that the eyes themselves were pink as roses.

Her name was Bruna. Or at least, that was the name she was going by in those days. The guards had given it to her as a sort of mockery—it was a German name that meant "brunette." She twisted the darkness of their intention for her own purposes, though, and wore the name with her own pale bravado.

"Phooey to dwarves," Bruna said. "Give me one of the cripples any day, or even one of the giants. You would agree with me?"

I was about to argue with this perspective, but Stasha interrupted.

"How did you get the bruises?"

Bruna pointed to the whorls of violet with pride.

"Ox gave them to me. For mouthing off to her. But she mouthed off to me first. If this were my hometown, my gang would take vengeance on her. I'd only have to say the word. Here, I have no gang. I miss it a great deal. I wasn't any kind of leader. But I was a good enough thief. A diligent one, you could say. Started with pockets but soon advanced to grander heists. Guess what my greatest theft was."

"A house?"

"How do you steal a house? People can't steal houses!"

"They stole ours," my sister pointed out.

"Mine too," Bruna conceded. "You are smart in that odd way, aren't you? But it's not a house. It's bigger than a house, because a house can't die. Guess! You're never going to guess, are you? Well, I'll tell you—a swan! I stole a swan from the zoological gardens in Odessa. Went to the pond and tucked it up right under my coat. I wore a very roomy coat in those days, just for stealing purposes. Of course, the coat wasn't so big as to hide the swan entirely. It was a young one, so it was smaller than average, and it bit me a little, here and there, but after I took it home, it was quite enchanted with our life, and I'm sure it would have lived with me forever if it could."

We asked what the good in swan-stealing was. It seemed a curious transgression, and hardly profitable.

"They were storming the city. They were shooting all our animals, any animal they could find. The soldiers liked to kick our dogs till they flew. Some of our animals—the horses—the men took for themselves. You do not want me to tell you what they did with our cats. Well, I wasn't about to let the greatest beauty in Odessa die by their hands. So when they stormed into my lodgings—I twisted her neck."

She illustrated this savage transaction with a wrenching of both her broad hands. It was easy enough to imagine her extinguishing that life. We might as well have heard the crackle of bones, seen the white length of a feathery neck go limp. It seemed doubtless that Bruna heard the crack and saw the limpness still; her pink eyes went misty with reflection, and she thrust her hands in her pockets hurriedly, anxious to dismiss the memory of this most useful violence. She wiped an eye on the shoulder of her pajamas, and forced a smile.

"But my gang—we were talking about my gang. We might not have been much but we took care of each other. Like I just took care of you."

"We will return the favor," Stasha promised.

"Of course you will," our angel said. "You'll do whatever I say."

Our faces must have shown alarm at the thought of being Bruna's handmaidens of crime, because she dropped her voice quite low, and she slung her arms across our backs and huddled us close.

"Oh, don't you worry," she cooed. "I won't ask for anything too bad or complex. It's not like I want you to murder someone. But I might ask you to organize some things for me from time to time. Just because you can get away with more here. Since you're twins and all. You could steal a whole loaf of bread with no punishment! A whole vat of soup, even! I saw the Stern triplets pull that one off, and a block of margarine to boot! They always share with me, since I taught them how to organize. Here, to *organize* is to steal, you know. You organize to live and to trade and to amuse yourself. Without organizing, I would go mad with boredom."

Stasha wondered aloud how one could be bored in this place, which seemed to require that one be perched always on the worst possibilities. Bruna scoffed.

"You won't wonder after you've lived here forever and are poked with needles every day. You won't wonder after they keep taking your picture and drawing your face while all around you, other people are losing their faces, their bodies too." She sighed and slouched, as if suddenly pulled toward the dust, then straightened herself, pushing her shoulders back with some concentrated effort toward uprightness. "Now that I have educated you, you must entertain me in return. I need entertainment. A trick, maybe. All you twins have tricks."

"You're not a twin?" Stasha seemed surprised by this, but the stupidity of this question was confirmed by Bruna's guffaw.

"Are you blind? If so, I'd be quiet about that if I were you. Or you'll get the gas."

"What is the gas?" Stasha wondered.

Our explainer of things became suddenly reticent and sorrowful.

"Never mind that," Bruna finally said. "Just do not let anyone think you're even weaker or stupider than you are, not even for a moment. Understand?"

She stood very straight and dignified, and she swept a hand from her face to her hips to indicate the extent of her pallor.

"Never seen an albino before?" she asked. "Because that is what I am. A genetic mutation."

"So you're like him." Stasha gestured in the direction of Mirko's retreat, and we saw him peek his head around the corner of the boys' barracks, where he'd apparently been eavesdropping on the conversation. He stuck out his tongue and then disappeared once more.

"Mutant! Pisser! Worm!" she shouted at him before informing us, "No, not like him at all! Better than him! But not as good as you twins. You—if one of you dies by accident, Mengele, he wails and stomps his feet. You are still objects to him, mere things. But precious objects. You are the grand pianos of this place, the mink coats, the caviar. You are valuable! The rest of us—just kazoos, canvas, tinned beans."

As she ended this little lecture—which she clearly loved delivering, delighting in such a neat summation of our troubles—a black fly careened near her nose, drawing a new stream of insults from her mouth.

"Tramp!" she screeched at the insect. "Parasite! Wretch! You think you can make me hate my life too!" She leaped after the fly, chased him this way and that till she lost her balance and collapsed in a white heap, the dust billowing about her where she fell. I leaned down to her, offered her my hand, but she shook me off as if possessed and turned her dirt-streaked face with those blackened eyes up to the sky, which was not the blue of a normal sky but a flame-touched blanket of gray.

"Tell me," she said, her eyes trailing the fly's escape over the fence and into the fields, "what does it feel like—to be of value?"

I said that I didn't know. A lie, obviously. I knew the feeling of value well, I'd known it until Mama and Zayde were taken away, and it still remained—though in an altered form—with Stasha, who valued me more than herself. But I wasn't about to boast of this to Bruna, whose frenzy had enlarged in such a manner that the whole of her quaked. The index finger of her right hand shook the most. She pointed it at a building in the distance, a building that I'd later come to know as one of Mengele's laboratories.

"Please," she entreated, "tell me when you understand? I would like to know."

September 7, 1944

The bread made everyone forget. That was one of the first things Bruna taught me. It was full of bromide, and all it took was a day's worth of crust lining your stomach to make your mind mist over. Since I was the half in charge of time and memory, I always gave the bulk of my portions to Stasha. One of us, I decided, should be encouraged to forget as much as possible, and I found other ways to sustain myself, with Bruna's help.

Bruna called me Smidgen One and Stasha was Smidgen Two. It was her way of owning us, but I didn't mind it much because it seemed better to be owned by Bruna than anyone else. She taught me all sorts of useful things. She taught me how to make a soup from the grass in the soccer field, how to stew it discreetly in a pot, and how to obtain a pot in the first place. She showed me how to ingratiate myself with the cook and how to carry supplies to the kitchen so that I might *organize* some things for us. A potato here, an onion there, a few lumps of coal, a book of matches, a spoon.

She sewed a little burlap sack for me to keep tucked into the waistband of my skirt so that I could be a stealthier thief. Soon enough, I held the whole of our world in that little sack.

I wondered what Mama and Zayde might think of our association with Bruna. On the outside, I would've feared her, but in a place swarming with treachery, she was family, and we did our best to repay her with our affection. She loved our games—they were more sophisticated than the standard grave-digging game that many of the other children favored—and she was always ready for riddles, or Kill Hitler, or the Classification of Living Things, which she was quite terrible at, as she had such odd opinions about what made a living thing superior or functional or worthy of life.

Bruna was only seventeen, but she'd been in Auschwitz for three years and had slunk from labor camp to labor camp for months before that, and so she knew, she assured us, what she was talking about. She said that where we lived was far superior to other sites that were unpaved, their only concrete poured into towers, their only decoration the crook of guns into the sky.

"More civilized here," she liked to say. "But that is not a good thing."

She kept herself occupied, this Bruna, and not only with us. She was always leaping up to help one person or to torture another; she was a busybody who presided over everyone. Much of the day, she stood on the top of a barrel outside the girls' barracks, shielding her eyes from the sun with one hand. Nothing escaped her attention. If a nurse wanted something organized for the infirmary, Bruna found it. If a twin was bullying another, Bruna bullied back, with pleasure. If Twins' Father required a book, Bruna procured it. If someone wasn't a great lover of communism, Bruna helped him or her find that love.

Still, even these activities were often not enough to satisfy her restless nature.

"I'm bored," she declared on our third day within the Zoo. "You should entertain me. I've shown you girls my talents." She turned her pink eyes on me. "Smidgen Two keeps boasting about your tap dancing."

"Stasha is exaggerating," I said.

"Show me," Bruna commanded, dismounting from her barrel with a showy jump. "I am a great appreciator of art. My life is proof of that. I stole a paintbrush once. I stole tickets to the ballet. I stole a dozen china figurines from a fine department store. They caught me for that one, but I stole those figurines all the same. I did time, paid penance. I suffered for art, you see, and so you can't refuse me."

She regarded me expectantly and then removed a few stones from the dirt before us to prepare a stage. I was shocked when she failed to toss them in the direction of any passerby, as she was known never to waste a potential weapon, but it seemed that she was occupied with a different form of anticipation.

"Come now, Pearl. Show me how you dance. Let me forget a little."

"I'm not going to dance here," I insisted. "I have no reason to."

"As practice for when we get out," Stasha said, and she bent to clear another stone away. "For the future. I'm in charge of the future, remember?"

"I won't."

Bruna folded her arms and watched us argue. This seemed entertainment enough for her, but Stasha insisted that I had to practice, I had to make preparations for the life we'd have when the war was over because my dancing might be the only way to provide for our family once the cities were destroyed and all the dead were counted up, once the fathers never came back and the houses never rebuilt themselves.

When I failed to accept this argument, she upped the stakes. That's what Judy Garland would do, she claimed. Judy would practice through her suffering no matter how much her feet bled or her stomach grumbled, no matter how much her head swam and the lice flocked to her.

"I'm not like Judy Garland," I protested.

But my sister remained unconvinced. So I danced in the dust, and Stasha provided some music by whistling. Her whistle was terribly feeble, all starts and stops, but I'll admit that it took me back, and for a moment, I actually did enjoy dancing, enjoyed it more than I'd ever have thought possible in such a place, and I might have happily danced for hours if my audience hadn't gained another member, an unwanted spectator who seated himself with a leisurely air on a nearby stump.

It was Taube, a young warden famous for his ability to creep up behind a woman and twist her neck, extracting her heartbeat from her body before she even had a chance to scream. He had yellow eyes and hair, and ruddy apple cheeks that bobbed as he spoke while the rest of his face remained still as stone. At the sight of him, I stopped, but Taube gestured for me to continue, and he crossed his legs neatly at the ankles, as if settling in at a movie theater for a much-anticipated performance. He pulled a bar of chocolate from his pocket and set to work attacking it with oddly dainty nibbles. Even from some distance, I could make out the semicircles of his bites, and it was easy to imagine the sweetness he enjoyed.

"Keep practicing," he ordered, his teeth coated in darkness.

So I continued. I tried to imagine an audience other than Taube.

"Faster," he instructed.

Heel and toe, I struck the dust. I thought that if I danced fast enough, hard enough, he might let the dance end. And then, to my relief—

"Stop!" he commanded.

I did. But Taube's apple cheeks bobbed irritably. It seemed that I'd misunderstood his directive.

"Not you! You keep dancing. Her!" He pointed to Stasha. "Enough with the whistling!"

Stasha shut her mouth with a snap, and her hands crept up to cover her ears. I could see that the sound of my feet striking the ground disturbed her. She could feel what I felt, all the pain, all the fatigue. Her voice whittled by fear, she begged Taube to permit me to rest.

"But Pearl's very talented. Don't you agree?"

"Very much so," Stasha quavered. She wouldn't look up from her feet, and I knew that they were throbbing like my own.

I might have been able to continue if I hadn't seen Stasha's anguish, but it tripped me up and I fell. Bruna offered me her hand, but Taube shoved her away, electing to pick me up by the waistband of my skirt. He then dragged me in the dust over to his stump, took a few steps back—so as to create a fine distance from which to study me where he'd placed me, like a toy on a shelf—and began to clap. It felt as if all our hearts were suspended in the air between his hands.

"Do you girls know Zarah Leander? Star of *The Life and Loves of Tschaikovsky*? The finest actress of all of German cinema?" he asked when the mocking claps finally subsided.

We did not know, but this didn't feel safe to admit. Instead, we gushed about her beauty and talent, and Taube grinned all the while, basking in the compliments as if it were him we praised, and not a distant movie star.

"Zarah is a family friend, and she is always looking for protégées. I am impressed." He stabbed my cheek with his finger. "You have good feet, and I hear she will be filming a new musical soon. Perhaps, if you work hard enough, your dancing will improve in such a way that I may recommend you to her. Wouldn't that be a nice thing to happen in your life?"

"I suppose so," I offered.

"We are very lucky to have met here, then," he said. His face assumed some facsimile of kind excitement. "I'll call Miss Leander immediately. I'm sure she won't hesitate—perhaps she'll get on an airplane and come whisk you away within the hour!"

An answer was expected.

"Perhaps," I said.

"Perhaps? Such a weak response—where is your conviction, your determination? You should pack your things! Why do you hesitate? Don't you know the life that awaits you?"

Only then did I notice that three other guards had gathered nearby to watch the spectacle—they laughed so hard that their cigarettes tumbled from their mouths. This laughter, combined with the effort of my dancing, left me sick and breathless, and I started to gasp. One of these onlooking wardens leaped to my side in concern—everyone knew that Mengele punished guards who let harm come to any of his twins—and gave me a gentle slap on the back.

"You should hope that the doctor doesn't hear about this," he warned his fellow guards.

"Just a joke." Taube shrugged. "Jews love jokes, especially jokes about themselves. You have yet to observe this?"

He placed a proprietary hand on my shoulder and shook me till my teeth clashed with my tongue.

"You love to laugh, don't you? Laugh a little for me now."

I wanted to appease him, but before I could manage the slightest titter, Bruna started to cackle beside me. She roared and guffawed and snorted with a mocking force.

"Not you!" For once, the whole of Taube's face was animated with disgust. "Communists have no right to laughter!"

He was too easy to bait, that Taube. Clever Bruna increased her cackle and turned and ran, and Taube trailed her, like a dog suddenly distracted by the prospect of a new, more challenging prey. By the wisp of her laughter, she led him away.

It was the sweetest thing she'd ever do in Auschwitz, but it made me never want to laugh again.

Once the yard was emptied of wardens, Stasha sat down beside me. She put my shoes on for me; she wiped my eyes with her sleeve. None of it, she saw, did much good. Deciding that one of our old games was the only thing that could cheer me, she positioned herself so that we sat back to back, spine to spine, hips to hips. It was the game of our youngest years. This game was played by drawing whatever entered our heads, at the same exact moment, and then checking to make sure that we'd drawn the same image.

We took up sticks and etched these images in the dirt. First, we drew birds. We checked. They were the same. Then, moons and stars hovered over the birds. They were perfectly alike. We drew ships. We drew cities. Big cities, little cities, untouched cities, cities without ghettos. We drew roads leading out of these cities. All our roads led in the same direction.

Then, without warning, I had no idea where to go or what to draw. My mind went blank, but I could hear my sister scribbling on with her stick, free of any interruption. I had no choice but to peek over her shoulder. Unfortunately, the shift of my spine from hers gave my intentions away.

"Why do you have to cheat?" she demanded.

"Who says I'm cheating?"

"I felt you move. You peeked."

I didn't try to defend myself against this charge.

"It's because you're different here, isn't it? They've changed us already."

She was not wrong, but I wasn't willing to accept this.

"It's not true," I told her. "We're the same still. Let's try again."

We would have tried again, we would have tried forever, but before we had a chance to try at all, a white truck with a red cross on its flank arrived. Nurse Elma emerged from the truck's door, her step so delicate and fussy that she could have been descending the ramp of a cruise ship. We had heard of this Elma from the other children in the Zoo, but this was to be our first encounter.

After spying Elma, Stasha drew a bullet in the dust. I drew bullets too, drew them faster and faster. For every step that brought Elma nearer to us, the bullets multiplied.

I tried not to look up at her, to focus only on the shadow she cast over our drawings, but Elma didn't give me a choice. Squatting beside us, she thrust her powdered visage into mine and pulled on the tip of my nose as if I were some rubbery thing without feeling. Elma had a fierce-angled face that Stasha would later claim was of an evolutionary design that allowed her to track her prey in the dark, but at that moment, when the nurse was near enough to sink her teeth into me, I noticed only the calculated nature of her beauty, the hair bleached to meringue, the mouth overdrawn with crimson. It was as if she did her best to look like a drop of blood in the snow.

"Aren't you too old to play in the dirt?" Elma asked, giving my nose one final tug.

Neither of us knew how to respond, but Elma wasn't looking for an answer. She was content simply admiring the slenderness of her shadow as it fell over our drawings. She pivoted to take in the view and then bent down for a closer look at the images in the dirt.

"What are those?" She pointed at the bullets.

"Teardrops," Stasha answered.

Nurse Elma cocked her head to one side, and smiled at our drawings. I think she knew that the so-called tears were bullets. She must've been charmed by our subterfuge, though, because she didn't handle us too roughly as she hoisted us up by our collars and steered us toward the red-crossed truck, her hands gripping the backs of our necks as if we were kittens she was dangling over a bucket of water but did not yet have permission to drown.

CHAPTER THREE

Little Deathless

I want you to know the eyes. The hundreds of them, in a constant stare. They could look at you without ever seeing you and when you met their gaze, it felt as if the sky were tapping at your back in warning.

It was on the day that the eyes saw me that I was changed, made different from Pearl.

But to tell you about the eyes, I must first tell you about his laboratories. There were laboratories for blood-drawing, laboratories for x-rays. One laboratory we never saw, because it sat at the foot of one of the cremos and held the dead. Mirko claimed to have been inside that laboratory once, after a fainting spell. He said he woke beneath Uncle's resuscitating hands and was saved, but others disputed the legitimacy of this account. See for yourself! Mirko always said to these naysayers, but all prayed that they never would.

The laboratories weren't places you entered but places you were taken to, on Tuesdays and Thursdays and Saturdays, for eight hours at a time. They were filled with not only doctors and nurses but photographers and x-ray techs and artists with brushes, all of them determined to capture the particulars of us for Uncle's medical review. In the hands of these technicians, we became picture after picture, file after file. Materials were extracted from us and colored with dye and placed between slides, set to whorl and fluoresce and live beneath the perspective of a microscope.

Late at night, when Pearl was fast asleep, her consciousness a safe distance from my own, I'd think of these tiny pieces of us and wonder if our feelings remained in them, even though they were mere particles. I wondered if the pieces hated themselves for their participation in the experiments. I imagined that they did. And I longed to tell them that it wasn't their fault, that the collaboration wasn't a willing one, that they'd been stolen, coerced, made to suffer. But then I'd realize how little influence I had over these pieces—after we'd been parted, they answered only to nature and science and the man who called himself Uncle. There was nothing I could do on their numerous, microscopic behalfs.

On the first occasion that these extractions were to be seized from our bodies, Nurse Elma led us down the hall of the laboratory. She held her fingertips to our backs so that we could feel the screw of her nails at our spines, and the airiness of her breath drifted down from on high, and our mouths were gagged by a perfume that made her sweeter than she really was. She escorted us past door after door, and when she trod on my heel I tripped and plunged forward and fell in a heap. When I looked up from this stumble, I saw Dr. Miri.

"Up, up," she said. Urgency threaded her voice as she offered her hand. It was gloved, but I could feel the warmth of it still, and thrilled to her touch before seeing that she regretted the gesture. She recoiled, and put the hand in her pocket. At the time, I thought she regretted touching me because a show of kindness could compromise her standing with colleagues like Elma. Years later, I would realize her sorrow arose from taking care of the children that Uncle claimed for his own. It must have been like stringing a harp for someone who played his harp with a knife, or binding a book for someone whose idea of reading was feeding pages to a fire.

But these realizations weren't available to me then as a semi-child, a hider-in-coats, a shrinking pretender to adulthood. There, in the laboratory, I knew only that we were flanked by two women who seemed to fall in interesting positions in the order of living things. They looked to be entirely without feeling, their soft forms walled with protective layers. In Nurse Elma, this seemed a natural state; she was an exoskeletal creature, all her bones and thorns mounted on the outside—a perfect, glossy specimen of a crab. I assumed that she was born this way, numb to everyone around her. Dr. Miri was differently armored—though she was gilded with hard plates, it was a poor protection, one that hadn't warded off all wounds, and like the starfish, she was gifted at regeneration. When a piece of her met with tragedy, it grew back threefold, and the tissues multiplied themselves into an advanced sort of flesh with its own genius for survival.

How long, I wondered, would it take for me to become like her?

I hadn't meant to wonder it aloud, but that's exactly what I did, because Elma's hand closed on my shoulder, and she gave me a shake.

"Are you talking about me?" the nurse chided.

"About her." I pointed to Dr. Miri, who blushed. But she was adept at covering for us children and negotiating Elma's moods.

"She only means that she wants to be a doctor someday too," she said, and her face, with its telling eyes, telegraphed that I should follow her lead. "Isn't that right?"

I nodded, and rocked back and forth on my heels as I stood before them, made myself smaller, more girlish. People usually found the gesture quite charming, for whatever reason. It worked for Pearl and Shirley Temple both, and it worked for me then, because the nurse released me.

"Well, then," she boomed, and she rapped her knuckles on my head. "Maybe if you work hard enough you will become a great doctor someday. Anything is possible here, yes?"

Will you believe me when I say that the weather saved me from having to answer this absurd question? We heard a knocking at the windows of the laboratory, a sound like thousands of tiny fists pummeling the glass. A scatter of nurses and doctors rushed about, closing the windows, fastening them shut, while beads of hail spilled down onto the floors. It was as if a sea's worth of oysters had been pried open in the sky and released the treasures that were my sister's namesake into the halls of the laboratory.

In this white tumult of hail, Pearl and I found ourselves unattended, and our interest was drawn to a room a few steps away, its door ajar. I stepped forward for a closer look at what lay within. Through the door slit, I saw walls lined with books, and I had a finger-twitch to steal one of the volumes. Surely, a laboratory book would be able to advise me on how to make my body withstand a place like this, how to fortress it and put the pain out. Books had never led me in the wrong direction. It seemed foolish to try to endure without such counsel by my side.

On tiptoe, I approached the room and pushed on the knob gently, but the sweat on my palm made it too slick, and the door swung open and the hinges tattled on me with a creak—Nurse Elma, her cap askew, stormed in and yanked me from the doorway, but as she did so, the door opened still further. And that's when I met the eyes, or when the eyes met me.

I remain uncertain as to how to classify the exchange of glances that took place.

All I know was that rows of eyes presided over the desk on the rear wall. They were fastened through the iris, pierced with pins, all assembled as neatly as children at roll call. They were colored like a pretty season: green and hazel and brown and ocher. A lone blue eye stood at attention on the periphery. All the eyes were faded in the way only living things that no longer live can be, their irises veiled with husks of tissue that stirred when a breeze lilted through the window. At their centers, the silvery winks of pins assured their captivity.

Though just a girl, I had ideas about violence. Violence had a horizon, a scent, a color. I'd seen it in books and newsreels, but I didn't truly know it until I saw the effects of it on Zayde, saw him come to our basement home in the ghetto with a red rag over his face, saw Mama go soundless as she bound his nose with the scrap torn from the hem of her nightgown. Pearl held the lamp during this procedure so that Mama could see, but I was shuddering so much that I couldn't assist her. I should be able to say that I saw violence happen to Mama when a guard came to our door with news about the disappearance, but I kept my eyes closed tight the whole time, sealed them shut while Pearl stared straight ahead, and because my sister saw it all, I felt the images secondhand, felt them burn on the backs of my eyelids—I saw the guard's boot glow and furrow itself in Mama's side as she lay on the floor. Pearl was angry that I was not an active witness, and so she forced me to take it all in, and when I begged her to stop subjecting me to such sights, she informed me that I had no say in the matter, because she would never look away, not ever, no matter how much it hurt me, because in looking away, she said, we would lose ourselves so thoroughly that our loss would require another name.

So, I knew violence. Or I knew it well enough to understand that it had happened to the eyes. I knew they'd been torn from bodies that belonged to people who deserved such better sights than what they'd last seen. And even though I was unaware of what the most beautiful sight could be, I wanted to give it to them. I wanted to travel the whole world over, from sea to mountain and back, and bring to them an object, an animal, a view, an instrument, a person—anything that might reassure them that even as violence tore on, beauty remained, and it remembered them still. Realizing the impossibility of this, I gave the eyes the only thing I could: a tear crept down my cheek.

"Why are you crying?" Nurse Elma demanded. She shut the door on the eyes, but not before they saw my tear.

"We're not crying," I claimed.

"Your sister's not crying"—she jerked her snowy head at Pearl and then crouched to face me—"but you are. What did you see in there?"

The truth was that I couldn't describe what I saw. But I knew that I'd never stop seeing those eyes, that they'd follow me for all the days I'd live, wide open and blinkless, hoping for another fate. I knew that I'd sense their stare the most whenever I heard of someone being born or wed or found. I knew that I'd try to shut my own eyes, just to have some peace, but I never would be able to shut them entirely. True closure, I was sure, would escape all of us.

"I saw nothing," I protested.

Drops of moisture from the hailstorm beaded Nurse Elma's face and they dove to the floor, one by one, while she resorted to her standard tactics.

"I know you saw something," she insisted as she shook me. "I just want to be certain that we saw the same thing. I want to know this, because I do not want the other children to be frightened by any of your wild stories. I am familiar with children like you. Lovers of fiction! There was a girl here once, she told a story about what she saw, a story that was not true, and do you know what happened to her?"

I told Nurse Elma that I did not.

"I can't recall either, not specifically. How can I be expected to remember? There are so many of you to look after. But know this: What came of her wild stories—it wasn't good. Do you understand my meaning?"

I nodded. This gesture served a dual purpose. Not only did it secure Elma's approval, but it allowed a second tear to descend my cheek without her notice.

"Now tell me, then. What did you see in that room?"

Searching for a suitable answer, I thought about rows mounted on the wall—even in their capture, the eyes had fluttered their pretty colors with a flighty animation, and the dust that coated them had the appearance of pollen. Many had likely migrated long distances. All received the treatment of pests. They'd been lured in, trapped, starved, pinched into submission, and then, when life had been sufficiently drained from them, they'd been pinned into place, mounted as curiosities for study.

"Butterflies," I blurted out. "I saw butterflies. Only butterflies. They weren't eyes at all. Just butterflies."

"Butterflies?"

"Yes. Row after row of butterflies. A class of insects. In the moth order Lepidoptera."

Elma put a finger beneath my chin and lifted my jaw toward the ceiling. I wondered if she would halve me, and just when I figured that she surely would, she released me and assumed the tone of a frustrated and imperious revisionist.

"But they are not butterflies," she informed me. "They are beetles. The doctor has collected them for years. Understand?"

I said I did understand.

"Say they are beetles, Stasha, I want to hear it. You made an error in describing what you saw. Correct yourself so Pearl understands too."

"I saw beetles," I said to Pearl. I did not look at my sister while I spoke.

"You don't convince me."

"I saw beetles, nothing more. Not butterflies. Beetles. Order Coleoptera. Two sets of wings."

Satisfied, she turned and walked on, her stride enlivened by the interrogation, and when we reached the end of the hall, she swung open the door to a room that would alter us forever. It is easy to think that there are many such rooms in one's life. *This room*, you might say, *that was the room where I fell in love*. Or, *This was the room where I learned that I was more than my sadness, my pride, my strength*.

But in Auschwitz, I found that the room that really changes you is the one that can make you feel nothing at all. It is the room that says, *Come sit in me, and you will know no pain; your suffering isn't real, and your struggles? They're only slightly more real than you are, but not by much. Save yourself, the room advises, by feeling nothing, and if you must feel something, don't doom yourself by showing it*.

Elma stripped us after we entered this room. Into her arms went the dresses Mama had sewn; Elma regarded the strawberry print with scorn. Even fruit could not avoid offending her.

"So childish," she observed while stabbing one of the strawberries with a red-lacquered finger. "Do you like being children?"

"Yes," we said. It would be the last word that we would ever speak in unison. I wish I had known that at the time, but I was too overwhelmed by the task of pleasing Elma, whose powdery face lit up with disbelief.

"How funny. I can't imagine why."

"I've never wanted to grow up," I said. This was true. Growing up held too much risk of growing away from Pearl.

Nurse Elma smiled her too-straight smile.

"Then you are in the right place," she said.

Yes, I should have deduced the truth about what she was implying about our future. But something about Nurse Elma upended me, and I couldn't think properly in her presence. Elma seated us on chairs, their steel backs so cold that we started to shiver. The room felt icy, then hot. A fog winged across my vision. I knew that fog well. It visited me whenever I saw cruelty. I tried to imagine Elma into a less cruel person as she set aside our things and arranged a tray of measuring instruments, but the woman's image had a peculiar solidity that defied any improvements my imagination sought to impose on her. Nothing about her was vague or negotiable. Some might call this a strong personality. I wanted to call it that, just to be human and generous. But it was obvious that what she really possessed was emptiness so vast that it managed to approximate power.

Maybe, I thought, if we flattered her, she would be nice.

"Tell her she's pretty," I whispered to Pearl.

"You tell her, if you think she's so pretty."

It was as if Nurse Elma detected our psychic efforts to like her, because she then crossed to the other side of the room and busied herself with the polishing of a pair of silver scissors, their legs gleamy in the light falling from the blocky window above. Though small, this window let in too much light for girls who had just been stripped. We crossed our legs tight, covered the buds on our chests with our hands; we clutched at these signs of growth as if hoping to make them feel so unwelcome that they might voluntarily up and disappear.

"They're more frightened of you than you are of them," I whispered to my sister, because there seemed nothing left to do but joke. Pearl giggled, so I giggled too. Naturally, our giggles soured Elma. She threw her scissors down on the surgeon's table with a clatter.

"Do you see any of the other children laughing?"

We didn't. In fact, we hadn't seen the other children at all, because the strangeness of this place had so dimmed our perception. But with Elma's direction, we saw that we were not alone.

There were five other children in the room.

Lino and Artur Ammerling were ten-year-olds from Galicia. Like us, they were new arrivals and had been subjected to some scorn by the Old Numbers. Hedvah—a girl who slept three bunks over from us and held the honor of being the most respected girl in the Zoo, due to her long tenure and ability to assert herself with Ox—had started a rumor that the Ammerlings weren't twins at all, but were merely passing in order to receive the benefits afforded to those of our station. Twins' Father had been known to pull such tricks, she'd said, changing the paperwork so that young boys could enjoy the salvation of twin status. Hedvah cited their different hair colors—Lino was a redhead, Artur a brunet—as evidence that they were impostors. But they had to be twins. I could tell by the way that they sat in their chairs. They showed the same shock, the same trembles, as the nurses counted and measured their every feature. Not a single gesture toward identicality was overlooked—their eyelashes were counted, their eyebrow hairs, the flecks in their eyes, the dimples at their knees and cheeks. They were added and subtracted and compared, two human equations who could only squirm in their seats.

And there were Margit and Lenci Klein, from Hungary. Six years of age. Whenever Pearl and I were immeasurably sad we looked for them, because they reminded us of how we'd been as younger girls—hands entwined, full of secrets and the occasional elbow-jab of annoyance. They were always combing each other's hair with their fingers till their strands shone and making whistles out of blades of grass. Their mother had left them with instructions to always wear purple hair ribbons to make it easier for her to spy them in a crowd, so they fastened them atop their heads every day, first thing, propping them up so that they stood like velvet ears on their heads. We watched as the nurses diagrammed their pale, goosebumped forms with red ink, circling a piece here, a bit there, until their bodies were rivered with scarlet.

The fifth subject stood alone, his thumb hooked in his mouth. He could have been thirteen or thirty-five or sixty, he was so whittled, so beyond age. His nurse was leafing through files with an air of boredom, as if there were nothing left to be done with him. Before her on a table were two folders, two sets of photographs, two sets of diagrams, two sets of x-rays. But there was only one boy.

And he was an iota of boy, a frail-boned brevity with an overbite and teeth that splayed themselves over his lips like a crooked fence. Tufts of white-streaked hair nested on his scalp and obscured his eyes, which seemed unable to focus on anything but the ceiling above. His veins stood so close to the surface of this boy that in the hospital's faulty lights, their clusters lent his skin a pronounced hue of illness. In his chill and suffering, he was near blue.

I fixed my eyes on him, hoping he might sense me and stare back, the way twins often do, but the boy only coughed showily, making no effort to disguise his sickness. The nurse frowned at him disapprovingly and boxed up half of the file—this action appeared to disturb the boy. I watched him sway where he stood and falter at the knees, and though I was sure that he was about to collapse, he simply stared at the box with all the reverence one might have for a grave, and then he reached toward it and tried to run a finger over the lid but the nurse slapped his hand away, and he withdrew like a wounded thing and inserted his thumb in his mouth again. The nurse declared him finished and gestured to him to dress, but he refused to accept his clothes, even as she thrust the garments forcefully at his sunken chest. It was as if he'd decided that nothing was graspable anymore, that there was no point in trying to hold anything other than a thumb to one's mouth. Agitated, the nurse threw the garments at his feet and stalked off. And still, he stood bluely naked, refusing to follow her orders. He turned only to cough in her direction, and that's when our gazes finally met.

I looked away as fast as I could, which was slow enough to receive his friendly nod and quick enough that I could avoid returning it. I couldn't face what he had endured, the horrors of which were made too obvious by the empty chair at his side.

"I understand what you are saying," he said to the empty seat beside him. "But our father, if he were here, he would say that curses curse their utterers. And our mother, if she were here, she would say—" And then he fell to coughing again.

It was the boy and his empty chair that moved me to decide: I would be more than an experiment in this world. I was not as smart as Uncle Doctor, but I could study his movements without him knowing, and learn about medicine, and use him to my advantage. Pearl had her dancing to look forward to—I needed my own ambition. After all, when the war ended, someone was going to have to take care of people. Someone was going to have to find the lost and put all the halves together. I saw no reason why that someone could not be me.

I planned to begin my practice with the boy. Not knowing his name, I decided to call him Patient Number Blue. I studied him, taking in what I could from a distance, but before I could think too much on his particulars, I was interrupted by a high, trilling note.

Uncle Doctor. He entered whistling with a sprightly step, smelling of peppermint and starch, the long white wings of his coat trailing against each surface he passed and erasing them. I'd come to learn that he considered himself an expert at whistling, just as he considered himself an expert on hygiene and culture and art and writing. But while his whistle was errorless, there was no mistaking its robotic lean. Even as it leaped about the scale, it was monotone at the core, a hollowed thing that couldn't know a feeling.

I tried to mimic this hollow whistle, but I found myself unable to copy the doctor's trill—when I put my lips together to blow, I could only sputter.

Uncle saw this mishap and smiled. It was an amused expression that might have seemed harmless to an outsider, but the arc of it made me shudder. After all, we were in his laboratory for tests, some of which were surely designed to ferret out our inferiorities and determine how long we might be permitted to live. It didn't seem impossible that one such test might be how well one could whistle. These Nazis had such stupidly vicious ideas of what constituted a person—I knew well enough to never underestimate their whims.

"I can whistle," I assured Uncle. "I swear. I whistled just a few hours ago." But he didn't acknowledge this—he just turned his back to consult with one of the attendants and paid me no mind.

I watched Pearl blanch with fright, and I followed suit. I was sure that my failure had doomed us both. In our defense, I considered listing our many other talents to the doctor, but I decided that it would not do to boast about Pearl's dancing and Pearl's poetry recitations and Pearl's piano skills. I chose another method to prove my worth instead.

"'Blue Danube,'" I announced to the room in an overly loud voice.

That did the trick. Uncle turned, curious.

"What did you say?"

"What you were whistling when you came in. That waltz. It is 'Blue Danube.'"

Uncle's face creased with pleasure. He picked up the tail end of one of my braids and pulled it, his manner not unlike a schoolboy's.

"You know music?"

I squirmed on the bench, discomforted by the singularity of his gaze. It was as if I were his only patient.

"Pearl is a dancer," I told him.

"And you"—this was accompanied by a finger-point—"a pianist?"

"I want to be a doctor someday."

"Like me?" He smiled.

"Like our papa," I said. It was the first time I'd used the word since Papa disappeared—those four letters, those two syllables, that sound that started hard and then went so soft, like a footstep that begins on a stair and ends in the sand. I'd tried to assign that word new meanings to erase the old one, to make a father into a ditch, a time, a false door in a library that one could hide behind and never be detected. After saying the word, I sank into myself, but Uncle was too delighted to notice, and I believe that when I said *our papa,* he managed to hear *you, and only you, Uncle,* because he beamed at me with a familial pride.

"A doctor! I'm impressed," he declared to the staff. "This is a bright girl." Nurse Elma looked doubtful at this proclamation, but she gave an expression of agreement before returning to the cleaning of the instruments.

Uncle stalked to the sink to wash his hands. Catching sight of himself in the reflective surface of a steel cabinet, he mugged a little, and then, upon noticing an errant lock, he fell to combing his hair with an obsessive attention, as if aligning the strands might bring his whole world into pleasing symmetry. After perfection was achieved, he sheathed his comb, resumed his whistle, and bobbed his head in the direction of an orderly, who set a chair before us for him to sit in. He wiped the seat of his chair with his handkerchief, rubbing disdainfully at a small stain on the wood, and then positioned himself stiffly before us. His posture resembled that of a person who finds himself at a family reunion after years of estrangement, eager to learn about the lives of others but preoccupied with hiding his own identity. As if it were our responsibility to put him at ease, I offered him a smile. I'm sure that it was not a pretty smile, but he saw my attempts to win him over in it, and I believe he saw my weakness too.

He clapped a hand over each of our knees, obscuring the cattle-car bruises that covered them.

"I have been thinking of organizing a concert here. Would you girls like that?"

We nodded together.

"It's done, then! I will have them play each of your favorite songs. Or maybe, to save them some trouble, I will have them play the same song twice!"

He laughed at his own joke. I laughed too, to cover my fear, and Pearl caught on and gave a giggle. Already, we'd learned how to co-ordinate our hearts in this place for protection's sake. But my heart must've been a beat behind, as usual, because the very next second, I was blurting something out in a move that was foolish, inevitable, and typical of me.

"I heard that you keep the families of twins safe," I said in a rush, my head bowed. As soon as I made this mistake, Pearl kicked the leg of my chair to prompt my usual apology.

"Don't be sorry," Uncle soothed, and he swept the back of his hand softly across my cheek. I wondered how many times he'd said that to people like us before, because the phrase appeared to feel odd on his tongue. The corner of his mouth twitched a little, and he chewed on the edge of his mustache. It was a strange tic for a man of his composure, a bit bovine and low, but later, I came to recognize that it usually surfaced when he was taking care in choosing his words. After some thought, the mustache was released from his mouth's grip, and he addressed us gravely.

"I do take care of the families. Is there anything you'd like me to do for yours?"

We told him that our *zayde* might look like an old man, but he was very young in his outlook, with a mind always prowling about in search of new things to poke at and study. In the cattle car, he'd made us promise two things: That someday we would learn to swim, and that, when we survived, we'd get a massive bottle of the finest wine and toast him. During this toast, we were to call for the obliteration of the murderers and wish on them a million mansions filled with thousands of rooms, and in every room, a hundred beds, and beneath every bed, a poisonous snake to bite their infernal ankles, and at every bedside, a doctor with an antidote, so that they might be cured and live to be bitten again and endure the same suffering over and over till the snakes got bored of the Nazi flavor, which would be never, because everyone knows that you can't bore a snake with the taste of evil.

At the conclusion of this outburst, Pearl glared and shifted in her seat uncomfortably, but Uncle appeared unbothered. In fact, he acted as if he hadn't heard it at all. He simply resumed chewing on his mustache and continued the inquiry.

"Does your grandfather like to swim?"

Oh yes, we said. Zayde swims and flips and dives like a fish.

"That is settled, then. We do have a swimming pool here, you know. I will arrange for an escort for him and inform his block supervisor."

I pointed out that Zayde would require swimming trunks.

"Of course! How could I forget? I'm sure it's unlikely that he brought a pair with him. We can't have that elderly bum-bum frightening off the other bathers, can we?"

I didn't find the thought of my naked *zayde* funny, but he did, so I joined him again in laughing, much to Pearl's alarm. I could only hope that she saw the strategy in my laughter, because when it finally subsided I made another request.

"There is someone else," I said. "Our mother."

"Yes?"

"She is our mother" was all I could say at first, because thinking of her emptied me.

"And?"

"She draws and paints. Animals and plants, mostly. She makes a history of the living things and the things that don't live anymore. It keeps her happy."

This was a polite way of putting it. I'm not sure that it kept her happy so much as it lessened her tears. I thought of the poppy on the wall of the cattle car, how the flimsiness of the petals supported her. But it didn't seem to be the time to hash out such particulars with Uncle. Already, a glaze of boredom was threatening to wash over his face, and I knew I wouldn't have much more time to barter with him.

"Brushes, then," he decided. "And an easel. Obviously, some paint."

We thanked him, we said that Mama and Zayde would be so grateful. It was more than enough, we said. Or, not more than enough, but—

"I know what you are trying to say." His voice was solemn. "It is good that you think of others, but your family should be entitled to advantages for bringing you into the world. Because you are special, you twins."

"I've been trying to tell Pearl that for years," I said.

"Maybe she finally believes you." His face was serious. "Do you believe now, Pearl?"

"I believe," she said. But I knew that this was not the whole of her sentiment.

Charmed, Uncle issued us both head pats, and then he rifled through a glass jar in a cabinet and handed me a sugar cube. Such a rare little igloo of sweetness—I couldn't waste it on myself. So I gave it to Pearl. He furrowed his brow, then handed me another sugar cube. I gave that one to her too.

"This is for you," he said, dropping a third cube into my palm and folding my fingers over it. "It serves a medicinal purpose."

"In that case—can I give it to Patient Number Blue?"

Confusion crossed his face and then soured into irritation. So I waved my words away and popped the sugar cube in my mouth. Pleasing him, I was discovering, was a great deal of work.

Uncle then plunged into an extended line of questioning that ventured into my most uncomfortable territories. He said he just wanted to know the fundamentals. Who we were because of who we came from. Or, more specifically, why didn't we have a father? Pearl eased the information out somehow. While she talked, I hummed in my mind so I didn't have to hear what she said. I hummed "Blue Danube" till its blueness began to cloak my thoughts, but even this blueness wasn't enough to drown out the whole story.

Pearl told Uncle that one night, Papa didn't return from the task he'd told Mama he had to attend to. She had tried to make him stay—it was past curfew, she'd argued, and why couldn't another doctor take care of our neighbor's ill child? Didn't Stasha and Pearl matter? she had asked. Papa did not argue, but he forgot his umbrella in his hurry out the door. We stood there, Mama with the umbrella in hand, waiting for him to fetch it. But he didn't come back that night. And then, Papa didn't return for day after day, month after month. Mama went to the authorities, who provided little in the way of explanation initially but later said that a man matching Papa's description had been found floating in the Ner River. Mama insisted that this couldn't be him, that some other violation must've occurred, and she was not going to believe it without documentation.

Uncle wasn't one to be put off by messy paperwork, though. Proof or not, he favored this explanation. Suicide was a Jewish epidemic, he claimed.

"Do you ever feel overwhelmed by sadness?" he asked us while shining a light in first Pearl's mouth, then mine.

"We never do," I said.

"What about you?" He gave Pearl another sugar cube, which she popped into her mouth to avoid conversation.

"Pearl is too good to feel sad," I said.

"I see."

"Pearl is so good—she can't even feel pain. See?"

To demonstrate, I pinched my sister's arm. But instead of her remaining silent, we both cried out at the same time. Uncle took note of this with great interest, but I don't think he could have understood what was truly happening. Pearl didn't cry because of my pinch; it was pure coincidence. At the very moment that my fingers twisted Pearl's flesh, we'd sensed the sorrows of Mama, who missed us so much that she was finding life too hard to bear. She had no idea of the blessings that were about to be visited on her because of our value as experiments. Mama was so fragile—we could only hope that the paint and brushes would reach her before it was too late.

I was about to impress upon Uncle the urgency of all this, but he grabbed my shoulder before I had a chance. His touch was firm, instructive—I tried to hunch over to hide my nakedness, but he was intent on making me rise and steering me through the room.

"Pearl will stay there and wait for you," he told me as we passed the other children and the nurses and made our way behind a screen that partitioned us from the room. There, he laid me down on a steel table and flashed on a light overhead. We were alone— it was just he and I and the white wings of his coat and the bright beam of the light—but I discerned another presence.

I sensed the gaze of the eyes looking down on me, even as I knew that not a single one had stirred from its pin. I knew those eyes saw what I saw. With them, I watched Uncle perform the magic of loading a needle with some luminous liquid. It was as amber as the amber stones Pearl and I had once collected from the Baltic Sea, and the color took me back to that time, shortly before Papa's disappearance, when we'd taken a boat and rowed out onto the waves—and then I forced myself to stop remembering because Pearl was in charge of time and memory, and I was in danger of trespassing on a history I wasn't sure belonged to me anymore. Yet

I was glad it did not belong to me. Because as I lay there on the table, beneath the stream of light, I knew myself to be in a place where time and memory brought only pain, and I was so grateful to my sister, my dearest friend from the floating world, for sparing me this affliction.

"I know what you're thinking," Uncle said as he approached me with the needle.

I told him that was very funny, because in the past, only Pearl had had that ability.

He smiled his laboratory smile, but I could tell that already, he was tiring of my jokes. So I made my face intellectual and severe, and peered at the needle with interest, as if I were in the front row of a schoolroom with a teacher I very much wanted to impress.

He tested the point of the needle on his fingertip.

"You're thinking that this is going to hurt. I promise—it won't. Well, it might hurt a little. But so little! And that will be a small price to pay for the reward you'll get."

What reward? I wondered.

He whispered it in my ear and then begged my permission. That is how I remember it, at least. Or how I remembered it for some time, before I regained my full ability to reason. But of course, it is likely he never asked at all.

Even still, desperation can riddle a heart with consent. Mine was heavy with it. This consent must seem odd—but in a place where a person could end so abruptly without a chance to save her loved ones, how could I hesitate when he offered me the contents of a needle that would make me deathless?

Yes, I said. I would like to be deathless, if only for a little while.

And Uncle coaxed one of my veins into cooperation, and the needle, it wheedled in, and as it wheedled I felt my cells divide and conquer other cells, and I went suitably cold.

As my memory lingers there, on that steel table, piled with its many instruments and confusions, you might ask: *Stasha, this death-lessness you believed you were dealt—did it dive into you like an arrow, or sink like a knife? Did it skip through you like a stone? Did it pour salt on your heart and shrink it like a snail?*

I would like to speak to the physical sensations of deathlessness, but in fact, I can't. After he plunged in that needle, I did not feel my body at all. I would continue not to feel for some time. The first moment I felt even a particle of this numbness lift? I was leaving the steps of an orphanage in Warsaw in 1945. I was failing and weary; there was a poison pill in my kneesock and a wail at my back, and just as I approached the gate, I saw the tears of a near-stranger min-gle with the rain.

But we will return to that episode later. For now, let's look at the needle. Such a simple pinnacle of Uncle's aims, with its fine sting and steady thrust into my veins. I could have lost myself watching it perform its labors, but I watched Uncle instead. His face was stiller than any face I'd known before. I wondered what feelings might leap behind his forced, placid expression, and then I stopped myself from wondering because I knew that it would not do me any good to know such feelings.

Once emptied of its amber, the needle withdrew. Uncle put a tiny cloud of cotton on the point of entry, brimming with a blood drop of sun.

"Your face is too white. How do you feel?"

Guilty, I wanted to say. Like I'd deserted all that was good and worthy. Like I'd escaped death by turning my back on life. All the cells in my body cried out, and I knew they cried not for me, but for all those who had been lost, and those who were to become lost, and there I was, someone who should not exist in the doctor's world, and yet—Uncle interrupted my thoughts; he was snapping his fingers beneath my nose.

"Stasha? I asked you a question—how do you feel?"

"I feel like I am a real person now," I lied, my guilt tucked away behind my shivers. "Not just a twin. But my own person. Stasha. Only Stasha."

"How interesting!" he mused, flattered by this development. I assumed that it made him feel powerful to undo the miracle of our doubled birth, to disrupt the bond nature itself had given us. I am sure, too, that he believed I might be easier to control in the absence of my twinhood. He thought me simpler and unfettered, a perfect experiment. As blasphemous as my words were, I saw that continuing this lie might be greatly beneficial.

"My own self," I declared. "I never dreamed that this was what I wanted to be—but now I know it. An individual, that's what I am. Not part of a pair, not just Pearl's sister. Just a normal girl, all alone and by myself, with no one else that I am compelled to love and live beside."

Showily, I renounced all that I held most dear and—do you know what this did to the innermost of me? My heart was visited by a trembling anger, and my lungs became aloof—they pretended they didn't know me at all. I could only hope that all of me, myself entire, would soon recognize my objective, that this was a deception undertaken to achieve the survival of us both. It was for Pearl and me, this sham. My sister, for so long, had upheld and polished me; she made me decent, lovable, significant—now, it was my turn to uphold her.

Mengele was fooled well enough. He was so amused by my declaration that he ruffled my curls with his fingers.

"Little deathless Stasha." He laughed. "You'll outlive us all."

As he placed the needle back on its tray, I realized that he'd complicated me; he'd imposed divisions on the matter I shared with Pearl, all that we'd both collaborated on in our floating little world. The needle made me a *mischling*, but the word took on a meaning different than the term the Nazis imposed upon us, all those cold and gruesome equations of blood and worship and heritage. No, I was a hybrid of a different sort, a powerful hybrid forged by my suffering. I was now composed of two parts.

One part was loss and despair. Such darkness should make life impossible, I know. But my other part? It was wild hope. And no one could extract or cut or drain it from me. No one could burn it from my flesh or puncture it with a needle.

This hopeful part, it twisted me, gave me a new form. The girl who'd licked an onion in the cattle car was dead, and the *mischling* I'd become was an oddity, a thwarted person, a creature—but a creature capable of tricking her enemies and rescuing her loved ones.

"You are the first, you know," Uncle said, and he prattled on, telling me that I was the latest in inventions, a girlish carrier of a startling future. He took out a magnifying glass and inspected my eyes, but no matter how closely he looked, he suspected nothing of my plans. Already, I was adept at trickery.

"Because I did this—my sister will be next?" In a world of questions, this was the only one that mattered to me. "You will make her deathless too?"

Uncle took a moment to line up the instruments on his tray. I could tell that he was stalling for time; he was trying to decide the best way to handle a Jew like me, a potential double-dealer, a probable spy. He told me that if I proved myself a worthy patient, Pearl would receive the same treatment, just like any identical twin should.

I promised that I would prove myself. Anything for Pearl, I said, and he nodded in an absent way and noted that he was happy to hear that, because it would not do to create a race of children who would live forever if such children could never outgrow the inferior origins of their blood.

As he spoke, I sensed what the needle had done. Within me,

there was a twitch, a fever. It was as if my cells recognized the sound of his voice—I could feel them branch and unfurl in their death-lessness, like blooms acknowledging an untrustworthy source of light—and I swore, on Pearl and her approaching deathlessness, that no child would have to listen to that doctor-beast much longer. She would join me as a *mischling;* we would be two hybrids together, two girls mutated beyond the laws of life and death, victory and sorrow. With our sophisticated gifts we would plot to overthrow him, we would wait and wait and then, in a vulnerable moment, catch him unawares, and we'd have the means to end him hiding behind our backs—perhaps we'd use the very bread knives they al-lowed us prisoners so that we could cut our morning meal, maybe we'd turn these dull blades away from our rations, toward flesh—and in the blessed minute of his death, Uncle wouldn't even know who was who, which was which; we would not identify which twin was freeing the world of him. All the duties that we'd par-titioned between us for the sake of our endurance would unspool and mingle. In this act, we would both take responsibility for the funny, the future, the bad, the good, the past, and the sad.

And we would know nothing more of pain.

CHAPTER FOUR

War Materials, Urgent

In October 1944, our second month of life as prisoners, we were no longer *zugangen;* we'd seen children come and children go like minutes.

Although I was the keeper of time and memory, I couldn't know exactly when something went amiss in my sister, but I think it happened during our first meeting with Mengele. After that day, she was a listless mumbler, her nose always stuck in an anatomy book or her little medical diary, a small blue-stamped volume dedicated to listings of parts and their features. She went on tours of all the systems and their organs, treating each to a diagram and description.

This blue volume was not unlike the ones we'd kept while bird-watching under Zayde's tutelage. But instead of larks and sparrows, she approached the features and functions of lungs and kidneys.

Of all the parts she listed, she seemed most preoccupied with those that appeared in pairs.

As morbid as such entries were, that interest was comforting to me, because though she professed—like all the multiples we lived with—an extreme interest in retaining our sameness, I had begun to feel as if a bit of her had broken off; her detachment reminded me of a crag of ice that frees itself from a floe and sets off, adrift.

Outwardly, she put on a fair show. All the cheeriness was there, the polite inquiries, the routine obedience. But away from the observations of Mengele and Elma, Stasha folded inward. She slumped through interactions, glanced away when addressed. Her attention went to her anatomy book alone, with all her furious scribbles in the margins. And whenever she paused in her studies, she sat with a thumb positioned solidly in her navel, as if it were the potential source of a leak and she was doing her best to hold herself together, to stave off collapse. I'd stick my thumb in my *pupik* too, just to copy her, but it did nothing for me. The sensations she sought were suddenly beyond my grasp—she was either lost or changed; I knew little, I knew nothing, so much of me had already been stripped away that it often felt that all I had was an ability to watch my twin become a stranger.

Mengele must have fastened some illusion to her ready imagination. That was the conclusion I reached. Ever since that visit, her voice was too bright and her eyes were always mid-blink and her mood was never what I thought it should be.

"How do you feel?" I asked her once after we emerged from hours of tests at the laboratory. "Do you feel like I feel?"

"I allow myself to feel only at sunset" was the answer.

"How do you feel at sunset, then?"

"I feel guilty because I get to live forever."

"What do you mean by that?" I laughed. This was hardly the sort of thing that one took seriously from Stasha. I'd heard so many stories from her over the years—another one didn't faze me.

She'd avoided looking at me since that first visit—that much I could be sure of—but never before that moment had the avoidance been so pronounced. I watched her lashes—all 156 of them, according to Dr. Miri's tally—brush against her cheeks, and saw the blue veins in her eyelids map out her distress.

"I shouldn't have said anything. I promised I wouldn't say anything."

I tried not to dwell on it, but late at night, as we lay in our bunk, blanketed by the body heat of a third child—a speck of a girl who would disappear in the morning, shuttled off to yet another prodding—I wondered what had put such an odd idea into her head.

My sister's head had always been a mystery to me, even during those brief flashes of connection where I found myself wading through her every fancy and sensation, but this was something new. Traditionally, it hadn't frightened me to conduct such forays—her mind was a sweet, mild place to visit, an island full of gentle animals, varying shades of blue, trees suitable for climbing, the books she wanted to read, the plants she wanted to know.

But when I looked into my sister's thoughts those days, I found them much altered. Where that peaceable island had once been there was new, unmapped territory, a realm where the chromosome held court and cells divided in reverie and the prospect of mutation was comfort, rescue, and the means to vengeance.

It was a place that believed she could be Mengele's undoing. She told herself that if she was clever enough—if she turned herself into the slyest of flatterers, a false protégée, a girl too girlish to draw suspicion—she could repossess what he'd taken from us, and set the Zoo free.

I found this belief, this strange territory in her head, to be nothing less than terrifying.

She called him an experiment, but I knew the boy named Patient Number Blue was more. I knew she thought of him as a brother, a triplet, yet another family member she could not lose. I warned her not to get attached. She accused me of insensitivity. She wasn't wrong to do so, but I couldn't help but be insensitive to Patient because I was so tired of being sensitive to the both of us. My body was overrun by pain; it didn't need Patient's pain too.

But I was helpless to stop her investigations. I could only sit and watch my sister conduct these inquiries outside of the boys' barracks, with her subject seated on a stump, the cremo behind him, looming in the distance. These examinations were redundant affairs, always touching on the same matters, the same explanations.

I remember the first one too clearly. I was sitting cross-legged next to Stasha and knitting a blanket as a cover for my real interest. The other girls in the Zoo, they'd schooled me in this craft, which they found so useful for passing the time between roll call and the laboratory or those inevitable hours in which you were separated from your twin. For needles, we used bits of wire torn from the fence and sharpened on rocks. For yarn, we used a pile of thread gathered from our unraveling sweaters. We had a small supply of this material, and each took a turn knitting a blanket large enough to suit a tiny doll. Once a blanket was finished, it was never used. It was simply dismantled, and the strands given to the next girl.

Finishing my blanket was always a good cover for spying on my sister. Whenever my fingers were busied with this project, Stasha didn't suspect that I listened to her. On that day, I remember that she opened her examination by inquiring after the white streaks in her subject's hair.

"Not always like this," he answered. "My hair turned old overnight. My brother's too."

"Overnight?"

"Or over a few nights. I wouldn't know when exactly. It happened on the way here. It's not like we had mirrors in our cattle car."

Stasha inquired about his background. The boy gave this a good deal of thought, screwing up his face in contemplation, before offering his relevant details.

"I've won five fights in my life. Three with my fists, and two with my teeth. Don't ask me how many I've lost. If you ask me how many I've lost, you'll just start a fight."

No, she insisted, his *background*.

"My father was a rabbi. My mother was a rabbi's wife. My father, the rabbi, he is alive still, probably. He was always saying that in the dark, all cats are gray. He had a lot of good sayings like that."

Stasha clarified: It was his medical background that she was interested in. And so they proceeded to discuss what Mengele had taken, punctured, and tinkered with. He spoke of instruments that clinked and saws that whirred, and when he was finished, he told us both to pray that we were never visited by these intrusions to the abdomen.

"You sound like Clotilde," Stasha said. "We don't pray. Our *zayde,* he prayed from time to time, but mostly he prayed to science."

Patient found the force of her protest amusing. He flexed his right biceps for show, biceps that resembled nothing more than a huddled pile of peas.

"I don't let prayer put me on my knees," he said. "But there's nothing wrong with asking to become a tiger, a lion, a wildcat, especially since I will be thirteen soon. I pray for the murderous stuff within me to overtake the damage that he does, so I can leave here someday and satisfy a Russian woman. And even if she isn't satisfied—well, she'll likely give me another go because I will be charming, and charismatic, a real gent. I wasn't always this way, this determined. But my twin—I have to carry on his legacy. You didn't know him, Stasha. But you can be sure that he didn't spend his time mooning after Mengele's lack of conscience. Even in his death, my double, the one so peaceful in life, so popular, so affectionate—now that he is gone, I believe he dreams about stringing Nazis up and setting their guts free of their bodies. Now, his dreams of vengeance live on in me. You can play nurse all you want, Stasha, but I can only be a killer."

"I'm not playing nurse—there is something else I am doing." Stasha pouted. She rested her book on her knee, glanced about to see if anyone might have overheard this confession. "Can you imagine that maybe I have the same interests too?"

"Tell me, what are you trying to do? What is this big thing, this plan that you have? Are you going to escape? You saw what happened to Rozamund and Luca."

"I didn't see."

"Shot!" He threw up his arms, staggered backward, and sank to the ground, mimicking the fall of the martyrs. "Shot for nothing. No good came of it."

"Well, it is a good thing that my plan is different, isn't it?" Stasha walked over to where he lay in the dust and took in the configurations of his bones.

"There are only two kinds of plans here," Patient claimed. "There used to be three plans, but that third plan—the plan to get enough to eat—has become impossible."

Stasha paused to consider this statement and then scribbled away in her book before declaring the examination finished. She said this in an overly loud voice in the hopes that Mengele might pass through the yard on his way to his tortures and stumble upon this testament to her nascent genius. To Patient, she said nothing of her observations about his health except that he shouldn't abstain from eating rats, given his condition.

"They're not kosher," he sniffed.

"Neither is the bread," she retorted. I was starting to think that the book was her way of avoiding eye contact; she ducked into it immediately, as if shamed by her own words.

Her charge just looked at her sympathetically. It was then that it became obvious to me: Patient was being her patient just so he could keep her alive.

And Patient needed saving himself.

The problem was this: Patient's brother was dead and so he wasn't a twin anymore. The twinless were expendable. When you became twinless, you had days, maybe a week, before you were reunited with your twin in the mortuary for study. These reunions never announced themselves, but we all saw the pattern: We knew Mischa had died, and we saw Augustus disappear soon after. We learned that Herman was no more, and we waved good-bye to Ari, his nose pressed against the window of the ambulance. Disappearances were inevitable, marked with red crosses on the sides of the vehicles that carried our companions away.

As the keeper of time and memory, I saw fit to put notches in the wooden arm of our bunk to record each day that Patient remained with us.

"What are these for?" Stasha had asked, moving her fingertip over the initial four indentations.

"The members of our family," I'd answered.

And when the notches numbered five?

"For the members of our family including our dead," I told her.

Satisfied, she ran her fingers over the grooves to indicate her approval. As the notches increased, I came up with new explanations. I said that they were for the things I missed, the favors I owed Bruna, the kindnesses Stasha had shown me.

Fortunately, the forgetful-bread made this deception easy. Every new explanation rang true to her so long as the bromide continued to line her stomach.

When the notches on the bunk recorded more than nine days, I couldn't imagine why he'd been spared for so long. I figured that Mengele was so busy with so many other bodies, he had momentarily forgotten about the boy. Or maybe he truly did have some respect for Stasha and was allowing her the fun of her own experiment. After all, Mengele was known for breaking the rules to foster his own amusements, and no one appeared to amuse him more than Stasha.

October 14, 1944

The white truck came to carry us off, chuffing up in the dust like some important beast with its false Red Cross insignia blazing over one side. And under the supervision of that false cross, stitched on the uniforms of nurses and doctors, splayed over the walls of the laboratory, Stasha's blood was taken and given back to me; my blood was taken and given to a bucket; Stasha's spine was prodded with needles while mine sang out with sympathy; we were photographed and drawn; we heard the cries of others down the hallway, saw the flash of the camera, and when the light got too bright, Mengele took Stasha from me with his usual long-dawning smile and a whistle of equal length. She looked back at me, over her shoulder, as they entered a private room.

The doctor would take special care of Stasha, Nurse Elma said.

Whether hours or minutes passed, I couldn't be sure. I knew only that when Stasha emerged from that room she held her head at a tilt, like a marionette with a broken string, and she cupped her left ear with one hand as if trying to prevent the entry of a single sound.

But even before I saw Stasha's injury I knew what made it.

I knew because as I'd waited in my chair I'd felt something pour and bubble down the canal of my ear; I'd felt it course and stream in a way that defied my understanding, and I cried out in recognition of this shared pain, which was very unfortunate indeed, because it attracted Nurse Elma's attention. She turned from the reflective surface of the medicine cabinet, where she'd been passing the wait stabbing at her gums with a pick and smoothing her curls.

"What is the matter, girl?" She sashayed over to where I sat and poked the dimple we had in our chins. "I'm impressed that you have the strength to shiver."

I told her it was nothing even as the sensation continued. I knew they were pouring boiling water onto Stasha's left eardrum; they were drowning her hearing forever—I knew this even though she did not scream.

Seeking escape from our thoughts, I looked through the window and saw guards pushing a piano through the yard. I was quite sure it was our piano, the one we'd lost when we found ourselves crowded into the ghetto. We'd grown up together, that piano and Stasha and me. We'd learned to crawl beneath it. It could have been anyone's piano, but I was quite sure that it was ours, and almost as soon as it appeared within the window, the guards pushed it out beyond the frame of my vision, and there was only a crash, a thud, a ruffle of keys, and a slew of curses.

I wondered where they were taking it. If I would ever see it again.

My vision of the old piano was then replaced with Mengele himself. He entered with his usual whistle. Mid-trill, he stopped and pointed to me, like a music teacher does when he's looking for an answer.

"Beethoven's Ninth?" I ventured.

"Ah, no, you are quite wrong." It was a triumphant statement.

I apologized for my mistake. I would have said that my hearing felt a bit compromised at the moment, but I decided it was best not to let him in on this mystery.

"Can I have a second chance?"

I'm sure he heard these exact words too often. He began to

laugh, and Elma gave him a look of mock reproach.

"Don't be so cruel to the girl!" And then to me, she said, "You are right, of course. Sometimes our doctor here, he just likes to have a little fun."

"To put you at ease," he said, nodding.

"I believe it had the opposite effect," Nurse Elma said. "Look at those pupils!"

"It works with Stasha," Mengele said. "That girl just loves jokes, doesn't she? You—you are a bit more reserved, yes?"

He removed his gloves and put on a fresh pair. He slid them on with the zeal of a boy suiting up for some sport, and then he held his hands up before him, in search of flaws. Finding none, he clapped a hand on my shoulder.

"Your sister has to rest a bit," he said. "Perhaps we should do something else to pass the time?"

He always worded things that way, as if he were merely making a jovial suggestion.

He and Nurse Elma consulted with each other for some minutes before arriving at a plan. I did my best to appear uninterested, but pieces of their conversation made their way to me. I heard talk of which was the stronger one, who was the leader, the superior subject, and then they returned to where I sat, so cold on my bench.

"Something new this time," he said finally, and with a smile. "Or new to you, at least. Your sister is already familiar."

He looked for a vein. He didn't have to look far. I cursed my veins for making themselves so available.

I don't know what was in that needle. A germ, a virus, a poison. But I could be certain as I shuddered and a warmth shivered through me, hand in hand with a chill and a shake, that it would eventually overtake me. A stronger person might have been able to fight what that needle held, but I was not as strong as I'd been before we'd exited the cattle car.

Satisfied, Mengele stood back and surveyed me. He cocked his head like a nasty parrot that once swore at me in a pet store. I hoped he would remain at that distance, but he drew up a chair and stroked my forehead so as to observe the fever that was quickly setting in, and then he took a little hammer and applied it to my joints. My legs and arms jumped at the urging of his hammer, and his face was a strange mix of amusement and intent. He scampered about me as I sat on the bench, the long, white sleeves of his coat falling over my nakedness.

"Do you feel any pain?" he asked as he hammered. "What about this? What about now?"

Yes, I said. No, I said. And then, No and no. Because I wanted to compromise his experiments. I wanted to make them as meaningless as I was.

Mengele didn't suspect a thing. He shone a light into my eyes, and I was grateful for the momentary blindness, because his face was so close to mine, and the smell of him was in my nose. It was scrambled eggs and cruelty, and my stomach rumbled against my will. He spoke over the rumbles, as if hoping to disguise the proof that he, too, was in possession of a body that answered to the normal demands of digestion.

"How has your day been, Pearl?" He asked this merrily, as if he could have been any of the people we passed by on our way home from school—the postman, the butcher, the florist, the neighbor— his inquiry innocent and casual.

"It hurts."

"Your day hurts? What a funny thing to say! And here I thought Stasha was the only comedienne."

On the other side of the room, Nurse Elma snorted.

"Pain has its reasons," Mengele said.

And then he gave me a piece of candy and commanded me to enjoy it. I carried it, fully wrapped, beneath my tongue for safekeeping. This was something of an effort because my tongue felt like dust and my head was swimming and my mouth was full of aches. Still, I managed to preserve this sweetness all through the ride back to the Zoo. Once in the yard, I spat the wrapped candy into the dust and watched the Herschorn triplets fight over its possession.

I didn't know whose side to be on anymore.

Stasha's injury made spying on her easier. She wore a mound of gauze over her now-bad ear, and she was in such a sleepy haze that I was able to read her blue book under her very nose as we both lay in our bunk.

October 20, 1944

Doctor keeps vials in a box. They are marked War Materials, Urgent. *I know that there are vials with my name on them, with Pearl's name on them. He is careful not to mix them up. He is careful in most things concerning organization, but I am beginning to wonder about his skills as a physician.*

And then she woke and caught me reading; she huffed a little, but she was too weak to care much about my intrusion. Nonchalant, she simply adjusted the white petals of the bandage at her ear.

"You know that you can't do anything about Mengele," I whispered.

"Zayde wouldn't agree with you. He thinks I can do anything I decide to. Ask Zayde, he will tell you."

"How will I do that?" I asked. For once, I made no attempt

to conceal my scorn about her illusions, all the strange beliefs she clung to so desperately that they'd begun to course and flex through her like medicine.

"I've been writing Mama and Zayde letters," she said. "I can add that part in."

She grabbed her book from me and rummaged around in her pocket for a pencil.

"Why are we pretending, Stasha?"

"Pretending?" She lowered her voice. "You mean, about Patient? Of course I'm pretending that he's fine. Any doctor knows that you don't tell sick people that they're sick. That only worsens their condition. They give up hope. Their bones start to fold in on themselves and before you know it, their lungs—"

"I mean pretending about Mama. About Zayde."

"Why wouldn't they be well? We're doing everything Uncle has asked of us."

And then she launched into her usual absurdities, saying that whenever a needle plunged into us, Mama was the recipient of extra bread. Whenever a sample of tissue was taken, Zayde was allowed to swim in the swimming pool with the guards. She insisted that she'd been more than able to manage these negotiations with Uncle. Now that she'd sacrificed her ear, there was no way that he could choose not to take care of the two of them.

I decided to say nothing about the piano I'd seen cross the yard— such proof of our loss, and all they'd take. This was not merely a charitable approach—it was also that I could not believe it still myself.

"Why not a visit, then?" I challenged. "Wouldn't that be the ultimate privilege? To see them?"

"I haven't asked for a visit."

"You don't ask for a visit because you know they are dead."

"It's not true," she said, her face so still. "I know it's not true. I have evidence. They are away from us but they are alive."

"What evidence?"

She sat up in our bunk and turned to me so that we were face to face. Suddenly gentle, she reached out her hand and closed my eyes.

"See that?"

"No."

"Try harder. I'm thinking about it."

She smoothed my eyelids with her fingertips till a soft blackness coated my vision. And then it bloomed.

"You see it now, don't you?"

I did see it. It was just as Mama had drawn it. But—

"No," I said. "I don't see anything at all."

"I know you're lying, Pearl. You see it. You see it as much as I do."

I continued to deny this.

"It's a poppy," she murmured. "You remember. The drawing Mama was working on? She was starting to draw a field full of poppies when everything changed, back in Lodz. And when they put us in the cattle car, she started drawing again, on the wall. She only got as far as one. Whenever I am too sad, I always see that poppy. I know that if Mama was dead, I would see many more. But I don't have to explain this to you—you know what I am talking about,

Pearl."

I wasn't about to admit this, though it was true.

"I don't mind seeing it, because it reminds me of Mama. But I don't like the feeling of it much. Sometimes, when things are too unbearable, the poppy threatens to multiply itself. If you were gone, Pearl—I'd see a whole field full. I hope I never have cause to see a whole field of poppies like that."

What she looked like at that moment I never knew, because she dove beneath the thin scrap of our blanket, concealing her whole head from view. I heard her grunt with discomfort as she shifted about and busied herself with untying my shoes. Ever since we were little she always liked to take my shoes away, just to make sure that I couldn't leave. I felt the shoes slip from my feet. I was glad that Stasha couldn't see in the darkness provided by the blanket. I didn't want her to realize that her shoes were in better condition—like new, in fact, because she hardly went anywhere besides the hospital and the yard—than mine, which were threadbare at the soles, worn from my trips to organize potatoes.

From beneath the blanket, she posed a question, the same question she'd ask day after day in an interrogation that would soon become so routine that I found myself answering it even as I slept.

"Have you practiced dancing today?" she inquired.

I wasn't about to tell her the truth, which was that I'd started to practice but as soon as I was in first position, a drop of blood leaped from my throat and into the air, as if it were trying to alert me to the damaged performance of my insides. In all its redness, the little drop made this clear: Mengele's plans to unfurl me had begun, and if I were to outlive the harm he'd wrought, it would take a miracle doubled and doubled again, multiplied to some impossible degree.

"What reason could I have not to dance?" I said.

CHAPTER FIVE

The Red Clouds

After Uncle hurt my ear, everything I heard carried an echo. This was good when someone said something pleasant. It was terrible when someone barked a nasty order.

I think I don't have to say which occurred more frequently, considering that Ox was charged with my care. That woman would never be pleased.

A second side effect: A constant peal of absence. A certain soreness, a raw pang.

A third side effect of this damage was more welcome. The puncture he'd left in my ear granted an easier passage for dreams to sift into my brain. I had all manner of dreams in the days after my hearing on that side went black. They were so beautiful that I almost forgave Uncle for the perversions he'd wrought on my eardrum. Because I could not turn down the opportunity, even in fantasy, to confront him with all the wrongs he'd done.

"Did you have the dream too?" I asked Pearl one morning after a particularly satisfying episode of revenge. I'll admit it: I was testing her; I wanted to see how aligned we were that day.

"Of course I did," she said. And she stretched out on the rough slats of our bunk and yawned a little, just to distract me from her unconvincing tone.

"What was in it?" I challenged.

Knowing that her face would give away the deception, she turned her back to me and stared at the bricks.

"Family," she said. "What else?"

I felt so guilty that I hadn't dreamed of family at all—not a glimmer of Papa or Mama, not even a figment of Zayde—that I went along with this lie she presented.

"A good one, yes. But I wouldn't mind if it changed a little from time to time," I said. "That part where Zayde turned the cabbage into a butterfly was pleasant enough, but the part where Papa reappeared every time Mother wept was terrible."

"It was dreary, really," Pearl said. "I'm not sure why we can't dream better."

"And I suppose these defects were all my fault? You were born first, after all," I said. "You always take the lead in such things. Even at the laboratory, they think you are the leader."

"That only proves how stupid they are," Pearl said. "Anyone with eyes can see that you are in charge of us."

I swung my legs around to the edge of the bunk. It could have been a good day if we were anywhere else. The sun was out and for once, the birds were determined to get their chirps in alongside the howls of the guard dogs.

"Out of bed!" Ox roared. She walked along the wooden railings, banging each with a spoon and reaching up to tweak a girl's earlobe whenever it pleased her.

I put my hands over both ears.

"Hear no evil, eh?" Ox said.

I nodded. My hands remained in their position.

"You'll see no evil too. Not today. A soccer match out at the field. Won't that be nice?"

I put my hands down, cautiously, and replied that yes, I was excited to watch the match.

My sister also cheered to this news. She'd been slow in recent days, but for once, she leaped onto the ladder and dressed in a hurry. But Ox caught her by the collar and pulled her aside.

"No match for you, Pearl," Ox said.

That's when we saw the flash of the ambulance as it rumbled past the door.

I began to wish, as I saw Nurse Elma collect Pearl, as I watched them disappear into the mouth of that trickster ambulance and roll off, that he'd blunted the abilities of my eyes as well, just so I could no longer witness the continued torture of my sister. But I was not to be spared the burden of sight, not yet.

We assembled in the yard, with Ox at the fore. She appeared to be a great fan of the sport, and she tried to raise our spirits, talking to each child about different plays and which guard was the best on the field. Dr. Miri and Twins' Father were less enthusiastic about the event. They walked among us, keeping a dutiful count.

Patient loped over to me in his knock-kneed way. His eyes were more shifty than usual.

"I have a present for you," he said. His arms were tucked behind his back.

"All I want is for you to be well, Patient."

He coughed in reply.

"And you're not well at all."

"It is one of those things," Patient said brightly, "where it gets worse before it gets even worse and then it never really gets better but who has the time to care because you're too busy fighting for a tin cup full of nettles."

This had become a popular saying at the time. I didn't care for it much. I turned away to avoid continuing the course of this conversation. I felt a whack at the rear of my skirt. And then a tap at my shoulder. Laughing, Patient held up an ear horn.

"It's for you," he said. "From Canada. They kept it because it is ivory, I think."

This antiquated ear horn must have belonged to a wealthy woman. It had that precious finish, and a horse's head for a handle. This horse was a defiant animal; its mouth quested, and its mane ribboned back, as if confronted by some terrible wind. I worried what Uncle might say about it if he happened to see me crossing the yard.

"Try it and see," he begged. "Put it to your bad ear and I'll say something."

I didn't try it. I stroked the horse's mane skeptically.

"You better like it," he said. "I traded for that with Peter. He stole it from the warehouse for me. It is easier to get things from Peter if you are a girl, because then you can pay with a fumble. I had to pay with a cigarette."

"I'd rather the cigarette," I scoffed.

"Cigarettes can't make you hear," he said, his voice ever reasonable. "I might say something valuable someday in your left ear, something you don't want to miss."

He had a good point. More and more, I was enjoying our conversations. I could speak to him about things I couldn't with Pearl. Things about ending Uncle. As in where to end him and how to end him, and the kind of implement that might end him the fastest.

At the match, we children spread out on the left side of the field and tried not to look at the right side, which was occupied by female wardens and some of the guards' families, all of them visiting for the weekend, every last one beaming and lolling on bright blankets with potato salads and rolls and sausages. The mothers were chasing their cherub-babies around the grass and reading picture books to their girl children and snapping photos with their cameras at all the curiosities of Auschwitz. I saw a camera pointed in my direction, and gave a deliberate blink. Patient mimicked the gesture. We were becoming, I noted happily, more and more alike every day.

After we opened our eyes, the game began.

We watched the ball fly back and forth between the guards in their trim athletic gear and the prisoners in their shabby stripes. Patient was particularly excited; I had to remind him several times not to cheer too loudly, if only for the safety of his insides. An unmodulated cheer, I warned, was sure to rupture the fragilities within him.

"And don't expect us to win either," I said.

"But we will win," he said to my good ear, thoroughly enraptured. "And when we win, the trains will move back on their tracks, through the forests, through the mountains. If we win, the ghetto will have never been, and there will never have been a knock on the door."

He paused for my approval, but only for a second. He was enjoying his fancies, all the powers of his imagination. We were alike in that way too.

"If they win," he continued, "my brother will be my brother instead of a dead boy. He'll never have suffered. He'll never have wondered where I was while he lay dying."

I wanted to tell him I didn't know if such a miracle could occur. I was privy to some of the secrets of this place and knew it to be strange, but a resurrection? That seemed impossible. But then I realized that I could not say that such goodness was unlikely because I had never thought the cruelty of Auschwitz was possible either.

But I kept these thoughts to myself, and if Patient was interested in what preoccupied my mind, he covered it quite cleverly by focusing on the match.

We watched the prisoners slouch across the field. But their

slouch was determined in the first round and valiant in the second. Some were whittled sleepwalkers, while others were enlivened by the possibility of victory, summoning strength that was sure to dissipate. The ball didn't care how feeble the kicks were, how sleepy the plays. It flew between the prisoner and the head guard as if trying to negotiate some impossible treaty. In the third round, a guard laughingly booted the ball off the field and replaced it with a sourdough boule, kicking it off from the starting point with a spray of crumbs. Even the crows perched in the trees knew better than to scavenge these crumbs; they turned their sooty heads toward the sun and ignored it. I saw that they were wise and followed their example, and Patient followed mine.

We looked to the sky instead of the match and we watched the clouds be clouds in their own way. Together, we read the shapes, in the style of children more innocent than ourselves.

"A clock," I said, pointing to a cloud.

"A Nazi!" Patient said.

I pointed to another cloud.

"A rabbit," I said.

"A Nazi," said Patient.

This pattern continued. Where I saw a bride, a ghost, a tooth, a spoon, Patient saw only Nazis. Sometimes his Nazis were sleeping or picking their teeth, but mostly they were dying Nazis. The dying Nazis died of an array of diseases, of run-ins with wild animals, run-ins with Patient's grandmother, and run-ins with the point of a bread knife held by Patient himself.

I tried to see what he saw, tried to follow his gaze from where he lay, his cheeks streaked with dirt. He coughed, but politely turned his face to direct this nasty exhalation into the ground.

"Explain to me how that looks like a Nazi," I said. I pointed to the latest puff, which he'd declared to be a Nazi dying of a poisoned arrow.

In answer, the boy took his bread knife from his pocket and dwelled on the blade. All of us in the Zoo were given these knives to cut our rations with; most were dull and leaned weakly from their hilts. But Patient's bread knife had a danger to its edge, a sharpness that he had cultivated from the backs of rocks.

"Someday I'm going to kill a Nazi," he whispered. And then he bolted upright.

"I want to kill one too," I whispered back. "But a very specific one. You know who."

Patient fell to stabbing the soil around him.

"They are all the same," he said. "I'll take any I can."

As he spoke, I felt a sudden pain. It was an interloper, one unknown to me. It tried to present itself as warmth, but really, what it carried was a sting so strong it was a wonder that I did not faint. Above me, the clouds rollicked without a care. Stupid clouds. I was beginning to tire of them. Not only were they unsympathetic to our plight, but not a single one was talented enough to attempt an imitation of my sister. As I felt this pain, I thought of Pearl in the laboratory. But I couldn't think of Pearl in the laboratory, not like that.

She was stronger than me, I thought, she would endure.

I forced myself to take a brighter view of things.

"Someday," I told my friend, "killing won't be necessary at all. Because the war, it will end."

"The world?" Patient furrowed his brow.

"No, the war," I said. "The war will end."

Patient shrugged. I wasn't sure if he shrugged at the sentiment or if he was reacting to the fact that the guards had scored another goal.

"World, war. These are also the same," he said.

It was then, in a fit of anger roused by the guards' victory, that he stood and thrust his bread knife at the Nazi-clouds, and his beleaguered body must not have been able to support even this small gesture, because he stumbled back, fell with a thud, and struck his head on a stone. His body shuddered and seized. Ox did nothing; I did less. I was afraid. I called for Twins' Father, for Dr. Miri. Patient continued to shake; his eyes flashed. The prisoner-goalie let out a cry and dashed over; he tried to cradle Patient, and he tried to fit a stick in the boy's seizing mouth so as to save his tongue. Seeing this rescue, one of the guards drew his pistol. Shots were fired. Two in the air, and one toward the flesh. Gut shot, the prisoner-goalie fell beside the twitching boy.

Uncle pushed his way through the crowd with a stretcher. He shouted furiously at all he passed, and he stepped over the body of the fallen goalie to retrieve Patient.

A premonition ran through my head as the boy was carted off on a stretcher: This was the last I would ever see of my friend. I looked down at my arms, which trembled around Patient's gift. I didn't need the ear horn to hear the shouts of Uncle as he screamed into Patient's still face in some hopeless attempt at revival.

And in the midst of these screams and cries, I felt the pain of my sister that I'd tried to dismiss because she was stronger, because she would want it that way, because I couldn't live with any other. Pearl's pain, it insisted within me; it ran and coiled and it said: *Do what you like with your share, but I will not be ignored, reconfigured, or endured.*

Hearing this, I dropped the ear horn.

It fell some feet away from where the wounded prisoner-goalie lay on the field, clutching his belly with one hand. How can it be possible that we remain so curious to the end, so intent on knowing and experiencing even as we are dying? Because, you see, when the prisoner-goalie spied that precious object, so strange and foreign on that soccer field, he dragged himself forward in his dying haze— it was as if he wanted to see if that ivory ear horn held something final for him, a message, a sound, a cry. But the guard, spying this interest, took him down with a shot to the back just as he grasped hold of it. Only then did the wounded man lie still. Red clouds bloomed between the bars of his uniform—I watched them seep and travel across the horizon of his shoulders.

CHAPTER SIX

Messengers

When Patient was borne away from us, so lifeless, my sister hushed. If she said a word about her grief, I did not hear it. But perhaps I missed this—after all, grief was difficult to distinguish from the other sounds of Auschwitz. It was late October 1944—planes plowed the sky above us; they drowned out the barking of the dogs and the gunfire from the concrete towers.

"Russians," Taube remarked bitterly to no one, his face tilted to take in the view. "If only I were coward enough to desert this hell now, before all of Poland falls to pieces."

"Such a shame!" Bruna mocked. "That you are so burdened by bravery!"

I held my breath, waited for the retaliation for her insult. But none came. Taube was too busy with his musings.

"We should bomb this place immediately," he continued. "Leave the whole lot of you writhing in the rubble. Let the Russians try to free your corpses."

"What is stopping you, then?" Bruna taunted him. "You miserable lump of deformity!"

Taube was so distracted by the planes that he did not even chase her. Or perhaps the engine's roars made Bruna's insults inaudible. In any case, she took advantage of this opportunity. "Foul pudding!" she cried. "You tedious sore! More worthless than a fish's ass!"

She had such fun with this, it gave us even more reason to hope the planes might continue their paths. But while the appearance of the Russians was useful to the dreams of many, they meant nothing to my sister.

Without her friend to tend to, Stasha found herself overwhelmed by open swaths of time. Everyone had a suggestion as to how she should put herself to use, but she turned down Bruna's appeals to organize as a team and the Lilliput matriarch's invitations to tea. Knowing my sister's love of babies, Clotilde gave her the honor of plucking the lice from her twins' heads, but even this enviable show of trust failed to move Stasha.

She no longer had time for distractions of any sort, Stasha said, and it was true, she couldn't be tempted by a single round of our diversions, the awful rouse of Tickle the Corpse, or even a Kill Hitler play. There had been a time when Stasha's pantomimes had threatened to unseat Mirko's—she had nearly outdone his Hitler impression with an act that was less dependent on mustache than most, relying instead on a mockery of his speech and a fine line of drool. I knew that she enjoyed making the others laugh more than anything else, but nothing could convince her to participate after Patient was gone. When I tried to persuade her by saying that games were good because they involved friends, she said that she no longer had time for friends either, and she issued this declaration as loudly as possible, obviously hoping that Moishe Langer, who had recently offered her a sweet and killed a roach before it could plink across her foot, might finally put his bothersome affections to rest and leave her be.

And where she wanted to be was on the steps of the infirmary with her bread knife across her knees. Those steps saw the feet of many—the sick, the nurses, the dead being carried out. Dr. Miri began to exit and enter the infirmary with the greatest caution, avoiding my sister at all costs—her demeanor said that she couldn't risk discussing Patient's fate. But no matter how quickly she ascended or descended those stairs, she was always confronted by Stasha, whose stony face would attempt an expression at the doctor's approach. She did her best to make her countenance into a question mark, a soft confrontation, but Dr. Miri only wrinkled her brow in an aggrieved fashion, and then—as if in answer to the cries of the dying within—smoothed it promptly.

I don't know how Stasha was able to listen to the cries. I know she sifted through them for some thread of Patient's froggy voice, but that was more than I could ever endure. I believe she was testing herself for times to come. Because when the Russian planes retreated, Stasha finally began to hold conversations with me again. But her voice had a new bitterness to it. It seemed older than us both.

"I see that poppy in my mind lately. I see it all the time. Do you see it, Pearl?"

I did.

"I can't see more," she told me. "Don't ever make me see a field's worth."

It was this warning that made me plan for her future grief.

I went to talk to Peter in secret. Stasha hated Peter, the exalted messenger boy who had procured the ear horn for Patient. He knew far more than we did about painting and books, which impressed the doctor to no end. Worst and most puzzlingly of all, he was twinless and sported none of the typical abnormalities or genetic detours that meant salvation. In fact, it was his Aryan good looks—what Mengele appraised as a heroic nose and strong chin—that enabled his presence in the Zoo.

From the very first, Mengele had anointed the boy as someone special, and he was given advantages that placed the fourteen-year-old above and beyond us all. If Peter was aware or ashamed of this, I couldn't tell. He carried himself differently—I'd watched him from the very beginning, looked on as he slipped beneath fences like a cat, prowling about with a look of grim concentration that betrayed his intent to subvert all the benefits of his post. He was gifted with adaptation, this Peter, but he was more civilized than Bruna; he approached matters with the utmost diplomacy, and it was easy to forget how young he was, given these skills. He stood out in this way, and more. Perhaps most notably, in this place of constant filth, he was an oddly clean boy. Never with any grime underneath his fingernails, unlike the rest of us. I often saw him smoothing his clothes with his hands and mending the buttonholes, and though he was as skeletal as any of us, he could be seen trying to exercise in the fields, performing endless series of push-ups and lifting stones above his head. He was captain of the soccer team and president of the boys' secret Zoo society, the Panthers, which was not very secret at all and seemed to amount to fits of meetings that ended in arm-wrestling matches.

But more impressive than any of these other achievements was this: Peter was one of the few who still had pride, and he dared to have it even in Mengele's presence, which seemed to be the greatest trick of all.

Yet the main reason for Stasha's envy was the fact that, since Peter was Mengele's messenger boy, he got to see all the sights and cross all the borders of our strange city. From block to block, from the men's barracks to the women's, through the coveted field of wildflowers and into the finery of Nazi headquarters, he roamed, carrying words from one place to the next. We were infinitely more limited. We knew the boys' barracks and the girls', we knew the length of the fence, the rear of the infirmary, the road to the laboratories, and the terrible insides of those laboratories. Of the rest, we could only dream. But Peter saw.

He saw Canada, the warehouses filled with all our lost luxuries. Heaps of gold, pyramids of silver. Forests of grandfather clocks, pillaring high. Stacks of china, enough for thousands of celebrations. Soft piles of fur and leather. He talked about it constantly.

He saw the secrets of the infirmary, witnessed the barter systems of the *kapos*. He saw people leave codes on the sides of the latrines, bury helpless messages in the dust. He talked about that, but in hushed tones.

He saw other piles too, the unmentionable piles of precious teeth and hair and flesh. He didn't want to talk about them.

His travels weren't without risk—while most of the guards were aware of his status as one of Mengele's pets and knew to leave the boy alone, there had been occasions on which Peter had been mistaken for a trespasser. One such incident ended in scarring—the lash of a whip tore a crescent of flesh from his ear. Mengele tried to fix it, but his clumsy handiwork only enlarged the wound. Peter didn't care about this disfigurement. He said that the resulting discipline of the officer at Mengele's own hand was its own reward, and he'd welcome future opportunities to repeat this sort of incident, because how else was he to inflict any kind of vengeance?

This torn ear only further commended Peter to me, because it reminded me of a stray cat my sister and I had loved when we were small, an animal we'd trained to run to us when we rang a bell. I'll admit it: I often found myself wondering what it might be like to pass my hand over that injury, to roll that scar between my fingertips, to know, before it was too late, what it was to touch Peter, to know the unique temperature of his skin.

I'd hoped to find him alone, though I had no real idea of what I might say.

But when I found Peter, he was with the Yagudah triplets, all of them leaning against the wall of the boys' barracks and practicing sleight-of-hand tricks. The triplets were trying to make white handkerchiefs act like streams of milk, to pour them out of one hand and into another. It was a trick that had made them very popular among the others because it provided an illusory proximity to food. Stasha had not been impressed by their magic. It had no utility to it, she complained, it was the stuff of dreamers in a world that didn't recognize dreams anymore. She'd been quite vocal about this opinion, and I hoped desperately that the Yagudahs wouldn't mistake me for my outspoken sister. Judging by their looks, though, they certainly had.

"What are you doing here, Stasha?" two of the three queried in unison.

"It's not Stasha," Peter said without the slightest upward glance. "Stasha is deaf now. This is the non-deaf one."

"She's not deaf," I said. "She's only half deaf. And her health, it's constantly improving."

The boys elbowed one another with glee.

"I'm sure she'll be dancing for Taube any day now," said one of the Yagudahs with a titter.

"Tell me," I said, cheeks burning, "how far does that handkerchief-milk go divided among the four of you? Are you stronger than the rest of us for drinking it?"

They balled their hankies in their hands and glowered, but I couldn't be deterred by such pettiness. I joined the boys against the wall. A silence followed. The boys and the girls of the Zoo didn't mix much. Before the cattle car, I'd heard older girls discuss the awkwardness of dances. I figured that this was the closest that I might ever know of that phenomenon. It was so quiet that I could hear my pain traversing new paths inside of me—it trilled as it coiled through me; it burned and sank like a stone. So I was grateful when Adam Yagudah leaned over to speak to me, if only for the distraction.

"You know that business about Taube being friends with Zarah Leander isn't true, don't you?"

"I'm not an idiot," I said.

"Well, your sister seems to believe it."

"She's not an idiot either," I said. "And don't you have any better tricks to do? If I were you, I'd make myself disappear before the Nazis do."

This prompted a peal of laughter from Adam's brothers. Adam himself wasn't amused.

"I wasn't trying to be funny," I said.

"Of course you weren't," Peter said, lowering his face to mine so that our eyes had no choice but to meet. "Being funny is Stasha's job, isn't it?" He spoke softly, without mockery, as if we were alone and not surrounded by an audience, as if we were in a real room and not outside by the dusty walls of the barracks. And then, as if embarrassed by his own earnestness, he wound a finger in my curls and pulled. Touch—it had grown so complicated and strange. The curl-pulling was a gesture I'd been familiar with all my life, or at least in the parts of my life where boys sat behind me in school, but this tease felt different. It carried a pleasant thrill, and I knew this was the closest I might ever come to an affectionate touch from a boy. But the fact that this could be my last thrill—it undid me. And Peter's torn ear—I could not look away from it. I wished for pockets in the skirt of my dress, simply so I could still the twitch of my hands as they longed to touch the badly healed wound.

"I'm only teasing," Peter said. "Don't worry, I won't tell."

I'd thought Stasha and I had kept our arrangement secret—I couldn't imagine how Peter knew. The triplets fell stonily silent, as if they themselves were familiar with such a coping tactic in their own lives. Peter must have seen my discomfort because he snapped his fingers, and the other boys scattered. I admit that I was impressed by this power. It was an odd thing, to see a sense of com-

mand so genteelly expressed in a place where a boot on the neck
was the most common order.

"Will you walk with me?" Peter asked. And he tried to give
me his sweater; he pulled it off and attempted to drape it over my
shoulders. I shrugged it off, just the instinctive reaction of an awkward girl. It wouldn't do to take too much from him, and I was
happy enough for this amble besides.

As we wandered, I saw that winter would soon approach. In the
distance, past the cremo and the soccer fields, you could see the
birches shedding the lit amber of their leaves, readying for snow.
And beyond those white-limbed trees, I knew there was a river,
hills, an escape. Like everyone, I'd heard the story of the rebel
lovers—Rozamund and Luca—who were shot as they'd attempted
that escape, how they'd died together, entwined in the mud at the
fence's edge, blood flagging their backs in surrender, after a month's
worth of sweet notes and covert courtship. I tried not to think of
that then, with Peter; I tried to focus only on the stumps that bordered the length of the fence. I walked ahead of him, jumped from
stump to stump so as not to touch the ground. It was easier to speak
to him this way, and during this exercise, I forgot my pain too well,
and was reminded of it only when I stumbled.

Peter plucked me up from the ground and pulled out a pebble
lodged in my knee with his knit-gloved hand. After all the prodding
of the nurses and the doctors, I shivered at the feel of a hand that
would never want to hurt me.

"I've heard the stories about you," I told him. "About how you
organize all sorts of things and taught Taube's dog to growl at
Hitler's name. About how you put a toad in Nurse Elma's desk, and
an egg in Mengele's house slipper."

Peter's hair had a habit of falling in his eyes. He used this as an
excuse not to look at me then.

"I've had some adventures," he admitted. "But the house slipper!

I can only wish. I don't know where these stories come from at all. They sound like some of your sister's inventions."

"I've heard less wholesome stories too."

"Oh? Well, perhaps you can convince Stasha to create more flattering fictions about me?"

"Not Stasha. Bruna. She is the one who told me about your visit."

He stopped short in our walk, disturbed.

"Then I assure you, the account is inaccurate. Bruna has no idea what that was about. You don't believe me?"

I was silent, too embarrassed to address the details of what I'd heard.

"I have been to the Puff only to deliver messages. But on one occasion, it is true that I lingered, because I saw an old friend. Did you know Ivan?" He paused, thoughtful. "No, you couldn't have—he was not here when you arrived. He was a couple of years older than I, but we grew up together, in the same neighborhood. I had not seen him for at least a year. All the men on his block saved up to take him to the Puff. I was shocked, but Ivan was so pleased by his gift—he even made me promise that if I ever saw his father again, I would let him know that he had had that evening."

"And have you seen his father?"

Distance entered his voice.

"Yes."

"And did you tell him?"

The distance increased.

"No."

"So you broke your promise."

Here, Peter hesitated. I could see that this was a story he was not longing to tell. But—

"Not really. Because when I saw his father, he was dead; he was lying alongside bodies. I don't believe in talking to the dead—if you talk to the dead here, it's not long before you stop speaking your true language, whatever it may be. So I wrote him a note instead. I wrote that Ivan had had a night that would have made him happy to know about, and I put it in his pocket. It was an awkward note to write." He paused. I wouldn't have taken him for one to blush, but he did then. "Do you think that was the right thing to do?" he wondered. "It bothers me. I think of it all the time."

I knew what haunted me. Was it terrible to take comfort in knowing what haunted him? Reflective, he ground the toe of his tattered shoe into the dirt, as if to make the thoughts that preyed upon him join the dust.

"Maybe now that I've told you, I can stop thinking of it. I can think of you instead." I hadn't known that a voice could be that tender. I also hadn't known that one day a boy would draw near and pluck a stray eyelash from my cheek, and I would hope desperately that Stasha would not sense how I felt in that moment.

I watched Peter rub the eyelash between his thumb and forefinger. "Nurse Elma will have to count them all over again tomorrow," he said, in an attempt at lightness.

I did not go to see Peter with the intention of kissing him. But that is what I did. I want to say that I only pressed my lips against his in manipulation, as a means to an end. I want to say that I maintained this position even as he kissed me back, cupping the side of my face as no one ever had before, that this was not the beginning of anything—not closeness, affection, love, the same wonder that had flourished in doomed lovers like Rozamund and Luca and led to their end.

Because it was wrong, I told myself, to become too human to anyone in this place, to try to imprint myself upon someone's memories, and, most pressingly, to give myself a first that might soon be my last.

When that final thought struck—I pulled away. He wondered

why I stopped but took a step back like a gentleman. Of course, this sudden reserve made me regret my action. But there were other matters of concern, and I forced myself to focus on them, despite my wants.

"There is something I need," I said.

"Oh. I see," he said wearily, and he sighed. "That is what this is about."

"You have dealt with this before? With other girls?"

He gave a polite shrug. I saw then that he had been careful to hold my eyelash in the palm of his hand. The wind picked it up and whisked it away.

I stood on the bottom rung of the fence so that I could reach his torn ear, and I put my feelings aside, and then I told him what I wanted. I needed this thing, I said, to keep my sister alive when I left her. And then with this business concluded, I touched the scar at his earlobe, that spot where his skin had struggled to mend.

A faint lilt of music cantered over, lifting and swelling from the orchestra practice in the basement. We'd heard music in this place before. It had been there to greet our cattle car at the ramp, and now that the transports had ended and no new prisoners needed its initiation, it accompanied the inmates' work as they built barracks and sorted warehouse goods and trundled carts full of bodies and dug grave after grave—alongside every labor, it rose and insisted and sang, *Come this way, to this, the latest version of your extermination, one that you can survive if you prove your usefulness.*

In all the smallness of our life, I had never thought I could hate music before. This place changed that; I cringed at every note, dreaded each swell and start, because when I heard it I could think only of the fatal toil that took place alongside each tune.

But I didn't hate the music then, as I stood with Peter. With him standing beside me, in his tattered sweater, his eyes fixed on the field beyond our fence and the birch trees that lined its perimeter, I welcomed it, because it was the sound of what we'd lost—the strains of those years that should have happened and now never would. I wanted to approximate a piece of those years. I wanted to understand what music meant when two people held each other and moved through the minutes with affection.

Like most boys, Peter couldn't dance. Still, I initiated a waltz, one ill-timed to the creaky melodies. Someone in that orchestra needed to tune our old piano, I could tell. While clasping the bones of one arm around me and treading all over my feet, he addressed my request with a mock-serious tone, as if we were two adults out in the world discussing some complication in our daily routine instead of the desperate captives that we actually were.

"You should know that what you're asking for will be very difficult to procure," he said. "Ox has taken to following me everywhere I go. And then there's Taube's new guard dog. That brute snores through his duties. But if I try to pass? He will wake."

I told him that it sounded like a challenge he would enjoy.

"Not for anyone but you," he said.

His grip on my hand was clumsy and warm; it trembled. Through his thin sweater I felt the rung of a rib. Every day, I saw bones; I saw them expose themselves under the skins of children who were slowly dying. But never before had I felt these bones in a boy so close to me—I blame those bones for what I said next.

"I love you," I said into his shoulder.

Peter stopped treading on my feet and cocked a half-closed eye at me in suspicion.

"You don't. You could—I think—in time. But you're just saying that to me because you think you won't have a chance to say it truthfully someday, aren't you?"

"Yes," I confessed. "I am."

"Then I love you too," he said, and I know we both wished we meant it. Still, I repeated the phrase into the bony ladder of Peter's chest. I did so soundlessly, shaping the words. I am sure he felt them, somehow. Because it was with great reluctance that, when the song ended, he turned from our waltz and headed off into the violet streaks of evening, assuring me as he left that he would get me what I so badly needed, no further kissing required.

I told him that I'd do as I liked in terms of kissing.

He said that he would never try to stop me from doing so.

Night—it had forgotten that it shouldn't be beautiful in Auschwitz. There was no stopping its velvet sway at the messenger's back.

October 27, 1944

By day, my pain worsened. Some mornings, I woke to find it fevering in my toes, and on others, it was sulking about in my guts. Every day, a new location, a heightened pitch. I tried not to wonder after the identity of my sickness—what could this matter?—but my mind wanted a name for it. Eventually, I settled for calling my sickness a weakness, with the idea that labeling it as such might motivate me to become stronger. I'd overheard Dr. Miri say that resistance and strength were at the center of this experiment, that the doctor was testing to see which twins were able to defy the travels of the intruders that entered our bodies through his needles.

Whether I'd been visited by typhus or smallpox or whether it was the work of some anonymous germ, I didn't know how I could hide my weakness much longer. I listened to the other children, tried to overhear their recommendations as to what might cure my ills, because I couldn't go to Stasha. They all had their tricks, my fellow experiments. They all knew how to evade questions that might result in being sent to the infirmary; they knew how to transform a cough into a laugh. When Ox inquired after the temperature of my suspiciously beaded forehead, another girl slipped the thermometer in her mouth while her twin distracted the *blokowa*. And so it was that my fever went unread.

Potatoes were commonly upheld as medicine by the whole of the Zoo. I was curious, though, if it was the complex process of procuring them that was the real cure, as it distracted me from my pain. Bruna was a great help in this, of course. We stole into the prisoners' kitchen together under the ruse of helping the cook carry a large vat of soup. As soon as the cook's back was turned, the potatoes went down the waistband of my skirt.

At our barracks, I bit into their brown jackets raw and felt my teeth wiggle in their sockets, keening like birds on a wire about to be toppled by the wind.

Day by day, potato after potato, I became weaker. And each day I went to Peter after roll call and he showed me the empty linings of his pockets. Then he'd tell me stories. About how he'd been asked to recite a poem at one of the SS parties and had passed off some Whitman as his own, with no one the wiser. About how the women of the Puff said that Taube was a crier and a drunk, a big cabbage-faced baby who proposed to the Jewesses when no one was looking. About the hollow book he'd been given by a member of the underground that held a secret store of gunpowder. He told the stories in an attempt to lessen the anxieties of the wait, but I think he could see, even as I did my best to listen, that I was pinned by some unseeable wound, some disaster that was biding its time within me.

A week after the initiation of his quest, he came to me, his fingers curled around what I wanted.

"I wonder," he said, "if you'll have any use for me after this."

He pressed it into my palm with ceremony. I couldn't believe he'd managed to sneak it from our captors. I tucked it into the waistband of my skirt for safekeeping, thanked Peter, and said good-bye. He didn't want good-bye. He wanted a new mission, he wanted to have to look for something; it was better for him, he claimed, to have this purpose.

"Ask me for anything," he said. "I need to have something to search for in here. Something better to do. Whatever you want, I'll bring it. Whatever you need, I'll get it."

There was a plea in his voice. I wanted to name something. But I couldn't think of anything. The pain inside of me was blotting out all of my wants.

"Ask like there's a future," he said. "Or at least another month, a week!"

The boy I'd known—or had started to know—suddenly, he was so lost, he looked nothing like the leader we children hailed him as.

Unnerved by my silence, Peter transformed it into a challenge.

"I'll steal real instruments for you," he said, and he tried to mask the falter in his voice with a jesting tone. "Not just pieces of pianos. Whole pianos! Baby grands! You doubt me?"

I didn't, I said. But this provided little comfort. I saw him eye what he had given me, and it was as if he wished that he could take that back, and more. He wanted to take back all that we had shared, that feeling, that moment, just so that we could relive it. This is what I suspected, at least. Because it was how I felt too.

But no amount of feeling for another can compete with the need one has to be alone with one's pain.

Zayde, he'd always told us about animals that crawled off to die, the injured and the weak that separated themselves from the others so as not to affect the endurance of their pack. I knew this was something I would have to do someday, that I should practice for that inevitable moment when I needed to turn my head and shuffle off, for the good of those better suited to survival, people like Peter and Bruna and Stasha, who had not been selected by Josef Mengele for deterioration and ruin. That was my role, my lot. I was glad for it—it meant that I did not have to watch my sister suffer as I did.

But I did not want to practice this abandonment with Peter, not then. I wanted a week with him. I'd settle for days.

"You can steal the whole orchestra for me," I said.

"Is that all?" He laughed, and he drew me close.

The object seemed too good to be real. I studied it; I turned it over in my hands. I'd thought I had wanted it for Stasha. But now that this object was in my possession, I knew I'd wanted it for myself too. I sat with it for a moment. And then two. Finally, I went to find Stasha.

She was sitting by herself behind the boys' barracks, scribbling in her little blue book, transferring anatomy diagrams into it. It was strangely quiet, or at least it was what passed for quiet behind the barracks, because only the guard dogs could be heard, and then, if you strained to part their barking, there was the sound of the cremo churning, spitting out its fire and snow with a dreadful efficiency.

Stasha's eyes were narrowed in study, and her mouth was drawn in a tense line as she penciled in her thoughts. The depth of her concentration drew my attention to how different we looked. It wasn't that change had touched only me, of course. I couldn't help but carry all the breakage of illness, but she too had been altered, though perhaps in subtler ways. Our youth had left us, but it had taken no pains to extract itself in equal measures. I said nothing of this, but she heard it still.

"It's true. We do look different," she said, acknowledging my thoughts.

"It's my fault. I parted my hair in the opposite direction," I explained.

"Why? Parting your hair differently won't bring anyone back," she said mournfully. And then she lapsed into her usual talk, the business about how she hadn't done right by Patient, that she'd failed thus far at ending Mengele.

Patient would understand, I told her. But there was nothing I could do to save her from her own convictions. So I braided her hair instead. She sat at my feet and I attempted to plait but my hands kept shaking and her hair kept slipping through my fingers.

"I don't know why I can't manage it," I said after the third try.

"It reminds you too much of Mama."

"Maybe so."

She put her book aside. The fact that she could even bring herself to do so startled me. I'd assumed that it had become my replacement, something she could love without the risk of losing it.

"Can we play the game where my arms are your arms?" she suggested.

"No."

"You forgot how to do it already? But it's so easy. You put your arms back and I put my arms through like they're your arms. And then I do funny things with my hands, like, say, wave and make a cup of tea and lose at cards."

"No." I made no attempt to be nice about this.

"Fine, I'll make you win at cards. Now will you?"

"Never." I shuddered. I had a good reason to refuse; the game no longer had appeal for me. Because while the Zoo had changed many things for us, its most severe alteration might have been the very damage it did to our notions of what it meant to be close to another living being.

The stories of this place, they alone changed our longing for attachment. Here is one such story: In the spring before our arrival, Mengele fastened two Roma boys together, sewed them back to back. First, they disappeared from their camp. Then, screams were heard from the laboratory, screams unlike other screams. The volume of their agonies unnerved the other experiments too much, so Mengele moved the joined boys to another location. Peter had told me this story; he'd watched as the boys were carried out on a single stretcher, and he'd followed the truck that transported them, at a safe distance, through the camp until it stopped. On the stone floor of a cellar, the Roma boys lived as a single entity for three days, each staring in the opposite direction, joined by a seam at their spines, and an infection.

The fact that they could not see each other's suffering was the only good to come of that.

I didn't want to speak of this, so I changed the subject. I had to say good-bye to her somehow, I had to slip it in so it didn't disturb her, I had to sweeten it so she overlooked its sting.

I assumed a cheery tone appropriate to such deceptions. I'd learned this from our mother, after Papa's disappearance, and I'd practiced it to myself down in our ghetto basement whenever I found myself alone and doubtful about our future.

"If you're so good at reading my mind these days," I said in a bright voice, "then what do I have in my pocket?"

Her eyes livened.

"You have a letter from Mama? From Zayde?"

"Guess again."

"A knife? A gun? What is it? Wait, don't tell me—I want the fun of a guess."

But it was too late. I had already pulled the object from my pocket and displayed it in my palm.

"A piano key?"

"More than that," I informed her.

She turned its whiteness over, and inspected it. Knowing how her mind worked, I understood she was already searching for another, lamenting its loneliness as a single key. She was confused by its lack of siblings.

"What's this for?" Her tone was not just unimpressed; it also carried the splinter of a conviction that said there was nothing I could give her in these times that would be of any use.

I explained that it was more than just a key, it was a key from our old piano—it was a token of our past, a reminder of something important, and whoever had it would be with me forever.

She bounced the piano key up and down in her palm as if handling a coin that she was about to gamble. Whenever the key was in the air she looked bright, thoughtful, anticipatory—but as soon as it fell into her hand, she went grim, as if the simple fact of gravity were enough to dash every hope.

"So if I ever leave you," I continued, "I'll never leave you. Because you have this, you see."

"This key, you mean. This is supposed to comfort me?"

I had no response for this. She buried her face in my shoulder, and my sleeve quickly grew damp. She shook a little. Enough to loosen her hands. The key fell, turning one whole revolution before clattering on the ground. Watching its escape, I wondered if the Roma twins died at the same moment, or if life, as it left them, had allowed one to ease the way for the other.

My sister put her lips to my ear and made a half hiss, half sob of despair, but managed nothing in the way of intelligible sound. What came from her was mangled and tortured, an attempt stopped short. I could only imagine what her words wanted to be. I couldn't imagine what the Roma twins had said to each other.

Had a good-bye been possible?

Or did the pain of their union render it unnecessary?

Thinking of these boys, I flushed and chilled; my pain made itself known, and I tried to push my sister away. It was one of those involuntary gestures, the kind that makes a person seem cruel, even though she's not aware of what she's doing. Simple as a reflex. Of course, my sister staggered back toward me; she threw her arms around my neck. My breath tried to leave me. I pushed her again, harder. The ache of this—it lit her face. She probably thought I was disgusted by the urgency of her cling, her pitiable illusions. I might have been, in some small measure, even though both had made the ruse of my piano key possible, but the truth was that, in that moment, I needed her to prove that she could manage without me at her side. The last time I pushed her, my force surprised me—she fell to the ground with a thud and sat there, blinking, as the first snow of the season began to fall.

"Get up," I ordered her. I was so cruel. I thought it necessary. I believed it was the only way in this place. She needed to live for herself; that's what the pain was telling me. I didn't know if she was the stronger or the luckier of us two—I just knew she had to live.

But my sister, she stretched out in the snow. At first I thought she was making a snow angel, but then I saw that this was a most different posture—it was one of surrender, though it was not without its angles of defiance.

"I won't get up," she whispered.

"Get up, Stasha," I ordered.

She rolled over like a dumb baby.

"I'll get up when you promise to never leave me," she insisted, her voice muffled against the snow-flecked ground. How terrible it felt, to stand over her like that, to maintain an impression of strength while she fell to pieces!

"I promise that a part of me will always be with you. Isn't that enough?"

She raised her head from the ground but refused to look at me. Her lips and nose were puffed with sobs, and I watched her bare fingers clutch the earth. They were so desperate, those fingers, to maintain a hold on anything at all that even dirt and snow would do.

"Which part?" She sniffed.

Her old fantasy—I drew on it. Had I ever truly believed in it? If I hadn't before, I certainly did in that moment, while my sister lay at my feet, so reduced.

"The part," I said, "that knew who we were before we had names or faces. Back in the floating world. Remember the floating world? We were just less than babies then, and still, we knew how to love each other. We knew these times would come, we just didn't know how, much less why. We had a lot of living to do before they came for us. That's why we decided to leave Mama early and start seeing the world as soon as we could."

"I don't recall making that decision at all," she said.

Stasha stared at the piano key glumly like it was some hateful thing.

"It's not enough," she said. But she got up. And in defiance of my pain, I bent myself at the abdomen, stooped to pick the piano key up from the ground. A tiny fracture branched out from one ivory corner. I displayed this new injury to her.

"Take better care of this," I warned.

CHAPTER SEVEN

─────────────────────

Come Make Me Happy

I was telling myself that the pain I felt was not Pearl's. Then I realized I was wrong. It had to be her pain. It was too pretty to have originated within me; it launched itself so delicately throughout my body, sending pirouettes of discomfort along my every nerve. Yes, I concluded, this pain belonged to Pearl—but before the fullness of this realization set in, I received a true blow. Bruna cuffed me on my ear.

"You cheated, Stasha!"

Bruna shivered with frost and anger. We'd been playing a game of cards behind our barracks. I'd thought it had been a pleasant one. But now, she leaned into my face so that there was no avoiding her rage. The powdered puffs of her breath smelled like winter and starvation, with a tinge of tin-cup coffee. "Don't deny it," she snarled between the snowflakes. "You knew exactly what you were doing. You're a cheater!"

I blushed and trembled. She was looking more fearsome than usual in those days. In an attempt to no longer be albino, she'd taken to coloring her white hair with coal so that it flowed down her back in a charcoal glory. This measure not only failed to deter Uncle's interest in her as an experiment but resulted in fierce streaks of black across her white face. This lent her the appearance of a raccoon, and a rabid one at that.

Much as I loved her, I feared her too.

Because it was true—I was a cheater; my survival in the Zoo was a slimy, privileged thing. No work was required on my part, no stealth, no desire—I was doomed to live forever without lifting a finger. The eye of a needle had sealed my immortality, thwarting any chance of release.

None of this bothered me until I realized that Pearl had not been given the same opportunity. Why had he withheld it from her? This was not what I thought we'd planned for at all. We were supposed to be deathless together, side by side, just as we'd been babies and girls together. Had he suspected my plan? Was he countering it with a plan of his own, some plot that would deny Pearl the needle, and me my sister?

And now, here was Bruna, my friend and protector, a lover of violence—she had found me out, she knew there was a fraud in me, a crime that allowed me to flourish. I did not know how to defend myself against such charges.

You could say that it wasn't my fault, the introduction of this lie. You could say that only Uncle could be blamed, because he had flooded my blood with it. And I would say that you were right, but while another child's body might have rejected this fraud, recognized it as a virus, a poison, an undoing, mine had embraced it. I had been too pleased by the prospect that we would survive, always we'd be together, to question what it might mean to outlive others more deserving of life. And now here I was, still the sole bearer of this cure, doomed as of this moment to spend eternity alone unless I was able to undo what he'd done.

Through my carelessness, I had betrayed my sister, and more. I was the lowest of Auschwitz. I had no right to shield myself from scorn, and yet—

"It was all Uncle's idea," I cried. "I shouldn't have let him do it, I know!"

Confusion set Bruna's eyes at an inquisitive slant. With her free hand, she motioned to the cards scattered across the snow.

"I don't know what Mengele has to do with this. All I know is that you peeked at my cards just now. I saw you! Admit it! Or don't admit it and you'll find a king in your mouth!"

She crumpled the monarch in her fist and tried to pry my mouth open. Only when she peeled my lips back and lowered the card into my throat, crown first, did I realize that her anger was about a different game, not the one I'd been playing with Uncle. Strengthened by this epiphany, I spat out the king and with it a splinter of confession, a mere fraction of my misdeed.

"You are never wrong, Bruna. I am a cheater."

"This is true. Don't you go forgetting it."

"I won't, I promise. You are the real winner here."

Bruna regarded the crumpled card in the snow, and the rarest of regrets crossed her face.

"I'm sorry for shoving the king in your mouth."

"It should've been the joker." I laughed, but it was a laugh unfamiliar to me. A desperate one, a bit ragged at the edges. A real beggar of a chortle. "But even a joker is too good for me! You would have to invent a card to suit my kind. The rot. The cheat. The germ. The disease—"

Bruna cocked her head in contemplation. I couldn't tell if she was disarmed or pleased by my abasement. That sort of innermost hatred? It wasn't common in the Zoo. Most of the others, they did not have the luxury of disliking themselves because they were too consumed with survival. This was not among my problems.

"The germ, maybe," Bruna concluded. "But the rest? You take things too far, as usual!"

I can imagine how I hung my head, but I couldn't feel it. I was numb. I assumed this to be a side effect of deathlessness, nothing more, because after the doctor had meddled with my ear, his toying with me had ceased. He took photographs of me to put next to photographs of Pearl, but this was the extent of his inquiry. Occasionally, I wished that my numbness might overtake me so that I could rally enough to see a new way to preserve Pearl, to finagle a switch at the labs and take her place as the chosen one.

Though I'd told my friend nothing of this sorrow, my face surely displayed it, because Bruna suddenly pulled me toward her in pity; she held me close and stroked my cheek with her own, as if I were just another swan in need of her rescue.

"Don't make me feel sorry for you now, Smidgen. You get me so angry!"

I apologized.

"Stop apologizing! You'll apologize yourself into the cremo."

I told Bruna she was right.

"Stop telling me I'm right! What if I'm not right?" She sank back onto her stump and stamped her boots, restless. I saw her eyes; they were sinking into her face. I saw her hands; the little bones in them were rising to the surface. "Let me tell you—I just don't know anymore. I am finding myself with nothing to say, nothing to look forward to. Stealing doesn't have the same satisfaction when it's stealing crumbs. Beating people doesn't mean much when they're already beaten."

I wasn't sure what I could say, so I said only:

"I miss Patient."

Bruna broke from the embrace and returned to her cards with a furious shuffle.

"I won't say that I miss him. But I'll let you say that without spitting in your face. That's pretty much the same thing, isn't it?"

I agreed that it was. Bruna pocketed her cards and glanced about to see if anyone was lurking. She waited for Ox to lumber past before confiding in a low voice, "Don't tell anyone that I miss him. People here, they need to see me in a certain way. They need to see my new sweater and know how I got it. You know how I got it, Stasha?"

"You stole it."

"Why, of course! But I'm not sure if it is quite stealing because I stole it for you. Just don't tell anyone. Not even Pearl."

"We don't have secrets, Pearl and me." This, of course, was me denying the fact that I was quite sure that Pearl was harboring the most terrible secret of all.

"Everyone has a secret here," Bruna scoffed. And then she draped her sweater over my back and gestured for me to join her on her walk. When I refused, she trotted off through the snow, eager to keep her daily appointment of teasing the Lilliputs.

The sweater was the finest I'd ever seen among prisoners, and it was large too; it hung from me so voluminously that I was sure that it could sleep Pearl and me through the night in an unusual degree of comfort. I should have been happier for this acquisition. It was proof that Bruna loved me. But happiness wouldn't have me, not then. Movement wouldn't have me either. And of course, there was that dull whine in my bad ear that made me want to shriek.

I sat watching the snow fall, watched it erase me. Surely, my captors envied the snow this talent. I was thinking about them more in those days. In earlier times, I'd been able to block them from my mind with my wild, *mischling* hope, but as Pearl's pain swelled and begged within me, as it fevered and limped through my every corner, searching for another solution and mocking my inability to save her, I'd found it impossible to continue without dwelling on what our captors had done to us, and in such an organized fashion that they made us turn on each other. I swore I would never turn on anyone but Uncle, and I solidified this vow by kissing Pearl's piano key.

One of Uncle's promises had come to pass—we were to be entertained the way that real living people were entertained. For an evening, we wouldn't have to amuse ourselves with another round of Tickle the Corpse or hour after hour of knitting a useless blanket out of barbed wire. No, on that late-October evening, shortly before the women's orchestra was to be dispersed, we were going to be able to listen to the music not from the distant barracks, but in the room of its origin. I knew that I was undeserving of such a pleasure, but I hoped that perhaps I'd be able to listen intently enough that I might later describe the music to Mama and Zayde.

"Stay still," Pearl commanded Sophia as the little girl squirmed. My sister had a tin cup full of snow that she dipped her fingers in to wash away the accumulations on the children's cheeks. A whole row of them lined up at our bunk to be cleaned.

Pearl had her doubts about this concert.

"It's a trick," she said. "Probably a selection in disguise. If they are presentable"—she nodded toward others in line behind Sophia—"their chances will be better."

For the past several hours, my sister had dedicated herself to the hygiene of any small girl who would permit such a fuss. She scrubbed their cheeks and chins, cleared their nails of grime with the edge of a pin. Watching her worry over prettiness, I was reminded of Mama, who loved to embellish us even though she neglected herself.

I wondered what Mama would have thought of how we looked, of the distinctions that had spread themselves across our faces.

Pearl had a grayness to her; silver moons had crept beneath her eyes, and when I caught sight of her tongue, I saw that it had grown its own fur. Pearl's tongue had always been much wiser than mine. I told myself that it had donned this ugly coat as a protective measure, to shield it from saying ugly things, and that my own tongue could benefit from such a precaution. But I could not trick myself into thinking that fur on a tongue was a good thing.

I hoped that I looked as ill as she did.

Naturally, Pearl detected these hopes.

"But it is good that you don't look ill," she told me as she dismissed Sophia and put her fingers to work on yet another set of cheeks. Alize, the tiny recipient of her attentions, regarded her dolefully, as if even she doubted that Pearl was strong enough to complete this simple operation.

I asked Pearl if there was anything I didn't know, and I warned her not to lie. I knew she was keeping a much larger suffering hidden from me. My insides told me so.

"Are you playing doctor again?" She laughed.

I told her that I'd put such pursuits—or, rather, the ruse of them—to rest after killing Patient.

"You didn't kill him," she argued.

And then she lapsed into the same narrative we'd lullabied ourselves to at bedtime for weeks, the one about how some live and die, some sacrifice and die, some cheat and die, and some simply escape and are never heard from again, and, yes, they probably died too.

I was tired of these explanations. Again, I insisted—what was this pain that she was keeping from me?

"I couldn't keep anything from you if I wanted to," she protested, and then she closed my eyes, her fingertips warm on my lids. "Tell me, what am I thinking of right now?"

My mind was so crowded with anticipation of the concert that it took some doing, but then, with a little focus, I saw constellations of hurt, little sparks of light on a background of numbness. The little lights appeared to glow in a maze that my thoughts couldn't quite navigate. I turned this corner and that corner and found suffering, but the suffering wasn't specific enough for me to recognize it. In short, I had no idea what she was thinking.

"I don't understand," I admitted.

The beginnings of a tear gleamed in her eye. She tossed her head back so that it wouldn't fall. And then I understood.

"You're worried about my ear, aren't you? You think that I truly am going deaf?"

She nodded, and then bit her bottom lip as she focused on Alize's hair. As she tugged her comb through the tangles, I saw cause for alarm. I wasn't sure how it had escaped my notice before, but I wasn't going to let another minute go by without addressing it.

"Give me your arm," I ordered.

"I'm working," she spat, but the child took this moment of distraction to bolt up and make a run for the door. We watched her dash off, saw her form grow smaller and smaller as it gained distance.

"I hope she doesn't regret that." Pearl sighed. "But at the very least, she can run."

"Your arm, please."

She outstretched it. It was clammy to the touch, bruised here and there. Most notably, it had more needle pricks in it than I'd ever had even when I was a frequent subject in the laboratory. Never had I borne so many marks. Pearl had dozens. Rosy scabs marched up and down the length of her flesh like questing ants. When I inquired about this curious swarm, she withdrew the be-scabbed arm with a start and tried to smile it all away.

"You know how clumsy Elma is," she said. "She's always missing my veins."

She waved me away, dropped her chin. Her shoulders too. The whole of her became limp; it was as if her bones were snapping, collapsing her from within. But as soon as another little girl presented herself for prettying, she resumed her normal posture.

"You've been busy," she said, her voice so bright that it drew my attention to the dullness of her skin. Her complexion wasn't far from the type I'd seen on children who were here one day and vanished the next. In all her preparations to ensure the safety of the others, she'd failed to fake her own well-being. I'd have to do it for her. I took up a trick I learned from the women who had traveled with us in the cattle car, wise women who knew the value of a rosy face.

With the point of my bread knife, I dug a little well in my wrist. The well offered me two drops of blood. I only needed one, but I didn't reject the other. Even drops of blood, I knew, liked to travel in pairs. With this redness, I affixed a false health to the apples of her cheeks.

I told Pearl that she had to look her best that evening, that there would be many people in show business at the concert who could discover her and set her free and put her in the American movies. Though I had no desire to live in America myself, I would be sure to follow her there, for the sake of her sunny career, and we'd all live together, Pearl and Mama and Zayde and me, in some place with a hummingbird in it, and a garden, a dog, weather that didn't want to do us any harm. It could be a fine life. Zayde would have the Pacific to swim in, and Mama would have more than just poppies to paint. A new set of seas and flora and exotics, that is what they needed.

But before I had a chance to tell Pearl any of this, Ox arrived at the door. In a strict line, we marched through our early snow toward an unfamiliar season, one that promised music meant for the living.

Inside, we arranged ourselves against the brick of the rear wall and watched the members of the orchestra tinker and ready themselves, saw them empty valves and adjust their reeds. They were a group of women with close-cropped hair, each aged beyond age, and their premature antiquity was emphasized by the girlishness of their clothes—uniforms of knife-pleated blue skirts, blouses brimming with scalloped collars. Their throats were sinewy, and every arm that held an instrument was elongated, as if their bodies had decided to compensate in length for what they lacked in volume. While the musicians' hands moved as if all were well with the world, their faces did not forget where they were, and they didn't let you forget either. Downcast of eye and drawn of lip, these performers were the grimmest figures in the room. Sadder than the Lilliputs, who were mourning the recent loss of their patriarch in their finest clothes. More melancholy than the women of the Puff, faded women in pastel dresses, their heads stooped like too-heavy blooms atop tired stalks, all of them milling about the tables set up for the enjoyment of the SS, tables piled high with cheese and sardines and pastries and meats. Even the aggrieved expression of the smoked pig, his scream plugged in his mouth by a lacquer-red apple, was outdone by the frantic sadness of the musicians.

The women had been playing since the early morning. Even though the transports had ceased, they had orders to play while the prisoners worked, accompanying their struggle with bright music that gave the impression of a hardy and cheerful place none of us were familiar with. It wasn't music that promised the gas or the grave; it didn't mention the forgetful-bread, the numbers, or the bones. I don't know what it was supposed to promise us.

I would've asked the Dutch pianist, Anika, her opinion on this matter if I'd had a chance. She had one of those all-knowing faces, eyes that moved in recognition of the unbearable. Many around me were in possession of such eyes, but Anika's burned a bit brighter at the time, their luminescence a remnant of what she'd attempted at the border of the electric fence days before.

The others had held her back. They said it didn't matter whether her little boy was alive anymore or not; she had to endure for him still so that she could tell someone someday what they had done to him. Why can't I tell the devil? she'd asked. It seemed a good question to me, but then again, I figured if there really was a devil, he already knew. And while I had no fear of the inventions Catholics like Anika believed in, I admired her willingness to face such a monster in demand of answers, simply because her pain was so great that it recognized only suicide as her friend.

And you'd think—given what the authorities said my father did—that I would have understood suicide long ago, that I would have known its color, its cry, its scent. And it's true that I'd been born with thoughts of it within me; it was my only difference from Pearl, and my greatest instinct until Uncle thwarted the very possibility of it. But it wasn't until I saw Anika's eyes that I truly knew the suffocation of this notion's friendship, the way it crept and curled within you, the way it said, *Look, here is another way, let me save you.*

Years later, the world would learn how common suicide was among these musicians. So few resisted it after they were freed. But I swear, that very day, I had some suspicion of it, the impulse that might follow them. I heard it in every note that the musicians played. The flutist squeaked, the oboist lowed, the drummer snared, and in these sounds there was written something else, a hidden meaning, a doubled message about beauty and its opposite.

Beside me at the wall, Pearl and Peter were ear-deep in whispers. They stood arm to arm, leg to leg; they managed a discreet clasp of hands. Pearl was wearing the sweater Bruna stole for us, and the strawberries on her dress had faded to dull orbs, like planets too pale to sustain life. Peter had slicked his hair back in an attempt to look like a gentleman. I'd heard he performed a thousand push-ups every day but saw no evidence of this. He appeared weak to me, just another moony boy, and I couldn't help but worry for him. Peter was attached to Pearl, and no good could come of that, because while he was a messenger boy, she was going places as soon as the war ended, and possibly even before that. Perhaps this very evening, I thought, someone would discover her and whisk her away to the new life she deserved, a life as a star or, at the very least, a life as someone who had a future.

Catching sight of my stare—I suppose it was unfriendlier than I realized—Peter dropped her hand and smiled at me in an attempt at a familial feeling.

"The orchestra's improved since they arrested more Poles," he said, too loudly, in my direction. And when I didn't grasp this offered thread of conversation, he flushed a little and mumbled something about having to excuse himself. Pearl tried to persuade him to linger but—

"There will be other shows," he said.

If I had known what was to happen, I would have begged him to stay. Years later, I would wonder if he might have changed what I could not, if he could have spared my sister even a portion of her pain.

But I was a stupid and possessive person, too attached to know real love, and so I didn't stop him when he picked his way through the childish crowd or the members of the orchestra or the throng of guards with the women of the Puff splayed over their knees.

"Where do you think you're going?" Taube leered at Peter as he passed the revels of this crew. "The Puff is empty tonight!"

He punctuated this statement by hurling a bottle at Peter's retreating back. We heard the bottle shatter at the threshold, and then we saw Uncle walk in, resplendent in a white suit, a silken Nurse Elma at his side, her neck beflocked with a string of minks, each of which surveyed the celebration warily, their beady eyes of jet telegraphing doom to whomever they glinted upon by chance.

"Quite a party," Uncle observed. He glared at the guards—their vulgarity in the presence of children annoyed him, but he appeared determined not to diminish his festive mood. He reached up to the toddler perched on his shoulders and tweaked his nose with affection.

It was an Italian boy, a non-twin whose handsomeness had endeared him to Mengele. He was three years of age, and others joked that he could have been the doctor's own son. In fact, this boy's resemblance to him trumped Rolf Mengele's likeness to his father. As I watched him bounce about on Uncle's shoulders and attempt to say the doctor's name, I couldn't help but wonder how many others might be seen as potential protégés. I hoped that they would not come between the doctor and me; it would not do to have my mission unraveled by a toddler. I vowed to apply myself to my work with renewed vigor.

I was interrupted in these vows by a sudden scuffle in the corner, a startled cry. Anika was pointing to the piano, a black expanse that stood like a beetle with one cocked wing. Taube strode over, his boots slapping against the floor, and she informed him of her instrument's deformity. Taube stared at her curiously and then bent stiffly over the piano to inspect the absence in the keys.

Pearl blushed—her cheeks carried the pinkest bloom of guilt I'd ever seen. I realized that this was the piano she'd mistaken for our own—this was an error so severe that I had to wonder after her mind-set. Ours had a charcoal finish and cat scratches on every leg. It had not been this pristine luxury. I said nothing of this, though. Already, she felt bad enough about what she'd done. She buried her face in my shoulder so that her guilt over this piano's pillage could remain undetected.

"You're responsible for this instrument," Taube was shouting at Anika. "And you will play it in this state. You will play it so that no one notices what is missing. Do you understand?"

Anika nodded and collapsed onto her bench. Her fingers hovered over the keys, hesitant. Then she began, her fingers finagling some solution to the absence. The orchestra played foxtrots, marching songs, songs sanctioned by the authorities. Looking down the row of girls, I saw Bruna tap her feet, saw the Lilliputs sway in time, saw Twins' Father lift up a crippled girl so that she might have a better view than any of us.

We were all moving toward forgetting, it seemed; we didn't know how hungry we were, how mangled and displaced. Our impurities meant nothing, our bodies were not unlike the other worthy bodies in the world, and not a death wish could be rooted out among us. The one person who avoided this rapture was Uncle.

He was bouncing the boy on his knee, but it was more a gesture of restless irritation than anything. I watched the boy's eyes roll in his head as he was jostled. A fear of Uncle had entered them, perhaps for the first time.

"Come now," he said. "Play my favorite."

The conductor's face was blank except for the false flush on her cheeks.

"Don't tell me you don't know my favorite?" Uncle demanded.

"Chopin's funeral march?" the conductor quavered. She pulled nervously at her skirt.

"A funeral march!" He boomed with laughter. "Is that what you think of me? That I'm a funereal sort?"

The conductor tried to stammer out an explanation but was able to produce only a squeak.

"I'm only joking, Marcelle." Uncle laughed. "Come make me happy."

The conductor stood stock-still, her mouth agape. The violinist had to poke Marcelle in the side with her bow to bring the conductor back to life.

"He means the song," the violinist hissed.

"Oh, of course," the rattled conductor said, and then the orchestra eased into "Come Make Me Happy." The flaws were frequent, because Anika was unable to make her instrument obey, despite her skill. The piano tripped and stumbled. I felt sorry for the piano. I wanted it to know that I understood its bereavement, that I feared nothing more than having an essential piece torn from me too.

Lacking his usual eye for precision, Uncle seemed unaware of these flaws and was merely roused by the song. Maybe it was because he was seeping with vodka. Maybe it was just his good mood. In any case, he deposited the boy on the floor and grabbed Nurse Elma for a dance. Everyone looked on with embarrassment and fear, as neither was a good dancer—Uncle was positively clumsy, and Nurse Elma kept trying to lead—and the couple's gracelessness was highlighted by the flawed music. Here was the perfect pair, the photogenic two, stellar genetic specimens, and they couldn't keep time. The oboist stifled a laugh into her instrument, which bleated piteously from this input. This sound startled Uncle and he dipped Nurse Elma precariously and then dropped her on her bottom. He tried to play this off as a joke, but no one could overlook his innate lack of coordination.

To distract from this failure, he strode before us and directed us to sing along, an impromptu maestro with an unskilled choir of ragged children. I'm not sure how many of us even knew the words to "Come Make Me Happy." I'm sure that many, like myself, invented words as they went.

But as we sang, we forgot our hunger and our filth, we forgot that we were splittable, faded, dim. For a moment, I even forgot that I was *mischling*. At the end, we hit the high note with the force of those who are usually powerless to strike, and I knew we were enabled because of the strength of our numbers, all the old and the new, and the force of our many pasts, small as they were; they conspired to make us sound beautiful. Even Uncle—I could tell he thought it so. And was it possible? Did the loveliness of our song make him reconsider the fates he'd planned? I swore I saw a bit of uncertainty cross his face as he swung an unseen baton at our chorus.

Work would never set us free, despite what they'd promised. But beauty? Yes, I thought, beauty might see us past the gates.

And then the song stopped abruptly when Anika's hands stumbled and the music soured. Boos rose and Taube, his face more massive and red than usual, threw his bottle at the beleaguered musician. It crescendoed at her feet.

Anika rose from her bench, glass crunching beneath her thin shoes, one with a high heel, the other cripplingly flat, in the mismatched manner of the footwear most women were issued. But even with this forced imbalance, she was able to stand upright, to put her hands in the air as if newly arrested. Her lips parted as if she wished to speak, but her tongue kept rolling out and saying nothing. She looked like an old doll I'd once left out in the rain, a toy stripped of its life through use and circumstance.

Taube directed Anika to lay her hands out on the wing of the piano. They quivered like two baby mice on the black lacquer while he took his time removing his belt, and the leather hissed like a snake in the grass as it whipped round his waist and entered his grip.

All was too quiet. I saw the belt. I saw her hands. I had never seen a room in such silence.

As I watched this confrontation, I felt for the piano key in my pocket. And when my fingertips lit on its surface—I tried to help it but I couldn't—I shrieked.

Anika breathed deep, Taube frowned, Pearl fidgeted beside me. And then Uncle, once again bouncing that boy on his knee, addressed me from across the room.

"What is it, Stasha? Why are you crying?"

But words had left me. I could only fidget with the hidden key in my pocket as he approached me.

"Tell me," Uncle insisted. He came to me, passed the flat of his hand over my forehead, and, finding no evidence of a fever, stooped to inspect my eyes. Finally, he withdrew and sighed. "You must not interrupt," he advised me. "Especially in matters you don't understand."

I promised that I would keep quiet from then on. He looked as if he didn't quite believe me, but he patted me on the head before striding to the piano, where Anika's hands still shook.

"Let the woman go," he instructed the guard.

"You are too kind, Doctor." Taube made no effort to conceal his surprise. It lifted every plane of his red face.

Uncle sauntered up to Taube so closely that his mustache must have tickled the guard. It was an unsettling proximity. He took his handkerchief from his pocket and dabbed at the corner of Taube's lips, where a bit of angry spittle had gathered. Taube went as white as the handkerchief.

"You are upsetting the children," Uncle said. His voice was slow and precise with anger. Chastened, Taube wove the belt back around his waist with fumbling fingers, but his face betrayed the fact that he would carry this insult with him long into the evening. Uncle folded his handkerchief, but just as he was about to put it in his pocket, he snorted with disgust to fully convey how much he loathed any further contact with Taube. Pinching the soiled hankie between his fingertips, he circled Taube like prey, all the while issuing that same half-smile that so many of us had received while we were being inspected by him and found lacking. Finally, when his intimidation was complete, he leaned into Taube's face for a long hiss, one so loud and pronounced that we could hear it from across the room.

"I never liked that song anyway," he said.

It was only then that I noticed that the piano key was slick within my hand. I marveled at this for a moment, thinking it had wept, before realizing that this was only the result of my guilty, sweating palm.

Uncle stalked back to his seat. We could hear the precision of his every footfall.

"I thought we were here to listen to music," he said merrily to the conductor, and she bowed her head obediently and gave the signal to the musicians to begin again, and then the famous singer entered the room, causing an immediate stir. She was a recent transport, so the guards had not yet had the time to get accustomed to the glow of her presence, and even they parted for her as she walked.

"Mama's favorite," Pearl whispered.

"Yes," I said. "It is too bad that Mama wasn't invited too."

She would have loved to be there, I knew. These songs—they were her friends after Papa left. He didn't mean to leave forever, I was sure of it. He only stepped out because there was a sick child down the street, a boy overcome by fever, and Papa was a good doctor, he couldn't deny anyone his attention. I'd spent so much of my time wishing that he had. Because he never arrived at the boy's house. The child died, and my father—he died too. He left too close to curfew, and the Gestapo caught him up in their clutches—that is what I think happened. But the authorities gave another story. They had a story for every disappearance. We didn't ask Mama what she believed. She'd shut herself up in the ghetto basement and refused to eat or change her clothes. We left food for her on plates, took it back in the morning, untouched. Playing the singer's music was the only thing she was able to do, and though the strains of it were sad, they uplifted her somehow. I know she was lonely, lonelier than any of us. She was a woman who had never had a twin, and before our very eyes, by and by, she became less motherly, and then less womanly, until she was reduced to a girl even younger than we were. She was restored to herself only when Zayde, the papa to our papa, arrived, his hearty embrace and booming voice a cover for the mourning of his son, and ordered that the music end.

I'd never wanted to remember such things—these images were Pearl's responsibility. But I suppose it wasn't her fault that my memory was so insistent. Looking at her, I saw that she was recalling the same things.

"She'd fall asleep listening to that music with her boots still on," Pearl mused.

"And her soup barely touched," I said.

"We were always putting a mirror to her mouth," Pearl said.

"To see that she still breathed," I finished.

We hadn't completed each other's sentences in some time—I leaned against the brick wall with a fresh contentment. I didn't even mind that Peter was standing next to Pearl and managing furtive grabs at her hand. All that mattered was the music.

It was a song I'd never heard before, an original piece that the conductor had created. Listening to it, I wondered if she had access to a window that the rest of us didn't. She must have been fed better, must've slept better, must've been allowed a letter from home, one unmarked by censors and full of good news. The song bore me up; it gave me a fuzzy feeling and a picture of the future I would someday have.

This future was at the movies—it had matinee tickets and a silver screen and a newsreel full of confetti and liberation. The future was Zayde and Mama and me, the three of us seated in blue velvet chairs waiting for the show to begin. I sat between them, surrounded by Mama's violet perfume on one side and Zayde's smell of old books on the other. The scents collaborated to create their own nature. Mama's hand was consumed by bandages, but she cupped my knee, and I saw her opal ring glint amid the gauze. We were trying to act as normal people act, but I still kept my ticket beside my tongue for safekeeping. I had all sorts of goods stored there, in a pocket of my mouth, and this disgusted my mother, who thought it no longer necessary for her daughter to carry razor blades in her mouth. But Zayde came to my defense; he kept telling her that the doctor had altered me in such a way that I might never be the same again, that I had impulses different than those of a girl who had not stared into the bright lights of a surgeon's table. Mama argued that yes, this was terrible, what had been done to me, what had been done to all of us, but it did no good to walk about always with one eye anticipating the next disaster.

And then the usher hushed us all because the movie was beginning. My sister was onscreen with all the greats.

It was a musical and Pearl played the part of me as well as the part of herself. Predictably, she was quite good in both roles, though I thought she could've been a little more mournful when she poisoned Mengele, because as bent on vengeance as I was, I was not a monster. The only element that troubled me more than this was the fact that the writers made us into orphans. This departure from the facts was a real insult. But I couldn't deny that Pearl excelled at the part since we'd come so close to being orphans ourselves—her tears were perfect splinters of grief that held real triumph.

What I loved most? The final sequence. After Mengele was felled, Pearl wore a white fur and clutched a tabby kitten while tap-dancing on top of a piano as lustrous as her name, and the camera loved her so much that it zoomed in on her repeatedly throughout.

This imagined scene—I knew it would be enough to pull me through, to make me survive the Zoo. I wanted it to go on forever. But it ended as soon as the singer stopped singing.

I turned to Pearl. I wanted to know if she'd seen what I'd seen, if she'd imagined it all too. But just as I was about to tap on her shoulder, my thoughts were flooded by gray, and my heart contorted. Was this a fit? I wondered. Was it a side effect of my deathlessness, some phenomenon where I'd find myself assailed by half-consciousness? When I woke from this state, I was on the floor with a number of faces floating over me, all of them angled with concern.

Pearl's was not among them.

I fumbled about to raise myself, and I pushed the faces away without knowing who they were, demanding all the while to know the location of my sister. And then I saw for myself—her absence, in full.

Where she had stood—now there was only a brick leaning out of the wall like a child's loose tooth. I called my sister's name. I called her by every name I knew, and then I invented new names for her. I even called her by my own name, just in case. She didn't answer to any of these. The music was too loud. She couldn't hear me. This is what I told myself while I screamed.

Then I saw her muddy footprints studding the floor. There were dirty quotation marks at the heels, brief flecks of mud that indicated that Pearl's departure had not been so sudden as to allow her to leave without a smudge. Such tracks are the marks of a stolen person. These imprints testified that Pearl was steadfast in her love for me, even as our tormentors removed her from this life. I wondered if—wherever she was—she saw the vision too, the vision of what I'd so dreaded, in all its multiplication.

CHAPTER EIGHT

She Said She Would Never Leave Me But

CHAPTER NINE

Million After Million

Auschwitz never forgot me. I begged it to. But even as I wept and bargained and withered it took care to know my number, and to count every soul that it claimed. We were so innumerable, we should have overwhelmed this land beneath us into nothingness. But this patch of earth would not be overwhelmed. Some claimed that we might overwhelm it when we fully understood its evil. But whenever we began to understand evil, evil itself increased. Others believed that hope might overwhelm it. But whenever hope flourished, so did our tortures. This was my belief: Auschwitz would end when Pearl returned. Where she had gone, I didn't know. I only knew that she was not with me.

And I also knew that I spent most of my time in an old sauerkraut barrel, which was an advantageous spot for my vigil, despite the cabbage stink I soon acquired. A perfect circle of isolation to enable a lookout for my sister. No *blokowa,* no Zoo fellows, no Twins' Father. Just me, my lice, and a peephole that held my view of the world.

"Are you in there?" Peter's fist knocked on the wood of my home.

I should note here that I believe that three days had passed since

Pearl's disappearance, though we both know that time was not my strength, but my sister's.

At first, I wasn't alone. Right after the music of the orchestra swept Pearl away, the lice came to keep me company. White lice, each thick as your fingertip, with black crosses splayed on their backs. I didn't mind them so much because they bit me and their bites kept me awake and I needed to be awake in order to find my sister. We struck a deal, those lice and I—I gave them my flesh in exchange for awareness, and by the grace of their jaws I kept a constant eye to the peephole of my barrel. I'm sure that we could've lived together quite beneficially for some time if it were not for the intervention of Nurse Elma.

Because those lice couldn't help but fall in love with Nurse Elma. They were always pacing my scalp, racked with longing for her. They oohed over her hips, her leather gloves, the cascade of her hair over her eye. The lice and I would get into frequent debates over her beauty. They likened her to perfection and I likened her to a parasite, which they took as a favorable comparison. At one point, a particularly tubby hustler had the temerity to pirouette up and away from the barrel as he professed his desire. Quite a leap for such a small insect. As soon as that louse said that he loved her, Elma grabbed me out of my barrel, hauled me to the laboratory, and reached for the razor. I'm sure he wasn't the first fellow to experience such a reaction, but I felt sorry for him all the same. Beneath her hand, the curls that had belonged to us gleamed in midair, then fell, and when my scalp was stripped, I saw my reflection in a steel cabinet. I did not recognize us in it. This frightened me, because maybe Pearl wouldn't be able to recognize me either. I slunk back to my odorous lair and slept. The guards knew of my presence in those barrel depths, but they let me be. I wondered if Uncle had told them to grant me this leniency or if they were intimidated by the sounds leaking from the barrel, because I spent all my time in that darkness sharpening my fingernails with my bread knife and practicing my snarl. The more I snarled, the faster my fingernails grew. The faster my fingernails grew, the more the guards trembled. They couldn't imagine the truth, which was that I sharpened my fingernails in the interest of words, not weaponry. I was writing letters to Pearl on the wooden slats of my home, inscribing it all against the grain. I wrote her once, sometimes twice a day.

November 7, 1944

Dear Pearl,

Is there music where you are?

Dear Pearl,

I know what you're thinking. Stop thinking that. There is no way that you can be dead.

Mere days into my epistolary captivity, I was already running out of barrel, even though I took care never to sign my name. And yes, I knew that there was no way for me to send letters written on this material. I just hoped that wherever Pearl might be, she could sense the scratch of every word and longing.

One day, bread crumbs flew through the hole of the barrel. I caught them like flies and threw them back.

"You bother me," I said to the visitor. This was my standard greeting at the time.

Because I had a lot of visitors. The other children visited my barrel to ask me questions; it seemed that my reputation as a smart girl had doubled in the wake of my sister's disappearance, as if I had been allotted all her genius. They had many questions, but none of them were meaningful, just talk-talk to take up space and time. They asked me what poultices were made of, how to cure a dog of crying, what it meant to dream of a swarm of bees. To everything, I answered, "Pearl!" That made them leave me alone. They didn't want to talk about my sister, because they all believed her to be dead.

In my pocket, hidden from view, my fingers clenched the piano key. I had no idea what to believe. I resented its presence, because it was a sad thing to have a piano key as the sole vestige of my sister. I hated how still it was, how mute, how inanimate. But I was becoming like that too. And like me, the key had no use for crumbs or visitors either. Still, the crumbs—they kept insisting themselves into my barrel.

"Save your crumbs," I said to the visitor.

"Stasha!" the visitor hissed. "You have to eat. You know what happens if you don't eat!"

It was Peter's voice. I'd heard from Bruna that he too had been suffering since Pearl's absence, that his stride had changed, that he no longer took pleasure in the freedom of his movements about the camp but tended to sit in the schoolroom all day, staring at the maps.

I told him I'd eat when Pearl came back.

"That may be a while. Long enough for you to starve more than you're already starving. Don't you want to be healthy when she returns?"

He threw another crumb. I caught it up in my hand and put it in my pocket. I told him that I knew Pearl would love this crumb when she returned and thanked him in advance.

"Fine. Wash, then. You have to wash. You know what will happen if you don't wash."

"Are you saying that Pearl will die if I don't wash?"

"Of course not."

"Well, then," I said. I could've added that there was nothing strong enough to cleanse me of certain filths that had been imposed on me through the experiments, but I didn't.

"Do you want to be *kaputt?*" Peter demanded.

I wasn't about to address the center of my concerns: I could never be *kaputt*. Through the eye of his needle, Uncle had prevented this. Never would I die. On his icy table, I'd thought I was doing what I needed to do to ensure the survival of Pearl and me. But Pearl was gone. I did not know if she was dead or not-dead, but I knew that he had never given her that needle, and I knew, too, that she would be ashamed of what I had done. Because after all this time in the barrel, I'd begun to suspect a few things. I suspected that my endurance was made possible by the deaths of others. My blood was thick with the thwarted survival of masses; it carried the words they'd never say, the loves they'd never know, the poems they'd never make. It bore the colors of the paintings they'd never paint, the laughs of the children they'd never bear. This blood made living so hard that sometimes I wondered if it was good that Pearl was spared deathlessness. Knowing the fullness of what I had chosen, I would not have wished her this fate—to live alone, a twinless half, forever burdened by the futures torn from others.

"Stasha? Are you crying in there?" Peter's knocks increased.

It was only my barrel creaking, I said. That barrel, it would insist on creaking for weeks.

November 20, 1944

Dear Pearl,

*The war is over. The Zoo is over. Mama and Zayde are living with
me now. We are planning a party for your return and installing a
carousel for the occasion. The guards are building it because they do
what we say now. There's a white horse for you. A mermaid for me.
When you return, we'll ride together, and when we go backward, it'll
be as if you never disappeared.*

I left my barrel for a limited number of reasons: roll call, bread-
eating, washing, and retiring to my bunk upon Ox's orders. The
only time I left my barrel uncompelled by these chores was to see
Uncle. I referred to him by this name still because I had yet to surrender my ruse—I still held hope that I might exterminate him yet,
by the skin of my charm. Was it strange, the relief I had in revisit-
ing the cold sterility of his laboratory? Even I was alarmed by the
fact that I was comforted by it, until I realized that it had become
familiar to my life, just as a schoolyard might be familiar to another.
Where my sister would have sat, there was only an empty chair,
but it was easy enough to pretend a person into a chair. Patient had
taught me that, so long ago.

As I pretended, I could hear my sister shaking, her quivers setting
the steel legs of the chair atremble. But no sooner was I closing
in on summoning some mirage of her than Uncle Doctor made
his presence overly known. Leaning over my shoulder to apply a
stethoscope to my back, he breathed too freely on the side of my
face, and the scent of his breath—sweet, but with an acrid tang—
made me wonder after his lunch, and I soon found myself adrift in
thoughts of food and was jolted out of my musing only by the intrusion of an instrument. He then tested the reflexes of my knees.

Left, right, left, right. And when he was finished, he inquired as to how I'd been.

I told Uncle that I wasn't sure if he'd noticed, but Pearl was missing.

"You don't say?" he said absently. "Now put on your clothes."

I expected him to turn to me with some suggestion of where to look for my sister, but he only went to the sink and washed his hands and combed his hair and popped a mint in his mouth. I obeyed his orders and put on my clothes. The fit of my skirt was predictably loose, so when I restored the piano key to its usual hiding place within my waistband, it clattered to the floor. He picked it up and eyed it with a curious smile.

"Explain this to me, Stasha."

I said only that I was sorry.

"Children like you often are. But what are you doing with this?"

I required a souvenir, I said, because I was afraid that I might forget this place one day. Seeing as I would live forever, that seemed a reasonable risk—how much could the deathless remember, anyway? So I'd taken the key from the piano before the concert. He drew his lips together in an exaggeration of a frown, as if he'd studied portraits of parental disapproval and found ones to emulate. There was nothing human in it, but I responded to it appropriately and hung my head in shame.

"You do realize that Anika was nearly beaten for your theft, don't you?"

I nodded.

"And you felt no guilt over this?"

"My sister" was all I could say. And then my voice gave out, or, rather, it pulled itself away from me as if tethered by some length of rope, the end of which was surely held by Uncle.

"There, there," he said, a flurry of mock sympathy contorting his face. "You have nothing to be afraid of."

I merely stared into his shoes, hoping that their gloss might reveal her location. But their usual shine was dressed in mud, and a tuft of dog's fur rose comically from the tip of one, like a clown's pom-pom. This was the first sign that something was awry. The second was his glass full of ice and whiskey. The glass itself was not unusual, but the many times it was emptied and refilled was alarming.

He left me sitting on the table, swinging my legs and dabbing at my eye with his handkerchief. His monogram was staked out at the corner, and I was careful not to let it touch my skin. As I dabbed, I allowed myself to peep around the handkerchief and take in the chaos that surrounded us. Never had I seen the laboratory in such disarray. Herds of folders were shoved into boxes, and the boxes were shoved into bigger boxes, and it appeared as if he were planning some great migration with all the pieces of us that he'd collected.

It is difficult to realize that part of you might travel for a lifetime with someone you hate, entirely against your own will. You may know what I speak of—maybe someone remembers you when you'd rather be forgotten; maybe someone has a piece of you that is impossible to retrieve. I can only say for myself that it was then that I knew that we were linked forever, the doctor and I, and I fainted before I could inquire about his future plans of escape.

The inside of my barrel became all but indecipherable, so thickly was it covered in letters to Pearl. I knew that if she did not return soon—actually, I knew nothing beyond the fact that my letters were growing angry and their lack of signature was erasing me. No one was counting bits of me in the laboratory anymore. No one was totting up the pieces of me. I did not know if this was because the doctor told people not to or because the best part of me was gone. Once, Bruna asked me, in her brutal and friendly way, why he bothered keeping me alive at all, and because I could not tell her that the doctor couldn't kill me ever, not even if he wanted to, I said that I expected him to end me any day, and she drew me close to her chest and vowed to spear him as soon as she had the chance.

I didn't know if she would ever have the chance. His presence was diminishing in those days. Here and there, from behind a curtain, I saw glimpses of him. He'd waggle his fingers at me pleasantly, give me a whistle. I had to find a way not to cringe at that whistle. In order to do so, I thought of my insides, all the tributaries of my blood, the inlets of my nerves, and wondered how hope fit into such a body. Because I had it still, that wild hope; it was as steady as a spine, and so pronounced I marveled that the nurses and technicians did not take note of this development within me and mark it on their charts.

There was only one other person besides Peter and the doctor's staff who reminded me that I was real, alive, a girl, Pearl's sister.

"Smidgen Two," Bruna whispered into the peephole. "It is the dead of winter now, don't you know? Can't you feel the cold in there? Our whole world—a snowstorm!"

"It doesn't storm in here."

"You can't live in a barrel anymore. You dear, stupid baby bedbug—come out!"

"I have to keep watch for her."

"Keep watch from a window."

"I don't trust the windows here."

"Keep watch from a door, then."

"I trust the doors even less."

There was a pause, and then—

"Maybe you should stop watching, Stasha." Never had I heard her voice so gentle.

I asked Bruna: "Should I stop watching because you have word from Pearl and you know that she's well, you know that she's just biding her time, just waiting until it is safe? Tell me that she's in a house somewhere. Tell me that she's hiding in a tree stump. That she's underneath someone's bed, and she is not who she used to be, but she is alive. I can take you telling me all of these things. Just so long as—"

"I haven't heard from Pearl," Bruna confessed. "My Smidgen One. She was my friend, that girl, my favorite—"

"Of course you haven't heard from Pearl," I interrupted with a snarl. "Why should you? It's not like you were important to her."

"Know this," Bruna said. "While you are in your barrel waiting for death, the Russian planes are back, more and more every day."

"Of course they are," I said. "They are here to bomb us."

"My people would never do such a thing." Bruna was indignant. "Maybe you should think, Smidgen Two, about how to prove yourself worthy of the freedom they are about to bring you. Decide now whether you are a cabbage or a girl. Fool! Barrel-dweller! How I miss you! You lousy coward!"

I turned away from the loving insults streaming through my peephole and retreated to my letters.

December 1, 1944

Dear Pearl,

I confess, none of that last letter was true. There is no carousel. The war is not over. But still, won't you return?

The next morning, I was surveying the snow from the peephole of my barrel when I saw Peter approach. His walk was hunched and slow and he had a wheelbarrow before him.

"Stasha! Come out, you have to see this!"

I removed the roof of my barrel and peered over the lip of the slats.

Peter's wheelbarrow held a bundle. The bundle was cocooned in a gray blanket, but the tips of the feet peeped from the frayed edge. A big toe frolicked in the wind.

I scrambled so quickly from my barrel that I overturned it and spilled onto the ground. This exit was as ragged and clumsy as my recent days of grief had been. A grief that, it now seemed, had been wholly unnecessary. I ran a hand above the length of the shroud as I'd seen a magician do once in a show. The bundle didn't animate readily, but that was just Pearl's way—she preferred a subtle showmanship.

"How?" I marveled.

"From the infirmary—just released."

"How long have you known?"

"Two days. I didn't want to tell you because I knew you wouldn't believe me. Go on—lift it."

You would think that after so much loss, I'd be eager for a reunion. But a feeling in me—one of the few feelings that Pearl hadn't taken with her—was hesitant to remove the blanket. What if Pearl had gone and changed without me? If she was not herself anymore, then who was I supposed to be? And then this hesitation was overcome by my eagerness and I peeled the blanket back.

The mouth that grinned up at me was now emptied of teeth. This was the face of a baby who had never been permitted a sojourn into the teenage but had skipped straight to manliness and then to old-manliness. His flesh was young but ancient; his eyes were new, so far as eyes go, but they'd seen too much. I am not sure how I recognized him at all, because his skin was no longer that be-veined, breathless blue, but a sickly white. Still, there was no mistaking his smile.

It was Patient. My Patient. I knew he would've been Pearl for

me if he could have. Sensitive to my disappointment, he clasped at
my hand, which was rather uncomfortable because my heart was
busy falling into the blackest depths of me, a locale unknown even
to Uncle, where it shed its skin, rolled in bile, assumed a new shell,
and grew thorns. Thus armored, the resourceful organ climbed the
ladder of my ribs and returned to its place. And I did what Pearl
would've wanted me to.

"What a blessing it is," I said, smiling as a fresh ache partnered
with my pulse, "to be family again."

It was as if Patient had been renewed somehow. Something had
done him good in his more than a month away from us—or maybe
it was just the light? In any case, it seemed that his cough was inter-
mittent. He clung to my side without any touch, warding off the
slightest separation.

In the yard, others gathered to view our returned boy. With wet
eyes, everyone joked about where Patient had been off to. Had he
been sailing, riding, sunning?

Patient shook his head, solemn. He wanted to joke in return—
but he couldn't.

Twins' Father clapped the boy on the back and then leaned in
for a whisper.

"When you leave next," he said softly, "it will be because we've
been liberated and I'll be taking you and all the other boys home.
It's a promise. And I'll need help with the little ones, so you'll be
my second in command."

Patient gave him a little salute, and Twins' Father left us to pursue
his duties, but not without glancing back a few times as he walked,
as if he still could not believe such a resurrection had taken place.

Bruna set to work pinching Patient's arm, her face lit with all the
pleasures of tormenting one she'd missed.

"Do ghosts bruise?" she inquired, pinch after pinch.

"I'm not sure, Bruna," Patient said, puffing out his chest. "I know only that your bruises are too embarrassed to be seen with you. I miss your white hair, though—you should wear it the old way. Charcoal merely dulls your beauty."

Apparently, Patient had learned suaveness and cruelty within the confines of the infirmary. Bruna was flattered and impressed.

"That'll do, flea," she said, and gave him the respect of a bow.

The others laughed, and then fell on him with questions. What was it like to be the first to return? Had he eaten anything interesting? Had he seen any of the others—to be specific, had he seen any of the others who went by the name Pearl Zamorski?

The last question was mine.

It was a great honor to be the first, he said. He hadn't met any pastries in there, but at the worst point in his illness he'd had the good fortune to hallucinate the smell of brisket. Pearl? She had been nowhere near, but all people tended to look the same in the infirmary, even though—

I slipped away, with the excuse that I had a letter to write.

He caught up with me quickly, his legs moving faster than they'd ever been capable of before, and the curious strength of this stride made me wonder if I was walking with the real Patient at all. Perhaps Uncle had sent an impostor back. Indeed, he introduced himself by a new name.

"You may no longer refer to me as Patient," he said. "Call me Feliks."

"Oh? Is that your name?"

"No. It was my brother's name. But I think I should have it for him now."

This made sense to me. Other things didn't. I asked this Feliks why he was alive.

"That's a cruel thing to say."

By all rights, I argued, he shouldn't have been. He was twinless, after all.

"So are you—and you still live. You look like the dead, though."

I made no attempt to dispute this.

"I bet you'll want to know what saved me, since you are curious about medicine and all," he said.

Then, as if to test my interests, he revealed the unique method of his survival. Jumping ahead of me as I walked, he shimmed down the loose waist of his pants and turned his back to me. A stump of a tail rode the space directly above his buttocks. The wriggle of this deformity—I could imagine Uncle's fascination.

"That's a fine trick."

"You can touch it." He reached for my hand.

"I don't want to touch it." My hand recoiled.

"If you touch it, it might bring you luck too."

Luck being unreliable in the Zoo, I continued to decline. He shrugged and lifted up his pants, thankfully concealing the little stub.

"It's always been with me. My brother was the same. The ambulance is never coming for me. I'm too valuable."

"Will you tell me more about the infirmary, Patient—I mean, Feliks? What was it like? I need to know."

He was only too happy to talk. He told me about row after row of beds, the thin soups, the crow that he could never see but whose caw woke him every morning. I listened and didn't question. Already, a map was spreading itself across my mind.

"I know what you're thinking, Stasha." He shook his head. "She's not there."

"Only Pearl knows what I'm thinking," I said.

But it was true that as I turned from him I had a fantasy in my mind, and in this fantasy people had disguised my sister, given her a new name. They'd probably slipped her something that made her forget about herself, because they knew that the separation from me was a great risk to her health. When it was safe, though, they would give her an antidote.

We would find each other still. This Feliks had proven it—a return was possible.

<hr />

December 8, 1944

Dear Pearl,

It is our birthday. But I am less certain of how old we are. We cannot be thirteen, not here. But maybe I am confused. I know you kept the time for us. I am not good at it. I am not good at any of our duties these days. Least of all the funny and the future. I am just glad that we did not give ourselves the task of finding the beautiful. There is nothing beautiful here, Pearl. I know only the ugly.

But here is one thing: The Russians have sent us a gift. The planes increased in number today. Can you see them?

The morning after our birthday, I woke to find a thread of smoke drifting around my barrel. I checked my sleeves, my shoes. Nothing appeared to be on fire. I pulled up my blouse, poked my belly button—I was sure that whatever Uncle Doctor had put in me was now scorching me from within.

Vermin! said the smoke.

I agreed with its assessment.

Out with you! said the smoke. It sounded strangely like Nurse Elma. But I obeyed, and bolted up, coughing. As soon as I exited, ash fell before my eyes. Nurse Elma loomed above, a cigarette wagging between her lips.

"You are needed!" she declared. "In the laboratory!"

I liked you better when you were smoke, I said.

"What is that you say? Speak up!"

"What can I do for you today, Nurse Elma?"

"Portrait time!" she declared.

I'd sat and stood and contorted for so many pictures already, all of them naked, all of them in the cold capture of the camera's eye, but every time, I'd done so with my sister. I'd never imagined that I'd be photographed without her; I wondered if I would even be able to stand for the photographer. But when Nurse Elma ushered me into a room in the laboratory, I saw neither the usual equipment nor any other subjects.

There was only a woman behind an easel, her face obscured by a canvas. Past its edge I could spy the crescent of an ear, a stretch of near-barren scalp tufted with gray. She wore the uniform of a prisoner and a gray shawl; her feet were shod with shoes of different heights. Though thin, the ankles above these mismatched shoes struck me as pretty in the way that I thought of things from my past as pretty: charm bracelets and potted violets in the window box, fires I built in the fireplace, Mama's Sabbath tablecloth.

Nurse Elma instructed the woman to begin and seated herself in the rear of the room to flip through her usual material, a magazine filled with actresses. I thought I saw Pearl's face on the cover, thought I saw her winking at me. *I miss you, Stasha,* the mouth on the cover said. *Things just aren't the same. But I am better here.* I was just about to ask Pearl whether the place she referred to was the afterlife or California, but then the mouth opened wide and the cover girl began to sing. That's when I realized it wasn't Pearl at all, but a cinema star, because Pearl's singing voice was far superior to that. *Do you know where Pearl is?* I asked the cinema star, deep in my head, where no one, not even Nurse Elma, could hear. I suppose I asked it too quietly, because the cinema star didn't appear to hear it at all, she just kept singing, and then Nurse Elma, seeing that I was staring at the cover girl, mistook my gaze for one of enjoyment rather than investigation and folded the magazine in half with a resentful flourish.

I could hear the artist pause at her easel while taking in this action, and then the movements of the brush resumed. I listened as it described my features. It seemed to mean well, but it moved slowly, as if it were having a difficult time deciding what to do with my face. I wanted to apologize to the artist for being so broken and ugly. I wanted to give her something redemptive to focus on.

Because beauty redeems the world, that's what Papa always said. He'd said it at a time when I couldn't imagine why the world might require redemption at all, a time when I wasn't even certain what redemption was. I was sure that Pearl felt the same way as Papa about beauty's redemptive powers, and for the first time, I found myself wanting to know if they were together at last, in the same place. Fortunately, Nurse Elma saved me from reaching the conclusion of this grim thought when she rose from her chair and stalked across the room to smack me on the head with her magazine.

"Don't look like that, Stasha."

"Like what?"

"Like you are about to cry. It changes the features too much."

"Should I smile?"

She raised her magazine again, ready to issue another crack, but then thought better of it—I saw her glance up, fearful that Uncle might have entered the room unseen, as he so often did.

"Do you look like yourself when you smile?" She smirked.

I look like my past self, I wanted to say, but I remained silent. Nurse Elma gave me an instructive slap on the cheek. I wondered if it would leave a mark. If it did, I was sure that the artist would not be permitted to render it.

"Of course you don't smile!" Elma crowed. "Smiles change faces too. What the doctor wants here is accuracy. Stare straight ahead, eyes open, mouth still. So simple, any infant could do it!"

She then returned to her chair, and contented herself with her magazine. I felt sorry for the cover girl—it wasn't her fault that she was a picture in a magazine that was forced to participate in Nurse Elma's abuse.

As instructed, I kept my gaze straight ahead. I focused on the brick-edged window that sat above the artist, hoping that a singing or cooing bird might light on the sill and provide the artist with something to listen to as she worked. Since Pearl's disappearance, I'd noticed that animal life had become increasingly rare in Auschwitz. There was little hope of any arriving just because I wanted it to, and when no bird appeared, I put one there with my mind. In its beak, I made it carry a sprig of olive branch. But the bird kept dropping it. Even my own imagination, it seemed, had abandoned me.

I was stirred from this fantasy by Nurse Elma. She rose with her magazine and, with a barking order for me to behave, banged out the door.

With her exit, the sound of the brush increased. I saw the artist peer around the edge of the canvas, exposing a single eye. The eye was sunken and dark, afflicted, but illness hadn't starved it of warmth.

"I'd like to see you smile," the artist said in a voice that matched the friendliness of the eye. There was something familiar in that voice, but I told myself that it was just the rasp it carried—that starved, battered edge that all prisoners eventually acquired. Still, there was something different about the artist's speech—even the coughing that ended her sentence had a rare charm.

"But Elma—"

"What does Elma know of art? She's just a monkey, a sham, a silly lady. Come now, give me a smile."

I gave my best attempt.

"Wider now, show your teeth. Do I need to tell you a joke? How can I make you laugh?"

I told the artist that as hard as I tried to smile, I hadn't been able to in recent days. Jokes only hurt.

"A story, then," she said. "I'll tell you a story about two girls. Would you like that?"

I nodded.

"Well, then," the artist said. "I'm not so good at telling stories. But I'll try. There were two girls in Lodz. Twins. Exactly alike in every way. When the midwife left after the birth, their parents couldn't tell them apart. So their father put their first initials on their feet. The next day, when he bathed them, the letters washed away. The father was distraught. How could he know which girl was which? He tried to convince himself that it didn't matter. After all, the girls had only had their names for a day. How attached to them could they be? He put fresh letters on the bottoms of their feet and didn't say a word to his wife. Later that evening, he confessed his error. The wife only laughed. She whistled in front of the babies. The one that stirs at the whistle, she said, should be marked *S*. She whistled, but neither of the babies stirred. Then the father joined her, and the *zayde* and the *bubbe* too. They all whistled together and when the whistling didn't work, they clanged pots and pans over the cradle; they got out Zayde's clarinet and played even though no one could play well. They woke the whole neighborhood in their efforts to find out the babies' names. Still, neither baby responded. Already, both were living in their own world. It was as if they were content watching everyone scramble to tell them apart."

"That wasn't a funny story," I said. Or at least I think that's what I said; I might have said something else, because I was so overwhelmed by the artist's voice and her story. "And you should have told me years ago, Mama. Because all this time I have believed that I'm Stasha, but now I might be Pearl?"

The artist laughed the laugh I knew so well, and then she became

Mama, my mama, though a Mama far removed from even the Mama of the cattle car.

"Is this your way of saying that you still won't smile?" she said. Or I think that's what she said. I'm not sure because her mouth was buried on the top of my head, since she'd risen from her seat to embrace me. Then, realizing the danger of this, she crept back.

We enjoyed the rapture of seeing and hearing and loving each other for the briefest of moments, and then—

"Where is your sister?" she whispered.

I told her I didn't know. I told her about "Come Make Me Happy." I told her about Pearl's footprints and the field of poppies.

Mama dropped her brush. The tip of it was loaded with white; it streaked an ivory swath of erasure across the floor.

"That can't be," she said. "I've only painted pairs of portraits. In every case, intact pairs only." And just as her voice began to climb in its despair, she rose and walked toward me and she embraced me with all the remnants of her strength, and she cried with what was left of her tears. "I am so happy to see you, Stasha. I could not be happier."

I buried my face in the star at her breast. There was so much I wanted to know. Why hadn't I seen her at the fence like so many of the other twins' mothers? I could see that Uncle was fulfilling his promise about the paint—though in a roundabout, very strange way—but was she getting enough bread? Was Zayde enjoying his swims at the pool?

As each question was asked, she gave me a kiss on the forehead, but at the last, she crumpled, and she begged me not to look at her—just for a moment, she said, don't look, she said, let's not do this this way, let's do it another way, when we're in a different world than this, a world that knows not to let such things happen. Don't look, she said.

I wish I hadn't disobeyed her.

Because when I saw her face, I saw Zayde. And he wasn't resting in his barracks; he wasn't throwing dice or talking politics or trading recipes or toasting the memory of a starling. He wasn't even dying in a swimming pool. There was no real hold, no center, nothing distinctive about what I saw. What had been done to him was the same that had been done to so many, and it continued still.

Seeing my horror, all Mama could do was say my name. She said it until she couldn't say it anymore, and then she started to say Pearl's. She said it over and over, as if in an incantation.

"Don't let them hear you," I whispered.

And then the last bleat of her missing daughter's name shifted into a cough, and we heard steps approaching the door, and Mama jumped a step back from me, tripping over her ill-fitting shoes. We were lucky that she had been quick to move, as Nurse Elma soon sidled through the doorway with her awful face. She was not pleased to see my mother away from her easel and so close to me.

"I had to get a closer look," she explained to Nurse Elma before scurrying back to her chair. "My eyes aren't what they should be. I couldn't get her mouth right."

"A fine thing—an artist with bad eyes!" Elma scoffed. "Do you think you can get it right now?"

Mother's voice dropped.

"I swear," she vowed. "I will make everything right."

If Nurse Elma had been at all attentive, her curiosity would've been aroused by the little catch in my mother's voice, by the way that she looked at me as she returned to her work. She even managed to sneak a nod and a grin to me while Elma stalked about in search of things to criticize. She paced the brief length of the room, and then stopped.

"Why is there paint on this floor? So clumsy and wasteful." She made a big show of her patent shoes as she toed the offending splotch of white.

"Clean it," Elma ordered Mama. "You have made this mess."

She flung a rag at my mother, who obediently stooped to the floor to pick it up but lapsed into another coughing fit. I took the rag before she could grasp it and moved it over the white paint until the rag was consumed.

The artist—because that was how I had to think of my mother while she was being kicked by Elma—apologized, and swore to be more careful. She greatly appreciated the opportunity to paint rather than work at the factory or in Canada or at the Puff.

Nurse Elma surveyed the canvas.

"I believe this will be adequate for our purposes."

"I am not finished," Mama said.

But Nurse Elma's face said different.

"Mama," I whispered. "Don't be frightened when you see Pearl. Because you will see her—she will come back. And we are still the same, all of us—"

"You may leave, Stasha," Nurse Elma said. She collared me in her usual style and led me out the door, so annoyed by my emotion and the tears of the artist that she failed to notice that I slipped the rag, an object blessed by my mother's touch, into the waistband of my skirt.

I slept that night with that rag pressed to my cheek. Some might think that strange, but I did it because my mother had just told me her belief. She believed us to be the last remaining members of our family. She hadn't told me in words but in the way that she'd painted my face. She'd painted it untrue, with hardly a real resemblance at all—this was a nice gesture toward subterfuge that I appreciated, but there was also an unmistakable element of mourning in it, the specific pierce of a mother's lamentation.

December 18, 1944

Dear Pearl,

Mama is alive. Are you too?

It was true, Mama was with us still. She painted our face, and, for a second or so, she and I had been restored to our real selves; we sat in our seats as if they were the chairs in our old house, and we looked at each other in a way that concealed our pain.

After I finished writing, I turned to the essential study of my anatomy book—this would keep me on my vengeful path. But before I could find my page, an ancient but boyish face appeared from above.

"Did he get your tongue?" Feliks asked.

I told him I was quiet because I'd seen my mother, and I hadn't seen my grandfather, but I'd heard of him.

Feliks responded with his own quiet, a quiet so still that it roused me.

"Do you think I'm stupid?" I asked in earnest. "For having thought I might outsmart him, change him, make him into who he should have been?"

Seeing that he had no intention of answering this, I climbed out of the barrel to face him directly.

"I think you like to see the good in people because there's been so much bad that you have to believe in good," he opined.

"Do you do that too?"

"No. I see the good in knives instead of people. Although there's really no such thing as a bad knife or a good knife, so long as it cuts."

"You sound like Bruna."

"I have arrived at my viciousness over time."

"I think I'm arriving there too."

He grew excited.

"We can have a lot of fun that way," he said.

"I'm not sure it will be fun at all," I said. "But it will be necessary."

He handed me one of Bruna's precious newspapers, a bit of contraband that circulated among the communists till it inevitably fell into the hands of a guard.

"I can teach you how to hate," Feliks said. "Step one: Read this. It says that they are coming for us, the Russians—those planes we have seen are theirs. It also warns that the heads of Auschwitz will flee at any minute, that they will try to destroy the place and us with it. This means that we have little time left to take care of Mengele." He shook the page at me meaningfully, urging me to read.

"I don't know Russian."

"I can teach you that too. It is a good language for hating Nazis in. Perhaps better than Polish. We can save Polish for other things— that would make our fathers happy, wouldn't it?"

"I don't need your instruction. I hate them all. I always have. It is just that I hate Mengele the most."

Never again, I swore, would I call him Uncle, not even in the interest of appearing innocent.

I saw that Feliks had a new respect for me as I spoke so nakedly of my hatreds, without the slightest attempt at concealment. He clung to every word I said, and wanted more.

"You should do something about this hate while he still trusts you," he suggested.

"That has been my notion all along. I have just been waiting for my moment."

"Do it now. You have an access to him that I envy. You know who else envies it? The whole of the Russian army; the American one too. We should exploit it."

He handed me two bread knives.

"Now you have three weapons," he said triumphantly. "That should be enough, I would think. I would recommend plunging the first into his thigh, the second into his neck, and the third into his heart. And when you get to the heart—give it a little twist and then kick it with your foot. Kick it till the heart squeaks and then you will know that he is dead."

I was too overwhelmed by the presence of the knives themselves to even think of the noises a heart could make. I made a point of writing this fact down in my anatomy book before returning to our plans and admiring the new trio of my weaponry.

"Why did you have two bread knives, Feliks?"

"One was my brother's. He would have been honored for you to have it. It hasn't been easy, holding on to it. Bruna looked after my weapons when I was in the infirmary, though. She knew what these bread knives meant to me, and what the cause is. It's too bad that Bruna isn't close to Mengele—she would be sure to get the job done. No hesitation with her." He lingered around the sentence admiringly, as if simply speaking of her brought him closer in his conquest of the whitest angel.

"I can be just as fearsome as Bruna," I said. I did not believe this, but I hoped I could make it true.

We conjured a plan. The plan was this: I would get Mengele alone somehow, preferably in an enclosed area. This was important, Feliks pointed out, because while the doctor was stupid—

"He's not stupid."

"So! He's not stupid. But isn't evil a form of stupidity?"

"Who told you that?"

"It is something I arrived at. I did a lot of thinking in the infirmary. More thinking than you know. I thought about good and I thought about people and I thought about evil. Evil was the easiest one to think about, since we are around it all the time. I know evil. It comes and sits inside me whenever I am in the laboratory.

The idea that evil makes a person stronger than good people—this is a popular misconception. But while Mengele doesn't have certain strengths that you have, he is stronger than you, more able, so it would be best to have him in a corner. Or on the ground. You must have the upper hand in these situations or someone will cut your hand off and then the rest of you will follow. Understand?"

It was then that I realized how misspent my education in this place had truly been. My hours had gone to Mengele, intent as I was on learning how to heal and fuse, how to stop the blood and start the heart, and, most important, how to make one thing match another, how to impose symmetry where none existed, all with the goal of impressing him enough so that I might gain the required closeness to fell him. In truth, though, Feliks was the real expert, the one I should've consulted. Because he'd schooled himself—through exposures to violent encounters that befell all of us, through the literature of rebel factions, through the scenarios he played out in his head—in how a body could be undone. He knew the place to stick so that one's victim might bleed out the quickest, the spot to target if one wanted to stun. He just didn't have the ruse, he claimed, to carry it out.

In me, he believed, there was a real opportunity for vengeance.

But Mengele wasn't as available as he'd once been. When the frequency of the planes increased, so too did the time he spent holed up in his office, shutting out his once-beloved subjects. According to Dr. Miri, he neglected new work, tended to the organization of files and slides, drafted frantic letters to his mentors. Boxes rose in front of the windows of the brick laboratory. Cars idled at the laboratory doors, and attendants shuffled in and out, bearing those boxes into the backseats.

For thirty-six days after Mama painted my portrait, I lay in wait for him. I replayed Feliks's plan for Mengele's death in my head, sifted through every move and shuffle. I whet the bread knives against the stairs. *We will never be sharp enough,* they sang. *We will never slash deep enough to get to the bottom of all this misery!* But I told them they would have to do.

Together, the bread knives and I waited. We waited anywhere the doctor might linger; we looked with interest at any footprint that spoke of his whereabouts. But the doctor's footprints were more reticent than your average footprint—when I looked at their whorls, I could feel only a boot at my neck.

On the thirty-seventh day of my wait, January 15, 1945, I sat on the steps of the hospital with my three knives in one stocking and Pearl's piano key in my shoe. I'd been waiting six hours, maybe eight, possibly two. Time, I'd noticed, passed differently now. I wondered if I would ever get real time back or if Pearl's absence would permanently change the function of the minutes, the way they trembled and circled the clock. I was always arguing with myself over which was best, to move forward or to stay still, and it was only when I'd decided on the former that the doctor's car pulled up.

He stepped out, unusually harried. The part in his hair was mussed and dust streaked the legs of his pants. Every feature on his face was drawn with stress. He ran up the steps, fetched a box, and nearly stumbled at the sight of me.

"Little Deathless? Why are you here?"

"You remember me by that name?"

"Of course I do," he chided me. "There's no forgetting you. Even if things here are not what they used to be."

"Not what they used to be," echoed the driver of the car, a ruddy man with the whiskered face of a catfish. His lips were slow and overblown and engaged in the consumption of a sandwich. I took notice of them as he spat from the window of his car in an expression of his disgust with some inferior meat. My stomach rumbled at the sight of the rejected food.

"Bolek would know." Mengele nodded at the driver. "He was here from the beginning. He helped build this place. Tell her, Bolek."

"It was 1939," Bolek said with his mouth full. "Back then, this was all swampland. Now look at it!"

He lifted his hand momentarily to sweep it across the length of the windshield. And then spat again, magisterially this time.

"Roads, gardens, music rooms, swimming pools, music rooms," he intoned lovingly.

"You said *music rooms* twice," Mengele pointed out.

"And why shouldn't I? You think they have those at Buchenwald? At Dachau? Some things bear repeating. Who can say Auschwitz is not a civilized place?" Bolek stared at me warily, as if I were the person to make that very accusation.

Mengele took to fussing with the boxes in the trunk, placing some of the presumably more precious loads into the rear seat. I spied a briefcase back there. The suit of a Wehrmacht officer was draped over it. Catching my glance to this strange costume, he was quick to cover it with his coat, but otherwise he acted like a papa readying the family car for a picnic.

"Just a brief trip. I'll be back soon. I have to do some rounds first, though—would you like to come with me? Perhaps we can look for Pearl?"

"Pearl is dead," I said. This was the first time I'd said it. Did the clouds flee when I spoke? Did the horizon march off to the sea while the layers of earth and dust came undone, each peeling itself back to reveal a lake? Did the ash shake hands with the dust while crows presided over the truce? Although such events should've been sparked by those words—*Pearl is dead, gone, over, Pearl is no more*—

I didn't know if any came to pass because the mere saying of such words stole my other senses from me. I stood there, tongue flapping, deaf and blind to all but the sight of Josef Mengele.

"Oh, is she? How funny—" He looked at me meaningfully. "I never signed a death certificate."

"But you sign so many," I said. I didn't say that he could've overlooked it; that wouldn't do. And if he suspected any hint of an implication of forgetfulness, he didn't acknowledge it.

"So I do." He sighed. "I do sign so many. But still, it couldn't hurt to look. You'd be amazed, Stasha, at the ways that people manage to hide in here. They make themselves smaller than you could ever imagine. I've found many a child folded in half and shut in a valise! And these are stupid children, not like our clever Pearl. She's so cunning, she could fit herself into a teapot!"

This praise for my better half resurrected her in my mind, and this resurrection—I admit, I was stupid, foolish, desperate—overshadowed what I knew him to be, just for a moment.

"You are very right," I said.

"Let's go find her, then," he said, and he opened the front door and gestured for me to get in. I did. The car stank of smoke and ash and a leathery oil. Bolek grumpily threw his sandwich out the window and watched the Yagudah triplets fight over it in the dirt. Mengele sat beside me, lighting a cigarette. The car rumbled outside of the Zoo limits.

There was a prolonged silence. It felt dangerous. The doctor moved his hand toward me very suddenly, to the vicinity of my neck. I flinched. I'm sure he noticed, because his affectionate manner with me increased.

"Stasha is my medical student," he noted to the driver. "She had lovely yellow hair once, but the lice—you know. Brown eyes, though—it is unfortunate."

"She looks very healthy," Bolek returned. His tone was familiar and approving, but his eyes in the driver's mirror told a different story, one that wished me little in the way of good.

I swallowed and fiddled with the key in my pocket. I couldn't tell you the logic of my nerves. After all, I had no reason to fear death, but the willful proximity to such a death-maker was unnerving. We were thigh to thigh. He directed me to lean my head on his shoulder. Did I obey? Of course I did. For the sake of ending him, I obeyed.

"What did you do with yourself this morning?" he asked.

"Studied," I lied.

"With Twins' Father?" His tone was scornful.

"I'm teaching myself."

"Good. Zvi is a nice man, but I'm not sure that he's the best teacher. You'd come out with a most inaccurate education. What are you studying?"

"Dr. Miri gave me a book. About surgeries. I'm learning about incisions. I learned about cesareans this morning."

"Interesting subject," he said drearily, clearly not interested at all. "You saw me perform that procedure once, didn't you? A messy business." There was a wink in his voice—he knew, even as he described it as such, that it was not a cesarean that I witnessed, but a vivisection. The woman—she'd had her child pulled from her, yes, he'd opened her and dispatched the child to a bucket full of water, drowning the baby before its mother's eyes, but that was not the end of her suffering. He sustained it for as long as he was able and my memory of this—I did not want it; I did not want even Pearl to remember it for me.

But if Mengele chose to remember this killing as a cesarean, then so it was, in Auschwitz.

"Usually, I send them to the gas straightaway," he added, seemingly for Bolek's ears. "But taking care of it before it has a chance for a single breath? That can be humane too, under conditions like those. In any case, Stasha, you should be commended for your interest in these procedures."

He paused thoughtfully, took a bottle from his valise for a drink, and gave my knee a squeeze as he swigged.

"But the arts—that appears to be your real calling. Dancing, isn't it?"

"That's Pearl," I reminded him. "I am a scientist."

He began to throw up his hands before remembering that he held a bottle in one of them. Liquor met my cheek.

"Of course!" he said. "But it really doesn't matter. Dancer, scientist—just keep yourself occupied. Dwell on your interests. Maintain your curiosity about the world. Curiosity has gotten me far. You lose your curiosity"—he shook a thick finger before my eyes— "and life, it will abandon you."

"I'm trying not to."

"But your voice—it says that your efforts don't come naturally to you. I imagine that you've found it very difficult to get on without your sister? I've seen many twins experience similar. I'm actually quite interested in that particular phenomenon—how one survives without the other after years of inseparability. So fascinating."

I offered the answer that I thought would keep me intact.

"I don't miss her at all."

"You don't have to be brave with me."

"I know she's just hiding," I said. "Until it's safe to come out."

"A good guess, that's what that is. You are a better detective than that, I'm sure. Now, take it further. Where do you think she might be hiding? Bolek, here, he'll take us there."

And so we traveled through the men's barracks and the women's. We crunched along the perimeter of the gates. I sat with my face pressed to the glass, and Mengele stared straight ahead. Everywhere, I saw Pearl. I saw her so many times that the true purpose of my trip grew muddled. I convinced myself, as the wheels rolled on, that my sister was merely in disguise, that she was one of any of the figures we passed. Her theatrical background and perceptive nature had likely conspired to create the perfect costume.

"That one," I said, pointing to a figure in the distance.

"That is a boy child. And a criminal at that."

"There's Pearl," I said of a different figure. "I was born with her. I'd know her anywhere."

"I'm afraid I know that woman," Mengele said. "She is a fine guard, but she isn't Pearl."

I had hoped that some revealing information might slip as we traveled. I'd hoped that he'd confess to his crimes, or at least to the deceptions he'd practiced on me. Zayde was not eating or swimming or living. Mama was starving; she painted only portraits of experiments for Mengele's archives. But as we continued to circle the camp, I knew that there was no sanity in that car. Not in him. And not in myself either, because every time I pointed to a person, I actually believed in the possibility that this he or she was my sister.

"It's her," I said. I pointed to a *kapo* with a cigarette, a boy with a shovel, a cook with a ladle.

"Who?" he'd always query.

"Pearl!" I would cry through the window. "It's Pearl acting as though she isn't Pearl."

And Mengele would command the person in question to come to our window, where it would become obvious—through an accent, a snarl, a scar—that the subject was not the loved one I searched for. It was only a *kapo,* a boy, a cook.

He seemed not to enjoy my disappointment, but I believe that he did like watching me inspect them. I performed this inspection just as he always had, employing similar gestures, asking questions of their origins.

"You should've been in our employ," he said with a chortle after I let the cook go.

I was about to ask Bolek to return me to the Zoo when I saw a woman. She was coated in soot, but even in their darkness, her cheeks shone innocent. A basket hung from her arms at an elegant angle. Seeing my stare, Mengele motioned to the woman to come to our window, and his interest caused her to drop the basket at her feet.

"Inspect her, Stasha."

I opened the door and stepped before her and I did as Mengele had done with us, lifting her chin with one finger. Beneath her jaw was a neat expanse of white, a brief reprieve from the soot.

"It has to be her," I said.

It would be like Pearl to disguise herself so humbly. This was, in my view, a clever move.

"You call those eyes?" he scoffed. "Just bits of tin or raisins. Hardly human at all."

Mengele gestured to the woman to turn around, to give us a show. She spun, slow but obedient, shuffling through each revolution.

"It's Pearl," I insisted.

"And does she speak?" he asked me. "Can she answer your questions, share a childhood memory?"

The woman blinked, her eyes snow-white against the soot. I saw then the milky cloud that veiled her irises.

"Glaucoma," he announced. "This is a Greek woman, midfifties. Probably birthed three children, at the very least. Widowed more than once, and miserable all the way through. Cleans the cremos here. Looks to have a fever, and she's going blind. Not much left of her, I'd think. Look at the scabs on her hands. Likely covered in them. What an infection."

I looked at the woman's fingers, speckled with injury.

"You are useless, yes?" Mengele said to the woman in a bright voice, his face giving the false impression of kindness. "You are an animal, correct? A low, stinking animal?"

And the woman simply bowed her head low and nodded, exposing a scalp riddled with bruises.

"You will get an infection, Stasha. Get back in the car."

But I wasn't convinced. So I told this mysterious human that I didn't care that she'd tried to go without me, leaving me only a piano key for comfort. If she was happier, that's all I wanted. I told her in Polish and Yiddish and German, and then I told her in the secret language special to our own two skulls and studded my affectionate plea with images of all the things that joined us in love—toward the blackness of her mind I threw the softness of a litter of kittens, the cherry-blossomed sleeve of Mother's dressing gown, the books on Zayde's desk. And when that didn't work, my efforts increased and I became resentful; I cast into her mind's eye the bleakness of my Zoo, the knotty curl of my spine against the barrack bed. Surely, I thought, these desolate images would rouse her, they would compel her to discard this flimsy disguise and vault back into her position as my better half.

They did not.

Instead, the monstrous version of my sister bulged her eyes in fright, and she inserted an elderly thumb into the puckers of her mouth, sucking like a frightened baby.

I ordered this demi-Pearl to stop. Thumb-sucking was no way to deal with pain. But the thumb-sucking continued.

So I stooped and searched the ground for stones. To this day, I remain grateful for the absence of them, because I know that I would have thrown them at her if I could; I would have tried to force her from the strange husk through injury. Mengele noted the trembling of my hands and drew me back into the leathery recesses of the car, but I was able to peer past his form to see the woman scamper off with an athleticism enabled by fear. She then huddled behind the bed of a truck.

Mengele sighed and clucked in a show of sympathy. He then produced a tin of candies from his pocket. These were not his usual gems of butterscotch, I noted, but a more evolved species of sweet. After administering this candy, he took up my hand and petted it comfortingly.

"So—she's not your Pearl. But the good news is that you may keep looking for the real Pearl. And here is the better news: You have forever to look for her. Your life will not end before you find her. How many may say this?"

I told him that this was not lost on me. He gave Bolek orders to drive back.

As the car roared from its idle, I gave one last searching glance toward the Pearl impostor, and it was then that I saw what I shouldn't have seen. I shouldn't have seen it because it should've been too dark, she should've been changed beyond recognition—by starvation, by anguish, by loneliness—she should've been obscured by those she rested with, those she'd likely come to know as family, her fellow dead whose outstretched arms should've covered the stillness of her eyes.

There, in a heap of others on the bed of the truck, was our mother, or the body that had belonged to the person who'd been our mother. The keeper of the poppies who once held within her a whole world of floating. I'd long accepted that to return to the floating world was impossible, but I'd never imagined that the woman who created it would end so savagely. The form on the pile—it was changed. I had no idea if she was supposed to be our mother still or if the death they'd dealt her had changed her into some unreachable thing—a star, a flower, a wave on the sea—that the surviving likes of me had no right to care for.

Don't weep, said my mother's tearful, wide-open eyes as they stared back at me.

And I knew better than to argue with my mother's eyes, but deep within me, hidden from her all-knowing view, my vow for vengeance renewed itself and I began to shake and I felt the cold kisses of the knives in my stockings as they pressed against my skin.

"Are you unwell?" he wondered. "So quiet, suddenly. Don't worry. You'll be with your family someday. We'll all have dinner together; Pearl will dance. How will that be?"

I thanked him, and as I did so, I nodded to my mother in an acknowledgment of the vengeance I would bring.

Mengele prattled on, but I could not converse. It was safer not to speak, because if I spoke I would have said to him:

Because you couldn't kill my mother twice, you keep me in this place to want and suffer a hundred times over.

Because you couldn't make my zayde less than ash, you leave me gray and small, a twisted thing to be blown by whatever wind will have me.

Because you had no power over the fact that I was born, you took from me what I was born with—the person who was my love, the half that made me entire—and now I am lessened into this dull thing, a divided person who will live forever, wandering in search of some nothing, some nowhere, some no-feeling, to mend my pain.

The blood he'd given me fled from my brain and collected itself into a fist. He might have made me immortal, I told myself, he might have doomed me to outlive everyone, but that didn't mean that I couldn't find some end, a death, a termination, in him. The knives in my stockings nodded in agreement. He leaned away from me to shout through the window at a passing nurse, making his back vulnerable. His neck was turned, his attentions were elsewhere. Now would be as fine a moment as any, the knives pointed out. But before I had a chance to act on this advice, he swiveled in his seat and regarded me solemnly.

"The future," he said. "We must always look forward to it. Understand?"

I nodded. In my pocket, I felt for Pearl's key. It was luminous, covered with shine; my fingertips felt glazed with light when they rested on it.

"I want to show you something," he said suddenly as the car

found itself before the Zoo. He removed a box from the floor of the car. It was one of the boxes I'd seen at the laboratory, a box he apparently loved above all the others, because while those receptacles were marked with the usual inscription of *War Materials, Urgent,* this one was deemed good enough to bear his name. *Dr. Josef Mengele* it declared in script so fine and practiced that I could imagine him rehearsing the curve of every letter. He clung to this box like a child with a teddy bear, a boy with a kite, and when he lifted the lid, it was with a careful affection, as if he didn't trust even himself with the marvels contained within.

"All of this here," he said. "Genetic material. You can't begin to imagine what we might achieve with these tiny samples. A different kind of human, a perfect person."

The slides clinked musically together in the box. I ran my finger over their edges.

"A perfect person," I repeated. "Like Pearl."

He grabbed the box away from me, closed the lid on all the little lives before I had a chance to memorize them. He took me by my neck, gripped it with his fingers, tilted my head back, and then, with a movement so deft that it seemed like a magic trick pulled on a stage, he drew a dropper from his pocket and squeezed a little bead of liquid into my left eye.

Oh, how it blinded and stung! That little bead of liquid—it embellished my tears.

"What is this for?" I gasped, and my hand crept to cover my pained eye as if to protect it from further shock.

"It is to remember me by," he said.

Through my tears, I told him that I didn't want to remember him, I wouldn't remember him. I refused to. Because he was so memorable, I feared that he would crowd out all the other memories. I said this as I reached for my bread knife. I fumbled blindly. All before me ran black, then white.

"You flatter me, Stasha. That's too bad." I could not see him, but I'm sure he winked. "Now, tell me—before I go—what do you see?"

I saw nothing. Oh, nothing!

"Don't worry, Stasha—it will be blue by tomorrow, I promise."

Then he opened the car door and pushed me from my seat and I tumbled out like some cast-off thing.

Soon after, on a night unknown to us, he left his Zoo behind. I did not know the time of his departure, what he bore with him, or if he ever glanced back.

I only knew that when next I saw him, it would all be different. We would be in a place that could prove one of two things: that the whole world had become Auschwitz, or that the world was no longer whole at all, that it, too, had split and sundered and ceased to be. On that mid-January day, I had no glimmer of that event, not an inkling. I could only retreat to the Zoo, like any poor and beaten animal, half blind, one hand held to my weeping eye while the other searched for the burrow of my barrel. I wasn't thinking of Mama's death; I couldn't think of Zayde's death either—I would never think of them, I swore, until I was able to avenge them both, and Pearl.

In that eye, there remained a blackness. For many days or weeks, it was just black on black. I tried to see the bright side of this. The bright side was that if I closed my good eye, I was blind, and if I was blind, every human that remained had the potential to be my Pearl. It was only when someone spoke to me that this illusion was ruined.

After my eye went useless, Dr. Miri pulled me from my barrel and installed me in the infirmary. She thought it would scare me into trying to live, and she put me in a private room in the back, with three other children.

"You know it is not a good thing," she said. "To be in the infirmary. They take people from the infirmary to the trucks."

I nodded.

"And the trucks—you know where they go—"

I did not make her finish this sentence. I indicated my understanding—I knew that the trucks took people to the gas. Dr. Miri couldn't know why the threat of this meant nothing to me. But I think she realized that I would go on any vehicle that might lead to my sister, and that was why she worried so and began to hover over me at any available moment.

In the night, I woke and traveled among the bunks of the greater infirmary in search of my sister. This thronged, howling place—it surpassed our Zoo barracks in its ability to pile one human atop another.

Row after row of bodies rested on bunks, in slots so tiny that the effect was of insects resting in a hive. The bodies were covered with white sheets and resembled clouds with heads affixed to them. Most of the heads were turned away from me, or buried in the mattresses, but all the bodies outstretched their hands, knots of bone and bramble, in a plea for food and water.

"I don't have anything," I'd cry.

The clouds didn't believe me, but they weren't angry either. They were too sick to be angry. They had dysentery and fever and germs that could kill. They had blood loss and family loss, and their hearts were slipping away from the standard heart-seat in the chest, more and more every day. What did these human-clouds have to live for? They merely rolled over and went back to sleeping or coughing or dreaming or whatever human-clouds do best.

As I trudged back to my room, a burst of light sparked against the window.

It was a rebuke, I knew. Wherever they were, Mama and Zayde, they were telling me not to be weak. They were ashamed that I had not fulfilled my purpose, and they emphasized this with a series of rat-a-tat-tats, as forceful and repetitive as gunfire. I didn't blame them for such extreme measures.

"I hope you understand," I said in the direction of the window, "that I'm not myself without Pearl anymore."

The loud noises swelled and increased. My bad eye saw only a blur, but the untouched eye helped me see the smoke that crept toward the building.

I hoped that smoke would take me till there was nothing left.

This thought must have disturbed Zayde and Mama more than anything. The windowpane began to rattle. Another rebuke. A spark, a flash of smoke. I knew the meaning of all of it. But I didn't know that I was weeping till I felt a hand wipe my cheek.

"I'm sorry," I said to Dr. Miri as she offered me her handkerchief.

Her face was oddly still, and then it began to crack along its every seam, and laughs and sobs began to pour from her.

"What are you sorry for?" she said between the fits of this display.

"All of this." I motioned to the flash of smoke passing by the bank of windows.

"This is not your doing," she said.

I assured her that it was, and just as I was about to confess—

"It is hard to believe, I know," she said, one trembling hand at my shoulder. "But the camp, it may be ending. We've been told the Russians have been approaching for weeks. It seems impossible, but all of this"—she gestured toward the knock-knocking on the panes by thick threads of smoke; the rattles; the hums—"it could give us hope if we chose it."

Even as she attempted brightness for my sake, her tone indicated that this was not a particularly large or impressive hope, but a hope that was a bit tattered and that introduced a new set of unknowns and troubles into our lives.

Three of the cloud-people rose from their beds and clambered over to the window for a look. They were told to lie down, to rest—I could see that the staff was worried; it seemed not entirely certain that the planes overhead were friendly. The cloud-people themselves demonstrated a division in this line of thought. It would soon be over, all over, some said. It will never be over, others said. I did not know whom to believe but looked to Dr. Miri's face for guidance. Her eyes were lit, active with optimism, but her mouth remained set in a grim line.

For three days we waited, with fingers in our ears, with eyes wide open, with our shoes at the ready in case we had to run. We waited while the bombs whistled a pretty tune, waited without knowing where they might fall. We waited while the snow mixed with smoke and the camp went gray with wondering.

I waited knowing that if freedom truly came, another wait would begin for me. I lay in my bunk and began another letter to my sister; I scratched it into the wall that stretched beside me, but I was able to execute only the salutation. *Dear Pearl,* I wrote, believing that someday, if only for a moment, she might leave the site of her capture—be it death, be it Mengele—and see this greeting and know that we were people, still, in spite of what we'd been told.

Auschwitz, its work was done, said the grim faces of the guards as they pursued the shambling of it. The place that had once welcomed their every evil impulse now threatened to be their undoing. We were accustomed to that burning-chicken-feather smell, that red sky, the ash always hunting us down, but this—now the flames leaped with tongues whose vocabularies were devoted to the destruction of Auschwitz. The SS set fire to the little white farmhouse where they'd gassed us; they had pyres of documents, they destroyed all they had built, but they were not systematic about this destruction the way they had been with ours. No, this was a blazing assault on the kingdom over which they had ruled, and the random nature of its dismantling placed us at still greater risk. The prisoners walked with bowed heads—meeting a guard's eye could only encourage his ruthlessness. While these guards had once answered to superiors, they now answered only to their desperations. There were rumors of what they might do, and no two rumors were alike—it was said that they would relocate us to another prison camp, that they would send the whole of Auschwitz up in flames to destroy evidence of their crimes, and that this was the beginning of surrender.

The last seemed most unlikely to me. I couldn't imagine that one would embark on surrender by enacting these particular violences, this tossing of children in the air to make them more challenging targets, this cornering of women to cut their throats, this mowing down of men with vehicles. Watching this chaos from the window of the infirmary, I wondered if a bullet or a scream could better pierce the sky.

On January 20, 1945, the movements of the SS festered into flights. We saw them load themselves onto the same trucks they had piled our loved ones on, and they fled. They scampered into cars and hurtled through fences, leaving twisted wire in their wake. Those who didn't flee were roaming about, extracting whatever power they could find. Along the rows of us, Miri was issuing strict instructions: "Stay inside," she said, "wait, wait, the Soviets are not yet here, but they are coming, and only then, perhaps not even then, will it be safe to venture out."

Being deathless, I slipped past her form. There was no keeping me within those walls. Not when I could see Bruna waving to me from the window, her arms full of supplies, her charcoaled hair thrown back, and her face drawn in anticipation of a good-bye. After I bolted down the steps she was there, around the corner, waiting with Feliks. She clapped a fur coat on my back.

"Jackal," she said, stroking the fur in benediction. I had never played a jackal in the Classification of Living Things, but it suited me. The coat shone with the determination of a clever animal whose reputation had been much maligned but who chose to endure.

Feliks was wearing a bear's pelt. It was luxurious, full of gloss and menace. In these additions to our own hides, we ran past the menace of uniforms, the goods that Bruna had given us bouncing in our sacks. We ran past the block where the orchestra had played, and the flames, they were eating all the instruments, they were gnashing with all the violent flicker entrusted to their kind. We heard the skins of drums burst, heard the oboes whimper as their reeds died. Thunder rose from the remains of the piano. But Pearl's piano key—it stayed by my side.

"Isn't it lovely?" Bruna asked, taking in the clumsy flight of the SS.

We agreed that it was and stated our delight in viewing such a show. We swore that we would stand by Bruna and help her contribute to these destructions. She did not care for this plan; she pushed us bodily away from her.

"You must go back to the barracks without me!" she insisted. "I have promises to take care of here."

Later, we would learn that Bruna's promises were to Dr. Miri. The two had developed an evacuation plan for the weakest in the infirmary if an event such as this came to pass, and the SS began to pick off the ill as they lay in their beds. Bruna had better things to do than deal with us. Of course, she would never have put it that way—our Bruna dealt only in benevolent insults.

"Go away, you babies, and hide in your bunks," she hissed.

"There, you worms have a chance. Your chances here—*pfft*—in this place you will live only by playing dead."

"We will do that, then," I argued, pulling on the lapels of my jackal fur coat. Already, I felt it sharpening my instincts. But Bruna did not share my faith.

"I doubt your ability to play dead well enough. You are too animated, Stasha. No, it is better for you to go to the barracks and wait. Wait for me to fetch you. If you don't go back and save yourselves"—Bruna paused—"I'll do awful things to you."

"Like what?" Feliks challenged. "Your worst is the best in all the world. I wouldn't have anything but the worst. All the other girls—"

She slapped him across the cheek with a resounding crack. He looked like he would swoon from the pleasure of the proximity, but her words ended that swiftly.

"I'll kill you, Feliks. You dumb bear. I may not kill you now. Or even tonight. Hopefully, it won't be necessary at all. But if one of these Nazis tries to kill you, you can be sure that I will beat them to it. I won't have my loved ones die at their hands. Only mine."

We saw the reason in this. We also saw the pistol in the waistband of her skirt. It seemed that Bruna and her fellow rebels had been prepared for this upheaval, even if they had not known, during their weeks of plunder and planning, the secretive missions undertaken in Nazi headquarters for supplies and the endless meetings, the breadth of destruction our freedom might bring.

"So," Feliks concluded, a forced brightness in his voice, "we will go. Back to the barracks. But only for now. We are leaving here together, yes?"

Bruna lifted her eyes to the flickering sky, as if she expected the flames to deliver her words for her, words she hesitated to give.

"Don't ever wait for me," she instructed us.

All of this meant nothing to Feliks. He cared nothing about the future if it didn't have a reunion with Bruna.

"We won't wait now. But perhaps—in case we are separated in this—we should establish a meeting place first?" he suggested. "That is what friends do. You are our friend, yes, Bruna? Only a friend would offer to kill you before others can."

I watched Bruna's face struggle to maintain its usual stony veneer. She was touched. It seemed likely that the term *friend* had never been uttered so nakedly alongside her name before.

"Of course," she said. "But it may be some time. Who knows what waits for us? There could be months of running ahead, years of hiding."

Feliks would not be deterred.

"Stasha and I will wait for you," he said. "Just name the place."

I watched the depth of his determination occur to her, saw it light up one pink eye and then the next. I'd always expected Bruna's tears to be as blush as her eyes but there they were, as clear and atremble as any I'd ever witnessed. She didn't seem to care that I saw them and even accepted the sleeve of my sweater for use as a handkerchief.

"I always wanted to go to a real museum," she said between dabs. "To be a lady for a day and see the art."

"A real museum, then." Feliks gulped. "In front of a statue, we'll meet. And tea afterward, maybe a nice café. I'll buy your ticket."

"That would be sweet," she said, and she gave him a kiss. "You are very sweet, Feliks."

I've never been sure what motivated Bruna to accept this invitation, to bestow this kiss. Perhaps she saw true possibility in it. Perhaps she was just humoring Feliks. Maybe she was sensing—as anyone with eyes and ears would sense—that a protracted conversation in the middle of gunfire and grand-scale selection was unwise for any who might want to leave that place alive. But I think she cared for him, truly.

"It's a promise," she swore to us, and then she shook my hand and smiled. I could feel the residue of her tears in that handshake.

Whatever else one could've said of our beloved criminal, we all knew that Bruna's word was true. Theft was not her genuine talent. A promise—that was her real gift. She could not help but dream of fulfillment and creation, even as she dedicated her present to havoc. She meant well, our Bruna. But of course, she did her best to mask her virtue. And so her kindness and generosity were cons, double-dealers; they skulked about, disguised as flaws—and then, suddenly, when you weren't looking, her tricks trespassed and broke inside you so that they could steal from you, bit by bit, until you hosted an emptiness in which your real goodness could thrive. In this way, she saved you. Bruna, she was our organizing angel.

Only when she let go of my hand was I struck by the stupidity of our pact. How many museums were there? Were we speaking of Poland or Europe or the world entire? It was a foolish plan.

In realizing this mistake, I looked at Bruna's face, half turned, that goodness on it still apparent, and before I had even a slip of a minute to ask for clarification about our future plans, Taube leaped up behind her and grasped her by the neck. He gave it the famed twist we'd seen him issue so many times before, but now it was visiting our own. As the bones cracked, a rare color rose in her cheeks. Her pale face filled with blood. After Taube finished breaking Bruna's neck, he snapped his fingers in our direction.

We were on our knees then, having watched her flutter to the ground like a scarf. The newly black hair she'd made for herself bannered with a flag's defiance. Taube caught up some of the coal-colored tangles and rubbed them between his fingers to reveal the whiteness she'd so desperately tried to conceal.

"She really thought she could be someone else, did she?" he asked no one.

Fearing Feliks might answer, I tried to clap a hand over his mouth, but he was too busy collapsing into the snow to speak. We looked at Bruna together. Her woolen skirt had upended itself, and the jumble of her white legs was exposed.

As Feliks moved to straighten Bruna's skirt, Taube interfered, placing a foot on the body to indicate that it had been thoroughly conquered. He stooped to draw the pistol from her waistband, balanced it in the palm of his hand, then redirected the muzzle at us.

"You two. You find this something to stare at? On your feet now."

Feliks offered me his shoulder, but his shoulder wasn't enough, and his bones were sharp enough to cut me besides. Still I clung to him. My shuffle drew attention to our furs.

"The coats. Where did you get them?" Feliks's mouth was still drawn into a silent scream. I turned his face away from Bruna, and I told Taube that the coats were a gift from the doctor.

"Tell me"—he laughed—"were you such a good liar before? Or do you have Auschwitz to thank for that?"

I told him I was sure I didn't know the answer, but it seemed a fair question.

"What is with this obsession with fairness? No matter," he said with a sudden cheer. "Keep your lousy coats. Who knows how cold it will be where you're going." He put Bruna's pistol at our backs.

There it was—we had lost the chance of escape that our dead beloved had entreated us to take.

Snow fell as flames rose. Both were outpaced by Taube. He was herding us, every last one—children and women and injured all. The usual efficiency had fallen away; it was all pell-mell stomping and dragging, people grasping onto other people, people stumbling, people trying to lift other people up.

Choiceless, we joined the swarm, that ever-enlarging multitude dotted with faces, scarves, bandages. We lost ourselves in it, and the loss was so thorough that the image of dying Bruna that had burned itself into the backs of my eyelids began to fade. It would reappear to me over the years—I would wake and see it in mourning—but in that moment I had to walk.

Feliks, though, I believe he walked with this vision of Bruna. Even as he supported me, he trembled and shook, and he spoke to me as if he were trapped in a dream.

"How many of us are there?" I asked him.

"Not enough" was all he would say.

Later, history would say that more than seven thousand people stayed behind at Auschwitz, emaciated and immobile while the rest of us were turned out in droves, dense marches of death and near-death. We in this particular death march numbered twenty thousand. Among us marchers, the hesitant were shot; the lame were shot too. Our numbers quickly dwindled. The soldiers entertained themselves with a trick of shooting one body so that it fell into another body, and that body toppled another in turn, and so and so pitifully on, bone-crack, hiss of bullet, snap on snap—our people fell, and the SS strode upon them, shooting whoever dared to stir.

I should've been one of the battered lame, one of the shot hesitants, but I fell into another category on the death march.

Of this twenty thousand, there were a fair number of people who managed the impossible, shouldering their supplies and falling into a steady pace. Feliks was one of these. He was able to walk so well that he even managed to whistle. He whistled for my sake, knowing that I enjoyed watching the miniature clouds spindled by his breath. I had a fair view of these whistle-clouds because I wasn't a marcher. I wasn't even a stumbler or a limper. I'd managed only a trio of wondrous steps beyond the gate before collapsing in the snow. Feliks responded to my fall by digging the blanket from his pack and unfurling the wool. It lapped at the snow like a red tongue. He'd gestured for me to climb aboard this blanket like a sleigh. In this way, we soon fell to the rear of the march.

People speak a lot about power. They say that it left them, or they summoned it. They talk about it in terms of exchange, of loss. Feliks, he had stores of it. I knew this, though, only because he was saving me. Would I have known it if he had saved someone else? I would like to think so. But when you have been halved and split, when you are torn, when you have been set against yourself by someone who claimed that he did it for your own good, it becomes harder to recognize the goodness of others unless their goodness is visiting you directly.

Feliks's power was made all the more visible as he slowed. Every fourth step was a stumble, every sixth step was an ache. The whistle-clouds receded. Night fell on us with its unbearable weight.

Still, he continued to drag me forward.

From my blanket, I had a view of many deaths. A woman stooped to drink snow and died. A man paused to ask a question and died. They died swiftly, bullets lodged in their heads.

In a hush, we spoke about where we were going. Would they march us into the sea, drive us off a cliff? Auschwitz had failed them, despite all its many innovations, so it was clear that they'd decided to end us all, to walk us to death, in the simplest of terms. I wondered how I would explain my immortality when a guard put a bullet in my head.

A cough took hold of Feliks's lungs, and he gasped for air. I ordered him to abandon me. He lurched instead of walked. He wouldn't let me go. And I wasn't his only burden. On his back he carried a sack of our possessions. He threw out the scarf filled with flour that he'd organized. The flour hit me and painted me white. He threw out the crusts of bread we'd collected over the weeks; the wind caught up the crusts. He tossed the potatoes out to the ice, but he was so weak that his aim faltered and the potatoes dropped at his feet and his feet tripped themselves up.

I thought it the end—he fell with a thud and a smack of skull, his limbs akimboed onto my blanket, while his parted lips kissed the ice. The procession stepped over us. Skirts and coats fluttered over my cheeks. The marchers were careful not to trample us, and the limpers approached us gingerly, but the pace of all quickened with the warning shots. All the while, we lay there, unmoving.

I whispered to him, I told him that it couldn't be this way, with him dying here. If you have to die, I begged, don't do it while I'm watching, and if you have to do it while I'm watching, do it while I'm not feeling.

He coughed, and the snow beside his mouth bloomed. I suppose I should've kissed him then, for Bruna. But before the thought even had a chance to occur to me, a boot lowered itself on his neck. Its sole gaped, exposing a grin of sock. I made my heart still. I like to think I made Feliks's heart still too. I watched his eyelids flutter.

Above us, Taube sighed. The boot moved from Feliks's neck. He stooped and plucked a stray potato from the snow. He bit into it with a great gnashing of teeth and then swore with disgust. "Rotten!" he declared, and he spat the potato-flesh on my scalp. The potato mustn't have been too rotten, though, because he took another bite. This, too, he spat out. It struck Feliks's forehead. He repeated this procedure again, and then once more. The warmth fell onto our cheeks and backs, on the snow beside us. It seemed that there would be no end to this potato.

And then, Taube's name rang out across the field. His evil was needed elsewhere. He stooped and sniffed us—he knew we were alive; I'm sure of it—and then, with a parting arc of spittle, he turned.

Let me be clear: Taube did not spare us out of a fit of conscience. He did not spare us in defiance of his superiors. He spared us for the same reason that he bothered to do anything—because he could.

Only after his departure did I realize that the rattle of gunfire wasn't as immense as it had seemed. We had walked surrounded, hemmed in by the noisy spatter of numerous guns. But while pretending myself into death, the curtain was raised on this ruse, the smallness of the rat-a-tat-tat. There were two guns, maybe three at most. An ineffective trinity, low on ammunition. They stuttered into the distance while Feliks and I played possum.

"Is it safe to be alive now?" he whispered.

I cursed him for lifting his head from the snow. What if someone looked back and saw him?

"No one's looking back." He laughed bitterly. "The whole world will never look back. And if they do, they'll probably say that it never really happened."

I was listening to him only in halves. Taking what I wanted to hear and dismissing the rest. What I wanted to hear was the part about never looking back. As I listened, I watched the velvet blackness of my closed eyelids. If I closed my eyes too suddenly and too tightly, I could see small sparks alight on that velvet, like footlights at the perimeter of a stage. I wanted to send my sister dancing across that stage, wanted to see her attempt something new. Some jump I'd never heard of, some turn that would reverse everything. But no matter how hard I tried to achieve this vision, only the blackness and the scattered lights remained.

"Stasha? Why so quiet? You're not really dead, are you?"

"I don't think so." I could never tell him what Mengele had done to me.

"Because I feel kind of dead myself. What if we are dead? My father the rabbi, he didn't believe in a heaven. But he didn't believe people would come and kill us someday either. So what if this is a heaven?"

I told him that this wasn't a heaven. This lousy, awful blankness—a heaven? This freezing, thunderous tundra—a heaven?

"It could be," he argued. "It could just be some special heaven-hell for people like us."

"It isn't a heaven-hell. It's not even a hell-heaven."

"How can you be so sure?"

There were, I figured, two ways of convincing him. The first was by presenting the fact that his brother was not there to greet him. Whether heaven existed at all was uncertain, but if it did, it would have no choice but to reunite us with our flesh, simply because all such systems depend on symmetry. And it was quite clear there was not a brotherly footfall about. But looking at his forlorn face, the cold-bitten hands—I couldn't speak of the lost brother to Feliks; he was so weak and frail and he had borne me across the vastness of an icy tundra, a white beckoning of fog and uncertainty in a place that still wanted to make us as insignificant as possible. We were nothing but two buttons loosened from the doctor's coat. Two specks beneath his microscope. Two samples of bone and tissue. As small as we were, Feliks remained the stronger, and I could not risk weakening his resolve with mention of his departed twin.

So I chose the second way to convince him that we were not dead. I spread the blanket, heavy with frost, on the ground.

"Drag me again," I said. "You will see that my weight is the weight of the living."

Feliks wiped his eyes and reached for my hand in reply. He looked for the sun, and I swore I heard his heart bow in his chest, as if in recognition of the great feat he was about to pursue.

We could have lain there forever. Because of him, we did not. How we were to survive in such a wasteland, we did not know. We could not even be sure what duties had to be divided on the journey ahead. Someone was going to have to find shelter, someone was going to have to find food, maps, shoes, hope. What it took to survive—even this was growing, and as it did, it diminished us both.

Pearl, I thought, *I never should have made you in charge of the past. I cannot endure this future.*

PART TWO

CHAPTER TEN

———————————————————

The Keeper of Time and Memory

I had a face still. I didn't know my name, but I was aware of others. I knew the name of Auschwitz. I heard it shouted out in whatever world lay beyond the boxes that I lived in. There were three boxes, so far as I could tell. One was a building, the second a room, and the third—that was the cage of wire and lock that kept me. It was the white-coated man who put me there. After he finished inspecting me on his table, he dropped me to the cage bottom with a thud and took away my blanket so I could experience nakedness in such a way that the wires dug into my flesh. He came, he left. He shone lights into my darkness and made notes about my squint, my response. He did more than that, but I chose not to remember this then. I knew his name when this occurred. But I chose to forget that too.

From this time—there is not much I want to recall. What I want to dwell on is different, and it is mine.

This may not be true for the world, but it was true for me, in my cage: There was a brief moment, a slip of rare time, quite unlike any time before it. Because when Auschwitz fell, the lives it took were restored—for the merest of moments—just so our dead could see it founder.

Our dead in this moment—they were not your ordinary spirits. There was nothing of the specter in them, not a bit of ghost. They were simply people who had been tortured but were now allowed to see a justice. I could hear their murmurs, their joys. Theirs was an afterlife of mere moments, a permission to witness the ruin of what had ended them.

Among the shouts and cries of millions as Auschwitz collapsed, two voices made themselves known to me.

I heard an old man try to toast but he couldn't find the words; he simply uttered the beginnings of them until his voice cracked. I heard a woman comfort him, I heard her assure him that the girls would not end, and that's when I knew she was my mother. She and my *zayde*—they watched over me while the camp burned and the guards fled and the prisoners found that they did not know what to do with their freedom.

I heard Mama suggest a game to get me by in this time. I knew games; they were familiar to me, the concept came from whatever sprawl of a life I'd had outside this cage. I told this woman whom I knew to be my mother that I wasn't sure what game would have me anymore—though I could move a little, I was sure I was a cripple, and though I could think, I was sure that my mind had been broken. But Mama insisted that I try.

My grandfather did too.

Play an ant, he suggested. *Ants lift fifty times their own weight. You need that strength.*

Play a chimp, Mama suggested. *There is no dignity in it, I know, but the intelligence is fair compensation. You must be smart.*

Just then, a pigeon landed on the windowsill opposite me, some ten feet away, and began to daven. A silver band flashed at its feet announcing its status as experiment, messenger, or property. I could relate to all three roles.

"I'll play a pigeon," I said.

The pigeon has an excellent memory, Zayde murmured in approval. *The pigeon navigates and rescues and delivers. This is good,* he said. *All will be well.*

A fine choice, Mama agreed. *All will be well,* she echoed.

But I could not even lift my arm in imitation of a wing. Simply crooking my finger lit a pain that soared through me. I asked them how I was supposed to treat survival like a game if the game would not have me, but their voices had gone. They'd witnessed the fall, and then they performed their own fall back into nothingness, into what I hoped might be peace.

This was how I knew that I was still alive, because I was not at peace at all.

But I continued with the game long after the voices were no more. *Play a mouse,* I told myself. *Play a fox, a deer, an elephant.* I recited the order of living things, and I ended them the way one ends a prayer. This was how my recitations went: species, genus, family, order, class, phylum, and all will be well.

CHAPTER ELEVEN

Bear and Jackal

When I looked up from my blanket, the parts of the world were before and behind me, the plains of snow extending on either side like the wings of a dove. The death march had slunk on, the guards had continued to torture our fellow prisoners at a distance, and we were left with the sound of despair in our heads. The wasteland chose us, but we didn't want to be chosen by it. There we were, moving so slowly across this eternal earth, readier for an end than ever; we clung to the winter beneath us, trying to remember that beneath it, there lay the heartbeats and mutters of a floral season. I knew I had to find a way to make Feliks stay alive, to see him through to that spring. I had not even a sense of direction without him.

I was stripped of location. Feliks could remind me all he wanted that we were in the forests of Stare Stawy, a village outside of Auschwitz. But where we were meant nothing to me. The Classification of Living Things, that meant something.

Because we were following the river, like animals do. Away from the death march, we'd been reborn; our instincts had reassembled themselves into a formation better suited to the wanderings of animals. Feliks was Bear—the protective forager, fearsome and charismatic, resistant to any human efforts toward taming. I was Jackal—the doleful creature, clever, stealthy, accustomed to ruin and abandonment. We were hungry, without direction. Little more than an hour stood between us and the death march we'd escaped. Or I should say that I believed it to be an hour. I really wasn't sure that hours truly existed anymore.

I knew I was not an easy burden, but though his hands were mangled and blistered, Feliks chattered easily, as he dragged me forward, with talk of his beloved city.

I never asked the city's name. How could I care? All I knew was that it had fallen. Its machines were abandoned, its books were burned, its synagogues turned to ammunition factories, its people stifled, disappeared. Still, Feliks said, he was sure the sun shone there still, and he insisted on spinning the place to me as we crept. He told stories of everyday kindness, stories that valued beauty. I knew he was trying to convince me that we should make a life there as brother and sister, with our brother-ghost and sister-ghost at our sides, and the stories were making me imagine myself into quite a different person, someone who could stop feeling as if her tongue were made of stone. This someone would not be an immediate someone but an eventual one, and I warmed, thinking of her.

"And someday," he concluded, shaking a fist purpled by cold, "we will leave that city, as beautiful as it is, and we will hunt down all the Nazis; we will make them pay. And after every thrilling capture, we will always return to the city, because it will be a fitting home for heroes like us."

"Your plans for this city aren't convincing me," I told him. We were deep in the woods now, with the stillness of the river in our ears.

"Who says it's you I'm trying to convince?" he spat.

He dropped the corner of my blanket and wiped his hands in an exaggerated gesture of disgust. From the parcel Bruna had assembled for us, he drew two bottles of water and a potato and planted them in the ground beside me. I watched his form retreat, watched his bear coat waver and blur before blending into the trees. I put my finger on the speck that was him in the distance. Ever since the cattle car, I had been denied good-byes. This was the first real good-bye I could have had, and yet I refused it. I didn't shout after him, I didn't even whimper. All I could do was stare at the dullard of a sun, so high above me, but penitent still.

It stood like a guilty trickster with his hands in his pockets. A sun with such a conscience—you'd think it could be easily manipulated. I thought if I stared at it long enough it might correct my vision.

Because what Mengele had done to my eye—it grew grimmer by the day. A consequence of the tamper with my vision: Shadows lilted around the edges of everything I saw. My shoes. My cup, my hat. Our sacks. I didn't understand the intention of this shadow. Why it insisted on cradling all I needed, I didn't know. Would it ever leave me?

"No, Stasha—I can never leave you." Because he'd returned and heard me speaking to myself, as usual. When he extended his arm to me, I saw his hand was outlined by that ever-present black. "I wasted time walking away from you," he said. "And even more trudging back. Now it is your turn to carry me, but you are unable. What do you propose that we do in such a situation?"

I promised that I would make him laugh at some point.

"I'm sure you will," he scolded, "but will it be for the right reasons?"

I stretched out my hand, and he hoisted me up. He shouldn't have had the strength even for this simple motion—he was stooped and twisted, and his hands were raw; he faltered a little at my grasp, and when he smiled, the force of his expression made the frost leap from his eyebrows.

"For Pearl," he said, and he gestured impatiently for me to walk.

I thought of my sister dancing. The tap-tap of Pearl's feet, the clap-clap of my hands as I watched. All of it in pairs, in repetition.

This is how I walk, I told myself. *One step, then another. This is how I walk with the sun, this is how I walk through the snow. This is how I walk in memory of Pearl, the girl whose every step could have been musical, and for all time, if only Mengele had fulfilled his promise and given her the deathlessness too.* That last thought—it made me stop walking again. But not walking would not do. I studied my feet and began once more.

This is how I walk beside someone I love who lives still, I thought, someone who should abandon me, but together, we walked until we found shelter—deep in the woods, a wall of fallen logs, and with the paws of jackal and bear we dug a shallow ditch beside this wall; we lay down and covered ourselves with leafy branches and decided that we would take turns sleeping and keeping watch so that no one could creep up on us in this feeble shelter and throw a match into our nest.

Feliks huddled beside me in his bear fur with all the closeness of a brother. Even in his sleep, he made vows. But they were not the vows of vengeance I expected to hear. Instead, he vowed to himself that he would never be alone again, he would never be parted from me, he would not permit separation to alight between us. When he began to panic in these vows, gnashing his gummy jaws together in grief, I saw fit to wake him.

"Your turn," he said, rubbing his eyes and peering into the darkness for intruders.

I tried to sleep. I begged my mind to give me a dream of Pearl. Not the best dream, the one in which the world never knew war at all, or even the second-best dream, the one in which Auschwitz remained swampland, but the third-best dream, the one in which Mengele gave Pearl and me this deathlessness at the same time, in unison; he plunged the needle down and we turned to each other and knew that while living forever was a terrible burden, this was something we could do together, in our usual style.

She would take the best, the brightest, the funniest.

I would take the guilt, the blame, the burden. And if she ever couldn't walk, I would do all the walking for her. Because now that I could walk again, I did not want to stop. It seemed a triumph to me, and yet both my ankles were braceleted by an ache that I knew not to be frostbite. It was an odd sensation, and not entirely unpleasant, due to the fact that it let me know I could still feel, and someday, I knew too, my walk would increase its pace, someday soon, I might even jump.

Papa, the good doctor—he'd told me that people who lost limbs and fingers and toes, they continued to perceive sensations in them long after, in the form of pangs and tickles, and to such an extreme that it felt as if they'd never lost any flesh at all.

But he never warned me about this.

The next morning, we heard the Vistula River crack, heard it shuffle its sheets of ice like a deck of cards. The morning was blue on blue; trees thrust their limbs into the clouds. The sky rustled like Pearl's blue hair ribbon when she turned her head. We shook off the blanket of snowfall and wondered at the fact that we still lived.

The river, fissured, was a great white expanse, and the cracks watched over us as we knelt toward the ice. Its surface was so milky that I felt welcomed by it—it seemed to me the freshest, most innocent surface on the earth. Despite the darkness crouching in the canopied trees, we found a rabbit struggling in a hollow.

"Cripple," Feliks said, noting a wounded leg. I looked away while the bread knife sank, but I made myself watch him hang the rabbit from a branch and strip the tufts of its fur. He popped the eyes in his mouth, wrenched the bones bare.

"Eat!"

"Why can't we build a fire? Just for a minute."

"You know why. There are people who would be happy to catch us in these woods. You don't even have to be a Nazi to enjoy capturing a Jew."

He was becoming like a father, this Feliks. He was impatient with me; his tone often dipped into severe registers. I didn't doubt that he would stuff my mouth with the raw rabbit if I continued to decline. It was better to be agreeable.

I watched him struggle to chew the bloody meat. His tooth loss made this difficult. So I chewed for him, then spat it out into my hand. Embarrassed gratitude—that was the look he gave me, but he accepted the chewed food from my hand and popped it into his mouth, swallowed as if it were medicine. He urged me to eat for my own sake, and this was harder to do—still, I was tired of arguing and gave it a try.

"We have to keep up your strength." Feliks nodded. "We can't achieve the vengeance we've sworn ourselves to if you are bones."

I agreed. Vengeance, it was what I longed for most, but I'd begun to doubt how it might be handed down from experiments like us. I'd made attempts before. Mengele was slippery, beyond cornering. In him, I saw a little boy life had long indulged. Life didn't always indulge, though, did it? Was there any chance that we, in such diminished states, might ever truly finish him? We did not even have a clue as to his location.

My companion stabbed a tree trunk with his bread knife. He issued pairs of gashes—one, two; one, two—in a meditative fashion. Then, inspired, he turned and looked at me curiously.

"There is something I must tell you," he said, cautious. "This city I speak of—it is not my city at all, I have been lying, but for good reason, to persuade you. It is Warsaw, and I have been trying, from the very beginning, to take you there."

I couldn't imagine what cause he might have to usher me into such destruction. The isolation of Auschwitz had not saved me from the knowledge that the place he spoke of would soon enter history as the most devastated city of all time.

"There is no greater ruin than Warsaw," I said.

He crouched in the snow and took to stabbing it with his bread knife. One, two. One, two. The motion was resolute, a way to steady his argument.

"But the man we want dead is alive there," he said. "I overheard him; he was speaking too freely in the final days. While I sat waiting on my bench at the infirmary, he was on the telephone discussing his future plans. He was going to flee to Warsaw. He was going to rendezvous with someone there. I think he was telling this to Verschuer. They have documents about us, valuable pieces. Research. Information, I believe. Or maybe bones, all that war material, those slides you keep talking about."

I couldn't understand why he was telling me this now. Why had he not been direct before? I joined him in stabbing the snow. Have you ever stabbed the snow to make sense of things? It is not something I recommend.

"Let's say that I do believe you," I ventured. "What else did you hear?"

"Oh, I don't know," he said, as airily as if we were seated in a parlor putting sugar in our tea. "Something about the Warsaw Zoo."

"It would be like him to want to go there," I offered. I thought of all the cells in a zoo, joining, dividing, engaging in all the tricks of variation that so enraptured Mengele.

"It would, wouldn't it?" He sounded oddly pleased, as if he'd had a hand in the sense-making of it all.

I will be honest—nothing in this wild story should have sounded correct to me, but I didn't want to doubt. It felt good to believe in something for once. It made me feel real. In believing, I was less experiment, more girl.

And so it was decided, there, on the banks of the Vistula, with its cathedraled branches of trees and snow: We would take Mengele's life in Warsaw. We would repossess his slides, his bones, his numbers, his samples. We would take and take from him until there remained only a single mustache hair as proof of his villainy.

He had tried to make monsters of us. But in the end, he was his own disfigurement. Future innocents, we swore, had to be protected, and then there was the matter of repayment for his misdeeds. In the name of Pearl, he would be our kill. I thought of his eyes, I thought of the terror that would color them when he spied my approach; I thought of his surrender, his arms flailing in that blasphemous white coat. He would cry out; he would beg. We would permit him to beg because we would enjoy the spectacle, but when his beggary ceased to amuse us we would put him down, and because our humanity had not left us entirely, we would be swift about it. Mengele's expression—the shock on his face at discovering our survival and pursuit of justice—that would be trophy enough for our violent souls.

And I knew that the animals in the Warsaw Zoo, witnessing the triumph of Bear and Jackal, would rejoice; I knew that they would lift up their voices in shrieks and cackles and guffaws so loud that even Pearl, in her death, would hear that vengeance was ours.

CHAPTER TWELVE

My Other Birth

There were things I knew still: There were doors that shut, there were shouts, there were scratches along the floor; there had been someone else, caged opposite me, who muttered poetry through the day and night, his voice melodious and familiar. I could not remember exactly when his recitation halted, I knew only that it had ceased, and then I wondered if I had ever heard a voice at all. Perhaps what I'd imagined to be a voice, one possessed by a lover of poetry, had merely been a leak in the ceiling. A meek drip-drop with a musical quality. This alone I could be certain of: I had tried to converse with the leak, I had begged for its help, but it did not help, it only stopped.

Rats squeaked their way near me where I lay and I remembered: species, genus, family, order. In the dim, I saw whiskers, snouts, tiny feet. I knew that these were not the same parts I had, that I was human, but still, I sniffed in mimicry and became reliant on my nose. I could smell rust, waste, the dried blood encircling my ankles, the stitches at my abdomen, a stagnant pool of water. I told the rats about what I smelled but they weren't impressed. I tried to smell more, I tried to smell all that I could, but the only other scent I could detect was death.

The scent of death is not frantic. When you have been around it enough, it is oddly respectful; it keeps its distance, it tries to negotiate with your nostrils and appreciates the fact that at some point, one becomes so accustomed to it that it is hardly noticeable at all.

Despite its politeness, I hated that smell. I wanted to train myself to smell other smells. This was an activity that was available to me, it was something I could do to pass the time. The rats, though, they refused to mentor me in this art. The pigeon at my window—he had departed long ago.

It seemed that I would have to instruct myself—if I could retain this sense of smell, I thought, the world might want me still, if I was ever freed from my cage. I began my recollections with the owners of the voices. Mama smelled like violets. Zayde smelled like old boots. My papa—I could not remember what he smelled like, but I didn't much care, because I found a different avenue of memory to traverse. Or my pain found it for me. Because when I became aware that both of my feet were clubbed and swollen, that the bones had been snapped at the ankle and my feet sat at the end of my legs like a pair of too-large lavender boots, I had a thought that he would fix everything: he would come and heal me if I only called.

Papa, I remembered, he was a doctor. I remembered that.

And this discovery was so great that it overshadowed that other, very different discovery—the realization that even if I were able to leap from my cage, I would not be able to walk.

On what I'd later learn was January 27, 1945, footsteps surged through the door. There were words that were close to the first language I heard in my head, but they were not my words. My words were Polish. These words were neighbors in sound and meaning— *They are speaking Russian,* I thought. The Russian chatter increased, and the stomp of boots rose beside them. A pair of red spots bobbed toward me, and then the spots became stars and I saw that they were worn on the caps of soldiers.

Someone trained a light to this corner and that, and then traced it up to the ceiling.

The boots and stars moved through the dimness. The lights multiplied. There was a stumble, a fall of materials—wire clanged to the concrete floor, there was a metallic clamor of instruments and trays—and the soldiers pounded fists into boxes and debated, as if on safari, who had seen the most interesting and grotesque of sights. What they spoke of—all the many horrors—made me grateful for a moment that my darkness had kept such sights at bay. I thought about contributing my own story to their conversation— they seemed interested in all the goings-on, after all—but when I opened my mouth to speak I found that I could only croak.

"You hear something?" a gruff soldier asked.

"Rats," said another.

Their flashlights found the wall opposite me, glanced over the wall after that, and then settled on my cage.

"What a shame," a voice said. There was a catch in it, a start. And the others agreed that it was a real pity—the child looked so young; it was too bad, what had happened to that little body.

Hearing this, I cried out. I wanted to speak to this child who was the focus of their concern. I wanted to say to this child, *I wish I'd known you were here! I hope you didn't think me rude. I didn't mean to exclude you from my conversation with the leak in the ceiling!*

But of course, when I cried out these things, there was only a rattle and an exhalation.

My voice was as good as smoke.

Above me, the beam of the flashlight shuddered.

"Is it dead?" asked the bearer of the light.

"How could it not be?" another answered.

"I swore I heard something. Like it tried to speak."

"There's too much to hear in this place. My ears haven't stopped ringing."

And he suggested that they move on to the next block, that they should permit someone else to collect my body—and I was sure that they were gone without another thought for me, but then they heard my whimper. The gruff soldier found my padlock and he fiddled with it and then he took up an ax and though I thought I knew that he was there to rescue me, I curled into myself as the blade closed in, and one of the other soldiers, he kept hushing me all the while, he kept saying, *"Na, na,"* which is a way of saying, "Nothing, nothing"—Zayde used to say this all the time to comfort me to sleep—and I wanted to agree with him, I wanted to say that I was a nothing, or at least that the man had made of me a nothing, he'd turned me into so little that I wasn't even sure that I wanted to escape that blackness because it seemed certain, as I shivered and bit my tongue and watched the little leak at the roof, that I was no match for living anymore.

But the gruff soldier was not to be reasoned with, he was determined to smash the lock and turn me loose, and so I let him reach down and take me up from my depths, and there I was, I was free.

Was birth like that?

I had to wonder.

There I was, gasping for air and squinting at the light. I was bare as a baby; my hands swung helplessly at my sides. Everything about me was infantile. But what kind of infant had these scars on her face? What baby is emptied of her innermost organs, a procedure indicated by the crude stitches across my abdomen? A newborn can't walk because she is new. I couldn't walk for a far different reason.

The gruff soldier clasped me to his front.

"I've never seen anything like it," he said.

"Don't cry!" his companion ordered, looking at me.

I opened my mouth again to protest. I might have done terribly within this box, I might have withered and lost the use of my legs, and I knew that there was something even greater in me missing, something so large that it was the equal of a whole other person, or at least a small girl. But I'd never cried. And then a drop lit on my cheek, and I realized that the soldier wasn't speaking to me but to the gruff man who held me, a man who trembled while my tongue crept from my mouth to find the evidence of his shock and joy.

"Look at it!" he said; he wept. "It is drinking my tears!"

CHAPTER THIRTEEN

The Straw Temple

When the woods fell behind us on our third day of wandering, we found ourselves near the village of Julianka, hunched and frost-threatened animals with two potatoes to our names. A vast azure opened up, and the clouds insisted on being formless and unread; they floated high above us and acted lofty, as if they feared nothing, not hunger or cold or the Angel of Death. I wanted to tell the clouds they weren't so mighty because I didn't fear him anymore either. Hadn't they heard of Feliks's plan? I shouted this for all the sky to hear.

A distant boom answered me. It was faint, but explosive, with a frayed edge.

Feliks's eyes darted about in panic, and he clapped a hand over my mouth, and he folded me over like I was an empty box. He held me close to the icy ground and glanced about to see if my foolish cries had been overheard. Fortunately, not a soul approached.

"Madness" was all he would say. But empathy shimmered through this statement. He felt mad too, I was quite sure, because we were emptier now than ever before; hunger toured through us during our rare intervals of rest, and winter was threatening to take the toes peeking through our holey shoes. While it seemed likely that we were crazed from all our deprivations, the booms were quite real. The following day, we would learn that these sound bursts were not gunfire but the work of Jewish rebels blowing up the tracks some miles away. In the grasp of that early evening, though, we had no notion of its friendliness.

So when, out of the emptiness, we saw a golden column at the farthest periphery, we ran toward its gleam, encouraged by the change in the scenery.

Like a brass bell sprinkled with snow, this straw temple rose from the earth with a steady determination. As we neared, we saw that we were not the only ones that this golden column had drawn in. It appeared that bales had been removed from the lowermost of this stack to create a burrow—we could see the discarded piles of hay flung about, their golden threads strewn on the ice, and through a flimsy panel of straw at the rear, we could see a peepery of eyes. They were scattered throughout in the manner of constellation, and with equal glitter. The eyes were friendly, I thought, but I'd been wrong about the friendliness of eyes before.

Was this a trap? A trick?

Another boom cried out into the night.

Before we could debate, Feliks parted the wall of straw and scurried inside. He dragged me with him, deep into the itchy burrow, on hands and knees. On all fours, we were rib to rib and so close to each other that I was quite unsure where I ended and he began. You would think this would have been a welcome feeling, considering the compromises of my hearing and vision, but it made me feel only amorphous and undone.

Adding to this discomfort was the general overpopulation of the haystack, which trembled with the shifts of its fugitives. We were not the only ones on hands and knees. Though it was dark, I could make out the forms of five individuals, all seated against the perimeter, and all so small that I assumed them to be children, not a one of them any older than the age of seven. But the curses that confronted us were quite adult; they tumbled toward us in Czech. We do not speak that language, we said. Then a few voices switched to cursing us in Polish. That is the way to curse us, we said. And we apologized for crowding them so.

"You can't stay here," a male voice hissed. His Polish was quite good, I thought.

"Why can't we stay?" we hissed back.

"No room! We did not escape to be crushed by strangers. You must leave!"

"But we are making it warmer in here for you," I pointed out. The temperature was most hospitable with this crowd of bodies, and the ceiling of this burrow was low, so low that when I moved my head, the hay tickled my scalp in a pleasant way. I cared little whether our hosts welcomed us or not—I could not ignore the welcome of this golden palace.

"It is true that you are warming us," the male voice conceded. "But we have warmth enough, and you are crowding my mother. This haystack is not as spacious as it appears. And it belongs to us. We carved out this burrow with our bare hands! Do you know how difficult a feat this is in winter? Only the most desperate men are capable of such miracles!"

I respected the speaker's message, but I did not care to move. It was too lovely in the haystack—like curling up in a summer I'd once known. The perfume of the hay was so sweet, and the perfume of its inhabitants—it was not terrible. For all time, I could live there, and my reluctance to exit made this clear.

A large sigh arose. It sounded as if it came from the depths of a matriarch. The eloquent speaker addressed us again.

"You have to leave, children! I am sorry—we have no room!"

Exhaustion possessed me and I could only weep. And I did not care who my tears fell on in this little crowd.

"Stasha!" Feliks whispered. "Collect yourself!"

All of the haystack hushed after this command.

"Stasha?" said the male voice. "Pearl's sister?"

At first, I confess, I did not know him, even as he expressed familiarity.

"Have you seen Pearl?" I blurted out, and my desperation nearly felled the haystack. "Or did you see what happened to her?"

"No, I haven't seen her," the male voice said.

A lie, that's what it sounded like to me.

"Who are you?" Feliks demanded. He was truly a bear in the tradition of the Classification of Living Things. A defensive lining, part growl, had entered his voice. Bruna and Zayde both, they would have been proud of this performance. But the speaker was not put off at all by this inquiry.

"I'm the one you call Sardine," he said.

His voice was even and brave. It had none of the oily flavor or shrunken nature of a canned fish. I couldn't imagine a more inaccurate term for this gentlemanly Lilliput, and I hung my head in recognition of the taunts he had so stoically faced.

"We're sorry," Feliks said. "Truly. We can't beg for your forgiveness enough!"

Because it was Mirko who presided over this straw temple alongside his family. Apologies were owed to the lot of them, because the children of the Zoo had referred to all the Lilliputs as sardines, at Bruna's instruction. Now, it seemed, sardines would be the preservation of us.

Upon realizing that we'd been reunited with fellow survivors, we felt as if the whole world might be held within this haystack; it was all that mattered. *In this pile of straw,* I thought, *there may not be happiness, but there is a hope that may impersonate happiness, if only for a small while.* We had lived through death together—how could we not want the intimacy of this haystack?

"This girl is my friend," Mirko told the other inhabitants. "I might not think much of her companion, but the girl—a gem. And she has lost so much."

Something in his voice made me want to ask how exactly he knew how much I had lost. There was a mournfulness, a knowing that indicated he was familiar with the workings of my grief.

"You hardly know her," another voice said. I recognized it as his mother's. "It's as if everyone from Auschwitz is a friend these days, no matter that they lived beside us for so long without a care for us. Is this how we will live—picking up every stray and pretending a friendship?"

The other inhabitants of the haystack appeared to agree with this statement. I could feel the straw tremble with the force of their nodding.

"She was Mengele's pet," Mirko said firmly. "She knows what it is to be us."

Even though he spoke in defense of me, I couldn't help but take issue with his words.

"I wasn't Mengele's pet," I said. "Not Pearl. Not me."

"I don't know what you were." Mirko sighed. "But he mixed his terrors with favors. How is that?"

"True," I said. Still, I felt defensive. I might have chided Mirko about the radio Mengele had given him. I might have reminded his mother about the lace tablecloth she'd eaten off of and confronted the whole lot of them with the palace of a room they'd been given while the rest of us were pierced by the splinters of our boxy little beds and given those black-crossed lice as company. I didn't say these things, though, and not just because Pearl wouldn't have approved of such an outburst. I had a more important question.

"Did you ever see Pearl?" I asked. "You had to have seen her."

Mirko acted as if he hadn't heard the question and breezed into another line of conversation.

"My grandfather, you know that he could recite all the passages of Ovid's *Metamorphoses*? It seemed such a feat to me, impossible. But in my captivity, I tried to do the same. Already I have the story of creation down pat. The beginning of the world, Stasha—what do you think of that?"

"I think you lie," I whispered. "I think you are lying about not having seen Pearl, and I don't appreciate it. You are trying to spare me her pain. But her pain after death—that is mine to take!"

I swore I could hear some of the haystack voices murmur in agreement. But Mirko remained firm, as if he knew my sister better than I did. I wondered what time they had spent together to allow him to form such a conviction.

"Pearl would want you to live anew," he whispered mournfully. "She would approve of this—she would want you to need the beginning of the world again."

I told him I was liking the ending just fine.

My friend replied with a recitation:

Before the ocean was, or earth, or heaven,
Nature was all alike, a shapelessness,
Chaos, so-called, all rude and lumpy matter,
Nothing but bulk, inert, in whose confusion
Discordant atoms warred.

As he narrated our supposed new beginning, I pared a little hole in the side of my haystack and looked out with my good eye. The heavens I saw, they had never been captured, but they were haunted like I was. Did they know the details of my sister's death? Those stars, they knew what suffering and renewal meant, they were forged from collapse and dust and fire. That wisdom should have been enough to justify their existence, I'd think.

But they insisted on being beautiful too.

"Do you see what I see?" Feliks whispered. Because he'd made his own porthole too.

"I see stars" was all I would say.

"I don't see the cremo" was all he would say.

Pre-morning glistened through the peepholes of our haystack. Like a litter of kittens, we'd slept, curled back to back into the family that adopted us, confronted only by the temple's golden lining. I rubbed my eyes and saw that it was true—there was hardly any room with the additions of us. The hollowed-out sections of haystack provided three square feet of space, but when I sat up straight, my head struck the ceiling of frozen straw.

Still, I told Feliks that I wanted to stay. I was earnest, but he laughed. I could've told him that I'd lived in situations just as trying. The floating world, opposite Pearl. Inside the folds of Zayde's coat. The vinegary confines of my barrel. And did I even need to mention the Zoo? But I chose to keep this logic to myself—I knew he'd mock me, and now we had company besides.

Mirko's sister Paulina was sitting opposite us with her two children, a boy and a girl, sleepy-faced charmers only as big as crumbs. Paulina was braiding the girl's hair, and I watched her fingers weave back and forth. Seeing me study this, she gave me a smile, and I was about to apologize for staring, to explain the longing it aroused in me, for touch, for family, but I was saved from having to do so when Mirko and his mother entered through the little thatch, each with a tin cup of snow, which one person passed to the next, lapping up any moisture that one could. Then Mirko took a roll of meat from his pocket.

"From the Soviets," Mirko explained to me and Feliks, opening his bread knife and sectioning the meat into pieces. "We charmed them after they entered. Sang to them a little. And they permitted us a ride in one of their tanks, took us all the way past Stare Stawy and into this field. It seemed as good a place as any to hide and plan. Mother, she was quite ill with exhaustion, but she has improved after a week's rest. If the trains are willing, we are going to go to Prague. We will be going back to the theater. Do you two have interest in joining us?"

I couldn't answer because my mouth was too full of food. I had tried to refuse it, but the matriarch would not allow this. She hopped over with a square of meat and insisted it between my lips, and then, as if I were a baby prone to spitting out foodstuffs, she held my mouth shut until I swallowed. When she'd decided I'd had enough, she cleaned my face with the corner of her shawl and tried to pinch the life back into my cheeks.

"Mother always wanted a giant pet," noted Paulina. And they all began to laugh, as if they knew they had to laugh again someday and it might as well be that moment. The laughter, though, it fell short; it was too soon, and they turned their attentions instead to drinking the melted snow from their tin cups, and gave Feliks seconds and thirds of wurst.

When their bellies were full, Mirko and Feliks began to discuss the problem of return. Our friend had many plans. He spoke of the parts he wanted to play upon his reestablishment in Prague, of the theater they planned to make their temporary home. He was so hopeful, I never should have interrupted, but I had to say the words that had been with me since I woke. They flowed from me in a burst.

"You never saw Pearl, that's what you tell me. I believe you. But I also believe that since you are Mirko, you are being an actor, you are twisting words, you are not being truthful."

Mirko lowered his head so that I could take in only the sea of his curls.

"I believe you never saw Pearl, the real Pearl, because she was already dead; she was just a body, she was emptied of who she was."

Mirko nodded, and then ducked his face into his scarf. I didn't expect a confession. But then he decided to give me one.

"I thought I heard her once," he murmured. "But it was just a hallucination."

"Where?"

"In the laboratory. A laboratory you are unfamiliar with." He motioned to Paulina to put her hands over her little girl's ears. She did so promptly, but the look on her face said she wished she did not have to hear this tale herself. Mirko covered the ears of the little boy, whose eyes darted curiously about as soon as his hearing left him. Only then did my friend continue.

"I was in a cage," Mirko said. "Is that what you want me to admit? That I was in a cage?"

I told him I did not want to hear such a thing. This softened him.

"I will say I was in a cage. But instead of the word *cage,* we will use the word *haystack.* This is more of my word-twisting, I know. Still, is this agreeable to you?"

I indicated that it was.

"So you see, I was in a haystack. I'd been in the haystack for three, maybe four days. The haystack itself was so small that I could not even turn around. I didn't eat, but water was given to me. This was at the end. Before they had a chance to initiate a single death march. The haystack was making me go mad. There were five other haystacks in this dark room, a room with two sources of light—the crack beneath the door, and a tiny window set so high in the wall that it looked out only onto the sky. Pigeons gathered on the sill. And rats scampered across the floor. These animals were noisier than the inhabitants of the other haystacks. I assumed them to be dead or so dazed from the injections that they could barely speak. I knew that I was the latter, because sometimes, lights flashed around me, and a great hand would unlock the padlock and pet my head and rattle things a bit. You know who that hand belonged to. Every day, another injection. The injections made me ill with a fever, and he marveled at the fact that I still lived. Of course, I wished myself dead, if only to get away from him. As time passed, I saw his hand grow shakier as he gave the injections. He seemed not to be his precise self. He even took no notice of the incompetency of my padlock, which was weak and rusted. Or perhaps he did notice, but he underestimated my ability to break free. Whatever the case, I assumed he was no longer in possession of his full powers— the end seemed near, and his cruelty toward me rapidly increased, as if he was determined to expel every last torture that occurred to him while he was still able. One day, another small body was lowered into my haystack. I felt the face on the body. It was dead. A child, maybe four—equal to my size. I had no choice but to sit beside it. I swear, there was no other option. It seems that Mengele was aware of Jewish prohibitions about contact with the dead. He told me that he'd take the dead body out of the haystack if I recited for him. I recited all day long, and into the night, though I had little voice left in me, and I knew that there was no hope. During my recitation on one occasion, a voice interrupted me with a cry and a plea. Mengele silenced that voice with a kick to its haystack, and I never heard from it again."

"Was it a child's voice?"

"It was a small voice."

"Was it a girl's voice?"

"It was a sweet voice."

I did not need to imagine it. I could hear it.

"My haystack was felled when the SS brutes came tramping through. This was during their sackings and evacuations and attempts at retrievals; the planes were above, and they were searching through the room, they were overturning it all, every last haystack, making us go, pell-mell. After their departure, I stood on top of the dead body in my haystack—apologizing all the while—and I fiddled with the padlock. This destructive romp of the SS had weakened it further—the rusty shank all but fell apart! I hissed out in the dark; I ran my hands across the bars of the other haystacks. Not a peep, not even from the one I thought held you. If one had lived there before—she no longer did."

"But you thought the voice was hers?"

"I thought it was yours at the time."

"Then it was Pearl."

"It was cold, I was starving more than the usual starvation, and Mengele, he was poking me, and when it wasn't pitch-black, he was flashing lights in my eyes. It is all difficult to recall."

"Maybe if I say what the voice was saying," I said, "it will confirm things for you. Do you think you can remember it, if I say what the voice was saying?"

"Perhaps." But Mirko did not seem to want to approach memory at all. I had to encourage him. I put on my sweetest manners.

"I know you'll remember," I said. "You are better than us all, Mirko. The smartest, the strongest to survive."

My closest companion did not take well to this praise. He looked at both of us with the wary eye of one who feels quite left out.

"If you flatter him," Feliks said, "you might change his memory."

Mirko bolted up, his head striking the hay ceiling and his fists trembling, as if ready for a fight.

"I will always remember this with accuracy. Until I choose to forget it entirely, which I plan to do after we arrive in Prague. As soon as I step over whatever threshold that remains—poof! You will be amazed, all of you, how much I won't remember!"

He stood, suddenly forgetting about his responsibility to his nephew's ears. Now his hands curled as if ready for a fight, and the matriarch scolded him softly; she tugged at his pant leg and eased him back to the earth.

"Which is all the reason now for you to tell me," I argued. "Tell me what the voice said so that I can repeat it and you can confirm and then forget."

"Might I tell you in writing?" Mirko asked.

"Of course." It would be better that way, I thought, because then I might carry the words with me. From Bruna's satchel, I withdrew one of my last bits of paper and the stub of a pencil. With these precious objects in hand, Mirko hesitated. He turned his back to me as he wrote, and the Rabinowitzes gave a show of hushing themselves, as if we were in the velvet cavern of a theater. When he finally handed the slip back to me, I read:

Tell my sister that I

Long ago, I might have thought that such words would be enough to end me. But in that moment, the five of them felt like friends.

Tell my sister that I

Looking at Mirko—it became painful in that moment. His was perhaps one of the last faces my sister had seen. For her, it could have been far worse, I thought. He was handsome and genteel in a way that you only imagine movie heroes being. His bearing within a cage must have given her hope. In him, there was a valiance I knew I would remember. It was too bad that he was no longer Mirko to me but Mirko, the Last and Final Sight.

I could not bear to look at him any longer, and I told Feliks that we had to leave. He responded by reaching into our sacks and thrusting one of the precious bottles of water at the matriarch. To this sacrifice, he added half of our potato, divided with his bread knife.

"You are leaving?" Paulina cried. "But it is not safe!" And she entreated her brother to stop us, to invite us to stay.

"We have to find a man," I told her. "We have to find him now more than ever."

And I ignored their pleas, their warnings. A jackal had no use for the likes of those. But I was human too. Here is proof of it: I put Mirko's note in my pocket, next to Pearl's piano key, and with every good-bye I said to the Rabinowitzes, I felt a tear knock on the door of my eye, a tear that acknowledged my sister's death and Mirko's proximity to her final hours. He pulled on the sleeve of my coat, indicating that I should lean down and lend him my ear. On tiptoe, he stood, so intent on the delivery of his parting message.

"Pearl is free now," he whispered, and then his voice divided itself beneath the weight of his grief. "Try to think of her, Stasha, as free."

And then, with his story told, we left our benevolent hero and his golden temple and traveled out into what the Rabinowitzes surely thought was our end.

CHAPTER FOURTEEN

The Russians Make a Movie

I would wander into my body and try to know it, to stake my claim within it. It was weak, this body; I was ashamed of it. It had none of the strengths I'd imagined it might have while still in the tomb of my box. I did not have the strength of an ant. I did not have the memory of a pigeon. All I owned was breath, really, and a single thought: that the numbers on my arm represented how many times I would have to prove myself useful in the world in order to remain in it. But even I knew that this was untrue; it was the logic of my cage and my keeper, and I had to overcome it.

It took bread to make me find my fingers and my hands. When the bread rolled down my throat, I found that I had a belly. I became reacquainted with my back again when the Russian laid me down on a bed within the infirmary. There, I looked out the window and occasionally faced the wall and sometimes the ceiling, and though there was no leak to converse with, I was the happiest girl one could know.

And though I took all of this in once I was out of the darkness of my cage, I didn't truly know I had eyes until I met the camera later that day. That is to say, I knew I had eyes, but I didn't know what they could do, as they were still adjusting to a world of light.

The cameraman in charge of the Russians' movie was a solemn, thin-lipped man. While many other members of the Red Army gave themselves to some wide-roaming emotion, he remained stoic. I imagined that the camera saw too much for him, or perhaps it provided details that he would rather have avoided. Strangely, the first time I saw him smile was when that camera attracted my interest.

He was moving a white cloth over the lens so tenderly. He held the camera to the light, took a look, cleaned it some more, and I found myself stretching out a hand, as if stroking the air that held such a magical instrument was contact enough.

"She doesn't reach for anything," the woman said, with awe. The woman—she had been the first to hold me after my retrieval, and she refused to leave my side. I remembered her doll eyes and her touch, but nothing more—I was told, though, that she was a doctor, that she could be trusted, that I didn't need to be afraid. I accepted this because I liked how she said my name, as if she'd known me for years.

The cameraman and the woman collaborated to give me a look through the lens. I passed from her arms into his, and I put my eye to the glass. I think I expected to see someone I loved in the eye of that camera. Someone I loved who still lived. But there was no one there.

Disappointment, that's what that camera held. I don't know why I'd expected the little black box to contain something better than a view of this place. All I could see were prisoners, tiny little prisoners whom the Russians had dressed in the gray-striped, voluminous uniforms of adults for the atmospheric purposes of their film. They were cold and sad and their faces said nothing of freedom.

Still, though I was unfamiliar with my personality, I had the impression that I had been an acquiescent sort, one interested in guarding the feelings of others, so I made a point of acting impressed as I looked in the camera, and when I was done, the woman picked me up, commenting on my lightness, and we joined the crowd of children to make the Russians' movie. We milled about near the fences, shivered in the snow. All us actors, so young and unskilled, were in a state of confusion. Why do we have to wear these clothes? we kept asking. We never wore these clothes before! we cried. Why are we marching but not leaving? But the moviemakers didn't care for our opinions—they wanted only to see us march in a tidy procession as proof of how free we had become.

We were lit with a snowy blur; all of us moved as if shaken from a long sleep. The camera loved two faces in particular, two small girls of ten, Romanians, who were pushed to the fore. Though these identical girls clung to each other as they walked before the lens, their postures were different. One was sober and demure, but the other tossed her head in the air and, ever so briefly, stuck out her tongue. Whether the gesture was deliberate, a cheeky reproach to the cameraman, or done out of thirst or reflex or simple girlish fun is uncertain. What is certain: Those twins would one day tell the world of the man who was not angel or doctor or uncle or friend or genius. They would speak of the man we experiments would banish from our thoughts except for when we had to warn others that people like him existed, that they walked among us without souls, seeking to harm others for sport and perfection and the satisfaction of some inborn cruelty. Someday, Eva and Miriam Mozes, they would not let the world forget what had been done to us.

But then, as the camera rolled, they clung to each other, so fearful of being parted, comforted only by their sisterhood. They were as bewildered as the rest of us. Confusion was the dominant expression of the photographed children. We were walking down a path, fences rising on either side of it, as if we were free—these gates were not the famed gates the world is so familiar with now, but another opening, unadorned by language—and then we retreated back as if we were not. By the time the movie was declared perfect, we weren't sure in which direction our true future lay, but the

Soviets assured us that we would be in every paper, in every movie house. People would see us; they would know that we lived.

And I noticed something during this constant march, back and forth and cut from and cut to: nearly every child was part of a pair. Each was like the other in looks and manner and voice, and they marched together, step by step, in unison; they moved as if one could not move without the other. It was then that I knew I was not whole.

What I knew was small, but it enlarged itself quickly. We were in a place where we'd been meant to die, but we'd lived. For what, I wasn't sure—but I was hardly alone in this. No one could tell me, not really, and there were so many sources of information too, all of them chatterboxes. They'd been bossed and corralled so often that they went wild in the infirmary; they spent their time shouting and jumping from bed to bed.

I envied that jumping. It was something I wanted for myself, someday, to leap and jump and run and dance, yet whenever I peeked beneath the bandages on my feet, the possibility of any of these seemed doubtful.

The shouting, though—I had no interest in that. But these freed children loved to shout. To their credit, these were quite organized shouts; they followed a strict pattern and held much meaning.

"No more needles."

"No more 'Heil Hitler.'"

"No more measurements."

And whenever one of these recitations ended, this little chorus would turn to me.

"No more," I said. "No more."

They took pity on me and supplied me with items with which to end the sentence. *Roll call. Root soup. Injections. X-rays. Elmas. Mengeles.*

The last made me shudder. I knew the name belonged to the man who'd lowered me into my cage. Hearing him mentioned made me not want to play this game at all. But I forced myself to participate.

"No more cages," I said to all of the infirmary.

It was all I could offer, as I could remember only the cage. I was certain of one other fact, and it was very curious: my name. It was scratched into the wall. *Dear Pearl,* the letters said. I liked to trace the letters in the dark and wonder after who had loved me enough to put them there.

That afternoon, the woman who carried me during the Russians' movie embarrassed me with her attentions. I wanted to ask her if we were family, because she acted as if she owed me every kindness she could give me. She bathed me and fed me and neglected her other charges in the infirmary to look after my needs. I wanted to point out to her that they suffered too, but I had the feeling that she was not easily influenced by others when it came to matters of suffering.

As she put me to bed in a private room in the rear of the infirmary, a man stepped inside and hesitated in the doorway, fully shadowed.

"Papa?" I cried.

"She knows who you are," the woman said.

The man was stern—I saw the shadow of his form shift, as if he was considering departure. But then he took off his hat and held it to his chest.

"Tell her I'm not her father," he said.

"Would it really hurt to say you were?" the woman whispered.

"More than you know," the man whispered back. He spoke for us both, I could tell. He was as discomforted by the prospect of necessary human connections as I was, it seemed. Though disheartened by this reaction, I began to sympathize with him in time. Over the course of our exodus I'd realized that the paternal figure had been living in a cage too, that he'd been cornered and pinned by the same torturer, though the assaults on his senses were quite different than my isolation.

He left the doorway and came closer, just near enough so I could see his face. It was a face that had once instructed me on the importance of remembering the other children's names. I felt a deep shame that I had long forgotten every last one, but fortunately, he didn't ask after them in that moment. Other clarifications were more pressing to him.

"I'm not your father, Pearl," he said. "Understand that. And this woman, she isn't your mother. And the rest of your family, your twin—"

The woman leaped up and hushed him. A confused look crossed his face, and then he nodded and left, unhappy with her intervention but not inclined to defy it.

Surrender was everywhere in those days. I suppose that was his.

And as for my own? I'd hoped that I'd left my ability to surrender in that cage, but I couldn't be sure.

When the woman put me to bed that night, she made their identities clear. The man was Twins' Father, and she was Miri. I was never to call her Doctor. I understood.

Twins' Father kept a list. All the children were on it, their names, their ages, their hometowns, even the barracks they'd lived in.

I peered at the list as Miri inspected it on the day that we departed, January 31, 1945.

I knew I was someone named Pearl. This was not new. The wall had told me so.

Apparently, I was thirteen years old. That made sense. If I looked at the other girls who were thirteen or near thirteen, we were of similar scrawniness, height. The fact agreed with me.

My hometown might as well have been a blank. *Unknown,* it read.

I watched Miri cross out *Unknown* and write *Miri* instead. She caught my glance, tapped her pencil.

"Is this agreeable to you?" she asked.

I told her that it was, and she received that as if I'd paid her the highest of compliments.

Twins' Father regarded this bit of information curiously when she handed it back to him but said not a word. He was too busy to care much, I think, about anyone changing her hometown to a person. He was scampering from child to child, asking after the contents of their packs—bottles of water, bread, sardines, candy from the Soviets—inquiring about the state of their shoes, and distributing fur coats pillaged from Canada.

The children's forms were made round and fat by these acquisitions. Their bodies were engulfed by supplies and fur, and their faces peered out from beneath their hoods. It was as if they were an army of tiny, directionless bear cubs, and Twins' Father handled them accordingly.

"Big ones look after small ones and small ones look after the babies, you understand? Keep up. Don't lag behind. If you lag behind—I can only wish you luck. Be soldiers now."

I watched multiple noses uplift proudly after this little speech. I wanted to feel so inspired. If only I had my half to walk alongside me, to lean over and joke to me as I lay in my wheelbarrow.

We were thirty-five children, all told, but my Someone was not among them.

"I know I had a twin," I said to Miri, "I just don't remember her. I tell myself that she must have been just like me in most ways, and different in other ways. But I don't know what I'm like either."

We walked and wheeled and trudged past the gates without the eye of the camera to note the grandeur of the event. Without costume. Without photographers. I didn't know it then, but this was what I wished the world could see: bundles of children footing their way across the icy path, the too-young paying no mind to the words at the main gate, the words that arched their way into Auschwitz's sky, and the still-young-but-now-too-old blinking at their meaning. I saw a fourteen-year-old boy with a torn ear and shaggy hair search the ground for a rock to loft at the gate's words. I saw him shuffle through the frost; he was telling Twins' Father that he had to find one heavy enough to strike those words and provoke a metallic clamor. I thought I recognized him as he fumbled through the snow. There was something familiar in the way he set his mouth, the way he searched for this stone, as if he were accustomed to procuring objects for very specific purposes. I tried to reach his name in my thoughts, but I could not. If he found a good stone, and he struck those words—well, then, I believed it might occur to me, I might hear it in the echo of a stone striking metal. But our march was moving swiftly on; Miri was carting me away, the children were sweeping alongside Twins' Father, and it began to look as if this boy would never find a stone mighty enough to achieve his purpose. The leader of our troop urged him on.

We were too late, Twins' Father told him, for life already. Better not to waste another minute looking back.

CHAPTER FIFTEEN

Our Marching Steps Will Thunder

Everywhere in Kolo, a sign, a message. Bits of paper leafed across the train station's walls. People wrote where they were going, where they'd been, who they were looking for. They wrote who they had been but were careful not to write who they had become.

I had never been to this town before, but I knew it by its former inhabitants: Kolo was a transfer point for Jews who were rounded up and deported to the Lodz ghetto. A couple of these captives became Papa's friends; they had met with him secretly in our ghetto basement. Papa's friends, they spoke mournfully of the town's history, its former hospitality to Jewish craftsmen. Their Kolo was not the one I saw from the windows of our train. This town, once so bucolic with its windmills and rivers, had become yet another place for Himmler to praise for its eradications.

I could hardly bear to look at it. I focused instead on the signs and the names.

Once, I saw Feliks scrape his name into the seat before us when he thought I wasn't looking. He performed this task with a hurried shame, embarrassed by the futility of the gesture and his compulsion to perform it. Because nobody was looking for us. Nobody even wrote our names anywhere. Nobody wrote, *If you are reading this, my greatest prayers have been answered, because it will mean that you are not dead after all, you are just away from me, which is the same thing, but somewhat more remediable.* I always wanted to write that to Pearl. But there was no room for such a lengthy message among those many names and scrawls. So many names—they darted across every available surface with violent urgency.

I would be lying if I said that I did not look for my name among them, written in Mengele's script. Because I was certain that he was looking for me still. On any one of these message depots—at the stations, on the backs of train seats—I told myself, he would have to be looking for us. I was happy that he was gone, yes, happy that I had to hunt him down, because this would be a greater demonstration of my love for Pearl. But I couldn't imagine why he was so willing to abandon me, his most special experiment. I was beginning to think I had never mattered at all.

I was a broken half afloat in a great nowhere, and the trains were determined to keep me this way. Let me say this about those days, when the war was still a war, but one soon to end, when refugees were roaming and tanks lay overturned on their backs like great tortoises and one was wise to avoid the marching streams of any soldiers, be they Soviet or German: These trains we never should have trusted again, they appeared to be our only way home. And so people packed themselves into the cars quite willingly and looked the other way when they failed to arrive at their stated destinations. I marveled at our collective belief in an eventual safety.

While the trains did not take us back to Auschwitz, they appeared determined to strand and confuse us. Their only real benefit was that they sheltered us from the snow, and we paid nothing for them. Feliks and I, we'd sit two in a seat, and when a conductor happened along to squint at us, we had only to shove up the arms of our furred sleeves and show him our numbers. Their blueness purchased whatever direction the train cared to carry us.

After leaving the straw temple, we had days of halts and reversals. We went east, and then west, our heads bobbing listlessly on our necks, our bodies jostled in our seats. And when morning slipped into dusk and we entered Kolo, we witnessed yet another ending: the tracks. A conductor urged us out. This was not a hotel, he explained. We huddled into each other, tried to act as if we didn't understand his Polish, tried to bargain this stalled train car into a place to sleep. But though the conductors weren't bothered by letting refugees ride the cars for free, our true comfort was another matter. We were plucked up by our ears, led to the car door, and forced out into the ice, where we wasted no time tumbling down an embankment. For once, even Feliks was slow to stand. The contents of Bruna's precious sack spilled out over the snow, and we leaped about, retrieving the one and a half potatoes and the bottle of water, the remnants of our sustenance.

Defeated, we trudged into the woods and found a barn. It appeared innocent. A pig lived there, fatter than even a pig had any right to be, and a sad-eyed Blenheim cow who mooed in pain, her udders overwhelmed by milk. Feliks showed me how to milk her, and I was impressed by this skill. We were cheered by the spaciousness of our accommodations—the cow and pig occupied two of the four stalls, and we claimed the furthermost slot, with the blankness of a vacant stall beside us. So sheltered, we drew our furs fast around us and dreamed of a morning when we no longer had to be Bear and Jackal.

Sleep comes so easy when you know you will wake to milk.

But when we did wake, it was not to sustenance but panic, to the neigh of a horse and the sight of a pair of boots, their muddy heels visible through the crack between the wall and the floor. As the owner of the boots secured the horse, Feliks and I tried to make ourselves very still; we flattened ourselves against the floor and possumed, and we would have gotten away with this, I'm sure, if it were not for Feliks's sneeze. This noise sent the wearer of the boots shuttling out of the horse's stall and into ours. She was an older woman in clean clothes and a decent coat. Her round cheeks bobbed like suns on her face, and the eyes above them were cloudy blue and suggested near blindness. I did not like the look of them, but when she approached us I convinced myself that they were kind, because we were lost and starving, living on beggar's time, and you can only live on beggar's time for so long until everyone starts to look like your salvation. She regarded us thoughtfully, as if calculating a move, and then, having reached her decision, plunged toward us with an open embrace.

"Children!" the woman cried. "I have been looking for you! I thought I'd never see you again!" She took us into her arms. She was a large woman, but she'd been diminished still—one could tell from her grasp; loose wings of flesh were enfolded in her sleeves. "Never run off again!"

I wriggled from her arms, huddled myself tightly against the wall of the barn.

"We are not yours," I said, calm. "I am Stasha Zamorski. Pearl's twin."

"Oh? Forgive me. And this is Pearl, you say?" She gave Feliks a punch on the arm.

"Hardly. He is a boy. But you're right to recognize him as a twin."

"I could've sworn you were my own lost children," she lamented. "I thought you'd returned. But maybe you can help me find them? I will give you food and shelter in exchange."

Feliks gave me a look, the kind of look that said this was my decision. For all the woman's suspiciousness, he had been disarmed by the prospect of comforts. If we had not been tossed about by trains and weather, if we had full bellies and proper shoes, and if the world hadn't been overwhelmed by white, I'm sure he would not have considered it at all. He pulled me aside for a consultation.

"If need be," he said, "do you think we could overtake her?"

I vowed that I would never allow harm to come to either of us. He received this skeptically but turned to the woman to present his plan.

"We will stay for an evening," he told her. "Just long enough— the girl is weak, you see. A meal too? We are hungry. And perhaps some bread when we go?"

"My home and bread are yours," the woman soothed.

"It is a deal, then," Feliks declared. "Madame, we will be eager to assist you in the search for your children." He gave a little bow, one shockingly graceful in its bent. And we followed the woman as she picked her way through the snow flanking the barn and onto a little path, where there stood a cottage so humble and white, like a child's overturned top, that I couldn't imagine any harm might come to us within it. Still, I knew that trusting such a stranger was a gamble. The woman's milky eyes did not warm to us, and as we walked in the company of her detached and blighted stare, I began to wonder if her true flaw was not a matter of her sight but her disposition.

My deathlessness was useful in situations like these. But Feliks? I had to make certain that no harm befell him.

The woman's lodging was simple. She had a rag-covered bed, snowshoes by the door. A drab braided rug, the usual harvest wreath. A bucket posed to capture a leak. The low ceiling made giants of us both, and the woman walked at a curvature so as not to crack her head. What must it be like, living at such an angle? She was crooked, I thought, but she must have been a good mother still, because the cottage was without spot or stain. The bench was cherry and polished, the cupboards plain and clean. A shiny hatchet lorded over the table from its nail on the wall.

"Your children—how long have they been missing?" I asked.

The woman didn't have a ready answer. I asked again. But she appeared to be a little deaf in addition to being nearly blind. I was not beyond sympathizing with her conditions and so I did not press the issue but simply watched as she busied herself with cutting a loaf of bread. It was then that the starkness of the house came to my full attention. I found it odd that there were no pictures of these lost children. Or any sign, really, that they—or anyone—had ever lived here. Not a book appeared on the shelves. There was no piano, no cat sleeping in a cat basket. Before my family's time in the ghetto, we had lived in a realm of objects, and sometimes I'd lie awake at night wherever Feliks and I happened to be sheltering ourselves and practice the memories of those things. I'd recite the details of Mama's dishware, the color of Zayde's telescope. I felt so sorry for the lost children because wherever they were, they had little to cling to in the way of reminiscences—this was a place where the candle had naught to flicker over. And then I saw the wishbone on the mantel followed by a procession of tiny ceramic angels. The sight of these objects comforted me—if I were a missing child of such origins, I would surely carry these tokens in my heart.

I asked the woman for her children's names, their faces. Instead of answering these simple questions, she poked me in the ribs, in the manner of one titillated by malnourishment, and insisted that I eat.

Feliks ate merrily, but I couldn't consume a thing. Eating bread required a talent that I no longer possessed. Raw rabbit—of that I was more deserving, as a jackal. But the civilized loaf of my past? Every piece of me had something to say about the fact that I did not deserve this bread if my sister no longer lived. What I am saying is this—I had no choice but to vomit on the table.

"What is wrong with you?" the woman cried, her voice entertaining a temperament quite different than the one we'd been introduced to. She raised her arm in the air. I could not tell if she was reaching for the hatchet on the wall or if she was settling for giving me a more standard beating, but I dove beneath the table and pulled Feliks down with me. "Vermin," she muttered, nabbing a broom from its corner. Thus equipped, she stalked across the floor and bent toward our hiding place. With the handle of her weapon, she issued blow after blow, striking us at our shoulders, our backs. We fled, overturning the table in our wake, and parted to different corners of the cottage. The woman closed in on Feliks's corner. Her broom handle flew about it in a chaotic fury, inflicting pain wherever it could on his body, and in a most disorganized fashion. Feliks shook, overcome by the reasonable fear of the mortal. But he did not cry out, not even when the broom handle landed on his spine with an audible crack. This crack made it clear: Now was the time to fulfill my vow of protection. My hand took up my hidden bread knife, and I crept behind the woman—she was so occupied with her abuse that my step escaped her notice.

But a knock at the door, merry and crisp, interrupted my quest.

The woman paused in her viciousness and her white eyes shifted; she crossed the room to the door and put an eye to the peephole. The sight it contained cheered her, and we understood why when we saw her company: a young man and a young woman in gray uniforms, thunderbolts riding their chests. The man introduced himself and the woman as heads of operations at the extermination camp of Chelmno. He was Heinrich and she was Fritzi.

"May you be blessed!" declared the woman, a nervousness riding the edge of her voice.

The man explained that Chelmno had been overtaken by the Russians. The camp officers had made a valiant effort to do away with the prisoners; to the very end, they'd risked themselves, even while fleeing, trying to leave no Jew alive. Unfortunately, the Jews, they were scattered all over the countryside. But Heinrich and

Fritzi and those who had been with the cause from the beginning were not going to let them scamper into hiding.

"I have two finds that will thrill you, then, I am sure," the woman said, ushering both of them inside. She gave us a nasty glance as we clung together, pressed into a single corner, shaking in our coats. She fluttered about, pouring tea and proudly displaying us to her guests.

"These two, they will not leave here alive. My husband and I killed Jews together for years. It was a holy obligation. You see that hatchet on the wall there? A good weapon against their skulls. I used to merely collect children for him, and he did the work, but now—he is gone."

The heads of Chelmno offered their condolences on her loss.

"Yes, he was a good man, so dedicated to the cause. Of course, finding Jews became more difficult over the years, due to the führer's efficiency! Once, we discovered a hiding place full of them in the woods, and from time to time, they even gave themselves directly to our hands, begging for food at the door. Collecting them is a much harder process without him. Now, if I am lucky enough to stumble upon them, I have to make them trust me. So I fill their bellies and then kill them while they sleep. You must understand my intentions—how else could I put these two at ease but with food?"

"A good plan," Heinrich said. "But such a terrible waste of bread!"

"I know," the woman lamented. "But I have no other way to gain their trust. I can't read, and we have no toys. I suppose I should have sung to them?" This last bit—it was tinged with sarcasm. I could tell that she was displeased by their reaction. She'd expected praise and thanks, an outsize appreciation of her cruelty. Strangely, this had not been offered.

Heinrich stalked over to our corner and squinted at us. I am not sure how much of me there was to see because I had so thoroughly curled myself into Feliks's side. We were just bear fur on jackal fur, trembling. The old woman joined Heinrich in looking at us.

"Maybe you will do the honors?" she said. "Or you could hold them down for me?" Her hand, mapped with green veins, clawed at the collar of my coat. I wondered why I was not running. Feliks tried to bolt, but in his fright, he tripped over his own feet and collapsed. Fritzi chuckled at his clumsiness, but somehow, her laughter did not strike me as wholly cruel. And then, oddly, the attentions of the heads of Chelmno turned to our hostess.

"You sing, you say?" Heinrich asked breezily.

"Yes," the woman said, her forehead crumpled at the detour of this question, and she rose up and smoothed her hands over her apron. "I was trained as a girl, in another life. What would you like to hear?"

"'Zog Nit Keyn Mol'" was the ready answer.

"This is a Yiddish song?" the woman wondered.

"You do not know it?" Fritzi asked, and, drawing her pistol and pointing it at the woman, she added, "It has become very popular in the camps and the ghettos."

Together, the two soldiers sang a song Feliks and I knew well, the partisan's song, the song of the Jewish resistance:

> *Never say that you have reached the very end*
> *When leaden skies a bitter future may portend;*
> *For sure the hour for which we yearn will yet arrive*
> *And our marching steps will thunder: we survive.*

And when they came to that last line, the old woman opened her mouth and began to squeak. Maybe it was an effort to appease them by joining them; we had no idea. We didn't hear a glimmer of her singing voice. The woman might have had a fine voice, one for the ages, one that would have pleased Hitler and Mengele both. Perhaps she was owed a far different life on the back of her musicality. I would never know. We never had a chance to hear her, because as soon as she opened her mouth a bullet buzzed into it, like a bee returning to a hive, and traveled through the back of her gray head. Upon its exit, the bullet performed a little jig into the wall and there it stayed, very still and quiet, as if it were aware that its work was done. The avengers coolly stepped over the old woman and loped around the scene they'd created, taking in the wishbone and the angels, their faces shiny with youth and excitement.

"You should finish eating," Fritzi said. Feliks rose, bumping his head on the table once again in his flurry, and reclaimed his seat. He tucked into his bread with zeal. I followed suit.

"Are those your real names?" Feliks asked.

No answer. They continued to stalk around the room. Fritzi had the attitude of someone at the intermission of a performance she was quite enjoying. Heinrich was equally mild. He took the third seat beside us at the table.

"May I?" Heinrich asked. He walked two fingers toward my plate, as if his hand were a person.

I pushed my plate to him. He didn't even notice that it was edged with my bile from my encounter with the bread. He was too busy admiring his partner. She took the cap from her head and it was then that I saw that her blond hair was coal-black at its roots. She cracked her knuckles as if preparing for a fight, and then she spat on the woman, on her clouded eyes, on her apron. Not a particle of her escaped this assault. Fritzi even took care to spit on the pool of blood on the floor. She spat and spat until her throat went dry, and then she eyed my milk, sniffed its whiteness suspiciously, and drank it down to the last drop. Her black eyes flashed above the rim of the cup like two ships traveling the horizon.

A great portion of difficulty with deathlessness is that you have an eternity to wonder who you have become. The death of a twin doubles this predicament. Though I would never cease being Pearl's half, I realized in that moment that I would not mind at all becoming someone like this dark-eyed girl avenger. My look for her must have been too admiring, because she turned from me with a grimace, as if to ward off my reverence, and declared, "You owe your life to no one."

I started to argue this point with her, because she didn't know Pearl, she had no notion that my life was owed entirely to my sister, but I could tell that the girl avenger didn't care to debate; she was too busy rummaging through drawers and cupboards and throwing objects in her sack. All the meat, all the cheese, all the bread. She took a box of cigarettes, handed one to the young man, and lit it for him while the corpse lay at their feet. Between them, there moved a feeling, something sweet and strangely innocent, and they didn't even seem to remember the corpse that they stood over until the girl avenger began to fuss with a spatter of blood that had lit upon Heinrich's breast pocket, bright as a boutonniere. Her fingertips lingered there, just for a moment, and then Heinrich returned to our table with a look of satisfaction and winked.

He ate some more, chewing quietly like a gentleman, and then he looked at Feliks and he looked at me. We did not need to show him our numbers. He knew who we were.

"And what will you do with your freedom now? You have plans for your young lives?"

He handed Feliks his cigarette and nodded for him to take a puff.

"My father the rabbi, he liked to say," Feliks began, attempting a puff before collapsing in a coughing fit. "He liked to say that the dead die so that the living may live. I did not understand that until now. In the case of our torturers, I think it more than applies."

Heinrich took this in appreciatively and raised his glass to the sentiment. Feliks had the look of one who had met his hero. I can't say that I felt any different. I wanted to tell the avenger my secret— I wanted him to know that while I appreciated that he had saved me, I hadn't required saving. It was only Feliks who was in danger. But all of the room was too absorbed with making plans.

"I assume you have had many torturers, though," Heinrich said. "It is quite ambitious to want to take them all on."

"We only want one," Feliks said. "Josef Mengele."

"You are too young to kill." This was the girl's opinion.

"I watched them open my brother," Feliks protested.

"It would ruin you, to kill. Look at us. We are ruined," the girl said.

I wanted to argue that they didn't appear ruined by any measure. To the contrary, they had a glow I hadn't seen since the war began. Feliks pressed on, determined to secure their blessing for our mission. "My brother was my twin," he said. "When the knife went through him, it went through me too."

"You are not strong enough." Fritzi clucked.

"That knife goes through me every day," Feliks said. "And still I live."

Heinrich and Fritzi exchanged glances. Will you think it strange if I say that love strung itself between them at every interval?

"Very well," Heinrich said. "Who can argue with the determination of the freed?"

So began our training. Heinrich spent the next hour schooling us on the proper use of a revolver. For my first shot, I took aim at the five ceramic figures on the woman's mantel. Even angels, you see, did not escape my fury, as they'd been quite content to observe our sufferings without intervention. The first angel splintered in the air, obedient. It knew what it had done. Then Feliks took a turn. We picked those angels off, one by one; we doomed their fragile souls to nothingness. After we'd each killed two angels, we turned to each other, both expecting a fight over this last murder. But all this shooting, it had a strangely civilizing effect.

"It is yours," we said in unison.

The avengers were frustrated by our manners. "On with it!" both cried.

And so Feliks took aim at the last remaining figure; he did so with great relish, and when the bullet struck this final angel, the avengers flung their sacks over their shoulders.

Of course, this made us wish that there were more ceramic angels, enough to keep killing forever, so that our new companions might remain with us, too intrigued by our executions to go. But they were determined to leave us. To soothe our distress, they addressed our need for better weaponry and treated us as peers in their mission. Fritzi said, quite airily, that we could keep the gun. Then Heinrich took the hatchet from the wall and handed it to me.

"It is a bit heavy," he said.

"We will manage it," Feliks said. He came up beside me and tested its edge with a fingertip, then he wasted not a minute in stealing it from my hands. "This hatchet didn't know what it was doing before. I will make it know its place now, in the heart of Mengele. And if not the heart, the guts. And if not the guts, the back."

I saw them mask their amusement. They were not successful in this. If they thought us a joke, though, they were fully committed to our comedy, because Fritzi bent toward me with a delicate smallness cupped in her hand. At first, I thought it was a pearl. But this misperception was due to my bad eye. Looking closer, I saw that it was a pill. A pill, Fritzi explained, that would kill one instantly after consumption. It was a pea-size ampule, walled with brown rubber, and its core was fatal: a concentrated solution of potassium cyanide. She deposited it into my hand, curled my fingers around it, and advised me to drop it into Mengele's drink before a toast, first crushing it to release its powers of brain-death and heart-stop.

I was overwhelmed by this. For death to seat itself in a pill held by my own hand! For vengeance to slip down Mengele's throat unawares! This pill had charms that I did not. It outranked my bread knives and, possibly, Feliks's new gun and hatchet. In my estimation, its powers matched the amber magic of Mengele's needle. I could only hope that handling it would not corrupt me as the needle had surely corrupted him.

I nudged the little poison pill along down one of the paths of my open palm, expecting it to unfurl like a beetle. It seemed like a living thing. On impulse, I put my ear to it—I had to decode its whisper. *I will always be strong enough,* it whispered. *In me, there rests a century's worth of justice.*

It had Pearl's voice, I thought. Or was it my voice? Did we still sound the same, now that she had taken on the duty of being dead, and I the role of the bereft?

I was about to ask the poison pill what it meant by this, but then I saw that everyone was watching me. Feliks blushed when I caught his eye, and he redirected his gaze, as if embarrassed by his association with me. The avengers chuckled freely at my haze.

But the corpse? Feliks asked what we were to do with it. That is for you to decide, they said hastily. They were eager to return to killing. From the doorway, we watched them enter a car, a sleek, boot-shiny thing with a Nazi flag waving pitifully from its stalk. Instead of a good-bye, they cried for revenge. *"Zemsta!"* they shouted, the word encased in blue puffs of cold that burst in midair, and then they sped away, and they no longer belonged to us but to the realm of Nazi impostors who sought justice at every opportunity.

We lingered in the doorway and then we remembered the body on the floor. We looked at the hearth and its severance of angels.

"What now?" Feliks wondered aloud, and he tossed a ceramic wing into the fire.

A shared thought moved between us. It flickered in him; it sparked in me. With the old woman's broom handle, we fed the flames to the curtains. The whole house was hungry for the fire; the flames moved over it in tongues, and sparks like birds fluoresced in the night. We watched it consume the rug, the table, the wreath, the wishbone. But as soon as it began to nibble at the woman's body, the flames crowning her temple, we fled without looking back. I was afraid of what I might turn into with such a sight in my mind. So I plodded on with Feliks and our new weapons; we stumbled through the snow, back to the barn that had initially promised comfort. The horse greeted us. He knew how we needed him. He saw the heaviness of our hatchet, our gun, our food—there was no way, his eye argued, that we could continue without him. After all the evil tours of his master, he owed us this, he insisted.

"He is old," Feliks said sorrowfully, stroking Horse's flank. "We would do better to eat him."

"Who would take care of the slaughter?" I wondered. Maybe Fritzi was right. Maybe we weren't suited to killing at all. I could not confront the fullness of the question, because what could I think of myself if I were unable to execute vengeance on my sister's behalf?

On Horse's back, we traveled on, tripping across all the fallen things of the forest, making our way toward a future we weren't sure wanted us at all.

CHAPTER SIXTEEN

Our Migration

Day One

I would reacquaint myself with what a day was as we traveled east toward Krakow. During the course of this journey, I'd see the sun and moon alternate, taking turns in their duties.

The sun took the hunger, the mile after mile, the swollen and weary feet. The moon took the nightmare, the unreliable road, the train tracks with the sudden ending, all that was no more. I was not sure which had the worse part of this deal. All I knew was that both shone.

"Look ahead," Twins' Father instructed. "I'll look everywhere else for you."

So we looked ahead, only ahead. But all I could see was what lay above me. First, I was swaddled in a woolen coat, and then a sheepskin rug, and then another rug, and these protections enwombed me up to my eyes. Above these layers was a sheet of cold air, a snap of frost, and this wintry skyscape was interrupted by my breath-clouds. I watched the little breath-clouds bear themselves into being and float up to Miri. She was most of the sky above me as she pushed my wheelbarrow.

Who needs a sun or a moon when you have Miri?

With myself below her, a dull, injured planet, she was determined to assume the responsibilities of both.

In our exodus, we were determined to make our leader proud, to conduct ourselves like the soldiers he treated us as. Some troops sing as they march, but we did not. In the beginning, we didn't speak, not even a whisper. All it took, we told ourselves, was attracting the interest of one bad man, or even a man who was not bad but fallen on desperate times. With these thoughts in mind we skittered down the demolished roads.

"How is she?" a boy was asking Miri. She nodded to me.

"Pearl, this is Peter. He is your friend. He has many friends. This is true, isn't it, Peter?"

Peter affirmed that it was. At least the part that we were friends, he and I. He didn't know about the other part. Most of his other friends were—

Miri would not let him finish that sentence. "Describe yourself, Peter," she instructed. "Leave nothing out."

Peter said his parents were dead. He was fourteen. At Auschwitz—

"Don't speak of it," Miri commanded. "Say who you are, what you do with yourself."

Peter swallowed audibly. He said that once, he had stolen a piano—

"This is Peter," Miri interrupted, her voice firm. "He is one of those people who is so smart that I'm not sure what he will do with himself. Always helping too," Miri added. "I'm sure you have faults, Peter? But I can't think of any right now."

I caught Peter staring at me with pity. Staring—that might be one of his faults, I thought.

"She is better than she should be," Miri told him. "Hardly remembers still."

"She must remember," he said in hushed disbelief.

"Put yourself in a cage," Miri tried to whisper, but I heard it all. "And then put the cage in a dark room. Once in a while, have a hand come through the top of the cage. Sometimes, the hand will give you food. Mere crumbs. Other times, the hand might shine a light or ring a bell or douse you with water—"

Miri could not bring herself to fully color the details of this scenario. I watched her grip on the handles tighten. Peter asked what the purpose of such an experiment might be.

Miri gave one explanation: Mengele wanted to know what might happen when identical twins, the ones most bonded to each other, experienced separation.

It was true, in its simplicity. But I could've given Peter another explanation: I was put in that cage because I loved too much. I had a great bond with Someone, a connection much envied by this man. He was cold and empty and he could not form attachments, not with his family or wife or children. All that coursed through him was ambition, and this empty man, like so many empty men— he was determined to make history. One day, he decided that the best way to do so was by discovering how two girls who loved each other too much might react to being parted. He tore us accordingly. I went to my cage, and she—I did not know. All I knew was that before he installed me in my cage, he hobbled me at my ankles, like an animal you want to keep but don't care to chase.

But just by my thinking of this story, the man's face began to follow me. I could not say a word. To rid me of that face, I asked after Someone's. If I could see hers, I thought, his would leave me.

"Were we identical?" I wondered aloud.

"The same," Miri confessed.

"Where is she now?" I asked. I knew of the death marches. I'd heard about the tumult when the Soviets entered, the many lives that had been snuffed out. And there was the unspeakable— Mengele. My Someone was extraordinary—surely he had known this; perhaps he'd taken her? There were so many terrible things that could have happened that it seemed foolish to hope that a good one might arise, but still, I thought Miri might present me with one.

Miri did not speak to any of these possibilities. But in her eyes, there surfaced a sadness, a bright and mournful quiver that said I was the sole survivor of my family. And then, as if she were desperate to change the subject, she enlisted Peter to join her in the task of telling me about things that were in the world we were returning to.

Miri listed places. Parks, she'd say. Open spaces where you could have a picnic, which was a meal taken outside. Museums, which were places with pictures and statues. Synagogues, places where you could assemble and study and pray. Peter focused on objects. Telescopes that showed you stars. Clocks that showed you time. Boats, which were vessels much like my wheelbarrow, but vessels that moved over water. Instruments, he said, and then added, as if this was supposed to have some meaning to me, pianos.

This was the second mention of this object. It did not have meaning to me. But he could repeat it all he wanted—I loved hearing Peter and Miri overexplain the world to me.

I could have corrected their overexplanations if I wanted to. But I did not, for good reasons.

For one, explaining the world gave them pleasure. For two, it made me whole.

I noticed, though, that neither attempted to explain a train station to me when we slunk onto an emptied platform that evening,

Twins' Father having decided that his little troop could go on no more. The other children slept, cocooned in rags, side by side, but I remained in my wheelbarrow, like an overgrown baby in a filthy cradle. Miri lay on the ground beside me, her hand raised to clutch the lip of the wheelbarrow even as she slept. The snores of my fellow children rose and fell, and I tried to pick out Peter's snores from the rest, but another sound took priority.

The nightmares of Twins' Father drifted past my ear as he defended himself in his sleep—who would be so foolish, he said, to create twins where there were none! Hearing his protest, I wondered if it was safe to dream, if there was any way to avoid this white-coated man as I slept. To make myself feel better, I renamed him. I called him No One.

"Good-bye, No One," I whispered. But the ache in my hobbled feet claimed that he would be with me always, even if I ever managed to take a step.

Day Two

Though morning came, it did not bring a train with it. Yet again, the sun had let us down. On foot and by wheelbarrow, we continued. And on this day, we began to sing a little, but haltingly, and with much argument as to which song we might sing.

None of Twins' Father's songs were appropriate, as he was a military man. Miri's songs were too serious and romantic and sorrowful. The only song we could agree on was "Raisins and Almonds," because all welcomed the thought of food. The lullaby sank us into our memories as we trod forward, and I felt as if I were not in the wheelbarrow at all but in Mama's lap. We sang:

Under Baby's cradle in the night
Stands a goat so soft and snowy white
The goat will go to the market
To bring you wonderful treats
He'll bring you raisins and almonds
Sleep, my little one, sleep.

On the third rendition of this song, we were swarmed by a dozen women, all of whom had been sitting against trees at the edge of a forest.

"Are you the last of Auschwitz?" a woman asked. "We are waiting for our children." Her face fell. "Should we wait? Is there reason to wait any longer?"

"There are others still," Twins' Father said, his voice hesitant.

The woman nodded at this information, receiving it with a guarded excitement.

"Children among them?"

"There are bound to be some at the camp yet—the Red Army has control. With me, there is thirty-five."

The woman was awed by this meager number; her face—I would never forget the wince of hope in it.

"Do you have a Hiram among yours? Little Russian boy."

"I do!" Twins' Father turned and addressed the crowd. "Hiram! To the front!"

A snippet of boy was pushed to the fore by the rest of the children. And then another small Hiram followed. The woman scanned both Hirams and then sank to her knees.

"Not mine," she whispered. "Not mine."

Everyone was too still for too long a time. It was as if all in our caravan were felled by the woman's grief and silence, and we were able to stir only when she rose and shook the dust from her skirts. She turned to resume her post at the tree trunk.

"Children, they draw other children, you know," Twins' Father said to her. "They see their own kind passing by, and they feel safe. You should join us. Maybe they will see us and find you."

"I leave a sign wherever I go," the woman said. She pointed to the tree trunk she'd been leaning upon. I assumed that she'd carved her child's name on it—I could not read it because the effects were indecipherable. Her knife must have been dull, her hand too shaky. "But it's not enough. Who is to say that they will even try to read it?"

I wanted to reassure her that children in captivity tend to read all they can. I wanted to tell her that as I traveled in my wheelbarrow, I was desperate to see any words on the horizon, words that could blot out the words of the gate I'd left behind two days before. I wished that the carved names could compete with the gate's power. I wished that they stood as upright and clear. Because the only fault with the woman's carved message was that it was tired and faint; every letter announced resignation.

Twins' Father was too good to critique the marks she left, as poor as they were, but he took his own knife and neatly reinscribed her message, and after he was finished with this task, he took up her pack and waved for her to join our procession.

"My friends," she wondered. "What of them?" And he looked at the women who'd returned to their trees, all of them so varied in age and suffering, and indicated that they should join us too. All he asked, he said, was that they record their facts on his list, to facilitate his communication with any authorities who might question our passage.

The women sprang from the trees and it was then that we saw that each trunk they had leaned against bore a message, a name, a plea. They would have covered the whole forest with the words if they were able. The face of Twins' Father—this had to be one of the few times I saw it become so overwhelmed with sadness while he was awake, outside the grip of one of his nightmares. But I watched him steady himself and pass about his list, and soon enough, the women fell to the rear of our march. They tried to mother us, and we did our best to resist their attentions politely.

We already had mothers, we wanted to say.

I thought of mine every second. I thought of her, and I begged her and Zayde to show me Someone's face. But neither responded. Had death forced them to abandon me? Or were they now so worried for my future that they couldn't bring themselves to rejoice in my survival? My fingers searched my face; they tried to know it so they could know Someone's too, but all they found were wounds, and two eyes that had seen too much.

We walked beside swarms of refugees. Face after face, body after body, all of them alive and searching, and not a single one of them mine. Was who I searched for already dead? I asked the sun and the sun told me to ask the moon—it claimed that the moon had taken the responsibility of answering inquiries with ugly potential. The sun was quite squirmy on this issue, I thought. It turned its back on me. And then a darkness lowered itself onto my eyes. The darkness was Peter's hand, attempting protection.

"Don't look!" Peter instructed. He was pushing my wheelbarrow at the time. I shrugged off the shield of his touch. I wanted to see what he saw. It sounded like horror. And there it was—

The body lay up the road, in a ditch. It was not a whole body.

"I told you not to look," Peter said.

"It is her," I whispered.

"It will never be her," Peter said. And to prove it, he defied Miri's instructions and veered close to the ditch so that I could peer at this corpse.

I did not know if it was male or female. I had no notion of its age—it was faceless and scalpless, and someone had cut off its legs so as to repossess its boots. That's what Peter told me when he saw that I refused to avert my gaze. He said that the Soviets had superior boots, and whenever the Wehrmacht found them, they took these boots for themselves in the most desecrating way possible.

"So, you see," he assured me, "it can't be your Someone. Your Someone would never have such boots."

I tried to find comfort in this. I could not. Did this mean that Someone was out in this winter with thin shoes?

"Look ahead, only ahead!" Twins' Father warned us.

"What does she look like?" I asked Peter as we left the body behind.

"She looked like you."

"I don't know what I look like."

"I bet you look like your mother," Peter said. "Do you remember what your mother looked like?"

I couldn't remember, not really. I decided that this would be another question to save for the moon. Its approach was nearing. I would ask it at any moment, even though I suspected that its answer was the same for all of us: We looked like death, one person after another; we were whittled and drawn, our eyes had sunk into our skulls, and the features that had once defined us had fled. Whether we would live long enough to be returned to our true selves—this seemed the greater question, and it followed me until we found our next shelter.

That night, we came upon a stone structure in the woods. It was too small to be a house and too large to be a shack. Inside, there was a constellation of teeth on the floor, and four narrow beds of marble. These marble beds had lids too, but only one remained closed. The other three gaped with empty blackness.

"Tombs," Twins' Father said before thinking better of it.

This structure was meant to house the dead. But three tombs had been overturned. Whether their disruption was the work of a fellow refugee or a pillager seeking to rob corpses of finery, we couldn't know. The yellow jawbone that had been tossed to the corner of the structure said nothing of this history. It sat, bereft of teeth, a silent, fossilized witness.

Though we were not its usual guests, this house of the dead did just as well to shelter the likes of us. Twins' Father cleared the emptied tombs of leaves and debris. They could fit a pair of children each. Peter stretched out on the lid of the fourth tomb and yawned. From the cradle of my barrow at the open door I watched the moon rise, answerless. Outside, a light snow fell and shook, like tiny white fists in the sky.

Day Three

A train ambled us a mere three miles toward Krakow. I looked out the window and saw roads filled with refugees, farmers returning home, Red Army soldiers slinking to unknowns. The frosty fields were scarred with the tread of tanks, and then we found ourselves in some untouched place, a row of intact farmhouses, as blocky and white as sugar cubes. Just as these farmhouses appeared, the tracks ended. We were forced to pile out, and as soon as all were accounted for by Twins' Father, we were confronted by a fierce pillar of a Soviet soldier, his face sweaty with enthusiasm.

"Pigs!" this soldier shouted. "Pigs!" He waved his arms about in a frightful manner. One of the arms held a long rifle. His face was gray and his eyes were like red-blue sores or loose buttons fallen from a coat. He kept repeating that word as our ragged troop advanced.

"Pigs!" he insisted. "Stop, pigs."

Twins' Father brought our procession to a halt. A rare fright overcame him—he looked as if he were about to fold in on himself and collapse. *Have we come so far just to end like this?* his face seemed to say. He began to approach the man with one hand outstretched, offering his list, which shook more in his grasp than any wind could shake it. But the soldier didn't even pause to look at the many names; he just raised his rifle to his shoulder and took aim. Children ducked behind smaller children. Miri's hands quivered atop the wheelbarrow handles. The eye of the soldier's rifle was our sole focus. We stared it down until the shot rang out, a shot that veered to the left of the road.

A pair of massive hogs, spotty beasts round as barrels, their snouts white with foam, were hurtling toward us, full of grunts and confrontations. The soldier's rifle struck them down, first at the forelegs, and then at the temples, and we watched their immense bodies sink to the snow with the moans and whimpers of tiny babies.

We were accustomed to blood-snow. The blood shouldn't have shocked our troop. But the confrontation dislodged something within us, because many began to cry in that silent way that captivity had taught them. The children shuddered and quaked, and then Sophia, a tiny four-year-old known for her queenly stores of dignity, collapsed in an uncharacteristic heap and wailed for us all. The soldier gave her a confused look—shouldn't a hungry girl be pleased by this bounty? He put down his gun, nodded at the kills in a self-congratulatory fashion, and shook Twins' Father's hand, and yes, we ate well that night, children and adults, without a thought to any law above the grumbles of our stomachs, but I could not forget the panic in those animals' eyes, not even as I comforted my hunger with their flesh.

I did not want to have a memory at all, not then.

As dusk fell on that third night, a farmer called to us from the side of the road. We saw him first by his beard, which bannered whitely in a peaceful manner. He offered us the shelter of his barn, and as eager as Twins' Father was for us to make our way to Krakow, which was rumored to be relatively intact, he could not pass up this offer, as his troops had begun to wilt. The Kleins moaned with every step, and the Borowskis complained of cold. Peter's toes had thrust through his shoes.

Most pressingly, David Herschlag was bent with illness—the abundant meal of pig had overwhelmed the poor boy's shrunken stomach. His skeletal body now bore a dangerous protrusion of abdomen, a belly so puffed that it looked to be filled with poison, and for the past ten miles, Twins' Father had taken to carrying David himself. So while our leader was always cautious in his approach to the peasants, he accepted the farmer's offer gladly.

We entered the sanctuary of a barn, occupied only by a speckled flock of chickens and their chicken smells and, here and there, a nest of eggs. It was warm and lively—a skinny rooster stalked to and fro and chased the busty hens. None of the chickens feared us because we still had the remains of the pigs to consume, and when our second hasty meal was finished—one that David could not take part in—Twins' Father shuffled off to a corner of the barn and attempted a fitful sleep while Miri traveled from one child to another, wrapping bandages and soothing feet and tipping canteens into mouths.

After each round, she returned to David, who lay on the straw, colored with illness, his brow thick with sweat. She looked at me with alarm and asked Peter to help her make a bed for the boy. Peter built a sturdy nest, covered it with my woolen blanket, and deposited David within it like a precious egg. David's face stirred with a smile—he stared up into the rafters at some sight we could not see, and Miri, she reprised "Raisins and Almonds."

Sleep, my little one, sleep.

Like a bird, she leaned over this nest, and lullabied the boy into something resembling peace.

Day Four

In the morning, we woke to the sight of Twins' Father kneeling. He bent down beside a form in the hay, and then he took up the form and shook it, as if he were trying to wake a person who refused to be roused. We could see, from the way Twins' Father held the boy, that David was no longer David, but a body.

"Zvi," Miri said. "You will frighten them." But she herself was undone by the loss. And Twins' Father would not lay him to rest. The boy appeared changed. I recognized him only by what killed him—the stomach that rose like a hill.

Miri put a hand to the man's shoulder; she tried to soothe him, but he would not be comforted. He fell to plucking feathers out of the still boy's hair, and he spoke as if he'd forgotten his troop entirely, as if the dead alone could hear him.

"I must have made at least a dozen sets of false twins," he said. He glanced at Miri for confirmation.

"Nineteen," she said quietly. "You made nineteen sets."

"Nineteen," Twins' Father repeated. "But David—and Aron— they were the first." Miri nodded as she removed her coat. She tried to cover the boy with it, but Twins' Father wouldn't loosen his hold on David.

"In the beginning, they had trouble with it—the lie. They were so young—only four and five years of age. And my Dutch is very poor—they spoke no other language—it was difficult to explain to them what I needed. But every morning, before roll call, I would remind them: You are twins! And I made them repeat, over and over again, the birthdate I fabricated for them, and the fact that Aron came first, and David second. The difference between them—I shrank a year into five minutes!"

He ran a finger over the bridge of the boy's freckled nose, in the manner of Mengele during one of his counts.

And this is where I tried not to listen to Twins' Father. I couldn't bear to hear him speak of the longing he'd had to be found out. How often, Twins' Father wept, had he wanted to corner Mengele in the laboratory and reveal, with a hiss, that the doctor's research had been tampered with, that his studies were jokes, idiocy easily undone by the lies of juveniles! He acknowledged that Mengele would have shot him on the spot. But it would have been better, he claimed, to die like that than to be doomed to save children only to watch them end like this.

Miri's face blanched and she tried to shoo us out. Her voice took on an odd pitch as she told us that we should go see if there were any chores we could do for the farmer. Not a peep arose from us. Even the chickens hushed. I tried to trace a path from the still-open eyes of the dead boy to the rafters above. What had he seen as he left us? I had never been dead, but I'd neared it enough to know that it was likely he had focused on that tiny fissure in the barn's ceiling, a crack just wide enough to accommodate the remote brilliance of a star.

"No need to lie to them," Twins' Father said stonily with a sudden, forced composure. The soldier in him had returned. He wiped his eyes on his sleeve and straightened the collar of David's torn sweater. "Let them say good-bye."

And so it was that we gathered around the little boy who had been felled by the food he'd long been denied. His face was not peaceful. Twins' Father gathered David into his arms and carried him out to the pasture, past all the frostbitten knots of fallow things, and though the soil was wintered and hard, it opened up to receive him. We filed past the brief grave, each bearing a stone.

But the farmer's wife interrupted our procession with her own ritual. She scattered poppy seeds on the grave. To feed the dead that come back disguised as birds, she said. I watched the poppy seeds turn in midair and settle in the ice. I didn't know why those seeds felt so dear to me, but I was lessened by the sight of their dark scatter. Already, the smallness of their lives were cold and stunted, and no sooner had our backs turned to depart than I heard the flap of a bird's wings slice the air, too eager to seize upon the abundance wrought by David's death.

In the bed of the farmer's truck, the troop propped themselves against the wooden slats. Red-eyed, Twins' Father surveyed us and consulted his list, dragging his finger down the weathered paper.

We waved good-bye to the farmer's wife, who stood with the bag of poppy seeds at her side, and to the six mothers, who had decided to linger at the farm, convinced that their children were mere steps behind even as the rest of their group had fractured, each of them wandering off on her own desperate quest. Yet still they searched the faces in the back of the truck, as if they had yet to accept that their loved ones were not among us.

Then the truck roared to life, a horn honked, and as we trundled off toward Krakow, I heard Miri say David's name into the wind—she said it softly, as if he could hear her where he lay, so deaf and cold beneath the earth.

"Forgive me!" I heard her whisper.

Miri's plea was puzzling—she was not responsible for David's death. She had cared for him to the end. But as mysterious as it was, it struck something inside of me.

The whole world might be obsessed with revenge.

But for my part—I knew I wanted to forgive. My tormentor would never ask for my forgiveness—this was certain—but I knew it might be the only true power I had left, a means to spare myself his grasp, the one that I felt close on me every morning when I woke. And if I could do this, if I took on this duty of forgiveness—maybe my Someone would return to me. Or at least maybe I would stop seeing my Someone's face on every refugee we passed, the dead and the living both.

CHAPTER SEVENTEEN

The Ruins Watch Over Us

Horse uplifted us. Mile after mile, we burdened this bony hero. In witnessing his enduring gallop, so unlikely for such a hungry animal, one could only believe that he, too, longed for the holy murder of Josef Mengele. But Warsaw would not be easily reached.

After four days of travel, we encountered roads thick with tanks and found ourselves turned about, choiceless, and pressed into Poznan. This had been Zayde's city; he had taught at the university. Poznan, he liked to declare, was a jewel of scholarly devotion, a maker of great minds, of believers of art. But violence seemed the only lesson we might learn here now. The Wehrmacht stalked through the city, its streets silent but for the warning rattle of their gunfire and the echoes of their songs, rowdy bits of verse that surfaced as they braced themselves for the Russian advance.

Fearing that these soldiers might tire of their music and seek to amuse themselves with the torture of Horse and two refugees, we undertook the utmost stealth in our passage. Feliks took custody of our sacks, and I led Horse by his bridle. Ducking down a street, its lampposts strewn about like uprooted weeds, we found our path interrupted not by a menace of gray uniforms but by a beggar whose palm fell open at the sight of us.

That anyone might see us as prosperous enough to approach for food or coins seemed a wonder. But we decided to strike a deal. Some bread for the date, Feliks offered.

"February," said the beggar. He said it could be the third day, it could be the fourth. I wanted to ask for our heel of bread back. "All you need to really know is that the Russians are coming. Leave now. This is my advice. And look," he continued, biting into the bread. "I am not even charging you extra for this wisdom!" Having imparted this information, he limped off into the evening, leaving us to wonder at the sight that loomed behind us.

There it was, the old museum: a collapse of walls, a shudder of brick, a stagger of columns. The remaining windows were pocked and rent, glassy veils. The grand doors had fallen in surrender, and through the jagged entrances in the facade, I glimpsed the museum's devastated interior. It appeared as if there was nothing to see but ruin. But when I looked still further, into my own memory, I saw the museum restored, its halls traversed by Zayde and Pearl while I lagged behind. I could see my seven-year-old sister pause on tiptoe before a painting while Zayde taught her what perspective meant.

Memory, it drove me into the museum.

I lied to myself and to Feliks, I said that we could find supplies in that building—in truth, this mattered little to me; what mattered was that I thought Zayde would be by my side if I entered. I might hear his whistle. I might smell the mothballs of his coat.

So we sat upon Horse's back, our heads held high, for entry into this wasteland. Horse picked his way delicately up the crumbled stairs, his white flanks flashing silver in the evening light. On the fragmented marble of the threshold, his front hooves slipped—he threatened to founder, his whinny draped the devastated foyer with echoes, and then, as Horse always did, he pressed on.

There should have been paintings for us to see. Pictures of things real and not real, of landscapes and people. But in that museum, we could find only a portrait of ruin. We watched a hurricane of black pigeons swoop through a hole in the eaves. The floor opened wide and threatened to swallow us. Where it didn't open, it hosted black pools of water. Light winced across the crumbled walls; rats philosophized from their holes.

"Blessed are the rats, for they at least believe in blood," Feliks intoned. "That's what my father the rabbi would have said."

As if angered by this blessing, the theories of the rats increased in volume.

"Turn back." Feliks shuddered. "That's what my brother would say. Turn back!"

But I couldn't turn back, because even in the shambles, I had this treasure: I was surrounded by what Zayde had loved. Though devastated, the museum still spoke of Zayde's compassionate logic, his will, his science, all that he loved. And what Zayde had loved, they could not smash or burn or plunder. What he had loved was my tradition.

And as we moved through the savage disarray, we kept a vigilant watch. Horse's eyes flickered in the dark. We let our path be informed by traces of brass, coins that pillagers had left behind, snippets of wire. Bits of antiquity minnowed among the gravel that peppered the floors, and we soon found ourselves in a room where a chandelier swung. Horse startled us by shattering a teacup beneath his foot, and we saw then that we were in a grand tearoom, the very kind we'd heard our pale friend say she longed to visit as a true lady, before Taube snapped her neck.

This ruin reminded us like no other ruin had—we still lived while our friend did not. With respect to her loss, we climbed down from Horse to pay tribute.

"I would like to buy another day for the lovely Bruna," Feliks whispered to the sky.

The wind offered nothing in reply.

"I don't accept your answer," he said, his voice dangerously veering from its whisper. "She was the bravest soul in all of Poland, and you let the world take her down."

He leaped onto a pedestal bereft of its statuary, and on this surface he posed and flexed and shook his fist at the God he believed in. Looking at this monument he'd made to our anger, I saw that we were children still, but mercenary children, half-murdered troublers. I had to wonder what such a child looked like. I stalked about the velvets of this tearoom looking for some opportune reflection. But the darkness was unrelenting; the shards of glass said nothing about appearances at all. I remarked on the blackness of this evening to Feliks but received no answer. Seeing that he had left his pedestal, I looked about in a panic. Whenever Feliks left my sight, even for a moment, all feeling but loss fled me. Distraught, I searched in the dimness for a single hair of his bear-fur coat.

This is when I felt a tap at my back. The touch was musical; it clinked.

And when I turned, it was to the sight of a silver fist, brandished high by an armored individual. It lingered above my head; its enmeshed fingers stabbed the sky. In the confusion of this darkness, I was certain that this was a warrior who was aware of my dealings with Mengele. I could tell by this warrior's bearing that he or she had a great love of justice and an awareness of my accidental crimes.

In my bewilderment, it didn't occur to me to call for Feliks. It didn't even occur to me to mount any defense on my behalf. I could've pointed to my greater scheme, my plans to thwart Mengele, my assumption that Pearl, too, would benefit from the needle.

Instead, I fell to my knees in the rubble, and I bent low. I made my neck vulnerable and ready for penalty. So bowed, I begged this warrior to punish me, to deliver me the greatest judgment of all, if he were able. I'd be happier dead, I declared, so long as I could be near my sister. I would bring death to myself, I swore, if I could!

"But I could never kill you!" the warrior proclaimed. He had a terribly pitchy voice for such a fearsome spectacle. It was the unmistakable squeak of Feliks. How could it be—was I so desperate to be delivered from my life that I mistook my gentle friend, clad in pilfered armor, for some divine hand of vengeance?

"Why would you make such a joke?" Feliks queried. "After all that we have endured! I understand your need for humor. But this?" He shook his silver head dolefully.

"I am not funny," I agreed.

Fortunately, he was too enraptured with his latest acquisition to pursue this further. He turned so I could appreciate his appearance as one of the old Polish winged hussars, but the armor was creaky and ill-fitting. The torso piece swung and gaped over his bear-fur coat, and he had only to take a step before the silver piece fastened at his legs loosened and fell with a piteous clink. Still, my friend desired praise for his ferocity.

Naturally, I informed him that he looked a grand figure. If I were a Nazi, I said, I'd take one glance and flee. To this, he thrilled. I wished that I could have shared his delight, but I felt only anguish. Spying my mood, Feliks did his best to cheer me with another find from the depths of the rubble. In the air, he raised a tiny flask. I caught it up greedily and took a sip. The embered sensation in my throat made it known: this was not water.

"Vodka," Feliks declared, repossessing the flask. "Good for bartering, but we could use some now." He attempted a tipple and I snatched it away. But just as my hand closed on the flask, I heard Zayde.

To Pearl! Zayde toasted. *Keeper of time and memory!*

I had to honor this toast. So I let Feliks take a swig on my behalf, but he was not familiar with swigs. He knew only indulgence, and drink promptly overtook the emptiness of his stomach. He staggered about like a tin fool, then collapsed in a silver heap. For a moment, it appeared as if I would have to drag him up. But then he peeled the armor off in disgust and swung himself up onto the back of Horse, who looked askance at his tipsy burden.

"You aren't fit to ride," I protested, but he would have none of it.

And what could we do but ride? The soldiers patrolling the streets outside cared nothing for the condition of a thirteen-year-old boy.

"Fine," I conceded, "let us go now."

With the ruins behind, distant villages floated before us. On horseback, we picked our way across the puddles of black pocking the snow, Horse sinking midstep into the mud. The same sky that had witnessed our imprisonment winked innocently above us. Such a naive sky seemed at risk of forgetting its involvement with our dead. Would it use the alibi of a cloud to deny all that it had seen? I hoped it would not. But doubt was beginning to overtake me. We were hungry, tired, lost—only bereavement bent us forward as we traveled on. We were forced by the Russian tanks advancing into Poznan to go in any direction available to us; we were turned and turned about in our passage toward the Warsaw Zoo, and as we rode, we begged our respective authorities—God for Feliks, fate for me—for the strength to end the man who'd lured such a wild hatred into our hearts.

CHAPTER EIGHTEEN

Partings

We arrived in Krakow and wandered through the city; we went from house to house. Here and there you'd see a sudden flutter of curtains—you could see fingers appear at the edge of the lace, and it was as if every adult had turned into a child in a game of hide-and-seek. Many did not want to look at us at all. Like the girl I saw—she was sitting before a wall papered with flowers and she was reading a book. I wanted to read a book someday. I wanted to read one that would tell me who I had been before my cage.

And on that someday, I wanted Miri beside me as I read. But since she'd spent the ride to Krakow begging for forgiveness beneath her breath, I began to wonder if her sadness might thwart the future I'd envisioned for us.

"It is not as bad as it could be" was Twins' Father's assessment of Krakow. He looked to Miri as if expecting agreement. None came. Her lips remained set with a silent dismay as we walked along the strings of houses and experienced a series of closed doors. Through the streets, we saw women chased by Russian soldiers, saw them taken into alleys, pressed into walls. We did not see them emerge. We saw beggars approach us for food and curse us when we said we had none. Most notably, we saw a man watching us from a bench outside a clock shop. He sat with a little book to write in and the day's newspaper, drinking coffee and listening to a woman whose distraught gestures made her appear as if she was petitioning for help. She was not the only one. There was a line of widows and refugees and townspeople, six or so, all waiting to speak to this figure. But when he saw the tattered assembly of us, he leaped up from his chair and dashed to Twins' Father's side to ask after our origins.

He was young, this man, but his face was old, windburned, and battered, as if he'd lived his whole life outdoors, hunting and hiding. In him, there was the presence of a soldier, but a soldier far different than Twins' Father. In his gaze, there was protective instinct—it was as if we had become his family simply by entering his city. Later, we would learn that he was deeply involved with the Bricha, the underground movement that helped Jews flee to other, safer lands. But at that moment, we knew only that this man named Jakub was determined for us to take shelter in the abandoned house adjacent to his own, a structure with boarded windows whose gray dreariness reminded one of a rotten tooth.

"I know its owners will not return," he insisted. Twins' Father hesitated at the door, noting the blank space where the mezuzah should have been, the paint there so bright and unfaded, but Jakub said, Don't be foolish, and he flung the door wide so that we had no choice but to enter.

So we had an abandoned house to sleep in and it had all four walls and a roof that leaked. Everywhere we looked, we saw the flight of the former inhabitants. The bookshelves were upended, and a woman's nightgown sat in a pale blue puddle in the sink. A trio of bricks had been pulled from the wall, revealing a secret compartment. A sheet of paper sat at the kitchen table alongside a pen, but only a salutation adorned it.

After we had gratefully surveyed the interior, dinner was announced, and Twins' Father doled out beets from a lone, mammoth jar in the pantry. We passed the beets around, each taking a bite, our hands pinked, our mouths encircled by their pickled blush. Miri alone refused. Outside, snowfall resumed, but for once, this seemed a celebratory frost. As we ate and passed around a single cup of water, the children made note of more absences.

"No Ox," they toasted. "No rats, no blocks, no gates, no needles!"

It was my turn. After the silence of my cage, I would never truly be comfortable with speech, but in that moment, the words found me. I don't know how they found me, but they were my *zayde*'s, and when they occurred to me, they fell as bright and easy as snowfall.

To the return of Someone! I toasted.

Miri raised her glass to me, but the smile that accompanied this gesture was wan and unconvincing. I wondered if she feared abandonment. Was she worried that when I found Someone, I would have no need of her?

I slept in fits and starts, always waking to the question of Miri's sadness. And whenever I woke, I saw that she hadn't retired at all; she sat in her chair, hands folded, utterly still. Seeing this, I realized that it was not Miri who had to fear abandonment, but myself.

Morning altered our borrowed house and drew my attention to a cage in the corner of the room. Its little wire door was open, hanging listlessly from a single hinge. The emptiness of that cage, the thought of the bird's flight, even if it escaped only to founder—it put a dream of motion in me. I wanted a pair of crutches. To move on my own, uncarried, toward the future I believed possible.

I told Miri about this fantasy as she thrust on her coat and readied to step out into the city. She warned me of the scarcity of crutches but said that she would inquire at the hospital. Already, she was embedded in new duties in Krakow, as was Twins' Father. He held a hushed meeting with Jakub at the kitchen table, one I strained to overhear while the other children ran up and down the stairs and romped in the rooms above.

Sometimes, it is fortunate to be a cripple. By not playing with the others, I learned our fate. Feigning interest in the birdcage, I spied as Twins' Father explained his sorrows.

Twins' Father was concerned about a woman. He said that she had witnessed the unimaginable, she had saved all she could, and now—she could not emerge from this unaltered, fully alive. He knew this because it was true for himself too.

Jakub paused before answering, thoughtful, as if he knew this matter too well. The burden saved you, he finally said, until you had a moment to examine it, to feel, for once, its full weight.

I think Twins' Father agreed. But his voice was too small for me to hear.

Jakub assured Twins' Father that the only thing greater than his devotion was the needs of the children. And then he gave a recommendation, one that put the identities of all in this conversation into sudden relief: The twins, he said hesitantly, should be put into the custody of the Red Cross. Only then could they flourish and the adults recover.

She will never leave them, Twins' Father replied, his voice hollowed by dread. I knew he spoke for himself too. Jakub urged him to reconsider. Thirty-four children, he said, all of them on the edge of one suffering or another. Jakub vowed to look in on us in Krakow and to send word to our guardians. They won't be forgotten, he swore.

But Miri, I thought. She is the forgotten one. Without us, she would not continue. Had no one seen the change in her since we'd lessened from thirty-five to thirty-four?

If this separation were to come to pass, I thought, I would re-member Miri. First, I would save myself with a pair of crutches. Then I would save her from her sadness.

I did not tell the others what I'd heard. The children had enough concerns. Already, they had an obligation to experience freedom. This was not as simple as one might think. Fresh from our journey, we still had leagues of hesitations, stores of panic. Even a pleasant laugh floating down from a window was enough to make us startle. But we were determined to make something of our first days in Krakow, so we spent the afternoon riding the trolley, flashing our numbers at the conductor for free rides. The townspeople were charmed by us—never before had they seen so many children who matched. Peter and Sophia and me, we were the lone strays.

Peter carted my wheelbarrow on and off the trolley, onto street corners and into shops, so we could inquire after crutches together. He swore he'd find a pair, and as we searched, I tried to tell him that it was Miri who truly needed help, because we would soon be leaving her. But I could not find the words to say this. Soon enough, I realized I didn't need to.

Because when we arrived at our adopted home, it was to the sight of a dim-eyed Miri seated in a chair, an empty cup cradled be-tween her hands. Twins' Father stood at the hearth and instructed us to gather round; he counted us, consulted his ever-present list, and when he said that it was time to discuss the future, all manners of plans tumbled out. The children spoke of reunions with their families, their schoolmates, their houses.

"You may return," Twins' Father warned, "but your house may no longer be your house. Your country may not be your country. Your belongings—they may belong to someone else."

As he spoke, he looked at Miri, as if expecting her to refute what he said. But she merely stared into her cup, as if she might find some other solution to our plight at its bottom.

"The Red Cross is better equipped to take care of you," Twins' Father said, and he began to speak of the arrangements, but the younger ones drowned him out with protest—they clambered over Miri in her chair, surrounding her with pleas, each tripping over the other in distress. She dipped her face into the sleeve of her coat as if to shut them out.

The older ones began to protest too but thought better of it and exchanged their outcries for a single question: When? they wondered.

The answer: four days.

Twins' Father consulted with each of us in turn. He informed Sophia that he would not leave her without a new coat; he assured the Blaus that they would not be separated. All of his reassurances appeared routine—but then, ever so softly, I heard him tell Peter that their plans for Krnov had been solidified. Peter caught sight of my confusion.

"A friend of my aunt's," he explained dully. "She says that she will be my mother now. She lives in Krnov. Twins' Father is going to take me there, on his way to Brno."

I was not the only one to be surprised by this news.

"How did you manage it?" the others asked. "Was it a trick? How did you fool this woman into wanting you?"

I could have told them: It was too easy to like Peter. He gave and fought and searched—who would not want his company? That was what I wanted to say to the other children, who now appeared to regard him as a mystery and—judging by their expressions, which ranged from light scowls to outright disdain—one to be resented. When I asked him why they were so angry, Peter told me that I should be angry too. A family was a rare thing these days, he said.

I knew Peter had given me much. Now that I knew we would be parted, I wanted to give him something too. But words were all I had. So I told him that I had ten memories. Of those, there were six that I really wanted to have. So, really, I had six memories. The first was Dr. Miri's face. The second was Peter pushing my wheelbarrow. The third was the gates, but only the gates in my hindsight as we left. The fourth was Peter throwing a stone at those gates. The fifth was Peter scouring the streets of Krakow for a crutch. The sixth wasn't really memory at all, it was more of a longing for a memory, and it was my Someone.

"You are in three of those," I pointed out.

He responded to this by increasing our search for a crutch. In our remaining days, we traveled up and down the streets in search of a pair, knocking on doors, asking passersby, inquiring at the hospital. We also checked with Jakub.

"Do you have any crutches?" I asked him on the first day of our search.

"Not crutches, but onions," he said, handing Peter a pair of yellow globes. One could see that refusing us anything pained him greatly.

That night, at our abandoned house, I put the onions in a soup pot and watched their yellow faces bob and revolve with unending optimism. I took their sunniness as a sign—by dawn, I thought, Jakub would have crutches for me.

And then, the following morning—

"Here for food, are you?" he ventured jovially.

No, we said. We thanked him for the soup. And did he have any crutches?

"I don't," he said, regretful. "But will you take this?" He folded a blanket into my wheelbarrow. I took its warmth as a sign—by dawn, I thought, I will have crutches.

But on the third day, Jakub hung his head at the sight of our approach. He couldn't bear to say no to me, so I did not ask. Grateful for our lack of inquiry, Jakub placed a pocketknife in my hands.

"That is all that I have to give," he said sorrowfully. We thanked him and then wheeled away. I studied the pocketknife. Peter saw my disappointment.

"Good for a trade," he assured me.

Back at the stoop of our abandoned house, I etched images over the frosty windowpane at the entry with my fingertip. I etched the image of one crutch, and then another, and as soon as I'd completed the second, a storm arose, erasing all I'd imagined.

I decided not to take anything as a sign anymore.

It was my responsibility—not fate's—to ensure that I was strong enough to look after Miri, even if I remained within my wheelbarrow for all my days.

When I wasn't with Peter, I was with Miri, who spent her mornings making rounds of the streets of Krakow. I was her attending nurse, or so she told me. Really, she just couldn't bear to leave me alone. Together, we went to the Red Cross and moved among the many cots. She knew that I was perpetually on the lookout for crutches, but she was determined to make me useful too, so I sat and wound bandages under her supervision. This work was good for me. But my guardian benefited even more, because Miri forgot her pain while surrounded by the pain of others. In tending to them, she was renewed. It was women that we looked after, for the most part, because not every soldier entrusted with the welfare of Krakow had been worthy of this task. Women and young women and girls that war had made women of too soon. I looked at them and wondered: Would they have appreciated the protection of my cage?

And every afternoon, when another doctor relieved Miri from her post, she took me to the station. There, we looked for a name. The name of Miri's sister. Or for Miri's name—in case Ibi was looking for her. The station wall was thick with names, but Ibi's was not there; she was not looking for Miri. Name upon name, letter after letter, plea after plea, and not a single one addressed to us. Until one afternoon, the day before the grand parting, Miri seized upon a flutter of paper and said that we owed the writer a visit. Her hand shook as she held this note, and her eyes were so overwhelmed with tears that it seemed a miracle to me that she could read it at all. All I could spy was the flash of an address. I wanted to inquire after the note's full contents, but Miri's demeanor told me enough: this was not a happy discovery but an obligation, and she steered me toward the address with dread.

In answer to our knock, a scarfed head poked out of the doorway. The woman's mouth was jam red and she had curls to match—a colorful person, to be sure, and behind her form, we could spy glimpses of a room that was once very fine, a parlor with gilt paper and furniture whose shimmer had been dulled by age and neglect.

The woman squinted at us curiously, and just as she was about to address us, a drunken man tripped down the steps with promises to return for fun the next day. That was how we knew this was not an ordinary house. Miri turned away, but the woman slipped down the steps and clasped the doctor's shoulders. With warmth, she studied my guardian.

"Very pretty," the woman said approvingly. "And I see you have a daughter to feed." She regarded me with pity. "But I'm afraid I have too many girls already—"

"I'm so sorry," Miri said to the woman. "We are in quite the wrong place."

She glanced down at the paper, and the woman took note of it too. Her eyes went wide with recognition. "If these names mean anything to you"—and she took the slip of paper gravely from Miri's hands—"then you are precious. We must speak." Introducing herself as Gabriella, she gestured for us to enter. "Do not worry," she said, spying Miri's dubious expression. "Nothing untoward for your daughter to see. Just a matron and her girls and a cup of tea."

So we followed the woman up the stairs, through the parlor, and into the kitchen, where a dour teenager, her limbs spotty with bruises, glared at Miri as if she believed her to be an old enemy. With a mocking bow, she pulled out a chair for my guardian.

"Away with you, Eugenia!" our hostess ordered, bewildered by this display, and the girl fled to join a trio lounging on the stairs, but not before casting a final look of disgust at Miri.

In the sweetly perfumed kitchen, Gabriella's softness increased; she lifted me from the wheelbarrow and onto a chair as if she performed this task every day of her life. Then she placed the note on the kitchen table and smoothed it lovingly with her hand, as if doing so achieved some proximity not just to the names, but to their owners.

"I left the note for my nieces," she said. "I do not expect their mother to be alive. She was lame, like your girl. I know that the cripples did not last."

Miri asked the woman if she had been at Auschwitz.

"I was in hiding here," Gabriella said. "This place—it was not my choice. I used to be a dressmaker. But who needs pretty dresses in war? What I know of Auschwitz I learned from my girls. Two of them came here from . . . the Puff, I think they called it."

Miri glanced at the girls on the stairs, the frills of their pastel underthings lending them the look of half-dressed parakeets. I knew she searched for Ibi. She did not find her.

"I have heard that twins were precious at Auschwitz. From Eugenia." She indicated the bruised teenager, whose sulkiness had yet to abate. "She insisted there could be hope if one was a twin. I assumed my nieces to be dead even as I left that note. But now you come here with their names in your hand—and you would not bring bad news?"

I thought Miri's silence strange. It seemed simple enough to reveal herself as the guardian of Auschwitz's twins, a caretaker who was losing pieces of herself to the stress of keeping them whole. But she said nothing. I took this as a chance to act on her behalf. And so, with an adult tone borrowed from my caretaker, I asked Gabriella her nieces' names.

"Esfir and Nina," the woman said, her voice wistful. Again, she caressed the note.

Esfir and Nina—these names brought back the memory of my first night in the Zoo. I thought of them dragging a dead girl from our bunk and stealing her clothes.

"Resourceful girls," Miri said carefully. "I was their doctor."

Gabriella was beautiful in this renewal of her hope. Her eyes shone; her cheeks pinked.

"Where are they now? Can I see them?" Her gaze darted about the house, taking in all that would have to change to make this place into environs befitting the two refugees.

Before Miri could say a word, Eugenia began to speak.

"A doctor in Auschwitz was not a doctor at all," she declared angrily. "Ask her who she answered to. Ask her what she did."

Bewildered by this outburst, Gabriella looked at Miri, whose eyes were needlessly lit with shame. Gabriella reached out her hand and tried to take the doctor's in it, as if the touch might prompt better news. Miri responded to this gesture with a start. Her tears were soundless, and they slid from eye to lips without the accompaniment of any expression at all. But in number, these tears—I have never seen them matched. One followed the other; they multiplied themselves; they became innumerable. I wondered how I might defend Miri.

And then the words presented themselves to me. At the time, they seemed to arise from a sweet nowhere, some place within me that I didn't know I had. I told Gabriella that I'd known her nieces too. They were good girls, kind girls, and their last act had been a brave one of which any auntie could be proud. I said that no sooner had the girls found themselves in the Zoo than they began to plot as to how to thwart the death-doctor. These plans consumed them down to the second. Always, they were sly, sidling up to him like little foxes and applying thick layers of flattery to his willing ego. They pretended to like what he liked, to think what he thought, and when they had him alone in a vulnerable moment, isolated within the confines of a car, they grasped the hilts of their bread knives, which were secreted in their pockets, and even though this plan proved unsuccessful, they had been more alive than anyone in that moment, and their plots to kill the doctor—however naive, however foolish—were the stuff of legend. Every day, I said, I thought of them. I thought of them with such an intensity that they often merged into a single person and I thought of this person as if she were my own heart.

Gabriella kissed the top of my head and held me tight; her embrace was such that I knew, in our closeness, that she imagined me into the girls she had lost. Her touch carried heartbreak, but her voice held only resolve.

"You have made life livable," she whispered. I thought her grip might never ease, but she suddenly released me, and she walked across the room and then back, as if proving to herself that she could continue, and then an idea must have seized her because she darted to a closet by the entry. Out of it tumbled all manner of things: scarves, umbrellas, hats, even the tuft of a toupee. She sifted through this pile, reached to the back of the closet, and, triumphant, she presented to me what no one else in Krakow could.

"Left by a soldier," she said. "A shrimp of a boy, and so ill—he is not coming back. Better for you to have these than some drunken lout!"

Though old, these crutches made me new. They made a version of me that could walk. Or at least, one that could do more than stumble. I could sidle a crutch forward and swing my feet before me, and even within a few steps, I saw the potential of what I might do. That I might remain broken, but I could be swift and broken, adaptable and broken, able and broken.

With these crutches at my sides, I could take better care of Miri.

As we left that place, Miri asked me where I'd summoned such a story, about plots and vengeance and dreaming this most impossible dream of Mengele's death, and I told her that it was something imprinted within me, and while I couldn't locate its origin, I knew it to be real, or half-real, or at least the warmth that ran through me—so intense that it cast a shadow I could pretend into family—felt realer than anything.

"Remember that," she advised me. And so, it was official: this became my first true memory of my sister, the twin that I'd once had.

On our final morning I woke to the sun peering through the cracks in the boarded windows, tossing its ribbons over the rows of sleeping children on the floor, all of us cocooned in blankets and rags. Sophia lay on my left, snoring mightily, her arms flung over my chest. My crutches were on my right, and seeing them, I remembered: I could go anywhere by myself, and take Miri with me.

But on that day, they would try to turn me over to the Red Cross.

As soon as I opened my eyes, I saw the preparations for our parting. Miri and Twins' Father, they were huddled on the kitchen floor, a pile of our many shoes between them. Miri was stuffing the holes with paper, and Twins' Father was binding them with twine. Shoe after shoe they mended in silence, and with hands that shook, both unsteadied by the nearing good-bye. I saw Miri glance at the packs stationed by the door, one for Peter, another for Twins' Father. She studied them as if she was trying to gather courage to speak, and then she addressed Twins' Father, her face downturned, her eyes still low.

"You never questioned my actions, Zvi. Why was this? The others—I would hear stories about myself, what I had done. And the stories, they follow me, even now."

She sealed the shoe's injury shut, tied the twine in a final knot.

"You were only ever good," he said simply. He faced her as he spoke, seemingly hoping that she might welcome this truth, and when she did not, he bent to arrange the mended shoes in rows, as if this could put matters to rights. But when he turned his back, Miri took the opportunity to slip past him, to the door. Spying my wakefulness, she gestured for me to join her, but Twins' Father was not willing to forgo the formality of a farewell. Looking up from the rows of shoes, he gave her the only one the ex-doctor might accept.

"Your children will miss you," he said.

Miri's eyes said that she believed him.

And as I hobbled out on my crutches, I saw Peter's head rise from where he slept, at the crackle of the fireplace, saw the hair ruffled on the back of his scalp. He looked at me in the haze of a partial dream. I had tried to prepare for this good-bye. "When we see each other again," I said, but I couldn't complete the sentence the way I wanted to. I couldn't say: *It will be better, I will be walking, you will be well, all will be found, we won't be imprisoned or without a country, we won't be hunted or starving, we won't be witnesses to pain.*

I couldn't finish that sentence, not then.

Twenty years later, I would have a chance to finish, but there was no need for it. We would be grown adults, waiting in a courtyard in Frankfurt. Peter would show me pictures of his wife, the one who understood why he bolted in the night following the ring of the telephone, why he kept boxes stacked beneath the bed filled with speculations as to the whereabouts of a criminal more slippery than most, a man whose initial escape from Auschwitz led to a transfer to Gross-Rosen, and then a flight into Rosenheim, where he found work as a farmhand, separating the good potatoes from the bad potatoes, putting them into neat little piles for the farmer's inspection, before settling into the ease of his final hideout in Brazil, where he wrote his memoirs and listened to music and swam in the sea.

But this is not about that man, as much as he would have liked it to be.

This is about Peter. As Miri had predicted, he was good at many things, so many that he found himself a bit lost after the war. He ran away from his guardian's custody and traveled; he roamed from country to country as if he would never shed the role of a messenger, a delivery boy, but his travels stopped when a woman loved him and married him, despite her family's warnings that he was damaged beyond repair, that she should not be surprised when their children were stillborn or, worse, born with mutations issued by the doctor's hands. But they had children. Two boys. They were healthy and beautiful; you could see their father in their faces. I could have studied that photograph all day, but we were in that courtyard with a greater purpose.

Her trial was over. We would be permitted to see Elma in her confines; we would be allowed to confront her with the facts of what she had done. Germany had given her a life sentence plus thirteen years. One of the more severe sentences handed down in the course of the country's prosecution of the criminals of Auschwitz-Birkenau, it determined that Elma's death would occur on the cold floor of her cell.

Peter went in first. What he said, I don't know. When he returned, he simply nodded me forward, without a word. Somehow, he had never stopped knowing what I needed.

Elma's cage was more spacious than the one I had lived in. And no one drove a needle into her spine, no one hobbled her at the ankles, no one broke into her body and sifted through its insides, seizing her ability to have children while still a child herself, before sealing her shut with a ragged stitch. Her hair was close-cropped, but she had not been shaved. Her fine clothes were gone, but she was not naked. She had been captured, but no one had taken her childhood, as she'd taken mine, and even from behind her bars, she tried to take more from me; she gave a little laugh at the sight of my cane, eager for me to know her defiance. But I knew that she would spend her days hearing nothing but the sound of her own thoughts. She had no Zayde or Mama to soothe her—she had not even the davening of a pigeon at her window. This seemed a rightful misery. I felt no pity for Elma, and yet—the sight of her troubled me. I could have given her a game or two, to help her preserve herself within her cage, but I doubted she would see the value of such things. Instead, I gave her something that was of value to me: my forgiveness. She spat in disgust. I forgave her that too.

Forgiving her did not restore my family; it did not remove my pain or blunt my nightmares. It was not a new beginning. It was not, in the slightest, an end. My forgiveness was a constant repetition, an acknowledgment of the fact that I still lived; it was proof that their experiments, their numbers, their samples, was all for naught—I remained, a tribute to their underestimations of what a girl can endure. In my forgiveness, their failure to obliterate me was made clear.

And after I was finished telling Elma that I forgave her, I reminded her of those who didn't have the opportunity to do so. I said their names.

Peter, he was the only one of the names on Twins' Father's list that I ever saw again.

All those innocents—I didn't wonder about their futures that day as I left the abandoned house. I couldn't know their destinations, their triumphs, their troubles. The ones who integrated themselves into new cities and forgot themselves in new professions, either forming empires grand enough to blot out a past, or failing to thrive because they couldn't get the sound of their own blood out of their heads. The ones who married other survivors, and the ones who wouldn't marry because they had nothing to offer a marriage bed but night terrors. The ones who took comfort and freedom in the soil of the kibbutz, and the ones who found themselves lying on a different set of tables, granting permission to other doctors to burn the branded memories from their brains, to take away, once and for all, the misery that he had imprinted upon us.

They were children, once.

When the truck bearing a true red cross came, I hid.

I heard the attendants collect the children. Some shrieked, kicked, clung to the doorposts. All thirty-two were forced to surrender their bread knives, and the blades clanged as they joined a pile on the floor. I wished I could have hidden them with me, but I could not risk discovery. I was in the yard, behind a snowdrift, with my wheelbarrow over me. I peered around the hedge to see the children shuffle into the truck. I saw Sophia jaunt merrily, a doll given to her by the attendant beneath her arm. I saw Erik and Eli Fallinger regard the attendants skeptically, their feet rooted to the ground. The Aaldenberg triplets hid behind Miri, and she coaxed them into the attendants' arms, her blank expression shifting with grief. And then—I watched her count the children, call their names, register my absence. I heard her cry out for me. The attendants tried to soothe her, but Miri protested that Krakow wasn't safe, the assaults were happening every day, no one could tell her that the girl would be fine, especially after what the girl had been through, and the girl, she continued, she was crippled besides, the easiest of prey for anyone who might hunt her.

I would listen to my guardian call for me till her voice deserted her.

It was cruel to make Miri wait, especially with such dangers in her mind, but I knew I could stir only once there was no risk of the Red Cross's return. Only without the interference of their presence could I convince her that we had to stay together. After a good hour of caution, I picked up my crutches and hobbled into the abandoned house. It was dark. I lit a candle. But I did not have a free arm to carry it. So I stood in the middle of the room and looked about at what I could see in this scant light. I wanted to tell Miri that we could start again now. But Miri was not herself; she was not even the version who sought forgiveness. This Miri was folded in the corner near the birdcage. She was awake, but absent. I thought that the game that brought me back could bring her back too, that it could make her recover from this want of death.

I dwelled on fish. I thought about species first, then genus, and then I reached the third classification, the one I truly wanted.

Family was my first thought.

But even family ends was my second. It was not a thought I wanted. I assured myself that Miri would continue to live simply because I needed her to—but when she would not shift her gaze from the thirty-two injurious reminders of all she'd lost, I recognized that she would end her world if I did not act—this possibility, it made me forget my crutches, and I stumbled forth for help. Desperation alone carried me, two steps, then three, and then I fell and cried out to the city, I cried for all of Krakow to hear.

CHAPTER NINETEEN

The Sacred Curtain

Here and there, lost, upended things: a bird's nest on a puddle of ice, shattered spectacles on a locket dangling from a fencepost. I opened that locket. One half held a lock of hair, the other rust. I knew how that half felt. I felt that way whenever I looked at the tree trunks and saw those many names, all of them loved and searched for, and mine not among them.

The beggars here were certain it was February 11, 1945. They wanted no payment.

We were in Wieliczka, just outside of Krakow, according to the signs I no longer trusted. Like many a place, we never should have been there at all. Leaving Poznan, we found the roads obscured by tanks, interrupting our path to Warsaw. Whether they were Russian or German, not one of us could tell; the darkness carried too much risk. We told ourselves that the roads would clear in only a moment, any moment, but we rode on Horse's back as we waited, and soon enough, our waiting turned into wandering.

Horse was annoyed; he did not care for the circuitous nature of our travels. Feliks accused me of stalling. While I was usually eager to accept blame, I could not fault myself for this. In all three of us, I knew, there had arisen a hesitation. Our fragile army couldn't possibly be up to such a task. Defeating Mengele! Even my new pistol had taken to mocking me, and its bullets chorused in terrible agreement.

My aim will never be true enough, the pistol said. *My aim will never be sweet or accurate or good.*

But you have your bullets, I pointed out. *You are not alone. And you have me besides. We are family, all of us. See how much Feliks and I have accomplished already, as brother and sister?*

What does it matter? the bullets murmured to one another. *Stasha's rotten eye has made her aim rot too—she is bound to miss.* I wanted to tell the bullets that they couldn't think this way, they couldn't question me, they had to dream themselves into the heart or the head of our enemy.

Hearing this, the bullets snorted. Pistol remarked on the presence of smoke in a manner of turning the conversation.

The smoke over the city smelled as smoke should—a tang of pine, a touch of balsam. The threads of it didn't write out a welcome, but they weren't the red furies of Auschwitz either. Still, there was evidence that our kind had been endangered there in the days that the Wehrmacht ruled. We stumbled over this evidence while rooting for a place to sleep.

Why had no one defended it? Or had its defenders been overcome? This wooden synagogue—I could only imagine the flames it had seen. I am not sure that we would have known our shelter to be a synagogue at all if it were not for the singed *parochet*—the curtain of the ark; blue velvet, its lions smote by soot, its Torah crown still agleam—that lay in the snow some feet away, as if it had managed to flee the pillage under its own power. When Feliks saw the *parochet,* he said not a thing, he didn't even say what his father the rabbi would have said, but he stooped and kissed it and he draped it over a singed post in the midst of the collapse to protect it from the earth. But the *parochet* fell once more, leaving us with no choice but to carry its sacred length with us.

Fallen rafters black as pitch thatched themselves across a floor that shimmered with broken glass. A corner of this structure remained intact, and it was into its shelter that we retreated, hitching Horse to a charred birch at the perimeter. Horse looked as if he could restore the synagogue to its former glory with his beauty alone. Though the protrusions of his ribs upheld their prominence, so, too, did the black spark of his eye, which he fixed on us with a vigilant stare, and whenever the slightest sound arose on the wind, his ears shifted with worry. In the sweet protection of Horse's observance, we were comforted.

We huddled together beneath the blue velvet and guarded ourselves. If one were to look in our distant direction, all he might see was a thatchery of torched wood, a luminescing horse shifting from foot to foot, and the briefest field of azure that was our *parochet*. It felt as if no harm could ever come to us. I was about to ask Feliks what his father would think of us using the *parochet* as a blanket, if he would praise our endurance or curse us for blasphemy, but already, he was fast asleep.

And so it was decided that Horse and me would keep watch. Feliks snored while we counted stars to stay awake. There were too few that night to outpace my thoughts, so I expanded on the usual by giving them names, and then futures. I gave them futures in all sorts of places that I'd never seen, and when these futures were complete, I took them away, because why should a star have a future when Pearl did not?

Eventually, the watchfulness of Horse's eye convinced me that it was safe to sleep.

A simple belief, the kind I needed.

I would like to say that although we woke to find Horse gone, nothing else was amiss, but more than his absence struck us in the morning. Where our pale hero should have stood, nodding his head while sleepily rousing, a red ribbon began. This trail of blood wove itself around the ruins and escaped across the field like a loose serpent, and we followed its path, all the stops and starts of it, for half a mile, until it flurried to finale before the arch of a stony-mouthed tunnel. Into the ensuing darkness, we peered.

"It continues," Feliks said. I was not sure if he was referring to pain or to the red path. He caught me by the arm and made an attempt to hold me back, but his grip was not earnest. He wanted answers as much as I did. We didn't care that it was to take place in the depths of a salt mine, that we were to follow a red path neither narrow nor straight into a briny underground, a place beneath the earth that seemed most hospitable to evil.

We were both blinded, I think, by this bloody ribbon that stretched before us, or, rather, we were blinded by what it might mean to our many losses. I took it as a message even as it was leading me toward horror. I knew I would not find my sister alive, I knew violence had seized Horse, but I thought perhaps I was being led toward understanding and restoration. How could I not think that while surrounded by such beauty?

Because the entry of this salt mine—imagine stepping into the tilted entry of a lily; consider slipping into coils of white, luminous beyond compare. Following the mine's wooden staircase, we turned into one gleaming corridor after another; we dead-ended ourselves in tiny cells strewn with tinsel; we stumbled into frosted dens of sodium that hosted flutteries of bats. Through these subterranean halls, we walked in witness to awe at the core of our world.

But even awe bottoms out. At the end of the wooden staircase, we saw that the lily that we traveled in held some nectar that had attracted an army of ants. The soldiers were all so alike in their uniforms and their misery. One would think, after all their crimes, that some godly, glowering hand might descend from the ceiling and lay them out, one by one, like gray dominoes. But no hand descended. Even if it had, it was far too late for Horse.

Because I was never an expert in bones, but I knew, seeing the scatter and the threads of red ribbon that led to a boiling pot propped on a primitive lattice of bricks, that we would not be riding into Warsaw on horseback, that Horse, this dear animal that had lent us his service had met with the same ineloquent brutality we knew so well.

The depths of the salt mine repeated my horror to the center of the earth.

Some people, they have heard so many gasps, screams, cries that they are deaf to them, no matter how much a salt mine enlarges their volume or reach. This seemed to be the case with these Wehrmacht soldiers. The six of them were too busy squatting here and there, picking at their plates, drinking. They had no fear or interest in bears and jackals. Only one turned to acknowledge us, the one manning the stew pot. He had a shuffled, disorganized bearing and metallic eyes that stood in his face like medals rewarded for terrible deeds.

"He wasn't yours to take," I whispered. I was certain that Horse had alerted his captors to this fact. After all, it is known that all animals speak while in the throes of de-creation. Horse must have shrieked that he belonged to us, that the three of us were on a sacred mission for the restoration of our souls, the taking of another's, and the avenging of Pearl.

I stumbled forward in rage. Feliks tried to pull me back.

The soldier tending the pot was dazed on horse meat and drunk on whiskey. He staggered forward and drew his pistol and then took another step. He tilted his head to regard us. He couldn't understand why we didn't run; he appeared to find our behavior novel, and he treated us like we were curiosities sent to interrupt his boredom and doom. I knew why I didn't run. I had nothing to fear. But

Feliks—why was he so rooted to the floor? He stood as if he had no choice but to stand by me. Both of us, we'd dropped our sacks, and we should have been lifting them in our arms and running, we should have been bolting up those stairs. The soldier stepped forward to inspect their contents.

We had a hatchet, three knives, two pistols, one poison pill meant for Mengele. We had a crust of bread, a bit of sausage, a bouquet of rags to bind our wounds. We had Pearl's piano key in a bag full of stones. I couldn't imagine they would be interested in any of this. He looked at the weapons in amusement. I worried not for myself but for Feliks. *Run!* I mouthed. He did not.

"You two are well armed," the man observed. "Have you come to kill me?"

"Another," I declared. "A real Nazi. You are all turning on each other now, yes? We can give you information about his whereabouts. You can make a deal with the Russians, with the Americans. Can't you? And maybe, in exchange, you will let us go and give us back our weapons? This person—he would be a fine capture for you. He's better than Himmler. Bigger than Goebbels. Greater than Hitler himself—"

"Josef Mengele," Feliks interrupted, breathless. "She is talking about Josef Mengele."

Not a single reverberation attached itself to his voice. Even echoes, it seemed, were not on our side that day, though they lent themselves freely to the soldier, who was inspecting our weapons, turning them over with metallic clinks that repeated themselves through the salty halls.

"We can tell you where he is—just let us go," I pleaded. "Anyone who captures him—they will be heroes. He is a prize—after what he has done, the whole world will want him."

But the soldier was unimpressed with this little speech. He was more interested in pointing one of our pistols at us. We watched the eye of the pistol waver in its focus. He shifted it back and forth. First Feliks. Then me. As if the pistol alone could decide. And then it chose Feliks—he leveled the muzzle at my friend.

My friend, with all his many vulnerabilities and braveries, the one who was now the root of my many dreams, the one who could tame a winter and lessen hundreds of miles and make sorrow eat from the palm of his hand. My brother. My twin. I knew I'd need Feliks all my life. I wanted to watch him grow and be a boy for all time, even as he shifted into an adult. I wanted to see the hair drift from his head as my own turned gray, I wanted to get him a new set of teeth so he could chew someday, and if he still couldn't chew, then I guess I'd continue to chew for him. When I looked at Feliks, my vision was only good.

I stepped in front of Feliks in hopes of absorbing this bullet. A bullet couldn't hurt me. But Feliks didn't know this. He pushed me aside. The soldier nodded the barrel of our pistol at us.

"The two of you—strip."

So it was that we shed the skins of Bear and Jackal, the outer layers that had protected us from night and winter and any misgivings about the nature of our true strengths. The bravado on loan from these predators—now it was gone. What an ache it was to watch the plush warmth of our borrowed skins fall into enemy hands! My dress followed, and then my two sweaters. I stood, feebly covering myself once again, and my body, it remembered everything for me, it took on Pearl's duty of the past, and it pointed out the march of needle pricks down my arms. I looked up at the ceiling of the salt mine because I could not look at myself or at Feliks. I knew that he was likely overcome by gooseflesh, that perhaps he'd wet himself in fear, and I heard him sniffle. When Feliks slipped off his pants, the soldier laughed at his tail and teased its tip with the butt of his rifle.

I wondered if this soldier knew Taube, if he had heard of the guard's merciful act and was determined to correct the situation.

Because he did not show any sign of sparing us. Taube, he had done so in a moment of insanity and confusion; he had taken his boot from my back. But this soldier was not confused as to what to do with us.

"Who said you could keep your shoes?" he barked at me. "Socks too," he added.

My poison pill was in my left sock. I thought of what the avengers would have done, and so as I bent to unroll the woolen sock, I extracted that ampule and slipped it into my mouth. I carried it neatly in the pocket between jaw and cheek.

And as we stood so bare, in the distance, I could see pieces of Horse's pelt, scattered like a torn blanket. How had I let Horse carry me for so long without noticing that he was piano-white, like the piano in Pearl's film? My good eye reported this fact, and curiously, for the first time since Mengele's drop entered my vision, my bad eye agreed. Its traditional veil of blackness had lifted. Both eyes were able to see the same white. There was no variation in it, no shades of gray, not a single suggestion of ambiguity. All was too clear.

This is what I saw: The soldier was touching all that I had left of my sister. Pearl's key. He'd taken it up from the sack, regarded it without interest, and then allowed it to slip from his fingers.

I could not let that piano key fall; I could not let it meet this dust. Pearl was dead, and that was my fault. But this—if I could not catch a key, I thought, I deserved all I'd been dealt. So I made a naked dash to catch it and threw myself at the soldier's feet, and it was such a glory having it in my hands, I wept with happiness even as he gave me a kick in the ribs. And then another. And another. I felt the little poison pill stammer between my teeth, the ampule's walls threatening to cave at the point of my canine. In my hand, there was my sister's life, and in my mouth, there was Mengele's death.

Even in that moment, I knew which one meant more.

I heard a shot ring out, and I presumed myself wounded. But it was not me; it would never be me who was truly at risk. I watched Feliks stumble back, watched him forget to hide his nakedness through the pain. I saw him clutch his shoulder, clapping tight a brimming wound.

I looked at Feliks and I looked at the soldier, and I'll confess to this madness—for a minute I thought I saw not the deserter but the doctor, the Angel of Death, standing there, the evils of his experiments so great that he could no longer live on the surface of the earth.

I wish I could blame this on the depths of the salt mine, whose dimensions were known to make people see ghosts and specters and illusions of all kinds. But the fault was with me. I wish, too, that I alone were visited by such a delusion, but so many, year after year, decade after decade, would find themselves followed by this same face. They wouldn't be children anymore and they wouldn't be prisoners either, but always, there would be the sense of his gaze, the prospect of his inspection. How many ways might he disguise himself? we'd wonder. And the world would look at us as if we were mad.

There in the salt mine, I was so sure that I saw him.

And the illusion shattered only when I took in the circularity of Feliks's injury. Mengele would not hurt us like that; he had more profitable and efficient ways to damage us. His brutality was too studious and elegant to leave Feliks bleeding from the shoulder, such a coarse and ineffective wound that contributed nothing to the advancement of his science.

The soldier took aim once more, but already we were fleeing; we tripped up the stairs, our speed quickened by the fact that the soldier who was following us appeared to be nearly blind with spite as he stumbled upon the stairs. I saw his boot slip and his face strike the wooden slats, and I paused too long to study his stupor and his tumble, his body thudding like a toy as it fell. It was as if I believed that in watching the descent of our enemy, all could be reversed—the trains would change direction on their tracks, the numbers would erase themselves, the point of the needle would never know my vein.

Even with a flesh wound, my friend was faster than I; he knew enough to lean his stunned body into mine as we fled up the stairs, he knew that I needed more to urge me on from the death of Horse. Yet again, they had killed a loved one, they had robbed us, left us defenseless. I felt no victory in evading that grasp. I could hardly see the point in continuing. If that poison pill would have ended me, I would have swallowed it with joy.

"Look," Feliks said with a gasp, and he lifted a tremulous finger to the sky. A dozen people were falling from it. We didn't know if they were friend or foe, but they had the clouds of a waning winter at their backs. My friend had the gleam of a bullet burrow at his shoulder, and yet this is what he saw. I watched his pained face marvel at their flight—the drifting freedom of it—and long for the same.

But what we had, it was only on this troubled and accursed soil. I had the poison pill in the pocket between my teeth and jaw, still intact and full of promise. The rest that we'd collected in our quest— gone.

Farewell, Horse. Our beloved. You were more innocent than Pearl on the day we were born. You were better than the best parts of us. You were who I wished the world could be.

Farewell, hatchet and pistol and three precious knives. You were fiercer and deadlier and sharper than I could ever be.

So long, fur coats. Farewell, Bear. Farewell, Jackal. You made us fearsome and possible, you vaunted us into the Classification of Living Things in a performance that I could not execute alone. In you, we became predatory in the way a survivor sometimes needs to be.

So stripped, I pressed forward in the snow, my friend draped across my side, and I dragged him toward the mercy of a row of cottages in the distance; we stumbled forth, hoping for relief, for someone to dress our nakedness and heal our wounds, while men parachuted above, so light and free. I shook my fist at them in envy. I gave them a reckless cry, not caring who might hear me and repossess my body once more. It had been taken from Pearl and me so many times already, I could not care anymore.

"Stasha," Feliks begged, "I see that you will die soon if you continue this way."

It was prophecy, warning, love.

Oh, that I could be a girl who needed to heed it!

CHAPTER TWENTY

The Flights

From our window at the hospital, I saw them, adrift in the sky like the spores of a dandelion. Parachutists—I counted twelve in number, afloat through our evening, on the edge of Krakow.

"Do you know who they are?" I asked Miri. I turned from the window and maneuvered my crutches so I could face her. I asked her who the parachutists were coming for, why they used that method. Miri said it was hard enough to tell, even up close, if someone had good intentions, but she'd been told that many in the Jewish underground used this method of travel in the transport of goods and secrets and weapons.

I did not get to watch the parachutists land—they floated down to a location beyond my eye's reach—but three days later, I would see a reconfiguration of the white silks that had bloomed above them, their soft lengths having fallen into the hands of a seamstress. Now, a bride glided down the streets; she drifted across the cobblestones toward the chuppah in this ruched wartime splendor, the parachute silks draped into a filmy bodice, the train wisping behind her like mist. The two mothers joined her; they led her beneath the lace. If you put your head out the window, you could hear the celebration. The bride circling the groom. The seven blessings. A shatter of glass sang out.

"There are weddings still?" I said in awe.

Miri rose from her bed and came to the open window to watch with me, to cock her ear and listen. She put her arm around me.

"There are weddings still," she said, a catch in her voice. "And I don't know why I am so surprised."

One ceremony, and then another.

In the abandoned house, when I had thought Miri was leaving the world, I'd felt as if I were in a different kind of cage. My hands didn't work and my vision blurred. All became distant and impossible. I didn't even consider my crutches as I stumbled out to the street in search of help. My voice moved far better than I could, and my cries drew the neighbors from their homes. Jakub, the giver of onions, our Krakow host, was among them. His was the only face I knew and trusted. I pointed to the open door and watched as he dashed inside.

I knew he would carry her out. But I didn't want to see her state. I didn't look. Not even as Jakub put Miri in an ambulance and placed me beside her. I did not open my eyes until we came to the hospital. I saw her look away from the nurses and the patients both—though they'd seen many with her affliction, she remained ashamed of it, and her shame did not lift as she was tended to and her vitals were taken and she was given a bed. She refused to lie in that bed; she just perched on the edge and studied the curtain that divided the room, and there she remained until a nurse showed Jakub inside.

His entrance was unusually formal; he gave a little bow at the door—it was as if he thought an extreme politesse might conceal his worry, though from my perspective, it only announced an attachment to the doctor. He looked about the room as if he'd never seen the inside of a hospital before, and then he asked me to give them some privacy. I did, in a way. I ducked behind the curtain that divided the room, and there, behind its cover, I still heard everything.

Jakub drew a chair next to the hospital bed and sat beside Miri's hunched form. He did not sigh or speak; he didn't even whisper. In his silence, there was a loss, a too-bright and borderless thing, a loss that understood: the survivor's hour is different from any other; its every minute answers to a history that won't be changed or restored or made bearable. Recognizing Jakub's loss, Miri spoke of her own.

"My husband," she murmured. "He didn't survive three days in the ghetto. Shot in the street."

I peered around the curtain's edge. The room was dim, but Miri's face was half bathed in lamplight.

"My sisters, both lost to me. Orli, dead, months after our arrival. Ibi, dispatched to the Puff. But before they were lost—he made me take their wombs myself."

She looked to Jakub, as if awaiting a response. None came. Jakub bowed his head.

"Of course, mine was not spared either. But I could not mourn it. I was too busy mourning my children. My Noemi, my Daniel. How many times have I wished that they were closer in years so that I might have told Mengele they were twins? In my dreams, I close that gap of time between them, I make them passable as twins. But when I wake, I know this was impossible, and I console myself with this: at least my children will never know what their mother did in Auschwitz." And here her voice began to slip away from her, as if it had become untethered from her thoughts.

Jakub tried to tell her that in a place where good wasn't permitted to exist, she had nonetheless enabled it. In a place that asked her to be brutal, she brought only kindness, a comfort to the dying, a defiant hope that crept—

But she would not hear it. The mothers, she said—she'd tried to keep the mothers alive, that was the logic of her acts.

So many more would have died without you, Jakub insisted, but my guardian drew only bitterness from this, a bitterness that plunged her into the unspeakable.

"A pregnant Jewess," she said. "Little offended him more. I told the mothers, 'If you and your baby are discovered, you will not be shot; no, you will not go to the gas. Such ends are considered too gentle for you. If your pregnancy is known to Mengele, you will become research and entertainment both, he will take you to his table, and, with his instruments, he will dissect, bit by bit, he will push you toward death. And as he kills you, he will force you to watch your baby become his experiment. For Mengele, such savagery is a treasured opportunity—as soon as he learns of a pregnancy, he places bets with the guards about the gender of the child, and they plot its death accordingly. If it is a girl, they'll say, we will throw her to the dogs. But if it is a boy, we will crush his skull beneath the wheels of a car. These are only some of the brutalities I can speak of. They are too innumerable and varied, so grotesque— I do not have the words. What I know for certain: the only true delivery he knows is that of misery. For every mother and child, he invents a new murder—in Auschwitz, one need not even be born to experience torture.'"

She closed her eyes as if to shroud the memory. But it would not be shrouded. Opening her eyes, she looked squarely at Jakub with the air of one who can only confess.

"So many times, to save a mother's life—I had to act swiftly, on the floors of filthy barracks, with dull, rusty instruments, and nothing to ease her pain. Alone, I pulled the life from her—my hands bare, bloodied—and I told myself, through the mother's screams, and my own, stifled tears, You are sparing this soul, this baby, the greatest of tortures. And when it was over—oh, it was never over!—but I would speak to the mother, I'd say, 'Your child is dead, but look, you are strong, you still live, and now there will be a chance, someday, when the world welcomes us back into its wonder, you will have another.' Each time I said this, it was not just for them—it was for me too. The grief was not mine, and yet all I knew was grief! So many little futures—I ended them before he could torment and end them, to enable other futures. And still, myself I cannot forgive."

Miri's hands fluttered to her face—she did not permit us to see her expression. But we knew she did not want her own future at all.

Jakub looked as if he had witnessed the events she'd described. His face grayed, as if struck by illness, and he struggled to compose himself. He tried to tell her that he knew what it could mean to save a life. That cost, he said, was unending, because in choosing who could be saved, he had also chosen who could not be saved. In failing these lives, he'd selected the color of these deaths, their scents, their violences. Every day, he murmured, he had to save his own life, even as he'd failed the most vibrant, dearest one, the one he'd wanted to save most.

And then he must have found himself unable to say anything at all, because he pulled the curtain back and led me to my guardian's side. She would not look at me, but she drew me close, she held me tight, and as she wept, I wondered if anyone else, the whole world over, could boast a stronger embrace.

Out in the hall, I overheard the nurses approach Jakub. The cost, he repeated. I know it well. I am sure that you know others too, working as you do, I'm sure you see us, desperate to shake these matters from our minds, you see us try to live until we try to die, and when we can't succeed at either, we try to coax ourselves toward death by trying to remember them, the ones we couldn't save, and when we remember them too well, it is terrible, and when we remember them too little, it is worse—

Here, a nurse burst into the room, her eager step announcing an intent to distract me from the conversation in the hall.

This nurse saw my need. She took off my shoes and laid me down in Miri's bed, so white and clean-sheeted, and there I pressed my cheek to my guardian's. That bed suited us so well. I could have stayed there forever, stroking Miri's hair and listening to the nurse's stories and telling some of my own. But the nurse said that I would have to leave someday. It was not good for me, she claimed, to be so surrounded by pain, and we needed to find a place free of it that I could go to.

"A place like that is real?" I asked.

I was asking not for myself, but for Miri.

It is a particular madness, yes, to long for a cage, and for the sounds of isolation—rat-scratch, leak-drip, my fingertips drumming on the bars—but there, at least, I had some expectation of suffering. I could speculate reasonably about how I might feel pain and how I might be torn, how I could die in a flash, or slowly, bit by bit, in increments so small that I was unable to tell the difference between my life ending and my death beginning. In that space, I'd kept my hope fast. But in places like the hospital, with their white sheets and scrubbed floors and modest stores of food, I was suspended in a perpetual wait. Everything that was good, clean, and plentiful reminded me, once again, how swiftly I could be diminished, and without a single warning. I could be underfoot and powerless in mere seconds, and the anticipation of this made the struggle to remain seem utterly pointless. What work there is, I thought, in being a real person after death!

I wondered how being a real person might feel after leaving the hospital. I assumed that one of us would be leaving soon, as a nurse had given us a suitcase. I also assumed that this person would be me. I would never be ready, I confessed to the nurse after receiving this gift. Ever patient, the nurse explained—Miri was ill, she could not take care of me. Polite, I protested—it was I who would take care of Miri now.

The nurse was not convinced. She merely folded two pairs of socks and placed them neatly within the suitcase. Then she left me with that dreaded object.

How odd it was, to own a real suitcase. We had become a people of sacks invented out of threadbare jumpers or emptied potato bags. These were easily slung over the back and were well proven in their utility. But a proper suitcase! When I took it up by the handle, I felt surrounded. By people and by wall. I felt as if I were boxed in, dust-covered; sweat pooled at my ankles and my ears rang with shouts and a panic burned too bright in my chest. I dropped the suitcase at my feet like a hot piece of coal.

Miri saw what I had seen, and drew me close.

"Believe that you are safe," she whispered, and she spent the evening scratching out the monogram—*JM,* it said, in silvery script—with a pin, and there was no mistaking that her efforts had such a roughness to them that she nearly put a hole in the leather.

Better a hole, she claimed, than a memory. I did not argue with this—Miri had more to forget than anyone, and it would do her good to impose large swaths of absence on her mind. But I hoped that as she pursued forgetfulness, a little memory of me might remain. Just a tiny bit, just enough so that if we were ever truly parted, she might seek me out again, someday.

I looked out my window while Jakub and Miri had one of their discussions. There were no parachutists in the sky, but the heavens were assuming a different blue, and the frost seemed soon to end. I consulted a piece of paper that one of the nurses had given me. On it, there was a series of boxes, little cages that represented days. We were halfway through the month of February. Did my Someone know this? I wondered.

Miri and Jakub spoke in hushed tones; they tried to conceal their plans. Jakub claimed that the time for worry was not ending, but it was changing a bit—the problems were different now, but so were the solutions, and he himself could escort the children toward one that was rare and brilliant. The authorities at the Red Cross confirmed the desirability of this scenario—already, they had selected eleven of Miri's children to participate in this plan. And, of course, there was Pearl—surely she would join this exodus toward safety? The good doctor was in favor of this venture, wasn't she?

Miri was not stirred by Jakub's excitement. She muttered something beneath her breath, something wholly unintelligible to me aside from the mention of my name. She said it longingly, or so I believed. Perhaps I imagined this. But when I turned at the window, I caught the trail of her gaze—it was fastened on me; her eyes, they appeared fixed on my injured legs.

Palestine, Jakub continued, insistent. First, a trip to Italy, which could be dangerous—some concealment was necessary—and then a ship that did not have room for everyone but would surely accommodate the twins. Hearing this, Miri faded still further—the voice I'd not believed capable of becoming any smaller lilted softly in query.

"This flight—it is our only hope?" she asked. "Still?"

I knew the tone she used. It was the tone I heard on all the streets when people turned and asked each other if it was safe to resume living.

"Would you like to take the risk?" Jakub whispered. "Is there ever a moment when you are not looking behind your back? Yes, it is over—we are free. Until they decide that we are no longer free—the war is not over, everything remains undetermined—"

This was an argument of proponents of the Bricha, organizers of the flight. We did not know it then, but peace was still over three months away. But who was to say it would come May 8, not July or the next year? While we lived in February's thaw, creeping toward spring, many believed that flight to another, more hospitable land was a necessary risk.

"She will be safer there than she is here," Jakub assured her. "I will see to it."

If there was a moment in which everything was decided, I suppose it was that moment.

Because my guardian did not increase her protest, and I did not raise one at all, and so it was assumed, by all three of us, that this was what would become of me. I would be shipped to Italy, where I would board a boat that held its own sea, a sea of numbered people like myself, young and old, survivor and refugee, and every last one a searcher seeking to purchase a new beginning.

Jakub had promised. It was to be a box quite different than the box I'd known—I was to bob within it next to Sophia, the two of us surrounded by the company of supplies: rolls of bandages, vials of medicine, tins of meats, bags of tea. But when the day came for my departure, a wooden box arrived at the hospital. It was a bit glamorous, so far as boxes go. It had a cherry-lacquered top rendered in the goyish style so as not to attract additional suspicion, and it was sized for a large adult. I could have rolled myself up like a blanket and lived in one corner. At the sight of my hiding vessel, Miri wept. Tears big as marbles rolled down her face. She tried to hide them with her hair, as was her custom.

"It's a coffin," she said.

"A trunk," Jakub corrected.

"I know coffins," Miri said.

I would only have to hide myself in order to cross the borders, he assured her. There were holes in the bottom so that I would be able to breathe. And there were other children that would be hidden alongside me, the ones that I knew so well from our journey to Krakow. We were to be quiet, but we would know we were not alone, and this, the man claimed, was a comfort.

Into the truck bed piled eleven of my thirty-two companions. While only a week had passed since I last saw them, they looked different from the children I'd known. Their faces were rounder; their eyes no longer carted hollows beneath them. Sophia had a new hair ribbon. The Blaus had gotten haircuts. One of the Rosens wore a pair of spectacles. They were ragged still, but you could tell that some hand had cared for them. I saw Miri's face as she took in the details of their transformations and I knew that she wished she had been that hand, but she only smiled at each of them and asked if they were excited about this latest journey, and she helped seat me in a corner of the truck bed, where I could lean myself against the coffin box for comfort.

Miri had a gift for me, which she presented with her ever-trembling hands. When I saw this gift, the fact struck me with all its finality. She was not coming with me—not then, and perhaps never.

Like us, the tap shoes were a mismatched pair. One was bigger, younger than the other.

All I knew was that one shoe was blush, the other white. I am not sure how she missed these differences. Maybe she hated the exaltation of symmetry after following Mengele's orders. I couldn't know. Both were kissed by the necessary metal at heel and toe. She shined them for me and caressed the laces with pride. She placed the shoes in my hands. She said she'd see me again.

"In Italy?" I asked.

"If I am well by Italy."

"And what if you aren't well then?"

"I will be well someday," she promised.

We would have a dinner, she said, and I could wear my new shoes. I wanted to point out that they were dancing shoes, and I could not walk, let alone dance, but she looked so pleased at the prospect of this reunion that I said not a thing. I put the shoes in the box and did not look at her as she continued to swear that this was not the end for us.

Her form, as the truck trundled off—first, distance diminished her, then the fog swept away her face. I tried to memorize Miri as the expanse between us grew, her eyes, nose, mouth, chin. Wordlessly, I said good-bye to each, until there was nothing left of her to be seen, and I told myself to be happy for this, this chance to say good-bye, to say that I loved her. My affections had found a home in her; she was not my mother, my father, my sister, my Someone, but she was who I wanted to be, she was born kind, but hardship kindled it, and her vulnerabilities did not live apart from her bravery. Miri knew what suffering was and still, she wanted to know restoration too.

I don't know if she ever truly believed that our reunion would come to be. What is more, I don't know if she thought she might live even an hour past my departure. But I believe she knew that she had to become well so that I could see her again, alive and re-stored. She could not do this with me at her side, as much as she would have loved to have me near. This was not abandonment, I told myself, years later. This was love, her dream for my future.

I'm not sure she thought much of her own future. She couldn't have dreamed of her triumph, I am sure. That she would be allowed a haven in America, that she would be permitted to resume her practice in the halls of a hospital, that she would enter thousands of rooms with her soft step, eyes fixed on the expectant patient.

Dear God, she'd pray as she washed her hands and pulled on her gloves and turned to the waiting mother. *You owe me this—the chance to deliver a true and vital life, a child that will never have to be known as a survivor.* And thousands would take their first breaths in her hands.

No, she couldn't have even dreamed of that, not then. We don't always know ourselves, who we can become, what we may do, after evil has done what it likes with us.

A decade later, we would find each other in a waiting room at a Manhattan hospital where I was to see a specialist. I recognized her as soon as I saw her back, those dark curls tangling at her shoulders, and her usual stance—a slight tiptoe, as if ready to tend to a new disaster at any moment. And though she'd been well prepared for our meeting, she could not help but call me Stasha when she saw me, and I spent the next minute or so begging her not to apologize for this error, which remained in my mind as a sweetness that I couldn't experience enough.

Stasha, she'd whispered, as if in memoriam.

And like the mother-sister she'd become, she remained with me as I was led to an examination room, as I was undressed and poked. She bossed the nurses a little, and she directed the doctor to be as gentle as he could, and when this inquiry of my insides were over, after I'd spent an hour reliving my girlish selves, all two of them, one the chosen sufferer, the other an intact half, I laid myself down on a couch in a private waiting room, and when the results were declared to be in, and the doctor took a seat to address me, I put my hand in Miri's.

Miri sat by my side as I was told the details of what he'd done to me, all the undetectable troubles that had begun to plague my health. Together, we learned that parts of me had never fully developed—my kidneys remained the size of a small, starving child's, a child caught on the cusp of adulthood, her growth interrupted by the fact that there'd once lived a man who had no soul, and he'd collected children and those he found odd, acted as if he loved them, marveled at them, and destroyed them. The insides that he'd tampered with—they did not meet the demands of my grown life.

Miri wept for me then. She took on the tears that couldn't pass from my own eyes. She did so as if there were some unspoken pact between us. She looked at me, so still, and wondered aloud after my feelings, and when I didn't answer, she said my name, and Stasha's too. She didn't care who saw her cry, she wanted all to know what he had done to me—she was so different then from the woman who'd forced herself to be stoic during our journey out of Auschwitz.

At our parting, I thought those tap shoes were all she had left me with. But when I was forced to enter the coffin while crossing a border, I found, in the toe of one of the tap shoes, a note. Opening it, I expected to see her say good-bye. I thought she might say that she was sorry, that she might detail how her burdens kept her from joining me in my flight.

But this long-ago letter, the one that wept in her blurred script?

It was not about her life, her loss, her sorrows. It was about mine.

And when we children were waylaid, when the roads clogged with tanks made us travel to the wrong city, and then the wrong village, I'll say this—it was not my will that kept me alive, it was not the canteen of water, the provisions of bread, the company of Sophia beside me or the other twins that rattled in their boxes in the bed of our truck. It was not even our system of communication as we knocked on the linings of what held us whenever we crossed a border or had to hide—one knock to say *I'm here,* two to say *I'm here, but there is little in the way of air,* three to say *I'm here, but I'm not sure I want to be.*

It was only what Miri told me about the Someone who had loved me. All the details she wrote about this person—all her games, her fondness for a knife, the way she'd made me dance—

those details kept the breath in me for three days of travel, till our truck was detained by a pair of Wehrmacht deserters so desperate for transit that they were not above forcing Jakub from the driver's seat. Seeing their approach, Jakub had warned us to take cover in our boxes. Whether he knew this was the end of his life, I don't know. All I knew was the sound of the pistol, and then the sound of a body hitting the ground beside the truck. I heard, too, the whimpers of Sophia as she lay beside me, and as we sped away, I told her that we had only to bide our time till the soldiers paused in their travels, and as soon as the vehicle stopped, we would slip out, the lot of us, head for the nearest village, and find another rescue. She pointed out that I was on crutches. I pointed out that we were twins, the both of us, even though we'd had our share of loss. I assured her that freedom was something we might achieve together, that my Someone had always said so.

And in that moment, having no one to share my duties with, I took them all on. I took the hope and the risk, the reckless determination, the stubborn belief that yet again, I would survive.

Inside my latest box, I put on the tap shoes and waited for the moment that my kick at the ceiling of my confines might turn into a leap.

CHAPTER TWENTY-ONE

Not the End

What kind of welcome did I expect from the ruins of Warsaw? In the place where Mengele's life was to end and lend a new beginning to ours, there was only the echo of peasants spitting in the streets, emptying their lungs of dust. And look at us—our weapons were gone, our furs had been stripped. Near naked, defenseless, we wore burlap sacks begged from a roadside farmer; we wrapped our exposed legs and arms in woolen rags discarded on the side of the road, we stumbled forth in too-large shoes, and my friend winced with every step, his hand constantly returning to worry at the wound on his shoulder, which had surrendered its bullet into my hand. With two fingers I'd pried it from his flesh as he shrieked, cursing the fact that my own affliction could not enjoy the same bloody and swift extraction. That, I told myself, was the last doctoring I would ever do. Destruction was all I cared for now, and Feliks shared this with me—together, we improvised fresh and clumsy methods of persecution. We collected a new sackful of stones to lob at our torturer's skull, we clutched sticks beneath our arms, makeshift spears, the ends of them whittled to points fine enough to pierce his chest, and we trusted that the meek power of these humble instruments would be transformed by our fury when, at last, we came upon Mengele, cornering him in the cages of his hideout at the Warsaw Zoo.

Warsaw did not recognize our destructive aims, as it was too possessed by its own restoration to know us. But although it did not note our entry, I trusted the city to host our mission. It had been destroyed like we had been destroyed. It was gutted and drawn; vacancies had been cleared until the city was little more than a cellar, a tomb, a waiting room with a telephone that said only good-bye, but everywhere, I saw people crushing themselves to revive it, I saw them expelling every breath they had into the foundations of the felled synagogues. They had the power specific to natives—they compelled the leaves to remain on the trees, coaxed the flowers to bloom and the skulls to stay in the ground, buried where no dog might unearth them—but we had the gifts of outside avengers. While they entrusted the city with life, we were there to ensure a death. Only when Mengele was finished would the leaves remain, the flowers bloom, and the skulls go back to sleep.

A violet night was falling and we heard a clock ticking in the air, addressing us, telling us that we were running out of time. Two steps farther, I realized that this sound was only the pound of my heart, though the message remained the same. The ticks quickened when we rounded a corner and saw a Red Army soldier paring an apple with a nail file and leaning against a wall alongside a broom. I wondered if that broom was so young that it had only the experience of sweeping ash and rubble. The soldier was so airy and nonchalant that I assumed everything had ended.

"You have captured him already?" I asked.

The soldier peered at me over his nail file.

"Hitler?" he wondered.

"Not him," I said. "The other him. The Angel of Death—have you found him?"

"I don't understand the question," he said. "Your Russian—very poor."

I knew that he understood well enough. But I pantomimed so that he could claim no excuse for not answering; I pretended as if we were playing the Classification of Living Things.

With my hands, I tried to depict a person born to German industrialists and affectionately known as Beppo. This was easy enough to convey. I stood on tiptoe and made myself look vast; I twirled a mustache, plucked a hair from it, and popped it into my mouth to approximate Mengele's nasty habit. Also easy to get across was the fact of his doctorhood. I swung the white wings of an invisible coat about; I plunged a needle, removed an organ, sewed children together, and caged a Lilliput. More difficult, however, was the degree of his evils. This I was unable to communicate in all its lowdown fullness, its beastly disrespect for all living creatures and their variety.

Yes, I failed at this as badly as I had failed in my cattle-car portrayal of an amoeba.

So I wasn't surprised when the soldier shook his head in confusion. I begged his forgiveness about the complicated message. I tried again. I left nothing out. The experiments, the shared pain, the Zoo, the days, the nights, the smell. All the dead tossed to the mud banks of the latrines. I did my best, but I realized that those who had not seen what we'd seen would never truly understand.

The soldier didn't understand. So I took another approach. Realizing that Mengele was a man that could become fully known only through his victims, I began to list them all in the dust. I wrote all the names that I knew. I wrote Pearl's. I wrote mine too, and then I crossed it out. The soldier bent to inspect the names, shrugged, gave Feliks his half-eaten apple, and then stalked off into the rubble chasing the vision of a pretty girl who'd begun to hang her wash on the ruins of a butcher shop.

"You didn't even try to help," I said.

"Not true," Feliks said through a mouthful of apple. "I stood by your side the whole time."

I told him I was beginning to think that he didn't want any outside assistance.

"You are right," he confessed. "I want it to be you and me, no one else. We are the only ones entitled to kill him."

For once, I could not argue. And we walked on in our quest, picking our way through these ruins. Men were crawling out from holes, puffs of dust and soot haloing their heads. Faces were covered with soot and ash and dust, but beneath these layers, determination peeked. They were singing to the city, these people, trucking their wheelbarrows to and fro. Children perched on fallen stoops with buckets. Cats surveyed the efforts with suspicion and made sudden moves to escape stew pots. Mugwort hung on the remaining houses, warding off traditional evils.

Feliks had a strange familiarity with this place, or as much familiarity as one can have with a city that has fallen. He'd had an auntie here once, he claimed, and so he knew the streets, and he took me through what remained of them. We found tattered clothing to replace our burlap bags, ragged socks and mismatched shoes for our feet. We inquired about the zoo to any who would pause to answer us. The inquiry always put people into fits of headshaking. We used to love the shriek of the cormorants, they'd say. We used to admire the canter of the zebras. And our downcast eyes told us that we would know this zoo by its destruction.

We came upon signs. The signs told of lives that should have been, lives that had burst or been diminished, lives that had wandered into the forest. Here, an aviary stripped of its feathers. There, the elephant house with its emptied swimming pools. Over there, in the middle of the green, tigers should have familied themselves into magnificence. Peacocks should have glinted, geese should have gaggled, apes mocked monkeys. The lynx should have given chase.

But where the grandeur of the animal kingdom should have made itself known, there was only scatter—an upturned moat, tufts of fur clinging to bars wrenched wide. The pheasant house fluttered with pages torn from a book; tourist maps clung to the mud. The polar bear's pool hid beneath a blanket of scum and moss. The only pride in the lions' house was now a litter of shells. In the monkey habitat, rope swings hung freely, ungripped by primate hands, suggestive only of the noose.

I traced my finger around the print of a hoof, laid myself beside it in the mud. Did anyone ever truly manage escape? The hoofprint did not seem to think so.

I'd come for Mengele, yes. But I'd hoped for life too. I hadn't known this, though, till I saw nothing of it.

To the left of the hoofprint, I spied a small mound of earth, a fresh heap of soil capping the ground. I turned over the soil and plunged my hand in. What did I expect to find at the bottom of this tunnel? My hand dreamed of discovering another hand; it wanted to find my sister sitting in a patient vigil beneath Warsaw's mud. But my fingers struck tin instead, and I smuggled out a glass jar populated with names.

I spilled its contents over the ground like seed, little slips of yellowed paper. There was Alexander and Nora. There was Moishe and Samuel and Beryl. Agathe, Jan, Rina, Seidel, Bartholomew, Elisha, Chaya, Israel. Not a Pearl among them. Feliks looked at the names and mourned. I was glad he did, because I didn't have any mourning to spare. We couldn't have known then that the names belonged to the children smuggled by the Jewish underground, children who had been assigned new identities and homes

and faces, children who sank their selves into objects—a bolt of
fabric, a pile of medicine, a slew of bottles—children who lived in
their mother's skirts, beneath floorboards, under beds, behind false
walls, so that they might someday rejoin life. But instinctually, he
knew enough to sweep up these names with his hand and bury the
jar again, admonishing me all the while for disrupting their hiber-
nation.

We crept through the habitats; we asked ourselves where a Mengele might lurk.

I wondered if he'd learned the art of camouflage, taken a suggestion from some animal at the zoo, an innocent that believed,
as I had, that goodness could be found within him. Chameleons
could be optimistic like that. But Mengele—he'd think too highly
of himself to blend with stone, dust, earth. Still, with every step, I
expected him to leap up beneath our feet, to bolt from an underground hiding place. I couldn't be too cautious. I kept one hand
fishing about in my sack of stones and readied the other with foul
gestures.

"Check the trees," I whispered.

But Feliks was not interested in my instruction. He threw his
makeshift spear into a copse of birches and shrugged. He considered
his sack of stones, and then laid the stones down, one by one,
as gently as if he were handling birds' eggs. Then he sank to the
ground and let the wind play over his face as he stared into the
evening sky above, with all its dusky drifts of clouds, and with an
odd air of resignation he played the game we'd played so long ago,
on the soccer field.

"I don't see a single Nazi among you," he said to the gathering
cumuli.

I said there was no time for this game. I promised that as soon
as we found Mengele, we could rest and read the clouds. We didn't
even have to kill him right away, I reasoned. We could secure him

in the tiger pen and take care of him later, to maximize our viciousness.

"I'm tired," he claimed, and he did not move.

In all our travels, this was the first statement of weariness I'd
heard. I'd seen Feliks struggle to walk, to lift his head, to open his
eyes, to swallow a morsel of food—but never had he voiced his
fatigue. This concerned me. I put a hand to his forehead, but he
wrenched it away.

"We should sleep and look for him in the morning," I said
brightly. "It would be stupid for us to confront him when we are
not at our best. Like your father the rabbi would say—"

"My father was never a rabbi," he said dully. "I lied."

He confessed this to me, but he said it to the clouds above.

"I forgive you," I said. "I lie too. I lie all the time since Pearl left.
Actually, that's a lie—I lied before she was gone. I always have."

This revelation did not bring him the comfort I thought it might.
I watched a tear slip from his eye and plummet down the side of his
face. He didn't bother to wipe it away.

"I am the biggest liar of all," he said. "My father was a drunk, a
criminal, an indigent. We lived with him in graveyards, back alleys,
anywhere we could find. He didn't even survive the invasion. My
mother—dead long ago. I don't know how. My brother—after our
father died, we went to live with a woman, a kind woman, she took
us in—"

I told Feliks that he could stop. This was not a contest about who
was the biggest liar. This was a contest about who could be the best
killer of Josef Mengele, Angel of—

He sat bolt upright, mouth twisted with confrontation.

"Let me finish! We lived here in Warsaw. Behind this zoo, in fact.
See that house there, so close? It was ours, once."

I looked at the remains of the house, its insides exposed like
the nest of a wasp. The sight of its skeleton laid everything bare.

I thought of his odd familiarity with the city, the way the people nodded at him as he passed, how he knew the name of every street. I told Feliks that I forgave him, none of these falsehoods mattered. The one thing I didn't understand was why he had acted as if this was a new place, as if he'd never been here before—

He did not look at me as he explained.

"I thought you'd love the zoo. I thought that once you saw the animals, you'd want to live again, and maybe you'd want to live with me. I thought—if you had that chance, that hope, it might even be possible for you to put this deathlessness aside. That ridiculous story he gave everyone! He told all of us that fib, you know. A bigger liar than myself!"

I don't know what my face looked like but I'm sure it showed my foolishness. For so long, I'd hoped that others would forgive me my survival. Just a moment before, I'd believed that the years of children and mothers were in me, the minutes of violinists and farmers and professors, every refugee who never managed to return from the seething country that war had put them in. And now it had come down to this: not science or God or art or reason. Just a boy—a traitor, friend, brother—who wanted to show me a tiger.

"You know that it isn't true? How could you believe it? Mengele told all of us, you know, every last—you were not the only one he put evil into."

Hearing this, I put my spear down too. I dropped my sack of stones, which thudded on the ground with finality. The stones took my side in this matter. The stones cried out, they agreed with me that, yes, I'd been a fool, but Mengele thought I was special, Mengele singled me out, he said I was a rare girl, the only worthy one.

My friend's mouth twisted with pity.

"If I had ever thought you believed that, Stasha—"

Seeing my distress, Feliks hurried to my side, and he went on to say that all I needed was a good night's dreaming and then a new

family, maybe an adopted family, and then a new country, complete
with a future. The soothing nature of his voice only riled me. I covered my ears to protect them against the force of his good wishes,
and I removed my hands only to reach down into my sack and pull
out a stone. It careened past his ear, toward the carnage of his home.

His face? The sadness in it told me we had been family.

I reached again, threw stone after stone. I threw them not to
strike but because I needed to no longer carry such burdens.
I threw them into the remaining window shards of his house.
The stones pleased me with their shatters. The last, in particular,
sounded distinguished, almost musical in its destruction. I did not
realize the reason for this until my target cried out in dismay.

"Your key!" Feliks shouted.

I looked into my sack. It was true, I had reached into its depths
with a careless, raging hand and thrown Pearl's piano key by mistake. Already Feliks was turning to run into the house to retrieve it,
and I was at his back.

If Feliks felt the recognition of his old home as he entered, he
did not say, but I watched him scan its insides warily from the doorway, I watched him step purposefully on a framed photograph that
lay just beyond the threshold. I looked at the photograph, and a
younger Feliks looked back at me. His twin looked back at me too.
I could not tell how long before the boys were herded into Mengele's Zoo this photograph had been taken. But though their young
lives had never been prone to ease, it appeared that once, they had
been immaculate; they grinned the same grins, these twins, their
hair was parted in the same direction, and their eyes were wide and
hopeful.

It was difficult for me to put that past down, but we had to move
forward.

We found ourselves in a parlor with armchairs and sofas in disarray, all of it covered in a fine shower of concrete and crockery. The

looters had searched the floorboards and pulled the china from the cupboards. The whole of this house was overturned and smashed, but its ruins were not pathetic in the way ruins can be—this place had struggled against those who came to overthrow it.

We climbed to the second floor, bolted up a staircase muddy with footprints, and found rooms aflutter with mosquito nets. They'd been suspended over every summer bed but the looters had ripped them and dragged them to the ground. This tulle, with its drapes and flounces, floated over the floors and furnishings, a ghostly blizzard. We sifted through this tulle foam for that white key; we bumped into this corner and that, and then Feliks stopped with a start.

"Did you hear that?"

I had not.

"A woman—crying," he said. "Listen."

And then it soared toward us like an invitation and we hesitated at a stair before bolting upward into the darkness.

"It's coming from the parlor," Feliks said. "And it sounds as if someone is hurt."

The weeping increased. I felt so distant from my body while listening to it. I could swear that cry was familiar. It sounded like a cry I'd heard all my life, one that I had once dreaded hearing but now welcomed.

"It's Pearl," I said to Feliks.

And then, as if in confirmation, there was a crash, a startle, the sound of something falling across a set of piano keys. I pushed past Feliks and, without the aid of candlelight, picked my way over the shattered glass, the furniture outstretching its arms.

In the parlor, I saw the piano. It was intact. Feliks rushed toward it, blocking my view.

"Who is in my house?" he demanded.

We received only more cries. I noticed, then, that these cries had a womanly note; they drifted out of an experience I was quite unfamiliar with. As we neared the piano, I saw their source: a figure swaddled in blankets. I watched Feliks approach this figure, and then slow.

"You have to see this, Stasha," he whispered.

It was a Roma woman. She was slumped against the side of the piano, but she lifted her face to us. Looking at her, I forgot Pearl's key. I wasn't even trying to look for it. The woman wilted before us—she was not unlike a petal struggling to remain on the stem.

"She's dying, isn't she?" Feliks asked. "That's why her breathing is so strange?"

I wasn't sure if the breaths were dying breaths. They sounded like a different sort of distress, though one just as life-changing as death. I was certain that I had never made such sounds. I was certain Pearl never had either. These moans carried a wisp of future in them— they were aggrieved, but hopeful too, as if the woman had some happy prospect in her mind even as she wept. But I said nothing of this to Feliks. Because I was too busy looking at this pitiable woman with hatred. Instead of my sister, she was this—a woman who had been hunted down, left to wander. A bereaved creature, much like myself, without too many gasps left. I wondered what had been promised her in life—a home, a husband, a child—and how it differed from what had been promised to me, but I couldn't get very far with that thought because I couldn't remember what life had ever owed me in the first place.

Feliks peeled back one of the blankets in search of a wound, and the woman exhaled with startling force. She flurried her hands at us—begging for pause—and then she reached behind herself and produced the arc of an immense knife. It may as well have been a miracle, that blade; we forgot ourselves looking at it and were impressed by her unforeseeable power. Surely, anyone who possessed such a weapon should be the true vanquisher of Josef

Mengele. Though prostrate and beaded at the forehead with illness, she shamed us both with her smiting potential.

We told her how impressed we were. If only, we told her, if only we'd had such a knife at our disposal in the wilds of the Zoo.

She was confused—drops of sweat were tossed from her brow as it furrowed.

"Not this zoo," Feliks said. "Another zoo, the one that made—"

The woman exhaled sharply. At first, I thought it was frustration. But when that exhalation multiplied into a series, I saw that it was pain, and in the midst of these spasms, she gestured for Feliks to lean in toward her. And into his grimy palm she placed the long blade with a ceremonial flourish.

"I thank you," he finally managed to say. "And I swear that I will kill a Nazi someday, in your name."

The woman cocked her head at him, gave another ragged exhale, and, by some miracle, capped it with a girlish laugh. It seemed that there were two words that she recognized. They were *Nazi* and *kill,* and though neither appeared to be relevant to her wishes, she seemed to appreciate their usage. She clapped as if we'd just performed for her, and then she crooked her finger at us apologetically, and pointed to her abdomen.

"We have nothing—" I started, but it didn't matter what I said because she was pulling up the hem of her ragged jumper to reveal a belly that was not the starved belly that we were accustomed to seeing but one of an unfamiliar fullness. A prick of movement encircled her navel. A ripple of life, that's what it was.

I moved to sit beside her, to hold her hand. I did this not out of familiarity but out of a desire not to faint. And then she drew my hand in a neat line beneath her abdomen. Her manner was instructive, her movements precise. There was no mistaking her petition. Feliks grasped me by the arm; he tried to force me back.

"You will kill her," he whispered.

I told the woman that I couldn't use the knife as she asked. She smiled at me and repeated the motion. She wanted to be my teacher, my reason to continue; she wanted to show me birth.

I told her I couldn't. But already, I was wondering if I could— she was dying, this woman, she was leaving the world with a life inside her, a life that could go on to know nothing of the suffering we had endured. A life with a real childhood. Didn't I owe something to a life like that?

"You won't forgive yourself," Feliks warned me.

I thought back to Mengele's charts. Once, I'd seen him open up a woman while I lay in the examination room. It was an unusual procedure, he'd claimed, a favor for a friend. I'm not sure what kind of favor sees a newly born child plunged into a bucket behind its mother's back, but he insisted on speaking of this as a charitable act, even though the cesarean soon turned into a vivisection before my very eyes. Before I had a chance to look away I had learned from this experience—I'd chosen to forget the bereaved mother's face, but I remembered the scars of such deliveries, their position, their length, their arc; I knew that such incisions could end children just as easily as they could deliver them.

And then I sank my knife in the way the woman wanted, the way my memory told me to, the way that Mengele never would have—I did it with care and the remnants of my love, and as she stopped crying, a new cry began.

For all my vengeful ambition, this was the first time I had had blood on my hands. We watched the woman's eyes dim, her posture slacken.

I think she saw the squirmer before she left. Its face was so humorous, shrimp pink and ancient. Why else would she have died smiling?

I passed my knife to Feliks and told him how to cut the cord. *Let him,* I thought, *be responsible for this final severance.*

"What do we do with it?" he asked.

I wiped the membrane of the floating world from the baby's skin.

This baby was so different than the camp babies. Its problem was not that someone was trying to kill it, but that no one in this house knew how to make it live.

In the morning, Baby wailed in my arms as I walked. I was on my way to the orphanage, crossing this street and that in my quest to put Baby where it belonged. Baby needed to be in hands that could properly care for it and see it grow into a child who could someday be more than an orphan. I knew this plan would be met with disagreement from my companion, so I'd crept out before Feliks could wake. His love of the impossible would make him want to keep the sweet unfortunate. And I did not want to be convinced. Because, you see, a new plan for my future had formulated within me as I'd spent the evening rocking Baby and watching Feliks dig a grave for the Roma mother.

He'd buried her near the glass jar of names.

The newborn cared nothing about this grave, but I knew Baby could feel the thoughts in me as I'd stood over the mound and placed the plume of a peacock feather where a headstone should have been. When the wind blew that feather away, Baby wailed. It wailed not only in grief, but as a negotiating tactic. It wanted to be known to me as a real human, and it saw that I respected grief more than anything. This was a shrewd plan, one much advanced for an infant, but as a hardened girl, I required more.

I looked down at its face now, wiped the sleep from its dark eyes with my shirtsleeve, and hoped that this attention to hygiene could serve as a substitute for love, but the infant mistook it for a gesture of true affection and blushed. Already, it wanted me as family.

I felt sorry for it for choosing to love me even as I moved toward its abandonment, holding it at arm's length while footing through the rubble.

During this walk, I noted what I was leaving behind. Once, I was Mengele's experiment. And now, it seemed that I would be an experiment for the war-torn countries, the disassembled, the displaced—how do you restore everything to its rightful home? everyone was asking. Of course, I wasn't alone in being an experiment in this way. There were so many like me, and I wondered how many among them would make the choice that I was going to make.

You see, the pill the avengers left me with, the poison intended for Mengele that I'd carried in my mouth out of the depths of the salt mine—it was secured in my sock. It took every step with me, whispering all the while into my ankle, which just so happened to carry nerves and veins that sided with my heart. This poison wasn't the bully I'd expected it to be but a strange comfort, a modern invention that knew my pain. It was wiser than I was; its chemicals had passed over the earth for centuries, and it was a well-traveled substance, practiced in human dismissal. From time to time, it tried to escape my ragged sock, but I only pushed it back and kept walking. The distance between myself and the orphanage was growing ever shorter, and I wanted to appreciate the walk because, though the city was gray and rubbled, it was the last city I'd see, and so I saw all I could—the old woman blowing dust from her photographs, the children collecting husks of bullets in a heap, the shop window full of stopped clocks and my reflection.

I pretended that the clocks had stopped for Pearl and me. I had failed at protecting her in life, but there was a chance, I believed, of finding her in death. She would want it that way, I told myself, and not just because she wanted to see me. Pearl would want me to die because she knew me, she knew how intolerable it was to my spirit that Mengele would escape unavenged, wholly beyond my desperate reach, my every wish for justice. Even if I was never reunited with her—I could not live with that failure.

And if there was a life for us beyond this death, we could embark on a new set of tasks and divisions.

Pearl could take the hope that the world would never forget what it had done to us.

I could take the belief that it would never happen again.

No one would know us as *mischlinge*. In that life, there would be no need for such a word.

And then I came to my destination. A red mitten was impaled on the iron gate, like a pierced heart. The paving stones before the remaining walls of the orphanage were upturned, the earthworms were surfacing in the exposed soil, the rosebushes were showing their roots, and the thorns were pointing the way to the iron knocker on the red door, a bold but tarnished lion. I wiped the dew from the doormat and laid Baby down upon it. I was no savage—I was careful to keep it wrapped in the blanket that had belonged to its mother. Baby appeared content—there were coos, a pleased thrashing of fist. I placed its thumb in its mouth. It was the least that I could do, I thought, though it began to wail a moment later. I started to leave, and I would've done so quickly, I would've passed through the gate and headed down the street to take my poison pill in a quiet corner, but I did not look where I was going and I collided with a man. He was coatless; his clothes were ragged, and his shoes were in pieces. He had no face—at least, none that I could see, because he held a Soviet newspaper before his head. The print shrieked across the front page. I begged his pardon. He begged mine. Or he almost did. For some reason, he stopped short in his apology. Then he clutched my numbered arm, and the paper fell at my feet.

There, on that front page, was a face I knew better than any other. It floated in a sea of other faces, behind the barbs of a captivity I knew too well.

From above, a drop descended to the page, threatening to blot the face out. Thinking it rain, I snatched the paper from the ground, and that's when I heard the crying.

You might wonder how I could recognize a man by his crying when I'd never, in all the years we'd spent together, heard him cry. Laughter had been his chosen sound, and shouts of frustration largely featured too in those last days before his disappearance, when he was trying to negotiate with the other men of the ghetto, all of them so interested in doing good, and all of them bearing conflicting ideas as to how to achieve it. But there, at the steps of the orphanage, it was his cry that solved our long separation.

"You are alive" was all I could say.

My father held me close. He sobbed. His sobs should have made him still stranger to me, but instead, they reintroduced a man who knew what it meant to search and press on, to ignore all doubts that wanted so badly to diminish him. I shouldn't have been surprised by this—Papa was never good at doubting, not for as long as Pearl and I had known him. And now, in our father's eyes, there was all the good I'd ever known, and there was good to come; there were days to see and stories to hear and weapons to abandon. From his threshold, nestled in his basket, Baby went quiet, so quiet, as he observed our reunion. They say the newly born see nothing. They are wrong. I can testify to this fact because in my own way, within Papa's clasp, I was newly born too.

When I saw Papa, the world rolled on for me. In seeing his face, so changed, I felt found by luck, by miracles. All became awe, and rain fell to join our tears. How strange, I thought, that rain remains rain after what we've endured! Some things were unchanged; this was proof. Another unchanged thing: my father lived, and as he pressed me to his chest, I could still hear his heart! It did not know quite what to say.

Papa was similarly speechless. He stroked my face with a bandaged hand, a hand that still knew, through its tribulations, Pearl's face as well as my own. When he tweaked the tip of my nose, I could not help but join him in his tears.

And through these tears, I tried to tell him that Zayde was dead, but all I could say was *Please, Papa, bend so I can see your face, a leaf is caught in your beard.*

I tried to tell him that Mama was dead, but I just said, *Mama, Mama.*

I tried to tell him that Pearl, our Pearl, my Pearl—he made me stop speaking, and he drew me even closer. I could feel his lips move against my scalp as he spoke.

"I am so happy to find you," he said. "The article said that the children are scattered all over. Displacement camps, mostly. Some orphanages. Gross-Rosen. Mauthausen. I have been traveling for weeks, one stopped train after another—I thought I might locate someone with information in Lodz, but I found myself in Warsaw. How could it be that I would discover you here?"

Papa laughed and I thought I heard Baby laugh too, in his newborn way. I couldn't laugh with them. I was too busy looking at the photograph in the newspaper that my father now clutched with one hand.

"That is not me," I said.

I said it not only to my father but to my sister's face, which peered out from the photograph, a look of capture in her eyes even as she floated above the place that tormented her, cradled in the arms of one of our few protectors.

"I thought it was you," Papa said. "The expression—it is yours." My father could not stop shaking, and yet he did not know how to move; we stood there, before the door of the orphanage, experiencing a joy so many would not.

"I didn't hear you, Papa," I whispered. "I am half deaf now."

It was a lie, somewhat. I just wanted to hear him say those words again. But there was no need to draw this phrase out of him. He was too eager to repeat his joy, to hold me close.

"I thought it was you," Papa said, and he increased the clasp of his arms around me so that I could hear his heart acknowledge our loss even as his voice refused to. "Look at the expression," he whispered. And this is where he crushed me, where he drew me so tight that I could not breathe. He held me so close I felt my ribs crowd toward each other, but curiously, there was no pain at all, and I wasn't the least bit worried about the potential suffocation of his embrace. My father was a good doctor, and he could do my breathing for me in a pinch, maybe not as good as Pearl could breathe for me, but I was beginning to think that, when I saw her—

I couldn't believe that I could even think such a thing.

Tell my sister that I, she had said.

Pearl was alive. Or at least, she had escaped the cage that Mirko told me of. She had been carried through the gates we had entered together. What happened after that, I couldn't know, but I was certain that her legs were moving faster than anyone's in her efforts to reach me.

I should have shouted, I should have danced, but this discovery was too sacred to be commemorated by anything we could humanly do. I picked up Baby, and Papa and I walked back to the zoo; we kicked up pebbles and watched them stonily confront the rain. We handed Baby back and forth, and we spoke to each other as friends invested in futures speak. Papa told me of Dachau, the camp the secret police had taken him to so long ago. There was more to the story, bits that Mama had never disclosed. Because the sick child he'd left us to tend to that night existed, yes, but so did the Jewish resistance, and Papa had been a part of that shadowy movement. With Mama's blessing he'd risked himself, smuggling weapons from the border of the city into the ghetto, and on that night, he'd risked himself too well; he was captured and beaten and then—he did not want to say, but I could imagine him being tossed onto the back of a truck or onto a train, traveling farther and farther away from us, till he arrived at a place that claimed, like so many others, that work might set him free.

I told him what the Gestapo said, that he'd plunged his body willfully into the Ner.

"I would never do such a thing!" he said. And then he hung his head and admitted that before the Russian newspaper gave him the company of that beautiful image, he'd thought of doing that very thing every day, soon as he woke, but with a rope, not a river. It was the inclusion of that last detail—rope, not river—that set my mind to realize that this returner was not the Papa of old but a new, broken man, one who no longer insisted on revealing the horrors of the world in discrete increments to his daughter, as they had already made themselves as plain as the new scar that careened across his forehead.

Papa asked me about what had happened to me, to us, to Pearl. I could not speak of such things. I simply told him that I wasn't fit to take care of this baby, as much as he thought we owed him a home. I had impaired vision, a bad ear. I was useless in matters of assisting another's survival.

Papa took out our beloved newspaper and unfurled it pointedly so I could not escape the face of my sister. She was ours, even in that picture.

"We will find her alive," he swore. "She would not leave this earth without you."

Already, the old nature of our relationship was returning to us, though with alterations. Our walk, that was new. For the first time

I could remember, I strode directly by his side. I knew he would have lofted me onto his shoulders if I'd let him; he would have held me high enough for all the city to see so that they could know that Janusz Zamorski was not only still a man, but also a father not entirely bereft of family, a man with two daughters, twin girls that he loved for all their differences.

But he did not try the old shoulder stroll of our younger years, because if I were to be carried in such a capricious manner, who would look after the safety of Baby?

Papa was immediately taken by the infant, you see. He appraised him as a good doctor does, admiring the broadness of his newborn chest, the steady intake of his lungs. You would hardly know, he said in wonder as he tickled Baby, that this was the face of a wartime child.

I could see that Baby would never be left in a basket at an orphanage, not as long as Papa had some say. I did not want him. Or at least, I did not want him until I had Pearl by my side, because only then would I know that my life truly could continue. Baby must have seen my thoughts, he must have known in that way that infants do, because he escalated his handsomeness in a snap; he parted his lips and made his need for food known so discreetly. I had to admit the child was a charmer, but his comely manners could not overwhelm my doubts, and I assessed the matter as we picked our way through the streets.

"He is hungry," Papa said, pointing to Baby's mouth, open with want. "We must find him something to eat."

Papa and me, we'd always spoken in bargains and bets. If I were to do this, I said, to take care of this baby, you must do one thing for me. What is this? he asked. He expected something playful. He expected me to make a joke. But I had none to make.

Please take this pill from me, I begged, please bury it where I can't find it.

We kept a list; we crossed off names. The names were of orphan-ages, displacement camps, nunneries, and monasteries, all the places one had to look in those days. A farmer gave us rides around the towns bordering Warsaw. We went to Zabki, Zielonka, and Marki.

"Have you seen a girl," Papa would say, pushing me forward, "who looks like this?"

"We've seen so many girls," the nun or the official or the monk or the guard would say.

"She has a number," I'd bleat, and I'd show them my own.

"This doesn't help us," they'd say, staring into the blue. Often, they seemed to lose themselves looking at it.

"She has other identifying marks," I'd say. "If she still has hair, she wears a blue pin in it. If she still has legs, they are knobby at the knee. You can't miss her—if you've seen her."

And they would smile and say that we should go to this place or that place. She was sure to turn up, they said. If she was alive, they said.

"Of course she is alive," we'd say, pointing to the photograph. "Look at this face!"

All we could do after the conclusion of these visits was look at the newspaper. There Pearl was, nesting in Dr. Miri's arms, with fences rising on either side of them, as if they were trapped in a gar-den with hedges of wire. If you looked at the picture long enough, you could sense the grip of the doctor's hands, or feel the prick of the frost. Whenever we returned to Feliks's house, the newspaper lived in Papa's dresser drawer, alongside our guns. He kept it there because I looked at it too much, he said. There were rules, he said, and they were imposed for my own health. He was not wrong in this. If I looked at the picture in the morning, I couldn't bring my-self to eat. If I looked at it in the evening, I could not sleep. And so my visits with the pictured Pearl were confined to the afternoon. If I looked at her with both eyes blurred, it was easy to imagine that she looked at me too.

Tears must have been invented for that reason, I thought.

On the first day of March, I confessed my stupidity about Mengele and my deathlessness to Papa. It was the weather's fault—it coaxed me with its beauty. Crocuses began to thrust up their heads in the animal houses. Birds returned. Buildings began to hold themselves high. Baby became round and hardy at the breast of a wet nurse. Humbled by this splendor, I could only hang my head and tell my secrets—I was sure that Papa would be ashamed. But he assured me that I did what I did in order to survive. And then he called Feliks over for a story.

"It is only because of a curse, or many curses, that I survived," Papa said. "When they first took me from Lodz, I marched with the other captives, on the roadsides, through fields. Often, we would come upon fellow Jews in disguise. I told myself that they would save us if they could. It didn't matter to me that they did nothing to support this belief. I took care not to look at them. I feared that if I did, they would crumble and be forced to join us. On a day I was sure I would starve to death, we were led through the field of a priest. Peasants were gathering potatoes, piling them in a wagon. On top of the potato pile sat an old Jewish man. Unlike others in disguise, he had never bothered to clip his earlocks. Seeing us, he suddenly crossed himself, as if horrified by the proximity to our kind—the gesture was unnatural; it was a wonder to me that he had managed to pass for so long without capture. But his next action made me realize I'd been wrong to question his resourcefulness, because he put a hand beneath his bottom, searched about the wagon bed, pulled out a potato, and flung it at me with a curse! Then again. One after another. For every curse, he threw a potato. His curses followed us until we reached the end of the field and came to the road, but we knew what they meant—these were the kind of curses that would keep us alive."

I wanted to ask Papa how he could be sure of this, but I didn't want to admit my uncertainty. So I pinched Feliks. He asked for me. Papa was unnerved by this connection that thrummed between us but he answered all the same.

"I saw it in his face," he said. "The curses were merely blessings in disguise. He meant for me to take up those potatoes and live."

He pulled on the end of his nose, as he always had in a thoughtful moment, and then he sank his head into his hands so I was forced to study the new seam that wound itself over his face and scalp.

"I know that Mengele's curse—there was no good intention in it, not at all. But I just want to say that you were not wrong to take that fool's curse—with all his lies and manipulations—and twist it so that you could survive by it. Understand?"

I did. And I lied and told my father that I would take comfort in his cursed-vegetable story. I know that he did. Because when Papa died many years later, eyes shrouded in illness, stretched out on his bed, Feliks and I saw him raise his hands in the air as if trying to catch an object. His fingers lifted with a strange urgency, unnatural to any deathbed, and we watched his sightless eyes dart back and forth, following the holy path of a potato in flight.

Papa did his best to restore us, but we knew soon enough that he was broken too. He went to Lodz alone, as he was worried about what he might find there. When he returned, he shook his head for days. We sought out the company of other refugees in Warsaw, every last one so hungry for reunion.

"Have you seen Pearl?" Papa would ask, pushing me forward.
None had.

Papa admired the resurrection of Warsaw and said that he would
stay to rebuild Feliks's house with him. But though Papa was a man
of skill, his hands weren't suited to the task of mending rooms and
righting walls. They were accustomed to the diagnosis, the wound
tinkering, the application of cures. And while Feliks was swell with
a hatchet, a knife, a gun, and could spin a lie to live in just as well as
I could, mending a house was not among his gifts. Still, both were
determined to rebuild, to follow the city's example.

I watched the two shamble about the house with merry shouts,
wielding mallets and breaking down the remnants of walls. I
perched with Baby while they fumbled with paving stones and fiddled with doorknobs and I often fell to wondering if they were
pursuing this rebuilding as a flimsy distraction from the unknown
whereabouts of Pearl. They would take up their hammers and their
nails and soon enough they'd find themselves too startled by the
sounds to continue. Rebuilding can sound a lot like war, a lot like
capture—all that bang and falling brick, all that smattering of stone.

As for me, I kept myself occupied by teaching Baby lessons from
Twins' Father, lessons from Zayde, lessons from my anatomy book.
The least I could do, I decided, was to give him certain advantages,
a distinct smartness, so that if he ever became an experiment too,
he would fare better than some. We had to get the words out fast
enough, before the words were snatched away. We had to establish
the words, make them whole. I spent my days memorizing all that
I could find so that in the event that we were recaptured, I'd have
words to amuse us with, words to let us abide. *Before the ocean was,
or earth, or heaven,* I'd say, in tribute to Mirko, *nature was all alike, a
shapelessness!* And to Baby, in hopes of installing his first word, I'd
whisper: *Pearl, Pearl, Pearl.* It was as if I believed that only the most
innocent whisper could bring her back. That if he cried her name,

she would be there, dancing. A crown of heather on her head. And good shoes on her feet.

I couldn't deny that in Warsaw, things bloomed. Baby cried enough to water a linden, and I did my part too, though I was careful to express my tears only in the vicinity of a wasp's nest, so that I might blame some assault if anyone happened to see my pain. People saw my pain often, though. Mostly, these people were ones who came to the zoo. The Jewish underground had operated through its buildings, in its many holes and caves. Now, refugees came looking for sons and daughters who had curled up within the burrows meant for badgers until it was safe to transport them to another location. Many of these seekers were mothers, and as they passed through, they paused simply to hold the child, and when they looked into his brown eyes they could not help but offer me advice. They told me to swaddle him tightly, and they showed me how to bathe him so that he looked less like a wild thing.

Whenever I bathed Baby in his bucket, the boy's life became too real to me. He was so vulnerable, a dark little duckling with a wee stem of a neck. While I made him clean, I wondered what I might tell him someday about his mother, how she'd made me kill her, how she'd guided my hand with the knife. I tried to invent prettier, more scenic deaths for her. Something with a snowfall. Something without a blade. But in Warsaw, my imagination had left me. I did not know where it went, but I hoped it didn't occupy anyone else the way it had occupied me. I wanted the death of my imagination more than anything. It had no place in this world after war. Once, I told myself, I was happy to live for another, to continue for her sake. But without her, I was just a madman's experiment, a failed avenger, a girl who didn't end when she should have.

Papa saw my sadness. He said that we had hope still. He said we had a country so cracked that it was easy for Pearl to slip inside and hide in the most unseen corners. He'd say this on our daily visit to the orphanage when we went to see if she had been shuttled into its care. But no one who looked like me was waiting at the window; no one who sounded like me was singing at the gate.

"If we don't find her," I began on the way home one time. But I didn't have a chance to finish this sentence. An odd correction was made to my thoughts when a stray dog appeared at my side and then promptly dropped at Papa's feet. This dog was a mud-covered scrap, ugly and mongrel. The state of his paws made it clear he had traveled a long distance in search of someone. On us, he could smell the same struggle.

Papa thought that the dog would cheer me. He was not wrong in this. I loved this mongrel's protective spirit, the way he barked like a pistol and snarled at anyone who raised his voice to me. This dog, I noted to Feliks, he would have been a match for Mengele. Feliks did not disagree.

"But I'm glad that he will know only this zoo," he said. "And not the other."

Together, we watched the dog dig tunnels through the animals' cages. This was something that pleased him to no end, and I could only hope that he would never dig up the poison pill Papa buried in the yard while he went about this business. I knew that if I saw that pill at the right moment—I could not resist the finality promised by its whiteness.

Feliks saw this temptation in me. He, too, assured me that Pearl would return. Maybe, he said, she was just waiting until the animals came back to the zoo. He said that the zookeeper's wife had plans to visit the grounds, and already, there was talk of the zoo's revival. Soon, the animals would march, two by two, into their rightful houses. I stalked about their cages in wait, and tried not to dwell on the cages I'd known.

But on the day I want to speak about, it was not an animal that arrived in Warsaw, but a coffin. I wasn't there to see it lowered onto the street. I didn't hear the cry of the mistress of the orphanage as she opened it.

I was in the fields with Baby and my dog. I was training him to be a stronger dog. He liked to beg, and I could not break him of it. Begging would not do in these vulnerable days. So I gave him a new trick to use instead—I taught him to dance. Whenever that dog danced, I heard Zayde laugh. I had thought I would never hear Zayde laugh again, but there he was, all chuckle and knee-slap. None of it ghostly or remembered, but clear as spring. That was fair motivation to keep up with the practice. Watching this shabby canine waltz—it made me dream again.

On this day, we were practicing in the field with Baby lolling in the grass, an uninterested audience. We had music too, of a sort. In the distance, you could hear the sound of paving stones being laid, one next to another—the stones sang out, their clinks carrying over the city and up into the drifts of the crab apple trees. Here and there, a starling asserted itself, warbling, its cry so forceful that its hasty body trembled. It was to this music of stone and bird and Zayde's laughter that the dog undertook his choreography.

I told my dog that he had to practice. Someday, I said, someone might discover his talents and put him in a movie. That could be our future—didn't he agree? My dog did not agree. He disliked practicing just as much as Pearl had; he had no interest in proving himself worthy of the art. But he danced for me all the same, and I applauded him after the full revolution of a turn.

When I stopped clapping, though—I still heard applause. Someone was clapping behind our backs. I blushed. Because dog-dancing is nothing to be proud of; it is a sport for the solitary, a sad sort of whirl.

But when I glanced over my shoulder, I saw myself. Or I saw a girl, a strong girl, a girl who was no longer lonely. The girl was happier than I'd imagined I could ever be again. She was clapping and smiling and the dog gamboled toward her and shimmied at her feet, abandoning any idea of a show. Still, the girl kept clapping. She clapped even as there were two crutches propped beneath her arms.

Have you ever seen the best part of yourself stationed at a measurable distance? A distance you'd never thought possible after so much parting? If so, I'm sure you're aware of the joys of this condition. My heart thrilled with reunion, and my tongue ran dumb with happiness. My spleen informed my lungs that they'd lost the big bet—*I told you so!* my spleen said—and my thoughts, my rosy thoughts, they kept thinking toward a future I'd believed long lost.

She put her crutches down and we sat back to back, spine to spine, in the manner of our old game.

I'll admit—I peeked at what she drew.

I peeked not to cheat, but oh—just because she was my sister. I had to see her. I am sure you understand.

CHAPTER TWENTY-TWO

Never the End

And we drew poppies. We drew them as tight buds that might never see a bloom, we drew them for Mama and Zayde, and then we added a river for Papa. We drew a train, a piano, a horse. We drew the children Stasha would have, and the children I never could. We drew boats that carried us far away from Poland, and planes that brought us back. We did not draw a needle, no; we did not draw a crutch, much less the man who had undone us. But we drew skies that would protect us our whole lives through, and trees that would shelter two girls who might never be whole, and only when we finished drawing did my sister even try to speak.

"Let's try again," Stasha said.

I didn't need to finish her sentence. I knew what she meant—we had to learn to love the world once more.

ACKNOWLEDGMENTS

I am grateful to the following:

Jim Rutman, for your gallant investment in my writing and the years of brilliant insights that illuminated the path for this book. It wouldn't be real without you.

Lee Boudreaux, editor-heroine beyond compare—I remain in awe of your commitment to every dream, sorrow, and longing contained within.

Reagan Arthur, Michael Pietsch, Judy Clain, Jayne Yaffe Kemp, Carina Guiterman, Tracy Roe, Kapo Ng, Sean Ford, Carrie Neill, Nicole Dewey, and the teams at Little, Brown and Company and Lee Boudreaux Books that I've been so fortunate to work with. Szilvia Molnar, Danielle Bukowski, Brian Egan, and the fantastic people at Sterling Lord Literistic. All of the amazing foreign publishers, for welcoming this novel.

The David Berg Foundation, for their gracious support, and my teachers and peers at Columbia.

Pranav Behari and Adam Kaplan, for always being my heartfelt and invaluable writing-family.

Stephen O'Connor, Lydia Millet, Joyce Polansky, Karen Russell, George Sanchez, Rudy Browne—that I have enjoyed your influence and friendship is a wonder.

The Konars, Cruzes, Kims, and Sos. Grandmama and Grand-papa—słońce i księżyc. Jonathan and Coco (for always taking the funny and the future).

My parents, whose optimism and attention to beauty have been my preservation. (Special thanks to Dad for giving me a field when I needed it most.)

Philip Kim—for the genius, animals, comfort, and jokes. How anyone writes without you is beyond my understanding.

And here, words can only fail. But I must try to thank Eva Mozes Ker and Miriam Mozes Zeiger for the inspiration of their sister-hood and their girlish spirits. And I must try, again, to thank Zvi Spiegel, Gisella Perl, Alex Dekel, and the innumerable, unnamed witnesses whose stories have compelled these pages. This book lives only in the presence of your memories.

AUTHOR'S NOTE

Mischling's initial inspiration can be found in the remarkable *Children of the Flames* by Lucette Matalon Lagnado and Sheila Cohn Dekel. Tremendous debts are also owed to the following: Sara Nomberg-Przytyk's *Auschwitz: True Tales from a Grotesque Land;* Tadeusz Borowski's *This Way for the Gas, Ladies and Gentlemen;* Eva Mozes Kor and Mary Wright's *Echoes from Auschwitz: Dr. Mengele's Twins;* Arnost Lustig's *Children of the Holocaust;* Elie Wiesel's *Night;* Diane Ackerman's *The Zookeeper's Wife;* George Eisen's *Children and Play in the Holocaust: Games Among the Shadows;* Isaac Kowalski's *Anthology on Armed Jewish Resistance 1939–1945;* Rich Cohen's *The Avengers;* Mary Lowenthal Felstiner's *To Paint Her Life: Charlotte Salomon in the Nazi Era;* Dr. Gisella Perl's *I Was a Doctor in Auschwitz;* Anne Michaels's *Fugitive Pieces;* Robert Jay Lifton's *The Nazi Doctors: Medical Killing and the Psychology of Genocide;* Primo Levi's *The Truce, If This Is a Man, The Periodic Table,* and *The Drowned and the Saved;* and the works of Paul Celan and Dan Pagis.

ABOUT THE AUTHOR

Affinity Konar was raised in California. She is a graduate of Columbia University's MFA program.

READING GROUP GUIDE

MISCHLING

A Novel by

AFFINITY KONAR

A CONVERSATION WITH AFFINITY KONAR

The following interview was conducted by Michael Silverblatt and appeared on the KCRW show *Bookworm*. It has been edited and condensed for this reading group guide.

Mischling is about the bond between two twins who are kept in Dr. Josef Mengele's "zoo" at Auschwitz. It's well documented that a twin knows what the other twin is feeling, sometimes over great distances. And the terrifying Dr. Mengele became interested in seeing whether if you tortured one twin, the other one would be in pain—if it was possible to sever the bond. Mengele was so terrifying, in part because he would present his concern for the children as a paternal concern—he asked the children to call him "uncle"—and he alternated between being kind and being vicious. Where did you first learn about Mengele and his zoo?

The book was called *Children of the Flames* by Lucette Lagnado and Sheila Cohn Dekel. I'm finding, as *Mischling* ventures out, that

Mengele is a name that you grow up with a strange awareness of, even if you didn't know everything that he was doing.

You've brilliantly put Mengele in the background behind the relationship of the two girls, Pearl and Stasha. How did you choose their names?

I always knew that I wanted Pearl's name to be precious. I wanted Stasha to be able to evoke her like a gem at every turn. In fact, I cut a lot of passages that were just Stasha riffing on the preciousness of her sister's name. As for the name Stasha, I was drawn to the sound of it. This will seem odd, but when I was writing the Stasha passages, I would imagine riding a horse. There was this sort of *clip clop clip clop* rhythm to those passages which is also reflected in the sound of her name.

What does *mischling* mean?

Mischling is a very charged term. It means mixed blood. It was used by the Third Reich to classify people. It's a very terrifying word, yet it sounds so innocent and lilting. I tried to confront that word throughout the novel, and its meaning changes over the course of the novel. In the end, Stasha rejects it entirely.

What difficulties did you face writing this novel? You worked on it for ten years.

I feel as if writing this book wasn't so much writing as it was a constant self-interrogation and negotiation. I couldn't shake the subject matter. It had been haunting me for years. It's hard to feel drawn to something that you also feel that you can't possibly do justice to.

It's a book that can't help but be written in a heightened language, and the language is often extremely poetic. There are pages where I found myself saying that if Sylvia Plath were taking on this subject matter it might sound something like this. In other words, intensity is the job of the prose. Also, to stay calm would do injury to the subject, yes?

Oh, I believe so. I felt very deeply early on that if I were to write this book, the language was going to be my entry point.

Many people left the camps unable to retrieve what had happened to them. You have created two girls who are giving us the gift of their recollection. It is a book of memory, yes? Why did you decide on that?

To me, one of the chapter titles, "World After World," alludes to the fact that Stasha keeps moving through this terrible world of Auschwitz while always imagining another one. And so it felt very natural to me that she be this collector of memories, that she needed to leap from world to world in order to endure.

Why twins? What was Dr. Mengele looking for? What did he think he would find?

Mengele conducted experiments to try to determine just how much pain of separation a twin could handle. And then there were also the genetic experiments, in which he experimented on one twin and kept the other intact to compare the effects of his experiments.

Stasha and Pearl are particularly precious to Mengele because they both have blond hair. But they lack the blue eyes of an Aryan, and at one point he puts drops in Stasha's eyes saying that by next week this eye will be blue. Of course, by next week the eye is blind. He also takes one of her ears away—he causes her deafness. I found it very, very painful to read. Did you find it as painful to write?

Just looking at the photographs when you're researching something like this, that alone kind of breaks you. I would often read Celan after looking at photographs—

Paul Celan, the great poet who said that after Auschwitz, after the camps, the German language was no longer usable for poetry. He had to invent a new German to write poetry in.

Yes, he meant so much to me when I was writing this book. It was about suspending pain within language.

The book is in two parts, and the second part is informed by the hopefulness of escape and the hopefulness of putting Mengele into the background. The twins have now been separated. Was it always your intention that they would meet again?

That was what I was driving toward the whole time, but I would question it occasionally. I would question whether that was what really needed to happen, or if my own longing for a happy ending was overriding what the book needed to be. But at the same time, I was always writing toward that last line, which made dwelling on the experiments and the aftermath and all the loss and all the grief bearable for me.

The last line is "We had to learn to love the world once more." Now, we more or less know from the first page of this book that these characters are survivors. Some people survived and some people did not, and, in a way, the people who did not survive are no different from the people who did survive. They all went through an experience that was unprecedented in the world's knowledge. So the book becomes an act of what? Recollection? Penitence? Refusal to forget?

Yes, the book is about remembrance and the refusal to forget. That was foremost in my thoughts as I wrote.

Did this book need a poet to write it? Did it bring out the poet in you? I feel that the experiences it renders are so hard to imagine in plain factual prose that only the extremities of poetry make it possible. When did you feel that you had the language, the ability, to capture these experiences?

I'm not sure that I ever really truly felt confident about having the language. I've lived in the shadow of the poets and the writers of these narratives, and I knew every time that I revisited their work I could never mimic or shadow or echo them in the least, but I hope that I could bring some sort of intensity to the material that could honor what they've left us with.

AFFINITY KONAR'S READING

RECOMMENDATIONS FOR *MISCHLING*

The Zookeeper's Wife, Diane Ackerman

Amen, Yehuda Amichai

Red Cavalry and Other Stories, Isaac Babel

Sefer Ha-Aggadah: Legends from the Talmud and Midrash, by
    Hayyim Nahman Bialik and Yehoshua Hana Ravnitzky

This Way to the Gas, Ladies and Gentlemen, Tadeusz Borowski

No One's Rose, Paul Celan

Playing for Time, Fania Fénelon

The Diary of a Young Girl, Anne Frank

Elegy for the Departure, Zbigniew Herbert

The Book of Questions, Edmond Jabès

Where the Bird Sings Best, Alejandro Jodowrowsky

Franz Kafka: The Complete Stories, Franz Kafka

Comedy in a Minor Key, Hans Keilson

Echoes from Auschwitz, Eva Mozes Kor

Surviving the Angel of Death, Eva Mozes Kor and Llisa Rojany
    Buccieri

Anthology on Armed Jewish Resistance, 1939–1945, edited by
    Isaac Kowalski

Children of the Flames: Dr. Joseph Mengele and the Untold Story of the Twins of Auschwitz, Lucette Lagnado and Sheila Cohn Dekel

If This Is a Man, Primo Levi

The Periodic Table, Primo Levi

The Truce, Primo Levi

Children of the Holocaust, Arnost Lustig

Fugitive Pieces, Anne Michaels

Selected and Last Poems, 1931–2004, Czeslaw Miłosz

Auschwitz: True Tales from a Grotesque Land, Sara Nomberg-Przytyk

The Shawl, Cynthia Ozick

Collected Poems, Dan Pagis

The Collected Stories of Grace Paley, Grace Paley

I Was a Doctor in Auschwitz, Dr. Gisella Perl

Homage to the Lame Wolf, Vasko Popa

Illuminations, Arthur Rimbaud

The Collected Poems of Muriel Rukeyser, Muriel Rukeyser

Life? or Theatre?, Charlotte Saloman

Sanatorium Under the Sign of the Hourglass, Bruno Schulz

The Street of Crocodiles, Bruno Schulz

The World Never Ends, Charles Simic

In My Father's Court, Isaac Bashevis Singer

Maus, Art Spiegelman

View with a Grain of Sand: Selected Poems, Wisława Szymborska

I Never Saw Another Butterfly: Children's Drawings and Poems from the Terezin Concentration Camp, 1942–1944, edited by Hana Volavková

Life with a Star, Jiří Weil

Night, Elie Wiesel

Mysticism for Beginners, Adam Zagajewski

QUESTIONS AND TOPICS FOR DISCUSSION

1. Did you have any prior knowledge of the medical experiments conducted at Auschwitz? What struck you most about the plight of those selected by Josef Mengele?

2. Music played a significant role in the workings of Auschwitz-Birkenau. Prisoners were greeted by music at the ramps, and Stasha notes that suicide was frequent among the musicians that provided this accompaniment. The idea of music itself, with its ability to distract from suffering, or to transport one to a life before imprisonment, could often be bittersweet. What place do you imagine music might have in the memories of a survivor?

3. In many of Mengele's studies, one twin was subjected to experimentation, while the other remained untouched. As the spared twin, Stasha is forced to witness Pearl's decline. How does this change her sensitivity toward her sister? What about her relationship with those around her?

4. The brutality of Auschwitz-Birkenau forced many prisoners to become resourceful in unimaginable ways. Discuss the hierarchy of Mengele's zoo, and the roles of Bruna, Ox, and Twins' Father within it.

5. We often think of acts of resistance as grand displays of heroism, but such acts can also be witnessed in small, meaningful exchanges among the prisoners. Peter's theft of the piano key could be classified as an act of resistance. Can you name other instances of rebellion, large or small? Would you classify survival itself as a form of resistance?

6. The Nazi regime used the term *mischling* to describe Jews of mixed heritage. Why does Stasha refer to this word while receiving the injection that will make her "deathless"? What do you think this word means to her by the novel's end?

7. Pearl tells us that she survives Mengele's tortures by listening to Zayde and Mama, and by playing the Classification of Living Things. How do these diversions inform her survival? Can you imagine other ways that one might endure such conditions?

8. In Part Two, Pearl focuses on forgiveness, while Stasha cares only for vengeance. Describe how the girls' perspectives inform their endurance and resolve.

9. What event convinces Twins' Father that he can no longer take care of the twins? Do you agree with the decision that he and Miri make?

10. Pearl gives us glimpses of the future. What do we learn about the fates of characters in the book?

11. Discuss the notion of "the survivor's hour" as described by Jakub. How does this apply to Miri's grief, and to her role as a doctor within the camp? Years later, Miri resumes her practice. Do you think she is at peace with her lifesaving actions?

12. Stasha survives the loss of her family. Pearl survives torture, isolation, and the physical damage of Mengele's cruelty. Is it at all fair to compare the two scenarios, and wonder which twin has endured the greater challenges?

13. At their reunion, the Zamorski twins draw images that refer to their quest for survival, but they omit any image that might represent Mengele. Do you see this omission as a meaningful indication of how the twins will resume their lives? What do you think the future holds for Stasha and Pearl?

14. *Mischling* asks how a survivor might "learn to love the world once more." When one has suffered the loss of family, home, and health, how can such a thing be possible? Can you imagine what you might turn to in order to restore your vision of the world?

LEE BOUDREAUX BOOKS

Unusual stories. Unexpected voices. An immersive sense of place. Lee Boudreaux Books publishes both award-winning authors and writers making their literary debut. A carefully curated mix, these books share an underlying DNA: a mastery of language, commanding narrative momentum, and a knack for leaving us astonished, delighted, disturbed, and powerfully affected, sometimes all at once.

LEE BOUDREAUX ON *MISCHLING*

One cannot approach *Mischling* without wondering, as Anthony Doerr so eloquently put it, if one's soul can survive the journey. But therein lies the magic of Affinity Konar's dazzling novel. While it is, indeed, among the most shattering novels I've ever read, it is also brimming with life and hope. It galvanizes the soul. It demands attention. It rewards that attention in a thousand unforgettable moments. And how did Konar achieve such transcendence? I put it down to her luminous and endlessly surprising language, which, to my mind, makes *Mischling* an absolute miracle of observation and expression. But we can't overlook Pearl and Stasha, young female characters of such strength, intelligence, imagination, and bravery that I know I will never stop thinking about them.

As I edited this remarkable work, I repeatedly found myself looking up some of the real people from whom Konar drew her inspiration: Eva Mozes Kor and Miriam Mozes Zeiger, Zvi Spiegel, Alex Dekel, and, most especially, Gisella Perl. I stand in awe of them, overwhelmed to imagine that *Mischling* will, perhaps, draw renewed attention to the largely untold story of the twins of Auschwitz.

Over the course of her career, Lee Boudreaux has published a diverse list of titles, including Ben Fountain's *Billy Lynn's Long Halftime Walk,* Smith Henderson's *Fourth of July Creek,* Madeline Miller's *The Song of Achilles,* Ron Rash's *Serena,* Jennifer Senior's *All Joy and No Fun,* Curtis Sittenfeld's *Prep,* and David Wroblewski's *The Story of Edgar Sawtelle,* among many others.

For more information about forthcoming books, please go to
leeboudreauxbooks.com.